ABOUT THE AUTHOR

Greig Beck grew up across the road from Bondi beach in Sydney, Australia. His early days were spent surfing, sunbaking, and reading science fiction on the sand. He then went on to study computer science, immerse himself in the financial software industry, and later received an MBA. Greig is still involved in the software industry but finds time to write and surf. He lives in Sydney with his wife, son, and an enormous black German Shepherd.

If you would like to contact Greig, his email address is greig@greigbeck.com and you can find him on the web at:

www.greigbeck.com

ALSO BY GREIG BECK

Beneath the Dark Ice
Dark Rising
This Green Hell
Black Mountain
Arcadian Genesis
The First Bird
Return of the Ancients: The Valkeryn Chronicles 1

VALKERYN CHRONICLES 2

THE DARK LANDS

GREIG BECK

VALKERYN 2
THE DARK LANDS

Layout by Cohesion Editing
www.cohesionediting.com

Cover Art by Mel Gannon
(Cohesion Editing)

"Wolves are not our brothers; they are not our subordinates, either. They are another nation, caught up just like us in the complex web of time and life."
Henry Beston

"To live among wolves, you must first become the wolf."
Nikita Khrushchev

DEDICATION

For Kathleen Joy – eternal beauty.
Funnest and smartest woman I have ever known.

ACKNOWLEDGMENTS

Thank you to the Native Americans, the Vikings, the Greeks and all the other cultures who wove the most magnificent mythologies to explain the world – they will forever be a gift to writers.

Cast of Characters

The Valkeryn Wolfen (remaining)

Sorenson – son of Stromgard, brother of Strom (deceased)

Vidarr – Valkeryn Archivist and oldest living Wolfen

Balthazaar – Royal Counsellor

Bergborr – the dark Wolfen, betrayer of the kingdom, enthralled with Eilif who does not know he was the betrayer of the Valkeryn kingdom

Princess Eilif – daughter of King Grimvaldr and Queen Freya (both deceased)

Prince Grimson – son of King Grimvaldr and Queen Freya (both deceased)

Arn and friends

Arnold 'Arn' Singer – The youth thrown into the future. Called the 'Arnoddr-Sigarr' by the inhabitants. His name means: 'bringer of victory' in the Wolfen language

Edward Lin – best friend to Arn

Rebecca 'Becky' Matthews – once the object of Arn's affection

Military Cast

General Ted Langstrom – military liaison for the US President

Colonel Marion Briggs – in charge of Fermilab and personally leads the Delta Force soldiers into the future

Captain(s): Samson, brutal Delta Force killing machine. Jim Teacher, Delta Force brains and brawn. Henson, defender of the gateway

Lieutenant(s): Weng, Doonie, Sharp, Brown, Simms, the Deltas who accompany Captain Jim Teacher into the Dark Lands

Lieutenant(s): Bannock, Farfelle, Miller, Wilson, Jackson, Diekes, Rodriguez, and thirty-five Other Delta Force elite soldiers

FERMILAB STAFF

Professor Albert Harper – brilliant senior scientist at Fermilab.

Guard(s): Chuck Benson, Leo Anderson, Dan Loeman, Jim Morgan, Zac Markson, Bill Porter.

PANTERRAN & LYGON

Queen Mogahrr – queen of the Panterran

Orcalion – Panterran Counsellor

Goranx – Lygon general, slayer of Strom and Valkeryn King Grimvaldr

Lygon warrior(s) – Drun, Brunig, Durok, Balrog, Unsaur, Murdak.

DARK LANDS INHABITANTS

Kodian – tribe of Ursa

King Troglan – tribe of Panina

Princess Simiana – tribe of Panina

THE ORIGINAL GUARDIANS

Big Fen – the first of the genetically-engineered guard dogs.

Morgana

Erin

PRESIDENTIAL TEAM

US President Jim Harker

Harry Vanner – Head of Science & Technology

Bill Weaver – Director of Public Policy

Secretary of Defence Frank Everson

OTHER CAST MEMBERS

Pratihba Singh – Nuclear Physicist, Pan Nucleonics.

Atom – Pratihba's ash-grey tomcat

THE STORY SO FAR

RETURN OF THE ANCIENTS: VALKERYN CHRONICLES 1

Arnold Singer, a normal teenager, is on a class outing to Illinois' Fermilab laboratories. Arn and his friends will be allowed to witness the firing of one of the world's most powerful proton-antiproton colliders – four miles in diameter, and able to send particles around its gigantic ring at 99.999 percent the speed of light.

Professor Albert Harper has developed an acceleration initiator, a pure red diamond, that will shoot a laser at the particles already travelling at near the speed of light, with the objective of pushing them to an even greater speed – a world first.

Arn finds himself trapped in the acceleration chamber when the laser fires. The resulting collisions are so powerful they tear open a hole in our universe. Arn is sucked through, with the red diamond, into a world far in the future. Humans have long left, and a new race now rules – the Valkeryn Wolfen.

Through what appears to be a stroke of luck, Arn saves the life of the Wolfen princess, Eilif, who has had dream-visions of him all her life. Though she and the 'Man-Kind' creature are vastly different, she finds herself strangely attracted to him.

Arn has arrived at a perilous time. The Wolfen have been in an eternal war with the Panterran horde – creatures that are without honour and known for their treachery and assassination skills. The Panterran now have a secret plan to end the war once and for all; they team up with the giant Lygon, monstrous beasts from the forbidden zone. Together, with the help of a Wolfen traitor, they make a final assault on the Valkeryn kingdom.

Back home, the hole torn in the universe remains open, continuing to grow and threatening all life on their planet. To close it, they need to retrieve the unique acceleration diamond they believe is in Arn's possession. Colonel Marion Briggs sends through a team of Green Berets to bring Arn back, but they encounter adversaries more powerful and ferocious than they ever expected. They are decimated, leaving one survivor.

The final war sees the kingdom of Valkeryn fall, the King and Queen killed, and Princess Eilif spirited away by Bergborr, the Wolfen traitor. But before the battle, the king had sent Arn on a quest to take his son, Grimson, from the kingdom and keep him safe. Together they set out, Arn looking for evidence of what happened to the fabled Ancients – mankind – and Grimson, seeking the legendary far Wolfen.

Their quest will be arduous, frightening, and the revelations will be world shattering.

PROLOGUE

Five-year-old Arn sat on the step of his grandfather's house. The old man sat next to him, sipping a beer and from time to time humming a tune that was both haunting and melodious.

Arn looked up at him. The man's face was the oldest thing he had ever seen – all lines and fissures and crevices. Long grey hair hung to his shoulders, and he smelled of old tobacco, fresh cut wood and warmth. He was full blood Shawnee and had a story about everything that ever was and ever would be. He caught Arn looking at him, and he smiled.

Arn studied his face some more and then frowned. 'Were you ever as young as me, Grandfather Singer?'

The old man laughed, and then placed his hand on Arn's shoulder. 'Yes, but it was so long ago that only the rivers and the mountains remember.'

Arn nodded solemnly: that made sense. He looked up again. 'And were you always good?'

His grandfather raised his eyebrows, and took a few seconds to answer. He tilted his head as he responded. 'Well, some days good, some days not so good.' He smiled some more. 'You see grandson, there is a battle between two wolves inside all of us. One is evil, and it is forged of anger, jealousy, greed, resentment, lies, and ego. The other is good, and it is joy, peace, love, hope, humility, kindness, and truth.'

Arn's eyes were wide, and he placed his hands on his chest, feeling for some sort of activity.

'Which wolf wins?'

His grandfather grunted softly, and looked down again with just one eye. 'Why, the one you feed of course.'

CHAPTER 1

GOD HELP THEM ALL

Dr Albert Harper was head physicist at Fermilab's scientific facility, and overseer of the Tevatron Project. It had been America's first test of laser-enhanced particle acceleration. He had hoped to find something unique, something fantastically new that could provide clues to the very genesis of our universe. He and his team had test-fired particles, hoping to achieve the speed of light. But the experiments had exceeded all expectations, and the particle velocity had moved well beyond those seemingly-impossible speeds.

Harper stood at his desk and lent forward, peering at the image on the screen. The acceleration chamber... or what was left of it. The tiny smudge of nothingness that had remained after the boy had disappeared was now the size of a dinner plate. It still looked like a flaw in the image feed, an indistinct and shadowy area, hanging in space like an oily substance smeared on the camera's lens.

But they all knew better now. It was a hole. A breach in their universe, and a gateway to a time and place that was both fantastic and horrifying. One moment, the Singer boy had been standing there, calling for help, and then he had been dragged away, to... where, when?

Harper had guessed that the 'where' was right here in Illinois, and, judging by the astral mapping they had been able to undertake, the 'when' might be some time in the distant future.

The strange creatures they had seen when they had sent a camera probe after him told of some sort of local terrestrial heritage. Harper had hypothesized to the military, now assuming control of the project, that for all he knew the boy was still within a few dozen miles – just not in our time. Harper believed Singer was in a different time-slice in the same dimension. It made sense, when everything else seemed not to.

The information had been enough for Colonel Briggs and her military masters. They had sent soldiers, but soon found the indigenous a little more… territorial, than anyone expected, especially Briggs' Green Berets. They died, fast and horribly. The only one to return was a shivering basket case.

As far as they could tell, and at least for now, the boy still lived. *What next?*

Harper switched camera feeds to a shot outside the acceleration chamber where a hole had been cut through the reinforced concrete wall, giving them access to the sealed acceleration ring room. Even though the outside areas had been cleared, there were now multiple objects stuck to the walls nearest the ring. It had started a week ago. First, small metal things; a bobby pin, or a paperclip from a report, sliding slowly across the floor. Then larger objects were affected; things like wristwatches, pens and rings.

People entering the outer chamber had needed all the old metal fillings in their teeth replaced by ceramics, otherwise the pull of the chamber would cause severe toothaches.

Harper smiled with little mirth – that didn't turn out to be the only pain from all this. Now, and more ominously, what they had originally thought was some sort of side-effect of the accelerator's magnetics running in overload had revealed its true identity – unnatural gravity forces. Things other than metal were now being attracted. Close to the chamber, anything not tied down was moving to the wall. Magnetic forces they could resist, but not the universe's very glue. Harper had unwittingly freed the gravity beast, and now that it was unbound, it was hungry and growing daily.

There was no precedent for this. There was no guidebook, no voice of authority or experience. Everything they were doing now would be judged in future days. Harper shuddered. If they were wrong, there might be no more future.

In searching for an answer, any answer, he had originally hypothesized that the original matter transferred, the boy, had created a dimensional imbalance. Since Singer, every time they sent something through, they tried to rebalance the mass equation: whatever went in, man or object, something of comparable mass had to be brought back.

Later, computer simulations had shown they'd never be able to coordinate the matter balance: whether they were out by a ton, or by a few atoms, the balance could never be restored. The stark reality was that the rebalancing was a waste of time. The dimension tear refused to close by itself. Every simulation now showed that they needed to refire the particle collider in the opposite direction to try to reverse the damage they had done. But to do this, they needed something else that disappeared with the boy – the original laser acceleration diamond they had grown to unique specifications in their laboratory. The perfect, tiny red cylinder was the key. Until they had it, the hole would remain open; voracious, devouring, and deadly to the present time and space.

Harper half turned to look over his shoulder. Soldiers stood guard on each side of the door. He knew there were two more on the other side as well. He also knew the project was not really his anymore. In the blink of an eye, or the firing of a laser, it had fallen under military jurisdiction.

His role had become little more than making educated scientific suggestions. The military listened, then did what they wanted. He sighed and turned back to the screen, flicking back to the view of the acceleration chamber and the dark wavering hole. He looked hard at the image, wondering if something on the other side of the breach was staring back at him.

Harper kept his eyes on the screen, and reached down for his cup. His fingers closed on empty space. Looking down, he saw that his cup had moved, slid a few inches towards the side of the table. He felt a ripple of fear in his gut. They were several floors above the acceleration chamber – the gravitational effect was growing.

God help them all.

CHAPTER 2

THERE ARE... THINGS IN THERE

'Arn, help me!'

Eilif was screaming as she was held back from him. She strained and bared her teeth, but couldn't break free.

Arn held out his hand but couldn't quite reach her. He was stuck, unable to move the extra few inches toward her. Eilif's ice-blue eyes were misted and her face streaked with tears. her head flew back and she let loose an unearthly howl that chilled his blood. The long torturous notes were like a blow to his gut, and they spoke of pain and betrayal, of love found and just as quickly lost.

A bag was pulled roughly over her head, and she was dragged down a corridor of concrete, steel, and fluorescent lighting. Soldiers were holding her, human soldiers. She was in his time, his world – it didn't make sense. He could hear her as she called his name over and over, muffled beneath the material. Each time she cried out it seemed farther away. His name echoed, echoed, and then was gone...

'Eilif!'

Arnold 'Arn' Singer sat upright, perspiration running down his face. His heart hammered in his chest and he worked to calm his breathing. It was the dream again, or at least more of it. As if a movie was being played in the deep-sleep corner of his mind, a few more minutes of the reel every time he closed his eyes.

He wiped his face with his hands and blinked away his broken night's sleep. Arn pulled in several large breaths, inhaling the dawn scents of the huge bowl-shaped valley spread out before him. From where he sat high on the cliff edge he felt he could see forever. Perhaps it was the height, or the fact that there was not an ounce of pollution in the crystal air.

He let his eyes move over the landscape; it was strange, almost prehistoric. If this was still Illinois then it had folded, sunk, and rearranged itself into something that looked completely primordial.

He waited for his heartbeat to settle. Blankets of floating mist hung in patches over the tree canopy. There was what looked like a volcano's crater-topped mountain to the west, and on the far horizon something glimmered in the weak morning sun, maybe a river or a lake. He'd look at Vidarr's map again to check the jungle's lumps, bumps and contours against its vaguely drawn landmarks.

Arn reached into his pocket and retrieved the only remnant from his own time – a pocket knife. Its small oval shape still shone, and pressed into its side was a compass the size of his thumb nail. He held it flat and waited a second or two for the tiny arrow to settle… north-east to the lake, river or inland sea, or whatever it was gleaming in the distance.

And then?

He grabbed a stone and started to draw on the rock as he let his mind wander. He scratched lines into the hard granite. He had originally planned to travel until he found what he hoped might be a sealed bunker with the gauntlet and lightning bolt insignia on its front. He pulled out the fragment of ancient parchment the old Wolfen Vidarr had given him; he knew the place; he had seen it himself a year ago. He snorted. *Perhaps a million years ago.*

He scratched some more lines.

If he found it, after all the hundreds of millennia, would he be able to be open it? Would there be anything inside other than a deep decrepit hole that, in the old archivist's own words, 'might contain things that crawled up from Hellheim itself'? Stay in the light, he had been warned.

He grazed a knuckle as he carved, and he lifted his hand, seeing the small lines of blood, as well as the silver wolf's head ring. Its snarling face and red eyes glared back at him, roaring out a challenge of the House of Grimvaldr, the kingdom of his friends. Now fallen.

Eilif had given him the ring. He fiddled with it – still a little loose. It now seemed so long ago that it could have been a dream. He wiped his hand and finished his rock carving. He smiled at the words – Arn was here.

'Arn who?' he said to the carving and lay back, placed one arm under his head, and looked up into the rapidly brightening sky. Blue, a few clouds, It looked the same. It had been a year since he had fallen into this world. A place where his own people were nothing more than a myth or legend, and in their stead now lived creatures, whole races different to anything he had ever known.

What would his grandfather have made of it all? *Yuhica ee-hahn blay* – the waking nightmare – he would have said ominously. Then the old man would have closed his eyes to think on it for a while, mumbling to himself, maybe even spirit walking, as he used to call it. Arn wished he were here now; he would have known what to do.

Arn was Shawnee. His family was one of the last few true bloods left in the state, and he'd spent years cutting his hair, ignoring his heritage, and forcing his body into normal clothes so he could conform. Looking like everyone else was, to him, more important than who he really was.

He sat forward and examined his hands and arms. The skin was darkly tanned, the muscles in his arms bulged and were whipcord strong from days of climbing. His long black hair was pulled back with a cloth band around his forehead. Now he probably looked more like a Native American than even his grandfather had.

He smiled ruefully.

Here, being a red man, or white man, or even a blue man didn't matter. Just being human was different enough – enough to get him killed and eaten. He still had the stone in his hand, so he stood and threw it over the edge of the precipice, watching it sail outwards, then arc down towards the ground thousands of feet below. He didn't expect to hear when it struck the valley floor.

A small figure immediately appeared beside him. 'That was a good throw. I think I could do that.'

Arn looked down. Grimson stood there with his hands on his hips, looking like some sort of jerkin-wearing Boy Scout in a Halloween mask. Except it was no mask. The boy, or rather the Wolfen creature, was, or had been, the prince of a mighty kingdom. His care was now entrusted to Arn, by the king… of a kingdom that by now had probably been overrun by creatures from some lunatic's nightmare.

'Be my guest.'

Arn picked up another stone, tossed it to him, and stood back watching the Wolfen as he drew his arm back. Grimson's fur shone in the morning sunlight, and his silver-blue eyes stayed on Arn with an evenness that was confident, honest and sharp. They were the eyes of a hunter, a noble born, and a warrior.

It was hard to hold the gaze of the young Wolfen and he looked away. The eyes haunted Arn, because they reminded him of the Valkeryn princess, Eilif. He felt a pang of regret, and a deep loneliness. Never had he met someone, some-*thing*, like her. She had disturbed and attracted him in equal measures. He had thought of her as a friend… but still couldn't stop thinking of her as something, more. Could someone love another who is so different? *No, impossible*, he thought, and flung another rock. *Gone now, all gone.*

'Are you watching, Arnoddr?' Grimson held his arm cocked, obviously waiting for an audience

'Huh?' Arn blinked and looked at the youth. He smiled and

motioned with his arm to the cliff edge. 'Let her rip.'

Grimson frowned. 'Let her rip?"

Arn shook his head. 'Uhh, I mean, go on… throw it.'

Grimson's arm swung forward and the small stone disappeared over the cliff edge, travelling about a third as far as Arn's. The Wolfen walked to the edge and peered down, following the tiny object with his keen eyes until it finally disappeared into the lumpy green treetops thousands of feet below. He turned and nodded. 'Hmm, yes. I think it went a little further than yours.' He wiped his hands on his pants and planted them on his hips. 'I'm hungry. Can we hunt now?'

Arn looked along the path, and then down. 'Yep, but first we need to get down there.'

Grimson stepped even closer to the edge and looked down over the precipice. His eyes moved over the landscape, as if seeing through the thick canopy of trees to what lay below. When he turned to Arn, his face was stony.

'That's the start of the Dark Lands. There are… things, in there.'

Arn laughed, slapping the youth on the shoulder, and holding on to pull him back a step.

'And there are things up here. They're called Arn and Grimson, and there be no creatures more fearsome in lands dark or light. Shall we make our way down, and scare some small things onto our plates?'

Grimson laughed, his trepidation forgotten. 'Some large things would be even better.'

The pair edged along the narrow path for another hour, sometimes moving just inches at a time with their backs to the rock face where the path was little more than a foot-span across. Arn closed his eyes for a moment, his foot almost daring him to step forward, knowing that one slip would mean all his fears, pressures and troubles would be over.

A small hand nudged his, and he looked down to see Grimson urging him on, a grin splitting the Wolfen's face. Just like a human boy, for him this was an adventure, and every day meant something new and exciting. Arn continued to shuffle along, forgetting his selfishness; he had bigger responsibilities now.

Slowly, slowly they moved around a bulge of dark granite and then abruptly, the path ceased to exist.

'Crap.'

An ancient rock fall had scoured the side of the mountain clean and dragged their track down to the valley in a heap of raw earth, boulders and crushed trees. Arn looked back the way they had come, then over the edge, and then again in the distance along the cliff face – it was near vertical, broken only by some dark holes that could have been caves, or just deep fissures.

Further on, their path resumed, but it was well over a hundred feet away. Too far to leap, too steep to clamber across, and not a single handhold on the scarred granite.

The raised slope they had chosen to cross looked to be about five thousand feet high, with a fairly easy slope on the Valkeryn side of their climb. But this side dropped steeply, was rugged, and Arn was sure from a greater distance it would resemble a giant tooth curving up and in towards the Dark Lands. In fact the entire cliff line had sharp peaks of similar shape, a gigantic set of open jaws waiting to swallow anything mad enough to enter.

Arn marveled at the forces that had created the barrier. A gigantic crustal movement had occurred when tectonic plates had ground up against one another. One part of their world had dropped, while a geological behemoth had been forced up elsewhere.

Our world? Arn wondered at the wisdom of the thought. Compared to the mountainous cliffs, he and Grimson were just two biological specks. He half smiled. *I am as old as you, Brother Mountain. Now, let me pass.*

Arn leaned out again and felt a steaming humidity rise up

past him, the first he had really felt in this strange world. To date the climate had been dry and benign. The mountain range was acting as a partition, separating one land from the next. He had crossed from a desert to a forest, and now was trying to enter a jungle.

'Can't go back, can't get across, and too high to jump.' Arn exhaled in a silent whistle.

'I can pray to Odin.'

Arn looked at the youth and smiled. 'Sure, why not... everything helps.'

Grimson nodded and shut his eyes, his lips moving silently.

Arn watched the youth for a few seconds. Praying might be all they had left, he mused. He guessed that the Panterran would soon be following them. The attackers of the Valkeryn kingdom, and their monstrous allies the Lygon, were ruthless, and the thought of falling into their hands again, and allowing them to capture the young Wolfen, made him shudder. It would be better to die trying than risk going back.

Arn leaned out from the rock face, and then looked up, moving his line of sight slowly back the way he had come.

'Maaaybe.'

Arn's voice made Grimson stop his praying and open his eyes. Arn tapped his shoulder. 'Back up about fifty paces.'

The youth did as he was instructed, and soon they both stood below a series of craggy bulges and fissures. Arn pointed at the scarred rocks ahead, working his finger up to a point above them. 'The rockslide started around our level. But above it, the mountain is still wearing its original face. I think if we can climb straight up about fifty feet, err...' Arn did a quick translation into the Wolfen numbering system. '... about twenty longs, we can edge across, and then drop back down onto the path.'

Grimson made a fist. 'You see. I knew it there'd be a way across. Odin always looks after the faithful.'

Arn smiled at the youth's confidence. 'Keep praying, Grim. The hard part is just about to begin.'

Arn turned back to the rock face, mentally mapping his route. He knew the climb would be impossible for the small Wolfen, as the scarce crevices, cracks and fissures in the stone they would use as toe and handholds were more than his body length apart. Arn was going to have to bear his weight – not impossible, as long as the Wolfen hung on tight and remained immobile.

'Okay, gonna have to carry you.'

'By Odin you will not, Man-Kind. I will climb myself.' Grimson backed up a step, his brow furrowed with indignity.

'I *will* carry you, otherwise we won't make it, and the Panterran will catch us. They'll be after us soon, if they aren't already.'

Grim's eyes narrowed, but there was a sliver of fear in them. 'The Panterran will never catch me unaware again. The next time they come, I'll cut their foul heads from their necks.'

'Maybe, but not today.' Arn reached for him. 'Remember, your father entrusted you into my care, and that means you are to do as I tell you. Now give me your hands.' Grimson put them behind his back, and turned his face away.

Oh Great. Remind me never to have kids, he thought and snorted mirthlessly. *Like that's going to happen here.*

'Do as you're told!' Grimson's eyes widened in shock at the harsh tone. 'Now, give me your hands.'

Grimson slowly held them out. Arn pulled his headband from his head, and unwound it. He then grabbed the young Wolfen's hands, and tied the wrists together. After much arguing, and a few choice curses, the youth finally understood what was expected. Arn carefully knelt and then looped the boy's tied arms over his neck. He stood up, Grimson hanging down his back.

Surprisingly, and thankfully, light, he thought. A year ago, exercise was something the jocks did, while he just watched. Now, he lived it. Arn looked up at the rock face again, grabbed

Grimson's swinging legs and wrapped them around his waist. He drew in a deep lung full of air, and leaped up a few feet to the first handhold. His fingers stuck, and he wedged his toe into a crack.

One small step, for a "Man-Kind", he thought as he pulled himself higher.

Hours passed, sometimes fast, sometimes agonizingly slow. If he was lucky he'd find a slight jutting bulge of stone that supported his entire weight, and he'd gratefully rest for a few minutes.

He missed his headband, as rivulets of sweat ran down his face and into his eyes, and more worryingly, coated his fingers and palms. Grimson hung on tight, and gave a running commentary on where next to place his hands, or which angle to start moving across. It all helped, and he tried hard not to think about the dizzying heights right behind them.

So far, they had made it just halfway across the raw scar on the rock face. Soon they would be able to ease down the fifty or more feet back to their path. Arn leaned in against the stone and relaxed slightly. He turned his face so the sunshine and breeze could dry some of the perspiration running into his eyes.

Arn sucked in air and blew it out. Right now he needed to focus. They were at the most dangerous point of the climb. The stone above the rock fall, where they clung, might also slide away, and as the rock face below them was gouged smooth, there was nothing to cling onto. It would be one long fall on their way down to the ground.

Arn stopped again and sucked in more air. His arms and shoulders screamed with pain from the exertion. He wished it was night, so the glow of the moon would fill him with the strange unnatural strength he felt every time it rose. He leaned his head against the rock, and inhaled its clean dry scent of sand, earth, and the hundred different minerals that had come from miles below the surface of the Earth.

Whispered words came to him.

[Give up]

'Huh?' He opened his eyes.

[It's all only a dream. Let go]

It was the sly voice in his head again – the creeping demon of doubt that had first appeared when he had crossed the wasteland, and obviously still lurked in the dark corner of his mind, hoping to undermine him when he was at his most vulnerable.

[You can make it if you let go... of the child]

He gritted his teeth. 'Never!'

'What? What is it? Grimson brought his face around close to Arn's, his nose cold and pressing into his cheek.

'It's nothing. Just, nothing.' Arn closed his eyes again, and licked dry lips. His arms now vibrated from the strain. 'It's just... I'm stuck. I can't...'

Grimson leaned back an inch and lifted his head. 'Odin, father of us all, give the great Arnoddr Sigarr your mighty strength so we may cross the mountain.'

[He's too heavy. Cut him loose or he'll kill you both]

Arn felt one of his hands slip just as Grimson shifted his weight, the youth leaning back even further as he yelled more prayers to the sky.

[Who will know? Who will care?]

This time the voice ended with a small, cruel laugh.

No, please, no. Arn squeezed his stinging eyes shut after the silent plea. His eyes burned, either from the sweat or from tears that were starting to form. Help me!

Tuweni Iyayekiy.

Arn opened his eyes.

TUWENI IYAYEKIY!

The furious words pulled Arn's face back from the rock. It was his grandfather's voice, deep, confident, angry. The old man's words were in the ancient tongue.

Tuweni Iyayekiy – never surrender.

'I will never surrender.' Arn tensed, then sprang, leaping across five feet of space to the next handhold. His teeth were gritted and his lips pulled back. He roared as he willed a bolt of aggressive energy into his fatiguing muscles. His body slammed hard and he clung to the rock, his fingers digging into the tiniest of cracks.

'There.' Grimson pointed with his long nose to the next small shelf. Arn swung again while he had the will and a few ounces of strength. He could feel his overworked heart slamming against his ribs, but he dare not stop now. He looked along the rock face, and waited while Grimson searched out the next foot or handhold he could use.

They'd make it; he knew in his soul now that the worst was over. While he clung, waiting, a shadow passed over him.

Arn frowned. It had moved far too quickly for it to be a cloud – a bird maybe? He pulled his head back, and as he half turned, the youth clinging to his back screamed. The darkness flicked by him again, this time catching an impression of something dark and leathery soaring past.

'What was that?'

Grimson clung to him even tighter. 'I don't know, but it's big and it's coming back.'

'Hang on.' Arn scrabbled up a few feet to another fissure in the stone, but resisted the temptation to rush. He couldn't afford to get jittery now – one small slip, and it'd be all over for both of them. 'Keep watching it.'

'I need my blade.' Grimson was becoming frantic on his back.

'Stay still!' Arn remembered he had tied the Wolfen's hands together so he could not let go and fall, but the kid obviously felt he needed his silver blade to protect himself against whatever was taking an interest in them.

With a thump something landed on the rock face beside

17

Arn. He sucked in his breath, and his overworked heart felt like it missed a few very vital beats.

Long claws dug into the stone, and glistening obsidian eyes were fixed on them from within a gargoyle face. Greasy dark fur surrounded a leaf-shaped nose, and a mouth filled with needle-like teeth. As big as a man, it clung to the rock beside Arn. Its enormous arms were cloaked with membranous wings, now hanging beneath its body. Arn saw it lift its head in their direction and he heard it sniff the air, taking in more of their scent. It scrabbled a few inches closer.

'Get outta here! Shoo!' Arn worked his mouth and spat at the creature. The giant bat-thing just dipped its head, and flicked out a thin black tongue to lick at the spittle. It edged closer.

Arn half turned his head. 'What the hell is it?'

Grimson was shivering on his back. 'I don't know, but it has the smell of a meat eater. It's going to attack us, I need my arms free.'

Arn's whipped his head back the way they'd come. His brain whirled; he couldn't move back, and the creature blocked their path. He couldn't use his arms to fight the thing, as he was barely hanging on as it was. He was loath to untie the youth's arms. One slip, and he'd lose him.

There was scrabbling on the rock face again, as the creature edged closer. Arn was out of options. He doubted the thing would be able to lift them from the rock face, but judging by its teeth, he reckoned it could probably rip a good-sized piece of meat from Grimson. He made a decision.

'Okay, put your hands in front of my face and get ready.' Grimson did as he was instructed, and Arn reached forward to pull at the knot with his front teeth.

'Hurry,' Grimson said.

The thing edged sideways and craned its neck to within a few feet of them. Arn could hear the sniffing again. Perhaps, like a true bat, it was better adjusted to darkness, and its eyes were near useless during the daytime hours. He might be able to use that weakness… if he got the chance.

Another thump from above, and loose rock rained down on them.

'Great Odin; it's another one.'

Arn remembered the dark holes in the rock face. They had probably been climbing right into the creatures' hunting ground. Arn ripped with his teeth and the cloth headband pulled loose. He used his mouth to reposition the knot and tugged again. This time the ball of material pulled apart, and he felt one of Grimson's clawed hands grab a length of his hair to hang on. The other he dropped to his scabbard, to pull free his short silver blade.

Arn watched as the cloth headband fell away and then soared up past them as the updraft caught the material, and like a frightened bird it sailed up and up towards the rim of the cliffs.

Arn was momentarily distracted as he envied its freedom. Grimson swung hard against his back as he slashed at the creature. 'Ha!'

It ducked out of the way and made an unsettling chittering sound, snapping its needle-filled mouth at the youth. But at least the thing backed up a fraction. More debris rained down on them as the one above inched closer while they were pre-occupied.

The first creature reached out a leathery wing with a long dark talon at the end, trying to hook the youth from Arn's back; he leaned away, and the young Wolfen continued to swing his arm and the blade back and forth. The bat thing merely pulled back a fraction, watching the blade, and waiting.

'Keep your arm away from it. Those claws will rip you to pieces. We need to move; hang on!' Arn swing towards the thing, causing it to release its grip on the wall, and peel away. It glided backwards for a second or two and then looped around, landing another twenty feet further along from them. It titled its head, watching Arn and Grimson as they edged across the sheer rock face for another few seconds, and then launched itself off the wall again.

When the thing took off, Arn lost sight of it. He concentrated on moving quickly but carefully. Grimson had repositioned himself, scissoring his legs even tighter around Arn's waist, and holding tight to a lock of his long hair, almost riding his back, as he bounced and waved his blade at the giant bat-like thing hanging above them.

Light and dark, light and dark – the sun was being blocked and then revealed as the thing circled them. Arn tried to move a little quicker, and wished he could wipe the streaming sweat from his face, when a smashing thump to his back crushed him to the rock face. The light was completely blotted out, and he was enveloped in a revolting acrid smell that was a mix of raw meat and feces. His arms were pinned and enfolded as what looked like long black fingers wrapped around his arms.

The vermin-ridden thing was blanketing him and Grimson with its wings. From under the membranous cloak there was frantic movement, a mad chittering from the creature and snarling from the Wolfen. Arn yelled Grimson's name, bucking and wriggling as much as he could to try and dislodge the thing using him as a perch before it could lift Grimson free from his back. He could already feel the tugging of the youth's legs at his waist.

The small Wolfen snarled and slashed, and he heard two sets of jaws snapping closed in a fight to the death. Grimson must have slashed his blade upwards as a jet of black blood sprayed the wall next to him, but was quickly followed by a chilling scream of Wolfen pain.

Grimson whined into his ear, and instead of struggling, he wrapped his other arm around Arn's neck, the fight gone from him.

Arn cursed and tried to launch his head backwards to strike the thing, but already it had lowered its gargoyle face to the Wolfen's exposed neck and back. Arn had sworn to the king he would protect his son, and he would be damned if he lost him so soon. He sucked in another deep breath, and dug one of his hands as far into a near crack in the rock face as he could. He then balled his hand into a fist creating a lock that would only be free if he opened his hand, or lost most of the skin on his fist. With his other hand he reached down to his own blade, like Grimson's, but longer and more formidable.

Grimson's long face was now buried at Arn's neck, as he tried to shut out the pain and fear of an attack from behind. His fight was over, and like an injured animal facing an approaching predator he waited meekly for his death.

Arn felt an explosive anger boil up inside him. He pulled his blade free, holding it pointed backwards, and then swung it in a single thrust up behind him, judging as best he could where the young Wolfen ended, and the belly of the beast began.

There was a satisfying feeling of resistance and penetration, and then a hot spray onto his knife-hand and an accompanying cough of pain. The creature stopped moving and peeled away from his back, dragging the long blade from his hand.

Arn whipped his empty hand around to secure Grimson and looked over his shoulder, seeing the thing fall to the ground, many hundreds of feet below. The creature's companion hung above them, watched it plummet for a minute, and then launched itself after the wounded beast. Arn doubted it followed out of any sense of kinship, but was instead tracking an easier meal.

'Are you okay?' Arn waited for a response, and only after he asked the question a second time, there came a feeble answer.

'I hurt.'

Arn nodded to himself, as the youth still had his face buried at Arn's neck. He carefully unlocked his fist, removing his

21

bleeding hand from the crevice, and laid his forehead against the cool stone of the rock face for a few seconds. He exhaled and licked his dry lips.

'It's okay, Grim; we're safe now.' Arn didn't believe it for a second.

CHAPTER 3

COME THE VALKERYIES

Sorenson tried to open his eyes. One was stuck closed, the lid glued with drying blood. The stench of opened bodies filled his nostrils; under him, on top of him, all around him. He was still on his battlefield, now piled high with corpses – many of them his enemies, but mostly his own brother and sister Wolfen.

He tensed his muscles, trying to sit up, but the weight of the dead kept him flat to the ground. He blinked some more and breathed in deeply, trying to regain some strength. He knew he was also wounded, but the damage to his own body was nothing compared to the hacked limbs of those around him.

Am I all that is left? he wondered in despair. As the rest of his senses slowly returned to him, his spirits lifted as he heard voices. Wolfen! Then he froze. There was also the Panterran tongue – the vile Slinkers were near. He drew up one arm, and carefully pushed some broken limbs away so he could see. His spirits sunk low when he saw the Lygon – like massive orange and black tree trunks – standing guard over a line of his kin kneeling before them. Chains bound them together, and their arms were lashed behind their backs. All were stripped of their armor, their battered evidence of a valiant fight, but he now realised, one that had been in vain.

His warrior pack was forced to kneel before the Panterran, while the ogrish Lygon ensured the torture and torment progressed uninterrupted. Sorenson felt a knot in his gut; as captives of the Panterran and Lygon, they could expect no mercy. But despite their injuries, all kept their heads high, their unblinking, defiant gaze on the massed creatures before

23

them. In return, the Panterran cowards, the vile, spitting, and whining assassins with yellow eyes and small goblin faces full of needle sharp teeth permanently pulled into a sneer, fought with each other for a turn to humiliate, taunt or torture their Wolfen prisoners.

Sorenson's breathing became more rapid as he recognized one Panterran amongst the many tormentors – the Queen's emissary, Orcalion. While Sorenson watched, he saw the Panterran questioning one of the Wolfen and then strike him when no answer was forthcoming. The Wolfen bared long white teeth and strained at his chains, causing the Panterran to step back. Even bound, the Wolfen struck fear into his tormentor.

Sorenson smiled grimly; he knew what the reward would be. A huge Lygon fist, encased in an iron glove came crashing down on the top of the resisting Wolfen's skull from behind, smashing him to the ground. He didn't move again, even when the Panterran kicked his body. The Slinker simply shrugged and moved to the next bound Wolfen in the line. And so the questioning began again.

Sorenson gritted his teeth, and tried to find a weapon... anything he could use to rush the gloating tormentors, and at least send a few more of the vile creatures back to Hellheim before he was surely brought down. He strained and then slumped back; there was nothing. In fact, he found he was also stripped of armor and weapons. Perhaps he had been taken for dead, and his body dumped with the other fallen.

Sorenson screwed his eyes shut, as the next Wolfen also refused to be bowed or answer Orcalion. There was no fear; he understood why. Valhalla awaited the battle fallen. The Valkeryies would descend and lift the brave to the golden halls, to sit before Odin, and await the call to the final battle. He wished he had his chance now. At the thought, he felt his heart sink. He had lost his beloved brother, Strom, and his king, and now the entire kingdom of Valkeryn was gone. He lay back and kept his eyes shut, willing the Valkeryies to descend to raise him up.

Orcalion lifted his voice, squealing threats into the face of the next Wolfen. Sorenson's eyes flicked open; he finally heard the words – where was the son of Grimvaldr? And then: where was the Man-Kind?

So, they were still free. Sorenson felt his spirits soar. His will to live exploded within once again. He had a purpose, a mission – this is why Odin had not called his *sáál* to the heavens. If they were truly free, he knew they would need his help. If he could find them… if he could free himself.

Soon, he thought. *Soon, I will have my opportunity.*

The Panterran screamed into the face of the Wolfen again, and then pulled a curved blade from the scabbard at his waist, thrusting it into the chest of the kneeling warrior. He made a dismissive motion towards the remaining prisoners, and the fearsome Lygon fell upon them, hacking at them, or raining heavy cudgels down, until they were nothing but bloodied heaps on the ground. It was over quickly.

Sorenson lay back with his teeth bared, willing his rushing blood to slow, but it wouldn't. Visions of axes cleaving Panterran skulls, long swords thrust into torsos and his own fangs ripping the throat from Lygon flesh flooded his mind and filled him up. His eyes burned and he only just caught the roar that wanted to burst from his lips.

Oh, he would live. He would gather his strength. Live to fight another day. He shut his eyes, praying silently to Odin.

Live to fight another day…. and by Odin's oath, there will be another day.

<hr />

Eilif hugged her knees and rocked back and forth by the stream. She stopped for a moment to stare into a calm shallow at its edge, seeing her ice-blue eyes reflected back at her. She remembered other eyes; those of the strange Man-Kind – dark, like fathomless pools. Her own eyes now looked sunken and miserable.

Bergborr, the dark Wolfen, sat a few paces away, preparing a small animal to eat and occasionally looking up at her, nodding and smiling his reassurance. She lifted her head and sniffed the air. She had sensed for a long time now that the war was lost. The ache in her heart also told her that her father and mother were no longer in Valkeryn, and by now were undoubtedly crossing the rainbow bridge to the golden halls of Asgard.

And what of the kingdom of Valkeryn, her home? She doubted it still stood. Eilif sniffed back some tears. Arn had left her and the kingdom before the battle. But she saw that now as only a good thing. If he had stayed then he might be lying cold among the fallen, and then what? She didn't want to think what the world would be like if he wasn't in it. She would follow him to the ends of the Earth, through time itself, if need be.

She sniffed again, continuing to stare at her reflection in the still water. From the moment she had regained consciousness, she had screamed out his name... much to the horror of Bergborr. She couldn't help it; she would never stop thinking about the strange creature from the past that had haunted her dreams even before he arrived.

He was something so different, so alien, that to some, her feelings for him were seen as either curious, or abhorrent. Perhaps that was why her father had tasked the strange Man-Kind with the mission to take her brother from the kingdom, to keep him safe. Maybe also to keep her and Arn far apart.

She looked hard at her image in the still pool. She knew Arn didn't feel about her the way she felt about him. She had offered her heart, and he hadn't refused it. But she wasn't sure he understood what it meant to her. Perhaps she was too different, too ugly.

'Ugly.' She touched her face as she whispered the word to the water.

Eilif looked down at her forearm where a recent battle scar was healing. The fur had not yet grown back, and the skin on her arm was bare, pink and smooth. She ran her fingers over the skin.

'Perhaps underneath we are more alike than he thinks.' She rubbed the warm skin, closing her eyes for a moment, and thinking of Arn's smooth brown hide. She sighed; there would be no other for her.

Eilif looked across to the smiling black Wolfen. She knew he still held out a vain hope of becoming her mate. When she had fallen in the great battle, he had rescued her, and though her memory of the events were hazy, she guessed she owed him her life. She smiled back sadly. *Thank you for saving me, but the competition for my affection is long over.*

She turned away, raising her head into the breeze and sniffing again. In her *sáál*, or soul as Arn had called it, she could sense him. She would find him. She knew where he would go – he sought the Dark Lands and the buried caves of the Ancients. He was trying to find his way home. She would track him.

Eilif got unsteadily to her feet, feeling the bandages binding her back, which felt tight from where the dark Wolfen must have closed her wounds. He had saved her life, but she didn't know yet if she could trust him. Still, he was a warrior of the Wolfen elite, and she was a princess. He was duty bound to help her, to get to the Dark Lands. She would tell him that they needed to seek out any clan remnants of the Far Wolfen, if they still existed. She didn't think it would be judicious to tell him of her suspicions about Grimson and Arn heading there just yet.

He still needed to prove himself. If he were honorable, she would tell him everything. If he weren't, then she would slay him without a second thought.

Sorenson kept his eyes tightly shut as the mound of bodies above him was pulled down. Next, his feet were roughly bound together. He heard the Panterran's guttural talk as the hundreds of other bodies he had been collected up. Now they were all to be dragged back to the Lygon camp for a victory feast... with the meat of his dead kin the main fare.

He used every ounce of his will to appear lifeless as the stink of the Lygons enveloped him. They had felt his arms and thighs, squeezing the flesh, organizing the corpses into grades of 'meat' quality. He was to be in the inferior category – the flesh on his long, hard and muscled frame too stringy and tough.

Just as well, for he soon realized that making the grade meant he could have been broken up for a quick meal on the way back to the camp. He tried to shut out the sound of the splintering bones and of limbs being ripped from their sockets.

He gritted his teeth – he knew fighting a Lygon while unarmed and unarmored would be difficult. But trying to fight a small army of them would mean death. He would need to wait. He knew that the closest Lygon camp was nearly a day's march – an opportunity would present itself. It must.

For now... he would lie still, and pray for strength.

The Lygons huddled and argued. It seemed that killing all the Wolfen had turned out to be a bad idea. Now, instead of making the prisoners march, the task of dragging all the fresh meat back to the camp would be the job of several of the Lygon... yet to be chosen.

The arguments quickly turned into physical confrontations and some of the giant beasts took to each other with hammer, club, tooth and claw, until a roar from one creature subdued them all.

This large brute pushed his way roughly to the front, slashing at the faces of the fighting Lygons. Sorenson lay still with his eyes half closed but easily recognized the beast – Goranx, the slayer of his king and his brother, and the leader of the Lygon army. Princess Eilif's broken arrow shaft still protruded from his wrist.

Sorenson carefully worked his head below a corpse tied next to him. If Goranx found him, even if he believed he was dead, he'd probably take his head, or mutilate his body just for the amusement it would bring him. Swinging at the monster's belt were the heads of some of the Man-Kind beings, and also his Wolfen brother, Strom. Sorenson turned away.

Another roar from the giant, and several dozen of the massive beasts shouldered the ropes, and started to drag the bodies, like bunches of bloody grapes. They bounced across all types of terrain, and Sorenson felt every rock and branch. Without armor, the travelling was harsh, and after several hours Sorenson knew that the fur and skin on his back was becoming raw. He couldn't afford to begin bleeding again – dead bodies didn't bleed.

They entered a deeper section of the forest, and now were dragged along overgrown paths and in amongst the bracken and fallen trees. Sorenson became alert – there was more shelter now, and it would only be a few more hours until they reached the Lygon camp. There, escape would be impossible. It would have to be soon. He tensed, alert for the opportunity.

Sorenson, like the rest of the corpses, had roughly a body length of rope tying him to the main bunch of dead Wolfen. He had observed that even if one of the corpses got itself snagged on something, the massive brutes simply pulled harder until it became free, worrying not if the body became torn, or a limb was ripped free.

Sorenson felt his heart leap. A chance approached – a tree stump up ahead, and to the side of the group where he was bound. He waited, praying that the brutes continued to face forward.

As he approached the stump, he quickly sat up, and jumped forward, giving himself some slack in his rope, which he then looped around the stump. He grabbed the length nearest his ankles and braced his feet, using the stump as a counter measure – either he'd be ripped over the top of the stump, the stump would be lifted from the ground, or...

The rope became taught, its fibers groaned for an instant, and the Lygons cursed. Sorenson strained to keep the rope in place, he ground his teeth, it was now or never, he thought as he silently prayed.

One of the Lygons began to turn, and Sorenson held his breath, but the others, too bored, or too dumb to care, simply bent their shoulders and pulled harder. The rope popped, and Sorenson rolled into the brush. He turned and waited, listening. Nothing stopped, no shouts came – just the low rumble of Lygon voices, receding, and the sound of his fallen Wolfen brothers and sisters as they were dragged away.

He quickly untied his feet, standing unsteadily, and rolling his stiff muscles. He balled his fists and raised his face to the darkening sky. Odin give me strength, he prayed, and then started to run.

CHAPTER 4

TIME FOR A LITTLE PAYBACK

The line of matte-black SUVs with darkened windows powered towards the Fermilab facility. To anyone watching, they looked like a line of aggressive, armor-plated beetles in attack formation.

Inside the lead vehicle, Colonel Marion Briggs leaned forward to look at the sky above the facility. Bruise-colored clouds now hung there permanently, and had started a slow rotation above the acceleration chamber – an airborne whirlpool forming in an angry sky. Strangely, just a few miles further out was clear. It seemed the weird weather was confined to this area alone.

Briggs sat back and thought about the scientist, Harper, and his warning about the potential dangers of trying to force the anomaly closed. Even if they nuked the entire site, burning a few square miles down to nothing but slag, it might not fully close the breach. It might just mean the freaking hole Harper and his pencil-neck boffins had punched through time and space was just buried for a while. And then by the time it did re-emerge, it would be too large to do anything about, other than bend over and kiss our collective asses goodbye.

But, there was another option – an extremely dangerous and potentially suicidal option. They could enter the vortex and retrieve the red diamond initiator themselves. She had already lost one team, but Briggs knew that the sacrifice had been worthwhile. After all, what price good intel... and they had learned a lot.

She sat back and smiled. Things would be done right this time. Because this time, she was going. Those freakish monsters were about to get some of their own lessons. Lesson-one: Earth has its own monsters, and she would make the introductions personally.

Briggs laughed softly. The US military had been working hard to move away from its image as an aggressor. Normally, entering foreign territory with any high-powered kit would be vetoed immediately, but this time the creatures had attacked their people first, and now they had a human as a hostage. That gave her mission full combat legitimacy – she was free to make war, under Presidential order. It was all too perfect.

She licked her lips and thought again of the image feeds that had been sent back to them by the probe. There was a whole world there – pristine and vast, and one she fully intended to appropriate on behalf of the United States of America. She snorted; how many soldiers got to make a righteous war, rescue their citizens, and potentially stake a claim on an entire world in the name of their country. She'd be famous. She'd be Christopher Columbus and General Patton rolled into one tough Special Forces kick-ass package.

This time she would not be unprepared. The giant creatures that had attacked her previous team had been enormously powerful, armored, and aggressive. Further they were non-human – no doe-eyed Eloi dancing around maypoles to tug at week-kneed, liberal heart-strings. You saw one of these big bastards up close, you wanted it dead... before it damn well ate you.

Briggs looked over her shoulder at the four hulking frames of her soldiers sitting silently in the rear of her speeding vehicle, with the rest in the other nine SUVs. She had forty Special Forces Delta Team – the best of the best – and she had something else... she had Samson. Her hand-picked Delta Ops captain, recommended multiple times for bravery awards, commendations, and also for immediate discharge on the basis of an aggressive psychopathic psychology. The man was a killing machine. But as a soldier he was fearless, hard to kill, and followed orders. He was perfect.

Those freaks got the jump on us last time. Time for a little payback, she thought, as they slowed at the entrance gates.

❦ ❦

At his desk, Albert Harper leaned forward on his knuckles and exhaled miserably as he watched the line of black vehicles slow at the security gate. The guard looked briefly at the documentation, saluted, and then stepped back to the booth to open the electronic fence. He hadn't needed to salute; he wasn't armed forces and didn't work for them. Seems the military assuming control of the project had confused just about everyone.

Harper sighed as his guard stayed at attention for each passing car. He guessed that Briggs had been in the lead car – her ferocious demeanor would make anyone obey or get the hell out of the way. *That woman's a nasty piece of work,* he thought. The SUVs accelerated in unison, almost as if they had been chained together. Bringing up the rear was some sort of massive eighteen-wheeler painted a non-reflective matt black. He could only wonder at what it contained.

Harper squinted at the screen. Crack drivers, as well as marksman, frogmen, hand-to-hand combat specialists, demolition experts. He shook his head. *Just as well they knew nothing about particle physics, or he might as well go home right now,* he thought glumly.

He checked his watch: they'd be here, in his office, in around ten minutes. He knew that Briggs planned to enter the anomaly gate with several dozen fully armed elite soldiers. The breach in time and space needed to be closed, and finding the boy, and the acceleration initiator, was the priority, but by now they had no idea where he was in the world, and the world was a big one. He snorted. Well, of course it was – it was ours – just at some distant point in the future.

Harper ground his teeth, to try and settle the niggling feeling he was getting in the back ones that had once held metallic fillings. He didn't know exactly how much time they had before a tipping point was reached, but based on how quickly the magnetic cores were degrading, he guessed it could only be a few more months, maybe weeks. But then what? He pulled at his lower lip. What happened if the distortion hole grew to a point where it started to pull large matter, all matter, into some sort of gravitational vortex? Would it be satisfied with just the building, the city, the continent, or would it continue growing until it scoured clean the surface of their world?

Harper straightened. Briggs had threatened to take him along for the ride this time. His colleague, Takeda, had accompanied the Green Berets on their first foray, and never made it back. He knew they had all died brutally The thought of it made him sick. Might as well shoot me here, he thought.

He looked at the monitor again and saw the cars slide to a halt. The hulking soldiers stepped from the vehicles. Briggs strode up and down their line, with her hands on her hips, the soldiers coming to attention. They looked professional, formidable, and deadly.

He turned to the door. Nothing to fear, but fear itself. *What crap*, he thought miserably, and went down to meet them.

• ┼◎◕◗ ⨯⨯◌◌⨯ ◌◗◕◎┼ •

Colonel Marion Briggs stood on the ramp at the back of the enormous truck that she had ordered parked across the front of Fermilab's main building. It was eighty feet long and thirty-five tons... and that was before they added another ten tons of armor plating. The monstrous vehicle was a mobile command centre, with enough ionized shielding to protect its occupants and their sensitive equipment against everything from a significant EMP wave to uranium tipped RPG strikes.

The 'beast', as it was affectionately known, would watch and listen to everything that went on – in this world or wherever Briggs decided to take her team.

Satisfied that everything was in order, she jumped down from the ramp so she could pace along the line of men and women assembled before her. All over six feet tall, they had been chosen for their aggression, skills, and unique ability to survive hostile terrain, and act as a fully autonomous unit on foreign soil. Where they were going was about as foreign as it got.

The Delta Force team's brutal and scarred faces, though young, reflected a life of hard trauma and pain, testimony to theatres of conflict all across the globe – though none of the missions would ever be found in any publicly available dossier.

Each of them wore a black, non-reflective uniform, interwoven with a Kevlar thread at the joints to give maximum rotational ability. Larger areas, like the chest, thighs and biceps were covered in ceramic plating, with armadillo strips down over torso – the composites virtually weightless but harder than steel. She nodded her approval.

The team stood stock-still, HK416 assault rifles strapped at their chest, with accessories for night vision, sound suppressors and grenade launchers. The carbine was a variant, replacing the M4, but with a shorter barrel for close-quarters combat. The A5 carbine had a gas piston kick to ramp up projectile velocity – it was short, light and deadly. Each carried a variety of knives at their hip, mostly K-Bar with night blackened blades and a tanto edge – like sloping chisels – guaranteed not to break or dull against rock, steel or bone.

She stopped in front of one huge man and looked him up and down. He stared straight ahead, his blue eyes unwavering.

'All right there, Teacher?'

'Delta is always right, ma'am.' Big Jim Teacher, or Teach to his comrades, stood a little straighter. He was one of her leading Specs Ops agents, an excellent strategist, as well as an unnaturally-gifted combat specialist.

'Good.' She put her hands on her hips, feeling her own blades nestling there. She nodded; they were ready. She turned and squinted at sound of an approaching Fermilab guard – slightly overweight and graying at the temples, he jogged towards them, puffing hard and holding up a hand. By his side, trotted an enormous German Shepherd dog.

The animal's eyes were like gun barrels, such was the intensity of its gaze… and focused directly on Briggs. The animal's eyes unnerved her. They were way too intelligent. The guard yelled to her, but she ignored him and turned back to her team, running a hand up and across her head, feeling the military crew-cut bristles spiking at her palm. Her mouse-blond hair, normally pulled back into a severe bun, was no more – in the field pragmatism was required, not aesthetics.

Briggs circled her hand in the air, and the team turned as one toward the large doors.

'Hold up, you can't park there.' The guard increased his pace, and tilted his head down to speak a few words to the dog, who sprinted forward. It immediately began to nose in amongst the soldiers, sniffing each in turn. When it came to Briggs she swatted it away. To her surprise, the dog stood on its hind legs, now taller than the colonel, and stared down into her face, the eerie cold eyes, seeming to burn right through her.

'Piss off.' She went to take a step, but the huge dog moved to place itself between her and the front of the building.

The guard chuckled. 'Don't mind…'

Briggs balled her fists. 'I warned Harper to keep these freaks outta my face.' She backhanded the animal across the nose – hard – the ceramic knuckles on her gloves ensuring it was a painful blow. She turned away again, and started giving a few more instructions to her team.

The guard's good humor fell away in an instant. 'Hey, cut that out.' He strode towards Briggs, and made the mistake of reaching out a hand to place it on her shoulder, and tug.

Briggs reacted immediately. Like lightening, she spun, grabbed his wrist and twisted, making the man cry out in shock and pain. She looked at his name-tag.

'Listen, Mr. Loeman...'

Things happened quickly. The dog snarled and leapt for the Colonel's hand, but before the animal could grab her forearm, one of the soldiers had materialized beside her. The man moved unnaturally fast and silently for someone who was easily six and a half feet tall. He landed a cracking blow into the side of the dog's head that sent it sprawling. The blow would have left a man unconscious, especially as it was delivered with the heavily-plated gloves.

But, a German Shepherd's skull is thicker than a human's and covered in a layer of fur, so the animal came back fast, this time its eyes round with fury and long teeth bared like white daggers. It leapt to attack. The soldier barely moved, just holding up one arm, the forearm horizontal to protect his neck and face, and also present an armored barrier for the dog to latch on to. The animal did as expected; it bit down hard on his arm. In a single smooth motion, the soldier pulled his longest blade from its sheath, and brought it up between the animal's ribs.

There was a bloodcurdling scream of pain, and then the animal fell away from his arm. He leant to wipe the blade on the dog's coat.

The guard came at the enormous Special Forces soldier, but Briggs shouted to him: 'Halt, or you'll be next.'

Her voice froze him. The enormous soldier with the blond flat-top crewcut stood motionless, holding the dark blade at his side, but kept an unwavering gaze on the guard. There was a slight satisfied smile on his lips.

The guard crumpled, going to his knees beside his dead animal. He cradled its head. 'Morgana!' He buried his head in its fur.

There was silence for a few seconds, before an eerie sound rose from a white dome shaped building in the distance, a cross between a howl and something almost intelligible.

Briggs frowned and looked around, her eyes settling on the Fermilab building. She snorted. Albert Harper was sprinting towards them. He skidded to a stop, and held both hands up to his head. 'What the hell happened here?'

Colonel Briggs spoke evenly. 'We were attacked, and we defended ourselves.' Without looking at him, she motioned to the guard. 'This man is lucky he didn't wind up as dead as his animal. I hold you personally responsible, Harper. I warned you that these animals would be tolerated as long as they did not to get in our way.'

Harper stuttered in disbelief for a second. 'H-He was just doing his job. You know all visitors need to be cleared, and the Guardians...' he pointed angrily to the dead animal, '... provide a non-intrusive and non-electronic way of doing that for us.' He stepped in close to her. 'Jesus, Briggs, each of these animals is worth half a million bucks, and owned by your military. You're going to have to answer to...'

'Well Harper, you can report that the military just field tested one of their animals... ' She grinned, but there was no warmth or humor in the show of teeth, '... and you can put in your report that your dogs need more work.'

She turned to the big man, who had sheathed his knife and stood like a colossal black clad statue behind her. 'That'll be all Samson, get back in line.'

He nodded and immediately spun to return in amongst the line of soldiers.

Harper spluttered some more, but she cut him off.

'Listen Doc, it attacked us, and now it's dead. Get over it.'

38

She went to turn away and then paused. 'And what the hell is that freakin noise?' She motioned with her head towards the white building.

Harper stood, his face red and his jaws working behind his cheeks, as though he was trying to chew and then swallow down the woman's unbelievable arrogance. After a few seconds, he exhaled and spoke slowly. 'That... is the animal testing facility, along with the dog compound. What you're hearing is probably a collective display of loss... and anger.'

'How do they know from over there?' Briggs turned her head, slowly scanning the open ground surrounding the enormous facility. She shrugged. 'No, I don't care. Now, do you want to rescue the young man you lost or don't you?'

Harper turned away from her, and knelt beside the guard who was cradling the dead animal. He put his hand on the man's shoulder. 'It's Jim isn't it?' The man nodded. 'I'm sorry; she was a good animal. I'll send someone out to help you.'

Harper went to stand but seemed to have another thought. He knelt back down and put his hand on the guard's shoulder. 'Don't take her back to the compound. I don't want the other Guardians to see the wound.' He lowered his voice. 'They'll know.'

He looked up at Harper, tears clearly blurring his eyes. After a second or two, he nodded and then Harper got to his feet. His face became stony as he turned back to the colonel.

'Your man will need an anti-mutagen shot. The animal fluids can affect human DNA – something we're still working on. This way.' Harper strode off with his shoulders hunched.

Briggs stood for a second longer and shook her head at the scientist's back. She then looked up at the sky – angry, iron-colored clouds moved in a ring over the facility.

'Stupid damn scientists.' She shook her head, exhaling long and loud for a few seconds, before turning back to her team. 'Let's move it.' She began to trot towards the massive doors of the facility, followed by the double line of her team.

Teacher looked down at the man and the dead animal. He shook his head and fell back into line to follow the group in.

CHAPTER 5

SHE'D BE FAMOUS

'This is sooo cool.'
Becky Matthews sat next to Edward Lin on the hillside, hunkered down against the wind that constantly swirled around their shoulders and threw sticks and leaves into their hair. Both had field glasses to their eyes, and Becky twirled the focus wheel at their centre as she moved her lenses a little to the left. Most days after school, sometimes on weekends, and even during the night when the urge took one of them, they would creep up into the hills overlooking the Fermilab facility to peer down into their grounds.

She half peeked at the young man beside her. It was strange the way things had turned out; look at her now, just sitting on a freezing hill in the evening with Edward Lin, an uber science-nerd, and about as far from being her type of friend as anyone could be. She in turn had been, was, one of the most popular girls at Nap High. Arn had brought them together, and he didn't even realize it. Not only brought them together but made them co-conspirators and potential lawbreakers.

Both Edward and Becky had been sworn to silence by the government – national interest you understand, they had said to her and her parents. But they couldn't control her – and when she wanted something bad enough, she usually go it.

They had watched when the soldiers had arrived, and then as the giant black-clad man had killed the dog. She had cried out in her anger at the brutal action, but thankfully she was too far away to be heard. She knew if she tried to tell anyone, the only ones likely to be arrested would be her and Edward

41

for spying. It was clear now that the military, or whoever they were, were controlling the facility.

'We should go.' Edward said and shifted beside her. She ignored him and pulled the thick down jacket a little tighter to her shoulders, and moved the glasses away from her eyes to look up at the sky. It was purple-black, and looked corrupt, and as if it was some sort of stained bathwater swirling down into a drain.

Thunder cracked over their heads, and Edward cringed, swearing under his breath, before talking to her out of the side of his mouth. 'C'mon, it's getting worse.'

She nodded. 'Yup, and then what?' She remembered what Albert Harper had told her the last time she had met him; they needed the initiator diamond, and that meant they needed Arn. They needed to bring them both home… or else.

Arn was the key. She wondered about the young man she suddenly found she cared about. Her brows knitted slightly. Did she really care, or did she care more for the excitement and attention? She had played him when he had been so close to her, literally just a few seats away in class. She had been aware of his attention. In turn she had pretended not to notice him at all. It just made him more determined to impress her, and try to stand out. Well, he'd certainly done that, and now, because of this tragedy, she found out she wanted him.

Harper had said he believed Arn was still alive, and could be found and retrieved. But there was something that nagged at her, something that didn't fit. If he was still alive, and could be brought back, then why hadn't he just come back by himself? She narrowed her eyes at the next thought – something, or someone was keeping him away. Maybe she needed to persuade him to return in person. After all, she was the girl of his dreams. He had told her as much.

She spoke without turning. 'If I got you in there, could you cover for me if I wanted to go after Arn?'

Edward's head snapped around and his mouth dropped open, mouthing words, but taking a few seconds before being able to release them. 'Are you... freakin... serious?'

She turned to stare at him with an unblinking gaze. 'I've never been more serious about anything in my life.'

He turned on his side towards her. 'Maybe, and maybe not.'

She frowned. 'Huh? What's that supposed to mean?'

'It means if you get me in there, then I'm going all the way. I'm coming too.' Now it was his turn to hold her gaze.

After a few seconds she smiled and nodded. She felt liberated, alive; at last she had a real purpose. When she returned with Arn, she'd be more popular than ever. She'd be... famous.

* * *

Edward continued to watch Becky, noticing the satisfied smile on her lips. Majoring in physics and all things sci-fi, he felt he had an understanding of what they might be getting into. Just before he had been ejected by Fermilab's new military minders, he had gleaned from Dr Albert Harper what was on the other side of the gateway – a whole new world.

He had been Arn's best friend for, it seemed, forever. But he still couldn't work out why Rebecca Matthews was becoming so determined to find him – she was acting like his long time soul mate, when really, up until the day he had been sucked through the wormhole, she treated him like he barely existed.

He shook his head. How was he to know what she really thought? Or for that matter, what any girl thought? He didn't understand them, and he'd never had a girlfriend, so he couldn't judge them based on his experience. He'd just have to go with what he guessed, or thought... or read in a book.

He'd go along with her plan if it meant getting his friend back. After all, right about now, any help was good help.

CHAPTER 6

ALWAYS WORKED FOR ALLIGATOR JACK

Arn jumped the last ten feet to the jungle floor, landing hard and going down on his hands and knees. His palms, knuckles and fingers were all shredded, and his shoulders and back muscles burned like fire deep in the joints and muscles.

He pulled Grimson from his back and the youth fell to the grass, immediately curling into a fetal position with his eyes squeezed shut. His breathing was faint, and the fur on his back was dark with blood – much of it his own, but also streaks of ink-black, a result of his fight with the bat-like creature from the upper cliff face. The young Wolfen had obviously got in a few good thrusts before he had been overcome.

Arn knelt beside him and wiped at the stinking black mess, but all he achieved was getting the sticky liquid over his abraded hands. He needed water to wash the disgusting blood from the back of his young charge – he had no idea what sort of infections that thing had carried. He also hoped to find some of the strange red-bloomed plants that Eilif had shown him, the ones with miraculous healing properties. He wiped his fingers on the grass and licked his dry lips. He also needed to drink. He was now so parched that his head pounded from dehydration… and if *he* was dry, Grimson, after losing so much blood, would be doubly so.

Arn sat back on his heels and looked around at the thick growth surrounding them. It was twilight under a tree canopy that reached hundreds of feet into the sky. He could smell decaying flesh, composting plant matter, and a thousand exotic fragrances. Birds and animals shrieked and screeched overhead, and looking up, he could make out small bodies weaving in and out of the branches.

On the trip down the face of the cliff, he had seen a 'V' indentation in the green canopy, and hoped that meant there was a watercourse – that or a ravine. He didn't want to think about any more climbing.

Arn wiped his face, feeling his fatigue settle on his frame like a heavy blanket. With both the light and his strength fading, he had to set off immediately.

He looked down at the curled Wolfen. Arn had already experienced a night out in the forest – there were weird vampire worms, centipedes the size of freight trains, and not to mention the vicious cat-like Panterrans. They were now at the edge of the Dark Lands, in a thick jungle, and there was no way he could leave the unconscious youth alone. He lifted the boy, who hung limply in Arn's arms. He might have less time than he thought.

Something glinted just off to his left, and moving towards it he found his blade – thankfully there was no sign of the creature it had been embedded in, or any of its cannibalistic brothers. He picked it up, and sheathed it.

Arn started to jog in the direction of the river. He hoped.

* * *

Only minutes ago the tree canopy inhibited light almost to the point of twilight. Arn knew there would be no starlight, and his ability to see in the dark was poor. He increased his pace; he needed to find the red-bloomed plants – *feninlang*, Eilif had called it – and then he needed to find somewhere safe to rest and wait out the night.

He tried to be quiet, tried to tread softly, but palm fronds and vines whipped at him or clung to his skin, rotten branches snapped under his feet, and his breathing was loud and ragged.

He slowed for a few minutes to catch his breath, and moved the youth to one arm. With the other he reached up to grab a thick vine, and used his knife to slash at it, releasing a stream of milky fluid. He held it up to his lips – he gagged; it burned and caused him to sputter and cough.

'Damn, always worked for Alligator Jack on the Discovery Channel.' He spat out more of the residue, feeling his tongue swell. He cleared his throat, coughed a few more times, and then started to jog again.

Arn ran on; for minutes or hours, he couldn't tell anymore. His vision was starting to blur, and his jog had turned to a stagger. There was next to no light now, and he felt a sinking feeling – without water, treatment for their wounds, and somewhere sheltered to sleep, there was a good chance they'd be found by predators.

'*Tuweni Iyayekiy* – never surrender - *tuweni iyayekiy* – never surrender.' Arn repeated his grandfather's words like a mantra. It was all he had left.

The soft pounding in his head from dehydration turned into a chant. Perhaps it was the ghost of his grandfather, seeking to help, singing to him. The words made him feel less alone as he staggered on.

Arn crashed to his knees, Grim sprawling to the ground in front of him, face down, still. Arn crawled forward, turning the boy over; his tongue lolled from his mouth, and his eyes had rolled back into his head.

'No, you will not.' He shook the youth, and then again roughly. There was a small groan. 'That's better.' He grabbed the boy by the arm, and tried to lift him, but seemed made of lead, the feather-light weight of only a day ago now more like a ton of stone. Arn lowered the young Wolfen's arm, and closed his eyes.

'What do I do, what do I do?'

His grandfather's deep voice again: *Listen...*

'Huh?' Arn tried to slow his breathing, and he shut his mouth to just breathe in through his nose. There was nothing except the sound of creatures moving in the trees overhead, something slithering in the leaf litter, and the noise made by something heavy crashing through the brush, a few miles away... and then.

'I can hear it.'

There was a tinkling, gurgling, splashing. Faint, but it was there.

'Thank you... thank you. C'mon Grim, we're almost there.' He dragged the boy up into his arms, and staggered back a few paces before getting himself into a forward gear. He blundered another few hundred feet, and then broke through onto a riverbank – grassy and shiny wet, down to a slow moving river, wide, and too dark to judge its depths.

'Maybe you used to be Lake Michigan. Or maybe you're something new altogether. I don't care... I love you.'

In the darkness the water was inky black, but even from a few feet away, Arn could smell its freshness. He staggered forward, lay the youth down, and then threw himself face first into the water, luxuriating in its coolness. He sucked in huge drafts, and rubbed his hands up over his face and hair, then sat back and tilted his head back to let the water cascade down his neck, back and chest. Arn reached for Grimson, and pulled him close, cupping water and rubbing it first over his face, nose and lips, and then scooping it to his mouth. Grim's tongue came out, and even with his eyes shut, he licked at the water.

'Good man... err, Wolfen; drink it down.'

No gift is free... It was his grandfather's voice again. Arn frowned; he didn't get it.

No gift is free – be on guard.

Arn's eyes widened, and he stood slowly, lifting the youth with him. He looked around – what was a favorite hunting ground of predators? Riverbanks of course . It was where the deer came to drink at sundown. Arn looked to his sides and then up at the sky. He could make out a glow coming from behind the clouds. He hoped it was the gigantic moon. He desperately needed to be bathed with its energizing rays once more.

He stepped back, and almost stumbled over a boulder sunk in the earth, and as he looked down, he noticed some blood red star shaped flowers sprouting from beside the rock. He went to reach down and then froze. Something was making the hair on his neck prickle. Something wasn't right. He remained frozen, just letting his eyes move over the bank, the dark water, then the overhanging trees and shrubs, first to the left and then to the right. Nothing...

There came a splash, and he whipped his head around. It wasn't repeated, but he straightened, and wrapped one arm tighter around the young Wolfen, who for now at least was breathing a little easier against his chest.

Arn frowned; the jungle had grown quiet. A rash of goose-bumps broke out on his arms, and his heart beat a rapid tattoo in his chest.

We're not alone, he thought.

He took a step back, intending to sprint back into the brush, but then stopped – he needed the red star shaped flowers. Without them, Grimson would probably die from his wounds. He might not get another chance. He reached down for the flower heads, and glanced briefly towards the river. He froze and felt the breath catch in his throat.

CHAPTER 7

NOTHING HERE BUT A THOUSAND OLD GHOSTS

Balthazaar sat in the dark, feeling miserable, hungry and for the first time in many decades, afraid. Close to him he could sense the old archivist, Vidarr, his breathing so soft and slow he wondered whether the old Canite was even awake.

Above them the sounds of looting, carnage and destruction had ceased – the invaders had departed obviously taking anything of value, or edible, but finding no potential prisoners.

'Vidarr, what if they set fire to the archives?' He continued to look up towards the roof, even though the stygian darkness where they both sheltered was complete.

Vidarr shifted beside him. 'It would matter not – an inconvenience, and nothing more. In fact, it would probably be better for us, for if they decided to make a thorough search of my archives, then they may find our hidden door.' He reached out, and grasped Balthazaar's forearm. 'We are many longs underground, and no flames can reach us. For the time being we are safe, my friend.'

Balthazaar's head was still raised towards the ceiling, but he closed his eyes, and breathed out slowly. 'The fighting is over. The Wolfen are no more.'

Vidarr's grip on his arm intensified. 'The Wolfen will never be gone. As long as Canite blood runs through the veins of a single being, then the Wolfen will rise again. The *sáál* is eternal, and can never truly die. Remember the words of the first of us all, the mighty Fenrir; as long as a single Wolfen stands, there will be a kingdom for us all.' He paused, and his hand fell away. 'The Man-Kind will keep the son of Grimvaldr safe.'

Balthazaar turned quickly. 'How do you know of…'?

Vidarr laughed softly in the darkness. 'There are no secrets for someone as old as the stone of the Valkeryn's walls themselves. Here…' He pressed something bread-like into the counselor's hand.

Balthazaar lifted it and sniffed. 'Fungus?'

'Hm-hmm, tastes like meat. You'll get used to it. You have to – you may be eating it for a long time.' He laughed again.

Balthazaar sighed miserably, and closed his eyes. Behind him, a tiny movement turned into a rustle, and then something that could have been a giggle floated up to them from far away in the darkness.

Vidarr's hand alighted on his arm again. 'Just the wind playing in the lower passages, my friend. Nothing down here, but you, me, and a thousand old ghosts.'

Balthazaar nodded, even though he knew his friend couldn't see it. He bit off a piece of the tough fungus, and started to chew without enjoyment. His ears remained firmly pointed to the rear of the cave.

⊰≺⊙⊜⊰⊱ ⋉∞⋊ ⊰⊙⊜⊱≻⊱

Arn was frozen to the spot. He held Grimson to him with one arm, the youth still unconscious. He watched the water, or more specifically the two yellow eyes just below the surface, gliding towards the bank. They seemed to glow and were focused on Arn. There were no pupils, just two golf ball-sized blobs of yellow, spaced about two feet apart.

He gulped, and the act of swallowing gave his muscles some movement. He looked around. The jungle cover was a few dozen feet back, and he was still at the waterline. There were a few broken branches littering the bank, but there was no shelter or anything to hide behind.

He took a careful step backwards, conscious that any movement he made might trigger the attack that was surely coming. The darkness wasn't quite complete, as a few silver edges of moon had snuck around some high cloud, and now, a momentary break threw down a curtain of silver light. Arn felt the enormous surge in his confidence and with it the familiar swell of energy rippled through him. But the light also revealed the creature as it came to the shallows.

He had been expecting some sort of alligator, but he was only been partially right – a long body, thick around as a horse, extended far out into the river. It was a giant snake, sliding beneath the water. As Arn watched, he saw it begin to fold in on itself just below the surface – he knew what to expect… as soon as it had enough power wound in its coils it would launch itself at them. Arn grimaced; the size of the head meant its jaws would probable easily expand to accommodate both he and Grimson.

The curtain of light disappeared, and like the Cheshire cat from Alice in Wonderland, just the two yellow orbs remained, their baleful stare fixed on Arn.

Time, sound, his breathing, even the air around him, stopped dead. Arn waited, but not for long. The head exploded from under the water, the two-foot wide triangular head catapulting towards them like a scaled cannon shell.

The moon came back out from the behind the clouds, revealing the riverbank in a silvery illumination. In the shafts of light, Arn saw the huge jaws dropping open in anticipation of the feast. Rows of teeth crowded the mouth, curving backwards – more like a shark than a snake.

The inward-curving white blades were designed for gripping and holding on – once the creature bit down on something, there would be no pulling away without a massive chunk of whatever it held being separated from the body. Arn guessed the powerful predator was designed for attacking far larger and more formidable prey than them. They wouldn't stand a chance.

The moonlight shot a jolt of lightning-like power through his limbs, and he leapt, flying ten feet to one side, taking the unconscious Grimson with him, his small body whipping like a loose doll in his arms.

The creature's head smashed into the riverbank where they had just been standing, gouging a deep furrow. It recoiled as more of its enormous scaled body slid from the water.

Arn's mouth dropped open in awe – the thing kept on coming, foot after foot, piling high, and yet still more of it trailed into the water. The coils smelled fishy, and dead, like a beached whale carcass, its body coated in some sort of slime. The most unsettling aspect of all was that the giant reptile never made a sound, other than the noise its plate-sized scales made as they ground against the soil of the riverbank.

Arn rolled, and came back to his feet, leaping again, as the thing exploded at him once more. He reached down to snatch up a tree branch and throw it over his shoulder as he kept running. The small log bounced off the scaled head, causing the thing to pull back momentarily, but it did no real damage.

Arn slid to a halt. 'Oh no.'

He had managed to run blindly into a dead-end in the darkness. He found himself ringed by a dense wall of some sort of bamboo, its stems so closely grown together it created a line of prison bars. He felt he could break through, but he'd need to put Grim down, and turning his back on the creature would be suicide.

Arn eased the young Wolfen down at his feet, and turned back to the creature sliding along the wet grass of the bank, most of its body now exposed and shining wetly in the moonlight. The yellow glowing eyes were unblinking in their concentration on its prey and Arn was mesmerized – he just stood and stared, momentarily becoming lost in their glow. He shook his head. *This is what snakes do*, he remembered – they hypnotize their prey. He stepped in front of the Wolfen, and pulled his blade free, still coated with the blood of the bat-like creature he had fought only hours before. *Welcome to Hell*, he thought.

He opened his arms wide and allowed the moon to bathe his sweat soaked body.

'Okay then, *kicizapi wicate* – a fight to the death, and I won't be so easy to swallow.'

The thing raised itself up, and as Arn watched, he felt the few brave words of his grandfather's language start to shrivel in his throat. The thing was now twice his height, and a even more formidable than he had expected.

'Well, looks like just a fight to my death then.' He took a step forward: his only wish was that the thing would be satisfied with him, and would leave Grimson alone… at least until he regained consciousness. And if it didn't, then he hoped the youth never regained his consciousness.

'He-yeeagh.' He slashed the blade back and forth in the air, and the thing started to draw back slightly, but Arn guessed it was in preparation of the next attack. Arn knew this time it would strike him – it had to, because if he leapt away, its strike would be upon Grimson.

Arn sucked in a huge breath, and drew his arm back. The massive head shot forward. Arn slashed down, and connected with… nothing. There was a thump that shook the ground beneath Arn's feet as the head of the giant reptile slammed to the ground not three feet in front of him.

Immediately there was an explosion of movement, as the giant creature coiled and thrashed, its attention totally drawn away from the two small creatures. Arn didn't wait for an explanation, instead reaching down for Grimson and pulling him roughly out of the way, down along the tree line, to shelter behind some thick trunks. He peered back as the sound of the turmoil was becoming thunderous. He could now see why the giant reptile was reacting the way it did – where its tail had still trailed in the water, it had gone tight. Either it had snagged itself below the water line, or…

The answer revealed itself as there came an almighty tug, and the snake was dragged back some twenty feet towards the river. Whatever had hold of it beneath the surface was big and strong enough to prey on the monstrous snake.

Arn remembered Vidarr's words in their first meeting, and how he had been told to give the waterway a wide berth. Because of what lives in the lake, the old archivist had said.

As he watched, another twenty feet of the reptile was pulled backwards. Arn stepped out, now confident that whatever was dealing with the snake would certainly hold its attention long enough for them to escape. He looked down along the bank; he still needed the blood-red *feninlang* flowers.

He sprinted down and grabbed a handful, immediately feeling the oozing sap bathe his injured fingers and delivering the stinging sizzle as it burned into his wounds. There was no fear this time; he knew it was healing him.

With one last look over his shoulder he saw the snake pulled fully back into the river, and then something mountainous humped at its centre, its coal-black body shining briefly in the moonlight, before it sank below the surface. There was nothing to show for the battle, except a few large swirls on the surface.

Arn grunted. 'Note to self – never cross deep water.' He reached down for Grimson and lifted the youth, quickly moving back into the jungle.

CHAPTER 8

YOUR JOB IS NOT YET DONE

Orcalion lay prone at the feet of his queen, his mind working furiously. He could hear Mogahrr's long talons raking the wood of Grimvaldr's throne, gouging deep furrows in the old dark wood as she stared down at him.

'I wanted the ssseed of Grimvaldr oblittterateddd. Youuu could not give thisss to me. I wanted the Man-Kind, aliiive, and yeett, you could not even bring meee hisss body.'

Orcalion kept his face pressed firmly down on the floor, and spoke into the wood. 'But I have given you more Wolfen heads in a day than any Panterran has taken in a hundred generations, my beautiful queen.' He raised his head a fraction. 'And the castle of the Valkeryn is now yours. Do you not sit now on the throne of the dead Wolfen king?'

She screeched, and many of the Panterran tending to the Queen stopped grooming her putrid body and froze. 'You thiiink I care for cold ssstone, and empty hallsss?'

Orcalion's head dropped to the floor again. 'But I have delivered Grimvaldr the Great and his beloved Queen Freya into your jaws.'

Mogahrr's eyes narrowed. 'If not for thattt, piecesss of your worthlesss body wooould be ssscattered over every field to the far horizon.'

Orcalion kept his head down, and swallowed, but his black lips had pulled back into a hint of a smile. He knew the Lygon were charged with securing the rear of the castle – it was about time those blundering oafs felt some of the queen's wrath for themselves.

'We Panterran did as you bid, but it was the task of the Lygon to ensure the rear of the castle and the surrounding fields were secure. I'm afraid it was this task that was not done. I only wish now that you had given me this job also, my queen. You would be dining on young royal Wolfen meat now, if it were so.' His smile widened as he pressed his face into the stone.

The queen's yellow eyes slid across to Goranx and the other Lygon generals, who stood like a small group of colossus at the rear of the room.

Goranx snorted. 'No creature passed us.'

Orcalion rose on one elbow from the floor. 'But how could you tell mighty Goranx? You were amongst the battle in the forecourts. I do not accuse you, but, perhaps Goranx did not have the information from his warlords that a general in battle deserves.'

Another Lygon thundered forward and held out a hand half the size of the Panterran, claws bared, and shook it at the smaller creature. 'You dare question our skill. No one passed our troops, no Man-Kind, no Wolfen.'

Orcalion got to his feet, confident now the conversation was heading in the direction he wanted. 'And yet, Hogar the brave, they all escaped, and right by... you.' He lifted a small hand and pointed one long talon accusingly at the giant creature.

The queen turned to whisper something to one of her attendants who nodded, and then quickly returned with a small box, which he placed beside her on the throne. She lifted the lid, and dipped in her hand, setting off a scuttling and hissing from inside.

Orcalion noticed the box and stepped back and to the side of the queen. The giant Lygon roared his fury at his ability being questioned. The small Panterran's grin split his face revealing the small needle sharp teeth inside his mouth. His eyes glowed with excitement and he kept pointing at Hogar's chest.

'Not everything can be won by brute strength alone, Hogar. Perhaps some better judgement, and concentration, might be of more use to all of us.'

The enormous Lygon lunged forward, even as Goranx roared at him to hold his place. Hogar swung a huge fist, with Orcalion easily ducking out of his way, and moving again closer to the queen... and in reach.

As the huge Lygon swung back around, Mogahrr flicked her hand out and scratched his forearm. Her long black talons were coated in a sticky green fluid.

The Lygon's eyes bulged and he gasped, grabbing his wrist. Immediately, his lips turned black and pulled back from his long teeth. He coughed and as the room watched in silence, he brought his hand to his throat as his breathing became ragged. Hogar's eyes dropped back in their sockets as though he was suffering the dehydration of a month in the desert. He dropped to his knees, his arms falling to his sides, and his head drooped. He seemed to shrink, and while they watched, his huge orange and black body collapsed in on itself, finally falling forward like a giant empty sack.

The room remained silent. No one needed to ask if was he dead.

Mogahrr was handed a goblet, dipped her hand inside and swirled her claws around in the fluid. Her eyes slid to Goranx. The stare burned viciously yellow and the entire gathering held its breath, waiting.

Goranx held the gaze, and bared his teeth, his chest moving like enormous bellows under his armor.

'Underssssstanddd?' Mogahrr never blinked, the golden yellow eyes like small windows to some horrid world of pain, torture and corruption. 'Undersssstanddd?' He held her gaze for another few seconds, and then finally he nodded and lowered his eyes. The silence stretched as Mogahrr searched out any who would challenge her. There were none.

Then, floating in through the windows, from somewhere out on the dark, far hillsides, there came a sound, rising and falling on notes that caused the queen to bare rotten teeth. The Lygon's heads moved on their trunk-like necks, the confusion clear in their luminous green eyes.

The recognizable howl continued for many long seconds. It pulled Mogahrr's eyes towards the open window and she hissed in return. She spun back to the room, fury burning like a cauldron behind her eyes.

'Seemsss all the Wolfen are not dead. Your job is not yeeet done, miiiighty Goranx.' She turned to glare at Orcalion, 'Fiiind me the Man-Kind, fiiind me the offsssspring of Grimvaldr. Killll all the Wolfen onccce and for all.'

She leaned in close to Orcalion's face, making him wince at the putrid breath. 'But the Man-Kind, the Arnoddr, mussst be alive, or you wiiill be the next disgusssting sssack of ssskin lying at my feeeet.'

Orcalion nodded and backed away, bowing all the way to the door.

***

Sorenson raided the dead bodies of his warrior kin. He knew that their *sáál* would long have left their crushed remains, but still, he said a small prayer over each. The brave battle fallen would have been gathered up by the Valkeryies, and together they would be crossing the bridge to Valhalla. He thanked each of them for their goods, promising to make their armor and blades repay the gift with rivers of Panterran and Lygon blood.

On a farthest hillside Sorenson turned to look back at the castle – he could still make out fires burning, and a miserable smoke hung over its once majestic walls and turrets. It was still his home and kingdom, but for now, a vile vermin had overrun it. The moon had risen behind him, and its silver light showed massive forms on the plain dragging the remaining bodies of the dead either into the castle or off to the camps of the Lygon to become another feast.

Sorenson, son of Stromgard and trusted warrior of the once great king Grimvaldr, felt a ball of rage rising up within him. His entire body almost vibrated with the fury and the pain and the burning desire for vengeance until he could hold it inside no longer. He threw his head back and howled, the long notes tumbling down the hill and valleys to crash against the castle walls. His hands crushed into fists and he held the note for many long minutes, letting whoever was inside know that the heart and *sáál* of the Wolfen was not yet extinguished.

With a snap of his jaws he bit off the sound and spun away into the darkness. He had many miles to travel if he was to find the Man-Kind or either of the heirs of Valkeryn.

Sorenson charged into the brush. He had rolled his armor into a pack and tied it over his shoulders. His sword was belted at his waist. The toughened leather garment he wore protected his frame as he smashed through the undergrowth; he couldn't afford to follow any of the known tracks with so many Lygon in the area.

He slowed as the forest opened out into a clearing, and he softened his tread. There were many Lygon and Panterran about, searching for survivors or picking over the dead bodies of the fallen Wolfen. The great orange and black brutes had no trouble with carrion, and a rotting corpse was just as palatable as fresh meat to them.

Grunting and snapping sounds came from up ahead. Sorenson paused and tried to search out the source of the noise before he was seen. Both Wolfen and Lygon had excellent night vision, their eyes managing to pull the most miniscule hint of light from the landscape.

He edged forward, inches at a time, scarcely breathing as he approached the open ground. The moonlight made the clearing appear as a silver-lit stage, revealing a Lygon crouching over a body. While Sorenson watched, the Lygon pulled and twisted a limb free, lifted it to his jaws and ripped at the flesh, swallowing it in great gulps.

Sorenson felt pain in his chest. Before he realised it, his warrior spirit had taken over. Where caution was needed, he instead broke into a sprint. Where silence was demanded, he instead roared a challenge, and when he should have discreetly detoured around the brute, Sorenson instead demanded the fight. As he flew forward he drew his sword.

The Lygon's head came up in surprise, and then whipped around, the shock clear on his ogreish features. He rose to his feet, throwing the half eaten Wolfen aside and towering over Sorenson, his eyes blazing a luminous green. One huge hand reached down for the enormous axe hanging at his belt. But he fumbled. Perhaps it was the sight of a still living Wolfen running at him, or astonishment that any creature would attack a Lygon warrior in full battle dress. By the time he had freed his weapon, Sorenson was already leaping at him, flying through the air, his sword making an arc in the cold night.

The silver blade flashed in the moonlight, and the beast's enormous head flew from its shoulders. Sorenson landed lightly on his feet, and turned to see the headless body, still upright, spraying blood as it toppled like a tree.

He snorted in contempt. 'Compared to the *sáál* of a Wolfen, you will always be the runt.' He walked back to the body and placed a foot on its chest. He threw his head back and howled once again, but this time it was no song of lament, but one of challenge.

The sound died away and Sorenson dropped his head, his eyes still burning. 'We are not all dead yet.'

He wiped his blade clean on the body, and then walked to the mangled corpse of his Wolfen kin. It still wore much of its armor, now dented and bloody. It was a female warrior, her face still caught in a snarl of fury. She had died fighting. Sorenson knelt down, and placed one hand on her chest. He made a fist and tapped the steel where the snarling crest of Fenrir was raised up. He closed his eyes.

'May you sit at Odin's feet and await his call.' He opened his eyes and stood. He went to turn away but paused. His lips pulled back from his teeth as he stared at the devoured remains. 'Be at ease, little sister, there will be oceans of blood soon enough.'

CHAPTER 9

I'M NOT ALONE

Arn woke with a start, and sat up quickly, spinning left and right, feeling there was something amiss, someone watching them. His neck tingled and he couldn't shake the sensation of something not being right. He waited, but there was nothing except the sound of the jungle waking at dawn.

He rubbed his face and inhaled. The humidity was already high, and his skin itched where biting insects had made a meal of him throughout the night. He looked down. Grimson still slept. Thankfully, it was more a sleep of the fatigued, rather than the coma-like little death he had been in the night before.

Arn slid a hand backwards through the short, silver fur on the young Wolfen's shoulders and neck, and saw that the wounds were now pink and mostly knitted together. There was no sign of any swelling or weeping coming from the wounds.

His stomach rumbled, and he crawled forward on his knees to the opening of their shelter. He and Grimson had found an enormous broken off tree trunk, still twenty feet high, but its base hollowed out – large enough for them both to enter, and sleep hidden from the jungle. Even if they had found a cave, he wasn't sure he would have chosen to enter – given what he had encountered in the darkness once before. Fatigued as he was, he wouldn't have been able to fight a mouse, let alone something the size of a freight train that spat acid, and had armor stronger than an Abrams tank.

The snap of a twig from just behind the brush line made him freeze. He dropped even lower and edged backwards a few inches, while keeping his eyes on the undergrowth. There was some snuffling and then something the size of a large rat pushed out into the open. It stopped, and its snout unfurled like a miniature trunk to pick at something in amongst the leaf litter.

Hello breakfast, he thought and slowly reached back for his knife. There would be no fire or cooking for some time. Aside from everything being mostly damp in the jungle anyway, he couldn't afford for the smoke to be seen rising above the tree canopy until he was sure there was no pursuit. It didn't matter – raw or not, food was food, and he and Grimson needed protein. He leapt.

Arn smiled and hummed as he expertly skinned the small animal. Not long ago, he was worried more about trying to date Becky Matthews, or cramming for final exams, and now, here he was sitting in the dirt, perhaps a million years from home, ripping the hide off an animal like his forefathers did.

'Talk about getting back in touch with your roots.' He laughed, and dropped the skin into a pre-dug hole in the dirt – best not leave bloody scraps around to be sniffed out by predators.

Arn used his knife to slice away some of the softer meat and brought it close to Grimson's nose. He put his hand behind the young Wolfen's neck and sat him up. The dark nostrils twitched and his mouth opened weakly. Arn pushed the meat between his jaws, and the youth made almost imperceptible motions of chewing before he swallowed. Arn repeated the process several times, before lying the youth back down.

'Need you up soon, buddy. We need to get moving.'

Truth was he had no idea what to do next other than keep moving forward into the dark jungle. He couldn't go back, and they were surrounded by dense, almost impenetrable forest on all sides. They needed to push forward. He'd carry the youth again if he needed to, but he hoped that with his wounds cleaned and healing, and now some protein, Grimson might spring back to health.

Arn sliced more of the meat from the small carcass. It was salty and still warm. He swallowed it down greedily; raw meat from something like a large rat suddenly seemed the most delicious thing he'd ever eaten.

Afterwards, he went to relieve himself a few paces behind their tree trunk home, remembering to bury his waste. Coming back through the cleared area around the base of the large trunk he froze. He frowned, and fell to his knees, lowering his face even closer to the earth. Arn gently picked away twigs and leaves, and then sat back to wait for his head to stop spinning.

He screwed his eyes shut for a moment and then opened them again – it was still there. He suppressed an urge to laugh out loud.

There, pressed into the soft dark earth, was a moccasin footprint; small, not perfect, but it looked definitely… human.

'I'm not alone.' Arn tilted his head back and closed his eyes. 'Thank you.'

CHAPTER 10

CREEPY AS EVER

Becky drove up to the front gate of the Fermilab facility and slowed, flashing the guard a big smile. 'Morning Mr. Wilson. How's the wife and that adorable baby boy of yours?'

The big guard smiled and nodded, touching his cap in a form of salute. 'Morning Miss Matthews. We're all fine and the boy is as big as a moose... and just as loud.' He laughed at his own wit, and then leaned into her car, quickly looking past her into the back seat, and foot wells.

She raised her eyebrows. 'Pop the trunk again? It's full of junk I'm afraid.'

Wilson thought about it and then shook his head. 'Nah, just a short visit to see Dr Harper again?'

'Sure is, and I bet I'll be straight back out after the usual "No news yet sweetheart" talk.' She turned her mouth down.

'Probably, but I'm sure things will all work out for you and your friend.' He patted her shoulder through the open window. 'Good luck this time.' He stepped back and waved her through.

Becky nodded and accelerated away from the gate, feeling the perspiration running down under her arms. She checked the rear-view mirror to make sure Wilson wasn't making any phone calls.

Becky turned around. 'Phew, you all right back there?'

There was the sound of muffled movement, and then. 'Yes, but it's really hot in here. Where are we?'

She laughed. 'Where are we? We're in... but that was the easy part, so it's about to get a lot hotter.' She grinned, excited and feeling like there was electricity running through her veins.

As she drove towards the enormous Fermilab building, she noticed one of the guard dogs had stopped and stood high on its back legs to watch her pass.

'Creepy as ever,' she whispered.

CHAPTER 11

VILE CROSS BREEDER

Eilif sat by herself and hummed as she worked her blade. The trek had been slow, and she felt she was dragging Bergborr along with her. He resisted every step of the way, and as she had refused to tell him the reason she was determined to travel into the Dark Lands, he had become more suspicious and withdrawn with every passing hour.

His earlier good humor, and his infatuated attention, had slipped away. She didn't care; she could tell he held his secrets deep inside himself.

A small sound made her drop her hands, sheath her knife and let a small piece of charcoal she was using fall to the earth.

'I brought you these.' He held a handful of long flowers of such a deep purple that they could have been made from crushed black berries.

She looked at them for a moment, her immediate notion was to reject them, but then decided that she could be civil to the Wolfen warrior. After all, he had saved her from a certain death.

'Thank you; they're beautiful.' She smiled up at him, and then looked at the blooms, so she wouldn't have to see his eager, imploring features.

He went to his knees beside her. It seemed her few words were encouragement enough 'They are as you are, my beautiful Eilif.'

She turned away slightly, the insides of her ears turning pink with embarrassment. She picked at the petals, pretending to further arrange the blooms in her hand. She felt him draw

71

closer. A hand fell on her shoulder. She shrugged it away, and flashed him an angry look.

'You should not make presumptions, Bergborr, son of Bergrinne. Your arrogance is tedious and lacks judgment.'

The hand on her shoulder pressed harder and then pulled her around. Bergborr pressed his face to hers, his mouth trying to find her own. Eilif lashed out, striking him with her fist and knocking his face to one side.

He ground his teeth and swung back at her. 'I saved your life.' He yelled the words into her face, spittle spraying onto her cheek.

She went to strike his face again, but this time he caught her arm, holding it easily. He smiled, but as he felt the arm, he looked at it, his smile falling away and instead being replaced with a look of disgust wrinkling his features.

Her arm had been scraped clean of fur, and a single small word had been carved into the skin. The wound had had charcoal rubbed into the word, so when the skin healed the design would remain tattooed forever. It was a single word, a name... Arnoddr.

He wrenched her arm in disgust. 'Ach.' He pulled it again even harder, jarring her shoulder, and with his other hand he slapped her face... hard. 'Lover of animals, vile cross-breeder.'

She pulled her arm away, and got to her feet. He rose just as quickly, grabbing her tunic and ripping it. 'How long until you desire to shave your entire body? You deceive yourself. Do you expect to make yourself a Man-Kind through the simply shedding of your outer self? Foolish, disgusting female.'

He held her by the torn shards of her clothing and shook her from side to side. He stared hard into her face. His eyes grew crafty and then lascivious.

'Where was the Man-Kind when the massed Lygon and Panterran attacked our home? Where was the Man-Kind when your father and mother fell? He was running away. But I was there, beside you, just as I've always been. But where was he? Where is he now? Stupid, stupid dreamer.' He shook her again.

Eilif reached up and tried to pull his hand away from her, but instead, he lifted the other and ripped downwards, tearing away a swath of the tunic front and exposing her small breasts. His eyes grew small, and his grin widened.

'Your problem is, you have never known what a real Wolfen feels like.' He kept his eyes on her exposed body. 'I can fix that for you.' He slapped her and she staggered backwards.

She was in shock and disbelief, but anger overrode her instinct to try and shield herself. Instead she pulled a small blade from her belt, and swung it, but before it could connect he slapped her again and then again.

Her head spun, and she felt him rip more of her clothing away. She still held the blade, but now her mind was turning to thoughts of using the sharp dagger on herself, rather than let this creature take her.

She lifted the blade, weakly this time, and earned a powerful blow over her eye, knocking her down. The world spun, and hovering above it all was the dark figure of the black Wolfen. She saw him pull away his own shirt, and then start to unbuckle his belt.

'No.' She held up her hand.

'Yes.' He pulled the belt free.

Tears ran down her face, and she suddenly thought that this is the day she will die. She would never see Arn again, or her brother, or even the mighty halls of Valkeryn. Instead, she would end up here, food for the worms in some lonely and forgotten corner of the forests.

The blurred figure of Bergborr filled her vision as he began to bear down upon her.

Sorenson had followed the twin pair of travelers – both Wolfen – for miles now. One large, the other smaller; a youth, most likely a female by the narrow prints.

His lungs burned, and his overworked muscles screamed in protest, but he would never let up. If it was one of the ones he sought, he would run until he was at Odin's door.

The forest became even denser, and he needed to slow his pace to thread his way through the crowded landscape. He leaned against a tree trunk, closed his eyes, and sniffed the air so he could concentrate on the minute sounds and scents. He was close now; he would be upon them in moments. He sped up, racing now, leaping over boulders and fallen trees, until the sound of a familiar voice burst across the landscape in a fearful scream.

Odin, give me strength. He sprinted madly – seconds would count now.

- ╫◈●▓€ ⋙⋘ ╕▓◈╫ -

The heavy weight of the dark Wolfen came down on her and she cried out. She landed weak blows on his head and shoulders, but he ignored them and lowered his face to hers.

'You're mine.'

Eilif crushed her eyes shut, willing herself to a place deep inside where just she and Arn sat in the sun. Where there was no war, no death, and her father and mother would be smiling, happy, and most of all, alive.

Her dream of escape suddenly shattered – a roar thundered out of the air around them, followed by an explosion of flesh, fur and teeth.

Bergborr yelped in fear and pain, and was knocked from her body. Something hit him, and continued on past, taking the dark Wolfen with it. She was knocked flat, her head striking a stone and leaving her groggy and making everything around her dreamlike and indistinct.

In her haze she felt, as much as heard, each of the thunderous blows, such was their ferocity. Fist blows, ripping, snapping of jaws, impacts, not just armor and steel as they came together, but of flesh, tooth, bone and muscle. The ground shook as the two creatures smashed into each other, and their movements were faster than her dazed eyes could follow. She tried to shrink back from the fight, but her body would not obey its instructions, and instead she just sat there, transfixed.

What happened? Was Bergborr trying to save her, she wondered. Finally, there came a screaming yelp, and she saw the body of the unconscious dark Wolfen lifted high into the air. He hung in one giant Lygon hand, and in the striped giant's other hand was a cruel-looking knife as long as she was. The Lygon took heads, she remembered.

'Halt.'

The whining voice was Panterran, and the cowled figure glided forward at the head of a small army of beings, some small, and others monstrously large. She recognized the vile creature, and in turn, it too recognized her.

The black grin turned from her to the large creature that held Bergborr in the air. 'Put him down; we need him.'

He turned back to the princess. 'We need both of you... for now.'

Eilif's world turned black as her consciousness fled.

Sorenson slid to a halt, seconds before bursting through the trees and into the centre of the group. His hand was on the hilt of his sword, but his rational mind had not left him – to engage them all would mean a certain defeat. He was bone tired, outnumbered, and out muscled. Even if he managed to grab the princess, he would be cut down, before he got to carry her ten paces.

He watched, sliding along behind the tree line to a better place of concealment. The princess was alive and for the time, safe.

Sorenson narrowed his eyes as he looked at the dark Wolfen still being held in one hand of the giant Lygon. He knew him, Bergborr – hurt, but alive. What was he doing here?

Odin give him glory, he thought, for managing to get the Princess Eilif this far from the Lygon and Panterran encampments.

He crouched lower. He would follow, he would wait, and soon an opportunity would present itself.

CHAPTER 12

I THINK WE GOT A BREACH

Harper watched as one of his guards escorted Rebecca Matthews into the facility. He sighed – he had to give the young woman ten points for dedication. But he didn't think she'd be allowed back from here on, as he doubted the military would be amenable to relatives and friends attempting to badger information out of anyone on site.

With Briggs assuming control of the project, batting eyelids or sob stories – even common sense – would get you about as far as whistling in a hurricane. He'd wait for the girl to come up to him in the command centre rather than go and meet her. He squinted at the screen; besides, looked like she'd already been met by one of the security detail, even though he hadn't sent one for her.

Harper looked back at the screen just as the two figures walked in through the front doors. He hadn't recognized the guard – seemed rather small to be one of his detail. Maybe a new guy, or one of Briggs' crew from inside the truck.

He shrugged and tidied away some sensitive material, sitting down to do some work while he waited for the persistent young woman to arrive.

＊ ＊ ＊

'Stand up a little straighter, will you?' Becky said.

Edward did as he was told, but was still only about the same height as the woman he escorted. He kept his head up and shoulders squared, trying to improve his bulk, but he began to limp.

'The things you gave me to put in my shoes are hard to walk in.' Truth was he felt like everyone was staring at him... and not just because he was walking like a cross between John Wayne and Quasimodo.

Becky snorted. 'They're called lifts, and they give you another two inches of height. But if you keep slouching, you'll look like my kid brother playing dress-ups. Keep your chin up higher.'

Edward straightened his spine even more.

She looked at him. 'Better, but try not to stand next to any other guards, or you'll look like their shrunken offspring.' She laughed.

'Thanks. You've got the card, right?'

'Duh; of course, and as long as they haven't noticed it gone, and rendered it invalid, it should take us where we want to go. And that is...?'

He nodded towards the end of the large room. 'It all started in the underground acceleration chamber. That's where all the action will be... so, that's where we'll be.'

'Okay, then lead on, Captain McShorty.'

Edward pulled the black cap down over his eyes as they passed a soldier standing beside a closed door. He tried to lift himself up on his toes and square his shoulders even more, but knew he still only came to the man's nose.

As they passed he turned and whispered to Becky. 'Just pray we don't have to fight our way in, okay?'

* * *

Harper handed the clipboard back to the waiting physicist, and then looked at his watch, frowning. He knew there was something nagging at him, something he needed to do.

He grabbed his coffee cup, and sipped at the cold dark fluid. *Yech.* Tasted like crap, and would probably make his breath smell worse than one of the dogs. Not that his breath mattered, as he only had one meeting... *Oh, good Christ – the girl! Meet with the girl!*

It'd been ages; what the hell happened to her? He went to his computer, and called up a list of contact numbers. Finding the one he wanted, he clicked on the code. Immediately the system displayed the image of a rugged-faced, forty-something male; Zackary Markson, head of ground security – at least until Briggs and her team arrived.

His voice came back over the screen's speaker. 'Hi Doc, what can I do for you?'

'Ahh, Zach, the Matthews girl. Where did your man take her? I expected her to be up here by now.' He checked his watch. 'In fact, she should have been in my office more than thirty minutes ago.'

There was silence for a moment, and then: 'Say again – the Matthew's girl?'

Harper exhaled, already exasperated, but more annoyed with himself for not noticing fifteen minutes back that she was missing. 'Yes, yes, Rebecca Matthews. I saw one of your men escorting her into the facility ages ago, but she hasn't turned up.'

There was more silence, and Harper guessed that Markson would be checking with his crew and rewinding the footage from the gate and front doors. After about a minute, Markson's voice came back at him.

'Okay, I see her coming in, but that's not one of our people, and frankly, I doubt that's one of Briggs' crew either. I think we got a breach.'

'For the love of God. Not now, not with Colonel bloody Bulldog Briggs in the house.' Harper dropped his head in his hands.

Markson came back on. 'I found them, Doc. They're on their way down to the basement.'

GREIG BECK

'Good… what?' Harper's hand went for the alarm codes and then froze. If he initiated a security alert, he was liable to have Briggs and her team spraying bullets about the facility. A dead teenage girl would be the final straw, and he wasn't sure just handing in your resignation would cut it with the military woman.

Harper dropped his hand, his mind working furiously. He pulled his key card from his pocket and sprinted for the door.

* * *

'This way, miss.' Edward tried to lower his voice a few octaves as he approached the guard. He also managed to keep his head and hat down, while maintaining an upright posture, but was sure he was dislocating every vertebra in his neck.

He lifted the magnetic pass card in front of the guard's face who briefly scanned the name and picture, looked at Edward and his uniform's rank, then nodded and stood back. Edward swiped the card across the elevator's panel, and the huge silver doors slid open.

Once inside with the doors shut, Becky flew into action. 'Phase two.' She pulled a lab smock from her bag, flapped it once to straighten the material, and then grabbed the dark cap from Edward's head.

Edward took the coat, pulled it on, and then pinned the pass card to his pocket. With his glasses and nerdish looks, it was a much more natural disguise than the military uniform.

On the way down, he looked at Rebecca. Her face was pale but her blue eyes shone like sapphires – she looked both nervous and excited. She turned and grinned.

'Almost there.'

He sucked in a deep breath as the elevator slowed. As the doors slid open, there was a pull of air, and everything not secured rushed from their bodies towards a grill gate that had been set-up over a large newly-cut door into the outer wall of the acceleration chamber.

Edward felt his teeth vibrate in his mouth, and a tingling at the base of his scalp. He had to hold onto his glasses, or they too would have been torn from his face.

Quickly looking around while trying to remain nonchalant, he noticed the other changes since he was here months back – racks for weapons, flashlights, water, and all manner of items necessary for a long trek. It was now an armory and goods depot, a bit like those rest cabins built high in snow-covered peaks for weary climbers.

A single guard sat at a empty desk, staring at them with a gaze that reminded Edward of a pair of colorless buttons. His expression was just as disinterested.

Edward nodded to the man, who didn't even blink in response. He felt his pulse start to race. *Be cool, fool,* he thought, and slid his hands into the lab-coat pockets, like he'd seen on a thousand medical shows on television.

'Dr Harper is on his way down. Final test on the chamber's integrity before the next trip.' He nodded and the guard ignored him, eyes instead sliding to Becky.

Edward guessed his own cover story was plausible, but why the hell would Becky, a student, be involved? Her cover was just to be herself. They continued to approach the man, who looked Becky up and down, his brows coming together in small frown.

She pretended to stumble and lean forward so her blouse swung open, letting her breasts jiggle before the man's eyes.

Good grief, Edward thought. *That's never gonna work.* He felt his face go hot. He was standing beside the man, who had pushed his chair back and was standing, towering over Edward by at least a foot.

'Going to have to see the paperwork, ah, Doctor…?' He went to step around the desk, his eyes remaining fixed on Becky's blouse. Edward grabbed one of the long mag-lights from a rack, and swung it like a club, hitting the base of the man's head, just above the neck-line. In the sealed room, the blow sounded like a baseball being struck with an aluminum bat. The man's head went forward, followed by his body as he collapsed to the floor.

'Yes!' Becky punched the air.

All Edward felt was dismay, and ran to the man, feeling his pulse and checking there was no serious damage. 'That's probably assault you know.' The guard was breathing heavily, out cold and probably concussed.

'Probably assault? Yeah, and he'll probably be angry when he wakes up.' She laughed. Behind them the elevator doors slid closed, and they heard the low whining sound of the large machine making its way back to the upper floor.

'We gotta hurry.' She kicked off her fashionable shoes, and pulled a pair of trainers from her bag, flinging the large car-ry-all to the floor. She motioned with her head as she hopped on one foot, pulling on a shoe. 'Whatever is happening, it's happening in there. Grab the guard's key.'

The metal mesh grill across the hole in the wall had an electronic control panel with a card slot – there was a matching flat metal card hanging from the fallen guard's uniform. Edward unclipped it and turned it over in his hand – it would work, or they were stuffed. Either way, they had no choice now.

He stood and dashed to some of the racks, grabbing flash-lights, water, food packets, and then his hand hovered over one of the pistols.

'Good idea, and grab one for me.' Becky stomped her foot into her second shoe and dashed towards him, plucking the key-card from his hand, and jamming it into the small slot. A light the size of his thumbnail went green, and the gate pulled open.

She stuck her head into the hole, and then yelled back over her shoulder. 'Smells like burning electricity wiring or some-thing.'

'Ozone'.

'Huh?' Her head popped back out.

'When oxygen is exposed to a huge plasma field, like when near some sort of powerful gravitational or electrical anomaly, the oxygen atoms are pulled apart, to immediately recombine in a three oxygen atom form – ozone.

'Huh?' She shook her head.

'Forget it.' He finished dressing.

Becky climbed in. Just as Edward followed behind her, the elevator doors slid open, and around two-dozen people poured forth like a black-clad waterfall. The mass of security guards exploded towards them, with the small figure of Albert Harper in amongst them screaming Rebecca's name. Edward pulled the gate shut, and then reinserted the card key – deep – bending it and snapping it off half way. It would be fairly easily extracted, with the right instrument, but it would buy them just a few more minutes – with luck, all the time they needed.

Edward fell the last few feet to the floor of the acceleration track tunnel. Becky was already standing before the bulge in the pipes where the particle collisions were monitored. Dozens of cameras and other equipment studded the walls and the equipment itself. She was hunched over, holding onto a length of the pipe, her hair streaming forward, blown by a hurricane that didn't exist. Strangely, there was no noise, just the odd dragging sensation, as if every atom in his body was being drawn toward the same place as Becky's hair.

She looked at him, squinting. 'It feels bad.' She pointed into the upper corner of the room.

He followed her hand. There it was, just as he expected, the small oily smudge that he had first seen on the screen in Dr Albert Harper's office, just a few months ago. It was bigger, now grown to the size of a dinner plate. The anomaly hurt his eyes and scrambled his logic, and even now it looked like some sort of glitch on a video screen, not something that was real. It hung in the air, floating, but it wasn't some sort of hot air balloon, it was a doorway.

Edward's eyes started to water as he continued to stare. He knew his brain was being tricked – the thing wasn't really the size of a dinner plate. Instead, Tardis-like, it was a doorway to something much bigger – a doorway to an entire world. He took a few steps closer.

'Are you ready?'

Becky stood rooted to the spot, grinding her teeth and still squinting at the strange phenomenon. Her hands clenched and unclenched. Edward understood what she was feeling. She was one of the few people on Earth to witness an actual rip in space and time. It defied comprehension, and even seeing it, knowing his friend had been pulled through to another place – he'd seen it happen – he still found it hard to believe. And if he found that hard to believe, then imagine if he ever tried to explain it to anyone else.

A noise from behind told him it was time to unfreeze Becky and move. He turned to where she stood.

'I said, are you rea —'

He never finished. The girl sprinted forward, and then dived. Like Alice in Wonderland sliding down the rabbit hole, she hung in space for a second, her body elongating, and then she was simply… gone.

Edward's mouth dropped open, and he felt a sensation in his stomach that worried him – excitement maybe, but more likely terror. Behind him, he heard the sound of the metal gate being wrenched open.

Go!

He ran and dived.

'Oh, god, what is that awful fart smell?'

Edward was waving his flashlight back and forth in the small tunnel and at the sound of Becky's voice, turned the beam back towards her. She was frowning and holding one hand over her mouth and nose, beckoning at him with the other. He immediately handed over another of the long black cylinders, and she snatched it from him, flicking it on, and pointing the beam down at her feet.

'Yuck, there's green water down here... and I think, poop.' Despite being hunched over in the small tunnel, Becky tried to get up on her toes, which were already waterlogged.

He nodded, knowing she couldn't see him anyway. 'Smells like rotting vegetables, and a thousand other dead things.' He moved his beam of light along the dismal corridor, and then turned to sweep it behind them. He brought the beam back once again. 'Judging by all the tracks, I'd say everyone went...' he pointed with his flashlight. '... thatta way. Let's go before someone follows us through and drags us back.'

Becky maneuvered herself into a stooped crouch, and started to head down the corridor, trying to step over the deeper putrid puddles, and around lumps of fallen stone or twisted metal. She stopped and turned. 'This is horrible.'

He came up behind her. 'Sure is, but imagine if you fell into here, without a light, and without any idea of how you got here, or where to go... like Arn. The poor guy must have been freaking out. At least we know now that plenty of soldiers have been through and probably cleared it for us.'

She didn't move on. 'Cleared it of what? You mean the debris? They did a pretty crap job then.' She turned away from him, and started to crab-walk further away in the dark.

Behind her Edward shrugged; that wasn't what he was referring to, but decided not to elaborate. Besides, he didn't really know what he meant, it was just a feeling he had. He turned around and sent the beam of light down the tunnel behind them.

'Hey! Bring that back to the front, I need the extra light.'

Her voice made him jump, and he did as he was told. When he spoke he sounded timorous, even to himself. 'Now, as we planned, we're gonna give this twenty four hours right?'

'I didn't agree to that. I said it'd only be for a day or so. And the "or so", could be as long as we need to be here. Don't worry, I'll protect you.' She laughed lightly and turned to scuttle further along the tunnel.

Her voice echoed, and the laugh seemed to go on and on, up and down the dark tunnel. Edward stopped; the giggling seemed to be coming from far behind him, and didn't quite sound like Becky's echo anymore. He had the urge to look over his shoulder, but was frightened of what he might see.

He hurried after her. *Nothing here but us chickens*, he thought, and hurried to catch her up.

Harper stood near the elevator doors and watched as the last of Briggs's soldiers came back through the hole cut into the wall. The tallest, a mean looking fellow with a blond crew cut and more scars than a back-alley pit-bull, stood quietly conferring with her, nodding as she give instructions.

Harper wished he was a lip reader, but guessed from the severe look on her face, it was little more than curses and invective, probably directed at the two teenagers, Edward and Rebecca... and probably him.

She dismissed the man and turned towards the scientist, her face like stone. He felt his heart start to race. This isn't going to be fun.

Colonel Marion Briggs stopped only a pace in front of him, planting her legs and stood with her hands on her hips. She wasn't tall, but she had an aggressive, authoritative presence that filled the room, and now, his personal space. She tilted her head to the side as she studied his face, her eyes moving from his left eye to his right, and then back. Harper waited, beginning to fidget.

'Friends of yours?'

He shrugged, trying to remain cool. 'Not really, I mean, no. It was Rebecca Matthews, Arnold Singer's girlfriend, and also Edward Lin I'd say, his best friend. I guess they are trying to find him.'

'Uh-huh.' She smiled flatly and with absolutely zero humor in the curl of her lips. 'You guess they are trying to find him; that's a pretty good guess. I mean they certainly knew where to come, and what to do.' Her smile parted to show her teeth ground together. Her pale eyes bored into him. 'The girl meets with you often... right?'

He looked away, feeling his stomach flipping over. 'It's your job to maintain security now. What happened to that?' He turned back to her and raised his eyebrows.

The unfriendly smile returned to her face, and she grabbed the front of his coat pulling towards her. 'You know what I think? I think those two kids just saved us a lot of trouble – now we don't need to worry about them anymore. After all, you saw what that freakin' world did to a full squad of combat professionals. How long do you think some teenagers with a couple of stolen Glocks will last?' She tugged him even closer to her face, and spoke in a whisper. 'We'll scrape up what's left when we go through... in... ninety-four minutes. Might even work in our favor – they can act as a distraction, decoys even, so we can travel uninterrupted.'

She snorted and pushed him back, yelling a single word. 'Samson.' It made him jump. She twirled a finger in the air, and the large, scarred soldier started yelling orders to the men and woman, causing them to file back towards the elevator. She turned away from him.

Harper shook his head and wiped some of the woman's spittle from his face. *How long do I think they'll last? Well, one other kid without a Glock has managed to survive for months*, he thought and jammed his hands in his pockets. He went to follow the soldiers into the elevator, but Briggs had positioned herself at the doors and she held up her hand in front of his face.

'You get the next one, Doc.' She half turned, but seemed to have another thought. 'Any other surprises we need to know about? Last chance.'

Harper shook his head.

She nodded, but her eyes were narrowed. He could tell she didn't trust him now... if she ever did. 'By the way, Doc, we left your men supervising floor safety and defense. Who's in charge of your security?'

Harper frowned. 'Markson, Zackary Markson. He's a very go...'

She shook her head. 'Not anymore, Doc. Tell him he's fired. In fact, tell them they're all fired. We'll assume full control of all internal and external security from now on.'

She stepped back but kept her eyes on him as the doors slid shut in front of her face.

CHAPTER 13

WHAT'S AN ELEPHANT?

A shadow fell across Arn as he was hunched down examining the footprint. He sat back quickly, landing on his ass, and fumbling for his knife.

'It's me.' Grimson stood over him, swaying slightly, his eyelids and nose paler than usual. He blinked constantly as if he was having trouble focusing.

Arn got to his feet, and hurried to the youth, grabbing him on each side of the head, and staring into each of his eyes, turning his face and looking for cloudiness, dilation in the pupils, or anything that might indicate some sort of permanent damage. Thankfully there was nothing obvious. And just as well – his medical experience extended to bumps and bruises, and anything else got treated with the *feninlang* flowers.

He nodded his approval and ran his knuckles up over the Wolfen's head. 'About time, Grim. How do you feel?'

'You saved my life again, brother Arn.' Grimson pulled away and wiped his nose. 'Hungry, thirsty… and sore all over. Where are we? Did I miss anything?'

Arn stood back and smiled. "Miss anything?' He shrugged and looked around with a slightly indifferent expression. 'Nah, not much. Oh wait, you did nearly die after being attacked by a giant carnivorous bat, there have been miles of jungle I had to carry you through, we ate a rat thing that looked like a miniature elephant, trunk and all, and…' He tapped his chin as if trying to remember an obscure fact. '… and, oh yes, we nearly got eaten by a monster snake… who itself actually got eaten by a bigger monster.' He raised his eyebrows, grinning and looked down at the youth, whose mouth had dropped open.

Grim shook his head in disappointment. 'Aww, and I missed it all.' He frowned. 'And what's an elephant?'

Arn laughed and slapped him on the shoulder. 'C'mon, we better get going. And don't worry, I've got a feeling there'll be more interesting things for us to discover on the way. By the way, look at this.' Arn pointed to the footprint.

Grimson smiled up at him, but then looked down at the track in the soft soil. He frowned and got down on his hands and knees to examine it. He sniffed it, and then got back to his feet, the frown still in place.

'Well?' Arn asked.

Grimson looked back at the print, and shook his head. 'Strange.' He seemed to be confused. 'Not… right.'

Arn shrugged. 'Okay then brother Grim, let's go.'

'Brother Grim?' He looked up at Arn grinning, before his face became serious. He brought out his blade and made a slice across his palm, then held the blade out, and his hand, with blood welling up from the wound.

'Brothers in word, in deed, and in blood,' he said, with a smile.

Arn took the blade and ran it across his palm, and then gripped the boy's hand. 'Brothers.'

The blood mixed, a portion of the young Wolfen's entering Arn's system.

⸺ ❧❦❧ ⸻

Eilif's finger traced the outline of the letters carved into the stone. She lifted her sleeve as if to check that the name was the same, but she didn't need to. She could never understand all of the complex writing of the Man-Kind, except for one word she had committed to memory. That one word, a name, was now, in turn, cut into her flesh.

She sniffed, and then threw herself forward to sniff again at the rock – a scent, his scent, in the smallest specks of skin where he had perhaps grazed himself against the stone. She sat back on her haunches feeling dizzy and excited – it was proof they were heading in the right direction and probably weren't that far behind now. She could find him in a matter of days.

She closed her eyes and laughed, quickly covering her mouth with her hand. It was probably the first time in weeks she felt any sense of hope, or dare she think it, lightness of being. She opened her eyes, the dizziness still with her. She couldn't remember much of the recent fight – was Bergborr attacking her, or saving her? And now she found herself a captive of a Panterran and Lygon war party.

Bergborr had told her that they were hostages, effectively being used to try and force Arn to return with them. He said they'd do as they were bid, for now, and soon as an opportunity for escape presented itself, they'd take it.

But, he had whispered to her, it was important that she follow his instructions. He was only pretending to be their friend, and she must trust him.

She frowned – why wouldn't she trust a fellow Wolfen? But still, something inside her urged caution. Eilif sat for a few moments with her head down in silence, listening; no one approached. She opened her eyes and looked again at the letters – no one else would know what the faint carvings meant. But she did – it was a message from him, to her and her alone, she was sure of it.

She could sense him and her brother, Grimson, in the air. *All may not be lost just yet*, she thought as she got slowly to her feet. They had made camp at the top of the cliffs, and Bergborr and the Panterran, Orcalion, had walked a few paces away and were looking out over the edge trying to find a route to the ground, which lay a dizzying distance below.

Eilif stood and looked out over the Dark Lands. They were feared by most Wolfen – a place of myth and mystery. The endless thick vegetation looked forbidding and mysterious. She took a deep breath. She didn't care. She would run head-long into Hellheim itself if it meant finding her brother and the Man-Kind. She would be patient. Time was still on her side.

Two Panterran approached Bergborr and Orcalion. One of them carried a small, crumpled object. She concentrated on the thing, and drew a little closer. The small hooded creature opened his hand and showed it to the Panterran counselor, who lifted it, and sniffed. He wrinkled his nose. It was a piece of fabric, red. The breeze was blowing towards her, and a few atoms of its scent drifted towards her sensitive nostrils and made her eyes burst wide. Reason fled from her as she sprinted forward, almost blind with determination. She covered the dozen paces between them in seconds.

The Panterran saw her approaching and each drew a curved blade; even Bergborr braced himself, perhaps thinking her plan was to push them both over the cliff edge.

Eilif lunged at the Panterran, ducking under the swinging slice of his sword, and briefly clasping the creature to her, while snatching the cloth and holding it to her breast. Fists and the flat of blades pummeled her, and she fell to the ground, curling into a ball. She managed to tuck the material down her shirt, and then covered her head with her hands as more fists and boots joined in the assault.

"No, leave her.' Bergborr covered her body with his own, and he too was roughly beaten before being pulled from her. 'She's still hurt.'

Orcalion leaned down and grabbed at the sensitive ruff at the back of her neck, and pulled her head back, hard. 'I said I needed you for now, Princess Eilif. But I never said anything about needing all of you. Try that again, and as well as losing your freedom, you might find you also lose one of your pre-cious hands.' He pushed her head forward. 'Bind her.'

She was dragged from the edge of the cliff, her hands bound in front of her, then she was thrown roughly against a broken shard of boulder. She stayed down with her back turned to them. Outwardly she was dazed, but inside her heart sang. Eilif half turned and listened for a second or two, before slowly turning back to her prize. She reached inside her shirt and lifted the small square of cloth to her face. She closed her eyes and inhaled – images flooded her mind. She laughed softly into the cloth. She could still see his midnight black eyes, and smile, teeth small, unlike a Wolfen's, but white and strong nonetheless.

She opened her eyes and tucked the bandana into her shirt. Her face lost its mirth, as she thought of the Panterran's beating.

'Vile creatures. It won't always be an unarmed warrior you try and beat on. There will another time, and as Odin is my witness, vengeance will come soon.'

She silenced her whispering as footsteps approached.

Bergborr paced back and forth along the cliff edge. He lifted his head and breathed in the scents on the breeze, slightly closing his eyes to concentrate. There it was, the scent of the son of Grimvaldr, and also the most hated being, the Man-Kind. He felt disgusted – the princess chasing after the freakish creature like some sort of lovesick cub. He ground his teeth; he had never wanted to kill another creature so badly.

He turned, lifting his head and concentrating. A frown creased his brow. It was strange; he also thought he could smell another Valkeryn warrior. He snorted; he didn't really see himself as a Valkeryn Wolfen anymore. He wondered if he ever did. He sniffed again – it was impossible; all the warrior blood of Valkeryn had been spilt and they were just bones by now... undoubtedly picked clean by Lygon teeth.

Turning back to the dark jungles, he narrowed his eyes; they weren't far ahead – perhaps only a day. Bergborr made a silent prayer to Odin, pleading for the chance to face the Man-Kind in battle. He knew Odin would approve of him keeping their race pure, and halt any chance of some vile union of races. His stomach turned at the thought.

He let his mind dance on the images in his head of facing the Man-Kind. He'd soon show the princess: the Arnoddr was a false prophet, and little more than a weak coward who relied on trickery and cunning. If he was an example of the mighty Ancients, then it was no wonder they had fled from the planet. His eyes narrowed as he imagined the fight – there would be no quarter given on that day.

A sting at his elbow startled him, and he looked down to see the flat face of Orcalion snagging his arm with one claw. Bergborr went to take a few steps away but the claws dug in, and the black slit of a mouth opened.

'Brave Bergborr, clever Bergborr, I'm so glad you were able to free yourself from the mighty battle and flee, even though you seem to have gotten yourself lost on your way bringing Queen Mogahrr the offspring of Grimvaldr.'

Orcalion continued to grin up at him. He waved one small arm at the dark jungle beyond the cliff edge. 'And now look. Now you have managed to guide us so quickly to the trail of the Arnoddr Sigarr, and the young Valkeryn prince.' Orcalion's claws pulled him around; his yellow eyes travelling over the many injuries Bergborr sustained from his recent fight with the Lygon warrior.

'So many wounds, so lucky to survive.'

Bergborr ripped his arm free in disgust. Orcalion nodded up at him, the black grin splitting his face even wider. 'Yes, so lucky to survive. Such a strong and clever Wolfen.'

Bergborr felt revulsion for the small creature. When the time came, he would take his head, and kick it around for pleasure. As if reading Bergborr's mind, the Panterran smiled even wider, revealing his entire mouthful of needle-like teeth.

'Friend Bergborr, so, there are now just a handful of Valkeryn Wolfen left in this world? Perhaps soon, there will be none, and your once mighty race will be no more.'

Bergborr bared his teeth. 'Careful, tiny licker of spittle, I gave the Panterran the Valkeryn kingdom, and for that I have Mogahrr's good grace and protection.'

Orcalion bowed. 'I meant no offence, mighty warrior. I was only talking of something that would sadden me if it were to occur.' He looked up with the guileful gleam in his yellow eyes. 'For then, whom would we war upon?' Orcalion bowed again, but Bergborr detected the soft sound of a wheezy laugh coming from under his cowl.

Bergborr looked away, detesting being in the presence of the small goblin-like creatures, detesting their ability to see into the soul of a being. They were unnatural.

Behind the Panterran counselor, there were dozens of other Panterran and a small war party of the fearsome Lygon. The large creatures were breathing heavily, from the exertion of the climb, and there was palpable excitement at the thought of getting their hands on more Wolfen... and perhaps even the Man-Kind itself.

Orcalion saw him looking at the formidable frames of the Lygon and nodded. 'Yes, I agree. We Panterran and Wolfen had better travel down the pathway to the Dark Lands first. Our large brothers might not prove so... agile on a cliff.'

Bergborr grunted. 'I'll see to the princess.'

Orcalion shook his head, the grin never faltering. 'No, we need her not. She goes back to the queen.'

Bergborr thought quickly. 'The Man-Kind thinks highly of her. Also, if she is gone, then we have no leverage over the prince.'

Orcalion narrowed his eyes. 'We don't need leverage. We just need to find them.' He looked back to where the princess sat. 'She is proof that Orcalion does what is asked of him.'

'No.' Bergborr advanced a step.

Orcalion held up a fist. Immediately several Panterran raised cross bows, aiming at the dark Wolfen's chest. Bergborr's teeth came together.

Orcalion started to turn away. 'She goes back.' He turned back to Bergborr. 'Be careful, or we may decide that we don't not need you either. The protection of the Queen counts for little so far away from her gaze.'

Bergborr could only watch as a Lygon looped a rope around Eilif's neck. She stared at him, her ice blue eyes penetrating him to his core. He watched her every step as she was led back down the rocky slopes, leaving him to scale down the cliff side, alone.

***

Sorenson had found another route down the cliff walls and climbed down in an almost reckless rush. He needed to be on the ground first, lest he be spotted on the wall when the Panterran and Lygon had reached the ground.

He was torn – follow Bergborr or try to free the princess. He groaned, indecision momentarily forming a knot in his gut. He knew Eilif was smart and tough; he would have to trust that she could survive for a while longer.

It would be Arn and Grimson he would track and, with luck, find first. He had the ability to see their trail. He was confident that while the Lygon and Panterran bullocked through the trees, he would dance above them.

CHAPTER 14

HUMAN, BUT THEN AGAIN NOT

I think it's a dead whale.' Becky sipped at the remaining warm water in the greasy looking plastic bottle.

Edward grunted. 'Maybe.' He walked along the line of chalk-white ribs. 'Maybe once it was. Maybe it started out as a whale... but it's not a sea creature anymore. Hey, did you know whales actually started out as land creatures?'

Becky turned her mouth down and shrugged.

Edward nodded and reached out to run his hand along a thick bone. 'Sure. It was called an *Ambulocetus*, looked a little like a furred alligator, and was only about ten feet long. It developed a taste for shellfish, and the rest is history.'

Becky sipped again and motioned with her head towards the long line of bones. 'Well this baby is more than ten feet long – more like a hundred.'

Edward nodded. 'Hmm, maybe it thought it safer to try its luck back on land. Done a complete evolutionary about-face – re-evolved the ability to walk on its limbs.' He looked around. 'I wonder if this was an ancient seabed?'

Becky scoffed. 'Safer on land? What the hell would scare this giant enough into wanting to drag itself out of the water.'

Edward grinned at her, an image of a giant whale-like creature running up out of the sea, chased by something even bigger lurking in the depths. 'No, I meant it would have taken a lot of generations, and perhaps some forced mutations along the way. I reckon a million years ought to have done it. Besides, it might have been pollution, sea warming or a hundred other things, rather than predation, and...'

'I don't care. Let's keep going, I'm boiling to death.' Becky started walking away.

Edward had wrapped his shirt around his head; his shoulders were now pink from the sun. He caught up, walking beside her for a few moments and examining her face. 'You okay?'

She looked at him, her cheeks glistening with perspiration. 'You're gonna have sunburn tomorrow.'

'Thanks Mom. But seriously, are you...'

'Yes, yes; just freaking hot and uncomfortable. We've been walking for hours, and I'm super tired.' She didn't look at him but he noticed her bottom lip was trembling.

'Don't worry Becky; we'll come to the forest soon, and hopefully find some shelter. We just need to keep following the tracks. The soldiers did it, and Arn managed to cross this desert with nothing but his determination.'

She looked at him and smiled, her eyes seeming to shine in her red face. 'I hope so. I didn't think we'd be walking this far, and I'm just about out.' She held her water bottle up and jiggled it. It had about a single sip left.

Edward's mouth dropped open. 'You're kidding me? Weren't you rationing?'

She pulled a face, giving him a look suggesting he was a dimwit. 'No-oo. No one told me to.' She finished it and threw the bottle onto the sand.

He raced after it and picked it up. 'We might need this. What do you expect to find in the forest, a 7-Eleven? Even if we find water, you're going to need take some with you.' She didn't acknowledge him. 'Where will you keep it? In your mouth?'

Becky increased her pace, leaving him behind. He shook his head. *Ooh boy, Princess Rebecca and her faithful hand-servant, Edward* . He sighed and pulled his shirt turban down over his eyes and plodded on.

Albert Harper tried to make himself as inconspicuous as possible as Colonel Marion Briggs walked up and down the double line of Special Forces soldiers. Each stood a head taller than her. The man standing at the front was another six inches on top of the tallest person, and seemed to be her second in charge. He had a stare that was pure psychopath.

Briggs half turned from them, and put a finger to the small stud in her ear before she spoke. Her words were loud so she could be heard over the screaming wind.

'Images?' She nodded. 'Sound… life lines?' She grunted. 'Good work.' She then turned to Albert Harper who stood white faced at the opposite side of the tunnel.

Harper's coat flapped and he held it down. The air was rushing inside the tunnel now, being pulled from both directions of the huge particle collision ring, and drawn to the oily spot hanging in the air. The tear in time and space was now large as a truck tire and looking like a toothless mouth – a hungry devouring mouth, waiting for its next meal.

'Count yourself lucky, Harper. I need you here in the event we need to technologically enforce an emergency exit strategy.' Her mouth turned down. 'Whatever the hell that might be.'

She half turned away from him and roared over her shoulder. 'Final weapons check.'

There came the rapid sound of metal and ceramic clips, slots and barrels being opened and slid back, of ammunition rounds, gas canisters and grenades being counted off, and bodies snapping back to attention. It all lasted only a few seconds.

Briggs turned, and walked up and down the line of soldiers, stopping now and then to stare into a face of one or another and speak a few words.

'Samson, no quarter.' The brutal man nodded.

'Teacher, you're on my three at all time.' This man looked both formidable and intelligent – probably an even more lethal combination.

Briggs walked on, hands clasped behind her back, her voice raised and her jaw set.

'This country is ours. We own it. We paid for it with our blood and our fore-father's blood, and by god, we'll rip a hole in anyone or anything that tries to take it away from us.' She paused.

'HUA!' the Delta's yelled as one. The word sounded like *hooah*, and was all a soldier needed to respond with, and all a leader ever wanted to hear. It was the combat professional's shorthand for Heard, Understood and Acknowledged.

She continued pacing along the line and then stopped to turn and face Harper. 'We own this goddamn beautiful country... now, tomorrow, and in the future forever and ever, Amen.' She grinned cruelly at scientist. 'Let's just make sure that those assholes in the future are clear on that.'

'HUA!'

Briggs turned to the gaping maw hanging in space, sucking in air and anything else not tied down. She balled her fists, and uttered a single 'forwa-aard', and sprinted at the dark void, leaping and disappearing in an instant.

Samson roared the same command over the banshee sound of the wind. 'On the double – forward.' He lowered a shoulder and ran, almost as if he expected to strike something that needed to be battered down.

Harper guessed the giant soldier approached every problem the same way. He silently watched, as two by two the several dozen black clad warriors leapt into the void. He shook his head and sighed.

'Look out Arn, your saviors are coming... whether you like it or not.'

Edward stood swaying slightly, feeling like he was on the deck of a ship, pitching and rolling in a swell, instead of the dry sands of a desert that was once Illinois. He knew it was just his balance going due to dehydration – his vision was blurring as well. His water supply was gone, the last few mouthfuls given over to Becky, who was probably in an even worse state.

He inhaled the dry air – he could smell earth, and in the distance there was a dark line that could have been mountains, or trees, or nothing but a shimmering trick of the light played out on the endless grains of quartz and silica.

He tried to swallow the dry lump in his throat. His heart hammered under his ribs, keeping beat with a pounding in his head. They staggered on, sometimes falling down, and then using up precious energy dragging themselves back to their feet.

The dark line was closer – not a mirage then.

'What is it?' Becky was gripping his forearm, not letting go, using him as a crutch.

He squinted into the distance. 'I, I don't know. But I think it's supposed to be a barrier. Maybe to stop us.' He swallowed again, and blinked. 'Oh no.' He felt the lump in his throat descend an inch or two, but threaten to immediately come back up, dragging with it a ball of sick.

What they had originally taken to be a stand of trees, or even some sort of wall, had turned out to be row after row of upright crosses, each with a body of some tortured being lashed to it.

'There must be hundreds of them.' He looked along the fence line of brutalized bodies.

Becky's fingers dug into his arm like claws. 'They're like scarecrows.'

101

He nodded. That was exactly what they looked like. 'And we're the crows.' He took a few more steps, and squinted up at the things. Their bodies looked strange – human, but then again, not.

Edward started to approach, but Becky held on, digging her heels into the sand. He tugged at her. 'Let's get closer – I want to take a better look.'

He had to drag her with him. She complained, but in the end knew they had to go forward, and fast – one way or the other, they needed to make it to the forest – they could never hope to trek back across the sands to the tunnel now without any water.

He plodded forward another twenty feet and stopped. 'What the hell is that? A man with a wolf's head?' He rubbed his eyes, not believing what he was seeing.

'Maybe it's wearing a mask, or they stuck it on.' Becky's voice was little more than a squeak at his shoulder.

Edward's scientific interest was piqued, and his intellect urged him on. He just needed to convince his legs and feet to agree and stop trembling beneath him. Taking another few steps, he stood close to the first cross, looking up.

The figure was shaped like a man, but bigger. Edward estimated about six and a half feet. Its body seemed normal – chest pectorals, stomach muscles, and arms and legs that were long-limbed and strong, but the whole thing was covered in a light sheen of fur. He grimaced; in this, as in most of the bodies, deep cuts and blue bruising ravaged the skin and fur. The figures were obviously dead, and flies feverishly jostled with each other over the wounds, eyes and mouth.

'Yuck, I can smell them.'

Edward ignored her, and walked to the next figure, this one suffering a deep slash from the side of the face all the way down its torso. Sticky blood still coated its legs and dripped to the sand a few feet below its trussed feet.

'Looks like they were tortured, and I don't think they were all dead when they were strung up. Why were they staked out here? Were they meant to be a warning, or were they meant to die facing something in the desert?' He went to reach up, and Becky grabbed his arm.

'Don't. Please don't touch it, Edward. Maybe they had been cast out because they had a disease, or they were criminals… or maybe they deserved it somehow.'

Edward pulled his arm away, and looked at her with disbelief, before turning back to the creature on the cross. 'A disease that was probably on the end of a sword or axe I'd say. Look at the wounds on him – at the wounds on all of them. These guys look like a vanquished army. Genghis Khan did the same thing to his enemies.' He looked at her again. 'And no one deserves something like this.'

Edward reached out again, this time placing his hand on the creature's foot. The thing immediately jerked as if shocked, and lifted its head, screaming out words at the sky in a language Edward had no hope of understanding. He fell backwards, colliding with Becky and dragging them both to the ground.

They scrabbled backwards on the sand, both breathing heavily and their eyes fixed on the wolf-being.

The creature opened its weary bloodshot eyes and looked down at them. The light-colored orbs told of pain and suffering on an unimaginable level, but the mouth and lips still worked to form words. Only two made any sense.

'Arnoddr Siggar.'

Edward stood again and hurried forward, clasping the creature's foot and looking up into its pained face. The thing repeated the words.

'Arnoddr Siggar.'

'I think he's saying… ' Edward breathed the words back to the creature. 'Arnold Singer?'

The wolf-man stared for several seconds, and then its body started to shake. It slowly lifted its face to the sun, sucked in one last deep breath, and roared out a single word.

'Valhalla-aaa!' The word stretched and as it ended, the creature's eyes closed, and the head slumped back to its chest.

'It's Arn. They know him.' Edward turned to Becky. 'Come on.'

Briggs was thirsty, and the black coveralls attracted significant heat regardless of the cutting-edge technology designed to draw away moisture and ventilate the body – there was only so much military science could do to keep you cool in temperatures over a hundred and ten degrees and humidity of around zero

The double line of men and woman marched at a pace close to five miles per hour – nearly jogging speed. They'd been keeping it up in silence for over four hours, and would continue to do so for many more. The recon told them there was fifty miles to cover and still twenty or so to go – they needed to cross at speed, without shelter, and without rest. And by the time they reached the tree line they still needed to be able to run, and fight.

Briggs smiled; every single one of her team would do it with ease. She heard the dry crunching sound of their boots on the sand closing on her from behind and she gritted her teeth; she needed to stay out in front. She was the squad leader; she was the one who led by example.

Damned heat, she thought, and put her head down to push herself a little harder.

Out on the sand plains, the two figures shimmered in the oppressive heat as they approached the tree line.

The huge bodied creatures watched, jostling and moving with excitement behind the trunks of trees.

One of the Panterran reached up high to dig black claws into one of the Lygon forearms, and hiss up at the figure towering above it.

'Mogahrr wants them alive – she has lost too many Man-Kind and will not take kindly to losing more.'

The orange and black creature bared its teeth, but nodded its enormous head and made motions to it companions to press themselves back behind the trees.

The two small figures ran the last few hundred feet, laughing at their good fortune and escape from the heat of the desert.

CHAPTER 15

THEY'RE DIFFERENT

'm itchy.' Grimson hunched his shoulders and pulled a sour face.

Arn looked down at him, pulled him closer and turned his shoulders to look at his back. The scarring from the bat creature's attack had healed over. The scar was still pink and uneven, but it was closed and there was no infection.

'Don't worry about it. It's probably just the new skin getting used to all your movement.

Grim shook his head. 'No, all over me – I'm itchy all over. It's too hot.'

'Oh that. Yeah, me too.' The oppressive heat was stifling – even though it must have only been in the high eighties, the humidity compounded the discomfort.

They had been following the river, staying a hundred feet or so in from its bank for safety. In some places it was as silent as a whisper, and others there was a thundering as if it was rushing over rocks and boulders. Now, as they crept through the thick bushes and ferns, there came a faint roar from just up ahead.

He listened for another moment, and then half turned. 'Let's have a quick look at the river, and see if it's any safer. Besides, that small lump we originally saw from the cliff tops is suddenly looking like a mountain. If the river started on top of it, then what we can hear is a fall of water, and that my young friend, means a bath.'

'No bath.' Grim turned away.

Arn shook his head. 'We'll see. C'mon, let's go.' He burrowed through the enormous leaves and vines, Grimson trail-

107

ing behind him, thwacking at the hanging plants with a stick. The going was getting tougher nearer the river, and after a short while, sweat ran from every pore, joining with the sticky sap, plant debris, and slow moving gnats to coat his body.

After twenty minutes of working his way close to the sound of the water, he saw the jungle brightening, and soon they had broken out of the dense undergrowth, and stood just behind the final veil of jungle vines. The hanging trees acted like a curtain, giving them a final bit of concealment so they could investigate their surroundings.

As Arn had hoped, the river they had been following pooled on broken rock at the base of a cliff. The fifty feet of sheer rock was scoured clean of plants, and looking up he could see the thick river pouring over the lip high above. Mist lifted off the falling water to sparkle momentarily in the sunshine before settling onto the giant green fronds of palms and tree ferns at the water's edge.

At the centre of the pool was a boiling cauldron of white water that spewed away from the downfall. Jagged rocks poked up from the froth like dark teeth, and the torrent would have been far too heavy for them to get any closer. At its edges, there were shallow overflow pools that were not connected to the river. He hoped that a quick dip might have been safe. *As safe as anything could be in this crazy world*, he thought. He might even be lucky enough to catch some fish, as he was getting tired of trapping the small elephant like rats from the jungle floor. He'd keep that to himself for now; fish and Wolfen did not mix.

'Wait here.' He cautiously stepped from behind the vines, Grimson immediately following him.

Arn turned. 'Hey!'

Grimson just shook his head, in a *no way I'm staying*-type gesture. Arn had to keep reminding himself that only a short while ago the young Wolfen was a prince, and rarely got orders from anyone other than the King and Queen.

Arn stayed still and silent, just letting his eyes move over the landscape, the water, and the cliff top.

'Is it safe?' Grimson was right behind him. Arn noticed he already had his shirt off.

'Maybe, Grim, but we'll be quick and alert, and you keep your eyes on me at all times, okay?'

The youth nodded. Arn tapped him on the shoulder. 'I thought you didn't want to have a bath?'

Grimson kept his eyes on the water and stepped out of his trousers. 'I don't like baths... but swimming is different.'

Arn laughed. 'Of course it is. Okay, there's a small pool over there that looks perfect.' A dozen feet from the falling water, the froth and spume splashed up onto the moss-covered boulders, pooling at their base to make a series of frothy ponds. Arn guessed they were far too shallow or agitated to have anything living in them, and would be perfect for a quick wash and cool down.

Before Arn could even unstrap his belt, Grimson quickly had the rest of his clothes off. He looked at the clothing – it was starting to wear through, like his own had days before. Arn was reduced to dressing like his forefathers in a breechcloth, flaps hanging front and back, with his last keepsakes hanging from a pouch at his belt. He kept the soft leather boots, but soon, without replacement soles he would be bare foot. Grimson still had trousers and shirt, but for how long he didn't know.

The young Wolfen waded into the largest pool and lay face down, rubbing his head, and then pulling it back to suck in a deep breath and smile. 'It's wonderful...' He lowered his face to drink. '... and tastes good as well. C'mon.'

Arn carried Grimson's clothes to a dry rock, and kicked off his boots. He stepped back carefully over the sharp boulders at the water's edge. Rays of light played on his skin, and with the cool spray from the waterfall it felt fantastic. He stepped into the pond, and he too lay down with a sigh. 'Oh yeah.'

He ducked his head under the water rubbing his itchy scalp for a few moments before surfacing. He noticed the slick of oil, debris and tiny struggling passengers that had been dislodged from his hair now floating on the surface. He decided, unlike Grim, that drinking from this pond was definitely out.

He lay back in the water, put his hands behind his head and reflected on his new life. How quickly life's priorities could change. One minute he was living a coddled life, in luxury that he didn't even appreciate, where the most important things in the world to him were getting good grades, keeping a lookout for bullies, and trying to impress Becky Matthews. The greatest risk to life and limb was the potential for getting hit by a careless motorist. Now, staying alive was a minute-by-minute blessing. He had been captured twice, tortured, saved, met races of beings – some noble and some morally decrepit – and he had made and lost good friends.

Good friends. His thoughts turned to Eilif. *Had she really existed?* If not for the Wolfen lying in the water five feet from him, happily spitting water in the air, he might have answered that question with a resounding no. Still, how could a creature really exist, so strange, so beautiful, so... loving? She still haunted his dreams.

His reverie was broken by Grimson's voice.

'I think my mother and father are in Valhalla now.'

Arn turned his head slightly. The Wolfen wasn't looking at Arn, but was laying back and talking to himself, nodding as he did so. 'Yes, I think they killed so many Panterran and Lygon that Odin himself wanted them as his personal guard... no, as his generals.' He nodded. 'They were great warriors.'

Arn kept watching the youth, who seemed unfazed by the possibility that both his parents were dead. He was proud of them, nothing more.

Grim turned to Arn. 'But not Eilif – she's not in Valhalla yet.'

Arn slowly sat forward. 'Hmm? What makes you say that?'

Grimson shrugged and turned his head back and closed his eyes. 'I know it. A Wolfen can sense these things.'

Arn grunted, and turned over onto his stomach in the water, resting his arms on a rock and his chin on his hands. He watched the waterfall cascade down and smash against the slick stone. Nonsense, but... He frowned and half turned to look at Grimson. The Wolfen did have extraordinary senses, well beyond his own. *Could it be true?* He lay back down. *No, nonsense.*

Arn tried to turn his mind to the path ahead. He hadn't really planned what to do if he trekked from one side of the Dark Lands to the other and found... nothing? Where was there to go back to? Valkeryn had fallen. Could he find a safe place to live out his life? Live, perhaps for another fifty years as a solitary and unique being. He snorted. He doubted anyone or anything lived a long life in this place.

He rolled over and spat water into the air. He could accompany Grim on a quest to find the lost Wolfen tribes. Although even Grim admitted they were nearly as much a myth as the mankind were.

He sighed, and thought about his last option – try and find his way back to the tunnel in the wasteland. Maybe he could re-enter the door that he had originally fallen through? But what of Grim? He could never take him back. What would become of a wolf-like creature in his time? He was a prince, who would end his days as a lab rat... or a circus freak. He shuddered as he remembered the dream of Eilif being carried away. He'd sacrifice himself before he'd ever let that happen.

Something dark came over the falls in amongst the cascading water. While he continued watching another of the dark objects came over the lip and disappeared into the frothing water. He got to his feet, and carefully walked to the water's edge. One of the objects floated towards him. It bobbed and tumbled in the current, finally being forced to the bank. Arn stared, and then bent for a closer look. He reached into the water and lifted it free – it was a fish, or what was left of it. But now it got interesting – it was the carcass of a fish that had been cleaned.

Arn turned it over; there was a spear hole in the head, and both sides of the fish had been expertly filleted – the meat cleanly removed by a sharp blade. He looked up as another one came over the waterfall. The thought struck him like a thunder clap – someone up top was cleaning fish. The Panterrans ate fish, but shredded the flesh, preferring to dig their sharp claws and teeth into the long silver bodies.

He took a step back, trying to see up over the fall's edge. The Wolfen hated fish, but he knew of one creature that ate fish, and cleaned it first. He scrambled back to Grimson.

'C'mon, we got to get up on the ridge. I think we've found something important.'

Arn completed the climb first, rushing over the boulders and steeper cliff banks, lest he miss whoever had been throwing the fish carcasses over the edge. He lay on his belly panting. Watching. Grimson soon followed and he flopped down next to Arn, his tongue hanging out, and a hoarse rasp coming from his throat. Arn didn't need to silence the youth as the roar of the waterfall still masked their sounds.

The climb had lifted them above the jungle's canopy. Strong sunlight poured down on the deep, basin shaped pool that fed the lip of the waterfall. Mist billowed up from the falling water, swirling in the agitated air, and cooling them. Still on his belly, Arn wriggled forward, and peered up over a fallen log.

Just across on the other side of the wide pond there was a large flat rock, and lined neatly upon it were about a dozen filleted fish, professionally cleaned, each resting on a broad leaf. Beside them were a couple of straight poles Arn assumed were the spears used to catch them.

'I'm not eating those.' Grimson made more disgusted noises in his throat.

'Shush; we didn't come up here for the fish, but the fishermen.' Arn lifted himself a little higher, and then crept forward. He froze as the bushes on the other side of the pond thrashed and then opened. Arn's mouth fell open – it was woman, followed by a man, both short and olive skinned. Even from where Arn stood, he could tell that neither of them was more than five feet tall, with slender waists and broad shoulders.

The woman motioned to the fish, and the man started to gather them up. Both wore a knife at their waist, and were wearing what was little more than a skirt. Both were bare from the waist up. Arn couldn't take his eyes off the woman, and not just because of her partial nudity. It just seemed strange to him now, after what he had endured – a real person, a real human female person.

Grimson had crept up beside him, and stared hard at the couple. He lifted his head, sampling the air. Arn stuck out an arm at the youth. 'Stay here, and I mean it.'

Grim grabbed at Arn's arm and held him. 'Wait.'

'Why?'

'Are they Man-Kind?' Grimson held onto him.

Arn frowned down at the Wolfen, not understanding why he had asked the question. He wondered about the quality of the youth's eyesight. 'Of course. Maybe a different race. I don't know if we'll even be able to understand each other, but they look human to me.' Arn stepped out.

Behind him, he heard Grim's voice. 'They look like you, but they don't smell like you. They're… different.'

Arn ignored him and stepped further into the sunshine. 'Hello.'

The man and woman froze, their black eyes round as they stared. Arn's skin had burned a deep brown, and his long dark hair fell to his shoulders – he hoped they recognized that he could have been one of them, except for his height.

Arn held up his hand, palm toward them. 'Hello. I am a friend.'

There was no response, and the woman looked briefly at the fish, and then back to Arn. Her eyes narrowed.

Arn waved his hands. 'No, no, I don't want your fish. I come in peace.' He took another step towards them.

The woman darted forward, snatched up one of the spears, and held it up, spear tip pointed at Arn. She said something over her shoulder and the male darted forward to gather up the fish pieces. He never took his eyes of Arn as he rolled them into the broad leaf, tucked them under his arm, and started to back into the forest. The woman began to follow him.

'Wait!' Arn started to wade into the water.

The woman's eyes went wide, and she screamed at him. 'No.'

Arn pulled up shocked, but his face soon relaxed into a smile as his brain registered the recognizable word. He waved. 'I just want to talk.'

He started to wade further out into the pool. He could feel the soft silt squelching up between his toes. The cool water felt pleasant against his overheated skin, and he continued on until it reached his waist. He took more steps and then felt a swirl of water followed by a small pinch on the front of his thigh. He looked down to see a flash of silver-orange, the same colors as the fish the couple had been catching.

There was another nudge and then a pinch to the side of his leg. Looking down this time, he noticed a small plume of red floating around his legs. *Blood?* he wondered.

The woman screamed to him again, and looking up, he saw she was motioning him to go back. Confusion was starting to turn to panic. She was pointing at the water, and waving him off.

Another pinch, more blood, and Arn realised that the original shout to him when he entered the water was a warning – the fish they had been catching might be good to eat, but they obviously returned the favor by finding people just as tasty.

Arn lifted his arms, staring down into the clear water. More and more of the orange-silver flashes started to swirl around his legs, their movements getting faster and more excited. Given he wore only his breechcloth, the thought of razor sharp teeth finding a hidden area of his body made his stomach, and lower parts shrivel. He covered his groin with his hands, turned and attempted a fast wade back to the shore. Pinches and nips accompanying him as he slipped in the slimy mud on the bottom of the pond.

He was closing on the bank, when there came a thud, and a shocking pain at his calf. Arn leapt the last five feet, and lay collapsed on the flat rocks beside the water. The fish had followed him right to its edge and boiled and tumbled in the shallows as though annoyed at his escape. He sat up and examined his legs – small grazes, nips and cuts pitted his thighs, but turning one leg over, he saw a good sized mouthful of meat had been taken from his calf. Luckily, they were all treatable with some of the remaining *feninlang* root, but he was glad he hadn't been further out – he knew whatever had taken that last bite was a lot bigger than the smaller fish he had first seen.

He clamped a hand over the wound and looked to the other side of the pond. The woman stood with her hands on her hips and a smile on her face. She waggled a finger in the air and shook her head. Even from a distance, he could tell by her expression she thought him slightly dim. In a flash she turned and disappeared back into the jungle.

He sighed. 'Well, you never get a second chance to make a first impression.'

Grimson came and knelt beside him. 'And was that a good one, Arn?'

'Not really, no.' Arn looked at the young Wolfen. 'Have you ever heard of Man-Kind living in the Dark Lands?'

Grimson shook his head. 'No. No they don't. I don't think they're really like you anyway.' He turned to look at the water's edge and the fish wrestling and tumbling in the shallows. 'Now do you know why I don't like fish – yech.'

Arn laughed and rubbed the youth's head. 'I'm sure they wouldn't dream of taking a bite from a Wolfen prince.'

Arn opened a leather bag he had strung at his belt, and unrolled the waxy leaf that still held some precious red flowers. He squeezed some sap from one of the fleshy petals, and rubbed it onto his wounds, gritting his teeth as the sap sizzled against his skin.

Grimson threw a rock at the fish still loitering in the shallows. 'What now?'

Arn kept applying the lotion. 'Now? Now, we find a way to cross the river, and find our new friends.'

CHAPTER 16

WELCOME FROM HELL, PUSSY

Brunig half turned to Durok, one of his Lygon comrades and whispered. 'There are so many, we can eat some. The old queen won't miss them all.'

Durok grunted. 'I have heard their meat is soft, and they are mostly already skinned. I agree, we can take half for Mogahrr, and eat the rest. But patience, we will wait until they come a little closer so they do not scatter when we attack.'

Brunig nodded and turned to whisper to the dozen enormous Lygon warriors hidden behind the trunks of the trees. They waited, green eyes focused on the approaching line of creatures, the orange and blacks stripes of their bodies rendering them nearly invisible in the dappled light of the forest.

***

Briggs' Delta force team had rested amongst the crucified Wolfen. Sipping water and eating protein rations, none of them look the slightest bit fatigued, even though they had jogged for almost an entire day through dry desert. The colonel had chosen to rest them in amongst the forest of carcasses so they had their first chance to study some of the indigenous life forms up close.

The professional killers examined the bodies for strengths and vulnerabilities, noting the musculature, the long teeth, and predator's eyes. They noted the position of vital organs, and felt the consistency of the flesh. They were satisfied in the knowledge that it was the same density as their own – bullets and knives would pierce them with ease. If the wolf creatures engaged or got in the way, they'd be exterminated. But every one of the soldiers knew the wolves were not the main danger, and the huge creatures that had taken out the Green Berets were the priority threat.

Briggs had them back on their feet quickly, and within an hour they were in sight of the forest edge. She held up her field glasses, moving the electronic dial for magnification. She smiled, and then pressed a stud, changing the vision to infra-red. It was what she had expected – phosphorescent orange outlines of huge bodies in concealment. Good, she thought, their first test.

'Well, well, we got ourselves a small war party lying in ambush.'

Samson pulled his gun from over his back. 'Orders?'

'We take 'em head on. Time to show them who the boss really is from now on.' She lowered the binoculars and half turned to the giant soldier beside her. 'Give me a wedge for-mation – you and Teacher lead 'em in.'

Samson spun and shouted instructions to the team, and they moved into a triangle, Samson and Teacher in front, a soldier at each of their shoulders, and so on. The sound of weapons being locked and loaded snapped back along the line.

Samson roared over his shoulder and started to run. 'Stay in formation – standard meet-and-greet – double time.'

The wedge went with him. Briggs jogged at their rear, doing her best to keep pace with the long strides of her elite Delta team.

When the soldiers were just a hundred feet out from the tree line, several huge bodies stepped forward. Any normal human would have been dumbstruck by the sight of the fear-some giants. But the elite soldiers had reviewed the footage of the Green Beret attack so many times, they knew how, who, and exactly what to expect.

Samson and the team kept up the sprint pace. The lead

creature roared, making a sound that rolled across the sand towards them with an almost physical wave of power. It swung a huge club back and forth.

The Lygon was protected by sheets of hammered iron many inches thick, and wore on its head a heavily studded and armored helmet. It would deflect bullets with ease – as the earlier GBs had found to their misfortune. But this time the Delta force had come prepared – uranium tipped rounds, grenade launchers and enough gas to choke a city block.

The huge beast roared again, took a thundering step forward and drew his trunk-thick arm back, preparing to fling the deadly missile at the approaching figures. It would be a flying battering ram, and carry enough force to shatter anything it struck.

Samson increased his pace and raised his rifle to his shoulder. His face was an expressionless mask. He fired a single round.

⊱•⊰ ⟩⟩⟩⟨⟨⟨ ⊱•⊰

Beside Brunig, Durok's battle roar was cutoff as his head snapped back. The giant Lygon seemed to stare skyward for a moment, a trickle of blood running down from under his helmet, below a tiny hole in the fire-hardened iron. The uranium tipped round had easily passed through steel and bone, and now continued to sizzle in his brain. Durok's knees bent, the club fell from his hand, and, like a colossal tree coming down, he fell backwards, dead.

The small group of Man-Kind continued their rapid advance, still holding the tiny black sticks before them. There were more popping sounds, followed by the clank of metal-on-metal, and more of Brunig's Lygon warriors fell. Brunig felt confusion, frustration, and something else in the pit of his stomach – something he had never felt before – fear.

He moved a fraction, just as a searing pain needled his shoulder. He reached up his large hand, and felt the tiny hole in his armor, the surrounding iron hot to touch. Blood spurted from either side of his shoulder. Whatever had struck him had punched a hole clean through his body – armor, flesh and bone.

A soft mewling whine escaped his lips. Confusion wracked him with indecision. These were not the soft-bodied creatures he had expected. They were nothing like the two Man-kinds they had captured only hours before. These were different; they were larger, and showed no fear. These must be the true warrior class of the Ancients.

Brunig backed up – he must escape and warn his clan – bring back more warriors and war beasts. He turned and lifted his axe, intending to throw the enormous weapon and then flee. But as he lifted his arm, there came a small puff of smoke from the lead Man-Kind, followed by a whooshing sound that grew louder in his ears.

His arm never finished its arc as his world turned white-hot and his body exploded in a plume of fire and huge gobbets of burning flesh.

That quickly, Brunig ceased to exist.

⚬⚬⚬ ⚬⚬⚬

Marion Briggs stood over one of the dying creatures and turned her head slowly, surveying the landscape. Armaments were field appropriate, all enemy down, no casualties or even a single scrape to her team. A good day's work.

She looked down at the giant beast at her feet, which was watching her with a single large green eye. She put her boot on its thick neck and drew her revolver, pointing it at the centre of the orb.

'Welcome from hell, pussy.' She pulled the trigger.

CHAPTER 17

STRONG BUT EASILY MANIPULATED

Bergborr crouched down, examining the ground. He exhaled with relief. The climb down the cliffs had been costly – six Lygon had fallen, the path crumbling under their broad and clumsy feet. Several Panterran were plucked from the cliffs by flying daemons that simply plucked them from the rock like ripe fruit and either spirited them away or dropped their bodies thousands of feet to the ground.

He hated them all, but for now he needed them. He could feel Orcalion watching him, knowing that the Wolfen were natural trackers, and it would be Bergborr that could find the fleeing offspring of Grimvaldr or the Man-Kind.

Bergborr snorted softly. He had no reason to leave the Lygons or Panterrans until he knew what they were up against. The Dark Lands were a place of myth and legend, frightening tales of monstrous beasts, sucking bogs, and strangling vines, all of which he could never overcome alone. Best to use the brute strength of the Lygons as his shield, and have the sly Panterrans keep the brutes in check.

He would put up with the Panterran Orcalion's arrogance a little while longer. He looked to the soil again. The tracks and spoor were faint, but unmistakable – the pair weren't far ahead of them. The Lygons wanted to rest, but there would be time for that later.

Orcalion glided up next to him, and placed one small clawed hand on his shoulder. 'An expensive climb Wolfen; we lost many brother warriors, and we have only just set foot in this most dangerous place. Let us hope we have something to show for it, hmm? Do you have them yet?'

Bergborr turned to look at the disgusting creature, and after a moment nodded. 'Of course, but they're moving fast, and we should to, or you will lose them… and it will be you that has to explain that to Queen Mogahrr.'

Orcalion smiled, extending and then digging his claws into the Wolfen's shoulder. 'The Lygons need to rest. They are a disagreeable force, and not one to be pushed too hard, even by me, or you, last of the brave Wolfen warriors.'

Bergborr stood, shrugging off the small hand, while trying to conceal the disgust he felt for the small devious creature. 'Tell, your brother warriors, we need to move away from the base of the cliffs, lest we suffer a rock slide that may dent even their thick skulls.'

Orcalion briefly looked up, then smiled and nodded. 'Very good, clever Wolfen, you are thinking more like a Panterran every day.'

He turned away to mingle with his own kin, before moving in amongst the Lygon. The huge creatures bent closer to listen, and after a few glances up at the steep cliffs the huge beasts straightened, and gathered their weapons.

Strong, but easily manipulated, Bergborr thought with interest and satisfaction.

* * *

Sorenson dropped to the ground from the trees to examine the spoor of the Man-Kind. He had already found the spot where they had made the jungle, and he had obliterated as much as he could. Still, he knew that Bergborr would be able to track them as he did.

He could tell by the impressions that the Man-Kind still carried the Valkeryn Prince. He prayed to Odin that the young Wolfen's injuries were not mortal. He leapt back into the trees and continued on.

Bergborr pushed, slid or wriggled his way through the dense jungle. The green vines, branches and fronds were thick and tough, and many times he had to slow down to drag in deep breaths of the humid air. Around him, the Panterran navigated the tangled vines and thick undergrowth with ease, but the lumbering Lygon brutes had to hack and slash every grinding step of their way. Many had pulled free their heavy armor and discarded it, trusting their own muscles and thick hides to protect them.

He had been following the tracks of the Man-Kind. There were none for Grimson, but he could tell by the depth of the human's tracks that he carried something heavy. Even though the man-creature staggered and fell as he travelled, they were making better time than he, since they weren't dragging a small army of dumb brutes with them. He couldn't help crushing his eyes shut for a moment and showing his teeth: every time he thought of the Man-Kind, he was torn by a rage that threatened to consume him. It was Eilif's fault – she had strangled his heart. Still, he would give her another chance, and probably another after that. She would love him eventually, and she would come with him, freely. What choice did she have? They were the only ones left.

If she still refused him? He punched a dangling vine out of his way. Then he would kill her. His *sáál* could never survive the insult to his honor.

Bergborr stopped and frowned. He backed up, and then walked in a circle. He looked at the tracks, confused For a moment it seemed like there was another amongst them – a Wolfen. A very large Wolfen.

In an instant Orcalion was beside him – the small creature was always watching him closely. His eyes moved from Bergborr's face, to the ground, and then back.

'The trail is not so clear after all, wise warrior?' The slit of a mouth hung open in a grin.

Bergborr continued to pace, and then crouched down to look at the ground. He moved aside some twigs and leaf litter and examined the last few footprints. 'The mankind and the young prince continued on, but...' he stood up, and raised his head, looking up at the green canopy high above him. Dots of light showed through the dense foliage like stars in a black night. For the most part the upper canopy was high overhead, but lower at mid-height, secondary branches, some with limbs a body-length across, intertwined and overlapped, creating an overhead highway.

He frowned and shook his head. Ghosts perhaps, he whispered. He continued to circle, spiraling outwards, his eyes moving from the ground to the branches overhead.

Orcalion snagged his sleeve again, in a fashion that was becoming irritating to the Wolfen.

'Perhaps they know of our pursuit. Perhaps they seek to evade us.'

Bergborr rubbed his cheek, and tilted his head. 'Maybe. It's getting dark; we need to push on as far as we can, before making camp. I think we should try and find dry wood to burn as we travel.'

Orcalion sneered. 'We do not need fire. The dark does not worry the Panterran or the Lygon. You have been pampered too long in the brightly lit halls of a rich castle keep, Valkeryn betrayer.'

Bergborr walked away, lest the urge to behead the revolting animal overtook his sense of self-preservation.

The night fell quickly, and beneath the canopy where there was an absence of starlight or moonlight, the darkness was complete... as Bergborr expected. It even tested the Panterran's extraordinary night vision. Behind them, Lygons grumbled at their fatigue and hunger, and their blundering ability to stumble into stinging plants or sharp objects in the blackness. Once again Bergborr felt the small creature glide up beside him.

'We must find a place to eat and sleep – somewhere defendable that will give us the space to be close together. It would be best in these dangerous lands if we are not to be strung out or hidden from each other behind thick foliage. Wouldn't want people getting attacked... or deciding to wander off.' The last bit of information was delivered with his peculiar wheezing laugh, and he turned to order several of the Lygon to spread out and find a suitable camping ground.

Bergborr turned and pressed on, keeping one eye on the branches overhead.

* * *

The huge Lygon warriors struggled through the thick foliage on either side of the animal trail the main group had been following for hours. Fifty feet apart, they searched for a suitable campsite in the rapidly diminishing light.

Drun, out at the farthest point, had been feeling the heat for some time. As the sun went down, the humidity settled over them like a warm wet blanket. He grumbled his displeasure, almost as loud as his stomach grumbled for food. Lygon were built for enormous bursts of strength over short periods of time, not for day-long wrestles with tough vines and creepers.

He cursed the Panterran. He needed to eat something, and sleep, or he might make a meal of the annoying little Orcalion. The thought hung in his mind – *who would know?* If they killed all the Panterran, they could then tear the last Wolfen to shreds. Who would know?

He was now far ahead of the main group, moving ponderously through the dark jungle. Even with his dark-adapted eyes, he could see little more than shapes and shadows. He couldn't even hear his brother warriors any more, though they were no more than fifty paces apart – the sounds of the jungle at night were even louder than during the day. Several times he heard large beasts moving through the dark – not his brothers, but other things, heavier. He froze until he had determined they were far enough away not to cause him problems.

Drun pushed aside a thick veil of fronds, breaking free of their tangle and into a clearing. Oddly, or perhaps conveniently, it was free of plants, nothing but a room-sized expanse of roughly-churned dark soil. It looked as though someone had been digging. He was tempted to hide and wait, in the chance that the digger was some sort of small foraging animal that might return to search for more roots or tubers. It might make a tasty morsel he wouldn't have to share.

He wrinkled his nose at the odors – the smell was appalling, even for a creature like him who smelt of meat and death and strong urine. He stood at the edge of the clearing, his senses screaming at him. He took a step, and halted, his huge head turning, trying to detect danger. There was nothing but soil with a few smooth stones churned to the surface.

He walked quickly out to its centre, standing with his legs braced, and his teeth bared, daring anything to come forward. There was still nothing. The ground under his feet was firm, but not hard-packed as he expected from the freshly-turned soil. He bent and flicked at one of the stones. It lifted from the soil, and exposed itself as a jawbone with a set of teeth. He looked around quickly; all the other shards were the same – bones. A killing field, then.

He stood and snorted in derision. It would not concern the Lygon warriors. If anything tried to attack even their small force, they'd feel a wrath and fury like nothing they had ever seen. It would turn into a killing field – theirs. He snorted again. *There wasn't much in this land that the mighty Lygon needed to fear*, he thought and kicked at some of the bone fragments.

Drun was satisfied that he had found a suitable site – he'd bring in his brothers. As he went to turn back to the jungle, he felt the earth slide under his feet. It was if something was moving beneath the soil. He stepped back and noticed that the dark earth was swollen in places. The more he watched the more swellings seemed to appear.

His senses screamed. He bared his teeth. His skin crawled and the fur lumped around his shoulders and along his spine as his body ramped up to fight. Drun reached for his belt, and lifted free the enormous axe. A soft, sticky sound brought his head around in time to see a pair of red eyes, peering up from the soil – no pupils, just fist-sized orbs that watched him for a second or two, before closing with the same mucousy noise he had heard before. Then they were pulled back beneath the ground.

The same sound was repeated from a different direction, and once again another pair of blood red eyes briefly examined him before pulling back beneath the earth. Drun started to pant, wishing he hadn't walked as far out into the centre of the clearing. Things seemed to lengthen, stretch and then coil underneath his huge feet. He backed up, swinging his axe, looking for something to strike.

Red eyes were opening stickily all around him now, some higher than the others, their owners still invisible in the darkness. They squelched closed, dropped, and then once again he felt the sliding sensation under his feet, as they seemed to move a little closer.

Drun had had enough and spun, preparing to bolt from the clearing, when he was confronted with a sight that froze the breath in his throat. A pair of the unblinking red eyes regarded him dispassionately, so close to him he could see the creature clearly now – a trunk-like segmented body. A massive worm with a triangular head, staring into his face.

The thing swayed slightly, and then beneath the eyes Drun

saw a circular hole open, displaying hundreds of needle sharp teeth, all pointed inwards – a mouth designed for gripping and holding. Drun roared and swung his axe, but the thing sprang back under the soil, and the mighty weapon cut through nothing but humid air.

The strength of his swing pulled him off balance, and he stumbled to one knee. Immediately one of the worms shot from the dark earth and fixed onto his leg. A searing pain shot up his body as he felt the sharp teeth cutting into his fur and tough flesh. He swung backward with the axe, but like before, the creature managed to disappear, taking with it most of his calf muscle.

Drun roared again, in frustration, pain, and fear. His bellow was also a call to his brother warriors. Supporting himself on his hands he tried to get to his feet, but more worms shot from the soil and fixed themselves to an arm, his flanks, and a shoulder.

The soil boiled beneath Drun now. He felt more sliding movement, more serated teeth latching onto his body, and then more of his flesh was ripped away. His blood spurted, covering the black sand, and he could see the earth surrounding him rise and fall like water as more of the creatures became excited by the scent of his life pouring out. Drun mewled in terror as he tried to drag himself to the edge of the clearing. Red eyes broke the soil's surface and cut through the dark earth towards him as another of the worms homed in, finally launching itself onto his already wounded leg, sawing until the limb parted at the knee. Drun weakly flung his axe back at it, but the worm and its prize disappeared under the soil.

Worms rose from the earth like weird plants, attaching themselves to his body. Soon the huge Lygon was dragged backwards, to the centre of the clearing, and then slowly pulled beneath its surface. Drun could feel the teeth burrowing into him, taking his body away from him, piece by piece.

As the soil reached his shoulders, his mind turned back to his previous brave comments – there was nothing on the land they needed to fear. It seemed, just like the legends of old, it was what was below the land that demanded respect.

His final roars turned to screams of futility, and as his vision dimmed, he saw his brother warriors appear at the edge of the clearing. With them, the small Panterran who was staring at him without care, and keeping his brother Lygon back with a raised arm. He must have bewitched them, for none made a move to help him.

Drun reached out one last time, his tortured arm immediately grabbed by a worm and dragged below. As the soil closed over his face, shutting off his screams, he saw the Panterran forcing them back, and lastly there was the sight of the dark Wolfen warrior, smiling.

· ⊩⊖⊖⊫⊂ ⊃⊃⊂⊂⊂ ⊃⊖⊖⊖⊩ ·

Orcalion watched the giant creature with interest as the sand worms bore it below the soil's surface. He ordered the remaining Lygon back from the edge of the clearing, and turned to the dark Wolfen, looking up at him with more good humor than the moment demanded.

'Nasty business, yes? 'Perhaps you can say a prayer to Odin to keep us all safe. Did not your Fenrir save us all from the time of great burning?' He smirked up at the Wolfen. 'Or was it us that really saved him? Hmm, so long ago, the legends blur, I think.' He wheezed out a small laugh.

Bergborr spoke softly. 'Be sure that Odin is watching. And be sure he has plans for all of us.' His eyes turned to rest on the Panterran. 'For none shall weep for the battle fallen. Valkeryies will descend and lift the worthy to the golden halls of Valhalla, where they will await Odin's call to the last battle.' He smiled. 'And that final battle is yet to come.'

Orcalion hissed. 'I fear there will be no more battles for the Wolfen. And soon, they will be myth and legend just like your Odin, Fenrir, and then even the betrayer, Bergborr.' He wheezed and turned, gliding away in the darkness.

CHAPTER 18

WE'RE ALL GOING ON A LITTLE TRIP SOON.

Pan Nucleonics, Northbrook – Private Testing Laboratory, 52 miles North East of Fermilab's Illinois Facility.

Pratihba Singh typed furiously at his keyboard. He had reviewed all the material sent by his old laboratory partner, Doctor Albert Harper, and made his own assessments and comments. The Fermilab generators were now running at ninety eight per cent capacity. It was if their acceleration lasers were firing and refiring particles, and then reordering the resulting collision into recognizable data, before firing again and again and again without stopping. The acceleration was self-generating now, and the result was the creation of a speed-of-light vortex.

Singh knew this had to be a false reading; even though the machines drew enough energy to run an entire city, no actual physical activity was taking place in the multi-mile ring. The sophisticated machines seemed 'locked' into full operational running mode – their objective apparently to feed the gravity distortion, nothing more.

Singh recorded his information and summarized it as best he could into short and sharp sentences – brevity counted now, when seconds were critical.

> *Dear AH, agree your findings.*
> *Energy tipping-point will be reached in forty-eight hours. Energy demand will then exceed output by generators. This will result in one of two outcomes – both equally possible:*

1. The high-speed accelerators will implode. Minor damage to facilities expected.

2. The gravity distortion will begin to seek energy sources external to acceleration chamber. Unchecked matter consumption limits – unknown. Potential sources: a) Planetary magnetic core, b) Planetary surface, c) Both.

Other physical consequences will likely be an extreme surface gamma flash that will be prevented from leaving earth's atmosphere by ionispheric shell – gamma radiation plume will travel globally in ninety-six hours, resulting in significant destruction of surface life, and gross DNA distortion for remaining populations for many generations. Biological mutation or sterilization inevitable.

Conclusion: Machines must be halted immediately. All vigorous containment attempts should be encouraged, or...

He sat back and read over his message. Even thought he had just written it, he felt it was alarming. He shrugged, he knew Albert well enough to expect he had probably already anticipated the potential catastrophe. Perhaps he just wanted a sounding board. Or perhaps he hoped that someone would find a flaw in his calculations.

Unfortunately, there was no flaw – it was as bad as the physics foretold. It was just maths, and maths never lied.

The option to detonate a ten-kiloton tactical explosive device over the gravity wound was firmly on the table. But here the math was a little more vague – there was a possibility it would simply feed the distortion and allow it to grow even quicker. In reality they needed less energy, not more. But if they severed the energy source immediately, would the 'wound' close, or would it be simply unbound; freed to consume at will?

He backspaced over the last word – there would be no "or". He felt they were all locked in the back seat of a speeding car, well away from the steering wheel or brakes.

Singh sat back, exhaled and ran his hands up through thick curly hair. He used his legs to wheel his chair backwards a few paces, looking back at his screen but not really seeing the words. The movement made the laboratory mascot, Atom, an ash-grey tomcat, leap out of the way and stare back at him with a level of indignation that only a cat can project.

Singh could feel the vibrations beneath his feet, could feel it in his teeth and behind his eyes, and he was over fifty miles from Fermilab. Raising his eyes he could see a new crack in the mortar above his head.

Atom slid past his leg, forgiving him for his previous sudden movement. He reached down and ran a hand along its back, and smiled. The cat looked up, its golden eyes half lidded, worldly-wise.

Singh nodded to it. 'Yes, I know. I think we're all going on a trip soon, my friend – whether we like it or not.'

CHAPTER 19

THE TIME OF CHANGE WAS COMING

Fen lay on his side with his eyes closed until he heard the hiss of the laboratory doors shutting.

Sitting up, he stretched, and then stood. Standing on his hind legs was becoming easier; the genetic enhancements had lengthened and straightened his bones and ligaments, and even altered the curve of his pelvic structure. For all intents and purposes he was now a biped, and all his offspring would share in the trait.

He also had other new abilities, having lost none of his existing characteristics. He lifted his head and sniffed. He could sense the changes in the atmosphere, and the rising radiation count was as obvious to his extraordinary senses as the rumbling of distant thunder was to the humans.

He reached through the door bars and entered the security code in the electronic lock. His finger-like claws had become more dexterous as they had lengthened. The door opened outwards soundlessly and he walked down the sterile-white corridor, past other barred chambers, each holding more of the Guardians – the altered security animals – his kind, his... people. All of them sat watching him. They had been waiting for him. He turned and nodded to each, and they in turn stood as he walked by.

He spoke softly to them – they all understood, and all were ready.

Fen was the largest and first of the true Guardians. He was unique, the scientists first successful test subject for a genetically-modified animal designed for combat and deep solar system space missions of the future. Strong, intelligent, agile and confident, bioengineered with a human physiology and intelligence.

In some ways, he was superior to his creators, as he still carried his canine characteristics but they were complemented by the elements of mankind. He also now carried a genetic resilience to high radiation. This meant Fen and his Guardians were armor-plated against the gamma and x-rays from the huge gravity distortion affecting the rest of the State.

He continued down the long corridor, knowing he could unlock all the doors when the time came, and free his 'people'. Reaching the end of the white tunnel he came to the sealed and fortified red chamber – Red Room 12, the experimental laboratory – where secondary biological life forms were tested for suitability. All had failed, their enhanced physiology and psychology proving too unstable or too dangerous for further test progress.

Standing high, Fen was able to bring his face close to the triangular glass panel in the red door and peer into the room. Beyond, there were further sealed chambers. They were quiet for now, but he knew there would be eyes in the dark, watching him.

Towards the back, larger cages stood, and within the first ranks, several sets of luminous green eyes hung in the darkness, staring for an instant or two, and then pacing away, only to return and glare again. They were like the slinking yellow-eyed ones, the cunning ones, but these were much larger and more ferocious.

He sighed, misting the glass. When the time came he would need to think about whether he would release these creatures. He was torn. He saw no good coming from their freedom, but he knew that in every creature there was a pure soul, and one day he might be able to unite them all under the creator's great tree of life. He made eye contact with one of the creatures, holding the gaze for several seconds before it spun away. Perhaps he just needed to work harder on these ones to reach them.

Fen lifted his head and peered down to the very rear of the darkened chamber. The largest cages of all were lined there; row upon row, all in shadow. Perhaps to keep the occupants comfortable or docile, or simply to hide the giant forms from the attending humans. Inside, the shape of the creatures loomed enormously. They already stood on hind legs, and as he watched, one stepped forward, its gaze on him. Three-inch long claws gently reached forward to grasp the cage bars. They tested their strength, the rods of iron bending outwards, but not enough to break. The stare returned. Fen felt a kinship in the gaze. Perhaps a balance could be struck with all the races after all.

Fen walked back along the corridor, stopping at one of the Guardian's cages. The name on the door read 'Erin'. He put his hand on the bars, looking in at her. She stood and came closer, her fingers wrapping around his. He nodded, and she squeezed his hand – he would lead, they would follow.

Back at his room, he pulled the door shut. He lifted his head again and sniffed – like a monstrous black storm that holds its breath for a second or two before unleashing a bone-jarring clap of thunder, he knew the 'time' of change was coming. He would be ready… they would be ready.

Chuck Benson, the Fermilab animal facility guard called over his shoulder without taking his eyes of the screen. 'Hey Porter, get a load of this will ya. Check out big Fen, he's doing his thing again.'

Benson leaned back and turned the flat panel screen so his colleague could watch as the big animal sauntered down the corridor, stopping at each room to stare inside for a few moments before moving on to the next.

Porter blew air through his lips. 'Even if I see it a thousand times, it'll still freak me out when they stand up like that. They look way too human.'

'There's a reason for that. I heard the docs talking; they used a mix of human and canine DNA when they made them.' Benson moved the camera down to the end of the corridor. 'Ah, I can't help liking them. Besides, it doesn't freak me out as much as those other weird things they keep locked up in Red Room 12. You seen the way those freaks look at ya? Don't tell me they're not thinking about a hundred different ways they'd like to rip you to shreds. Just be grateful there's only a few dozen of them. Imagine if there were an army – now that would be a world I wouldn't want to live in.'

Porter turned back to his own work. 'Don't sweat it. I hear the Doc is about to issue a termination order on our Red Room guests.'

'Good.' Benson pushed his chair back. 'C'mon, let's go down and change the codes again. Not sure what good it will do, as it only takes Fen about an hour to work out the new ones.' He turned and shrugged.

'At least it keeps him occupied.'

CHAPTER 20

I COME TO YOU IN PEACE

Becky Matthews had never felt so sick and scared in her life. She and Edward had been tied together with loops of course rope around their necks and their wrists bound behind their backs. Already, she could feel the rubbing rawness at her collar, and her shoulders ached worse than the time she had slipped in gym class.

They had been forced to stand together while her captors made camp, a pair of exhibits at a gruesome funfair while the monsters, large and small, prodded and poked at them. It was worse now that night had fallen; in the dark their eyes shone like devils – some yellow, red, some green, and always unblinking.

She burbled her tears as she tried to talk to them. 'My father is rich. He'll give you anything you want if you send me back to him.'

One of the small hooded creatures came over to lift one end of the trailing rope in front of her. It looked up, its mouth hanging open in what could have been a grin – or nothing more than the way the black slit under its almost non-existent nose normally looked. It yanked on the rope, making her yelp, and seemed to relish the pain it inflicted.

Behind her she heard Edward gag at the sudden tug. She half turned, but quickly snapped her head back, not wanting to look up at the lumbering things that stood just behind them. The biggest stood around nine feet tall, orange and black, like something from a horror movie. The huge mouths of the brutes seemed to be continually hanging open, as their huge chests pulled in great lungfuls of air through teeth as long as her fingers. To Becky, they looked angry, fearsome, and were dressed in armor that was inches thick and ground and clanked as they moved.

She sobbed again, and tried to wipe her face, as her nose was streaming down onto her chin. It was impossible the way her hands were bound, and she could do little more than smear her face on her shoulder. She turned to one of the horrible little goblins beside her and burbled weakly again.

'What do you want from us?'

It stared and grinned for a moment, before simply ignoring her and walking on, in its weird gliding movement.

'Give it up Becky, they don't understand us. Something tells me, it's not a handful of daddy's greenbacks that'll set us free, that's for sure.'

She ground her teeth and yelled over her shoulder. 'Shut up Edward; why don't you try and help, instead of making fun of me?'

The small creature in front of her yanked again, making a wheezing sound in his throat, and grinning at the angry interaction between her and Edward. Becky smiled down at it, as you would to a child. 'Hi there little one, I'm your friend. I want to help.'

She held her smile, even though she loathed them with every fibre of her being. The ugly thing continued to stare, always staring and staring with those horrible little piss-yellow eyes.

'I came from Earth, and I come to you in peace.'

Behind her Edward cleared his throat. 'They also come from Earth, and...'

This time when the yank came Becky was pulled off her feet, making her shirt ride up off her waist and exposing the handgun. The Panterran's hand whipped out like a striking snake and pulled it free. He sniffed at it, waved it around and felt its weight in his small hand. The gun looked oversized and lethal in the tiny taloned fingers. With the safety engaged, even a few presses on the trigger had no effect – which was unfortunate as a few trigger pulls came while a deep examination of the barrel with one eye was taking place.

The goblin thing spoke to one of the giant lumbering brutes behind them, who stepped forward and cut Becky's bonds from behind her back, freeing her arms only. He then handed her the gun, and made motions to her and the weapon – the implication was clear, how does it work?

Becky took the gun, and held it out in front of herself. She had it pointed directly at the small creature's face.

'Don't do it.' Edward whispered from behind her.

Her thumb flicked off the safety and she continued to point it. 'Untie my neck, you little piece of shit.'

'Don't... do... it. They can't understand you.' Edwards voice was rising behind her.

'Untie me now, or so help me god, I'll put a bullet in your flat ugly face.'

'Becky, please, whatta you going to do, shoot them all? And then we're going to try and run out of here tied together like the human caterpillar? Think for a minute, goddammit.'

'Shut up Edward.' She continued to point the gun, the strain on her arms making it shake in her hands. Behind her, Edward was talking softly and slowly again.

'Just... calm... down, Rebecca. Remember, Arn survived here, so we can too. Just take it easy, eeeeaaasy.'

She gritted her teeth, her face sweating as indecision washed over her. She might never get another chance, and she had no idea where they were headed, or what was in store.

She screamed her anguish and moved the gun slightly to the side, firing off a round into a tree. The small creature in front of her hissed and dived to the ground, and immediately confusion exploded all around them.

The huge Lygons roared and lunged, pinning both her and

Edward to the ground. The gun was pulled from her hand, and when she opened her eyes, she saw that the goblin was once again holding the gun in his hands.

He had the weapon pointed at her, his fingers properly placed and safety still off. He grinned and moved the muzzle around, pointing it at another of his kind. He pulled the trigger, and the bullet blew the small target off its feet, and ten feet back across the small clearing. The shooter's mouth dropped open, and after a few moments he spoke quickly to the huge beast that had one enormous foot pressed into her back. Immediately multiple hands commenced a rough search of her and Edward, the examination ripping their clothing to shreds and leaving them naked in the dirt.

Flashlights, Edward's gun, empty water bottles, and anything else they had managed to bring was piled at the small goblin-like creature's feet.

'And now they have guns. Great.' Edward lowered his head.

'Shut up Edward.' Becky sobbed again, but at least with her hands free she could wipe her nose.

CHAPTER 21

A MAN-KIND FOR A BROTHER?

Arn and Grimson spent the night sheltered in amongst a small outcrop of broken boulders, and the pair was already following the riverbank in the pre-dawn glow. The ever-present fish kept pace with them. Arn took it as a good sign that there were no larger predators lurking in the depths.

'I feel like the Pied Piper.' The orange-silver fish glided beside them, one lidless eye always fixed on Arn and Grimson, as though willing one of them to renter the water.

'Who?' Grimson threw stones out into the centre of the pond. Sometimes the fish would race away to investigate, but would soon reappear to tag along.

'He was a piper who saved Hamlin from a plague of mice.'

'Mice?' Grimson sped up to walk beside Arn.

'Tiny creatures that live in holes in the wall.'

'And this Hamlin needed saving from them?' Grimson frowned up at him.

'Yep, because there were lots and lots of them.'

Grimson nodded. 'I bet the piper ate them all.'

'Speaking of which.' Arn slowed. The fish slowed with him. The school glided just below the surface of the clear water. Arn lifted a branch he had sharpened into a spear and launched it at a rather large one – a direct hit.

He had to dance down quickly, reaching out to lift the spear without entering the water, and also gathering it up before other fish picked it clean. He had eaten the muddy tasting flesh with relish many times now, and even managed to get Grimson to swallow a few slices, even though the cold, fishy meat was not to his taste.

143

The young Wolfen marched beside him, and for a while had been watching Arn's face.

Arn smiled down at him. 'Penny for them.'

Grimson frowned, and Arn translated.

'What's on your mind, Grim?'

Grimson tilted his head, and tried an imperious look. 'You know Arn, if I had a big brother, he'd be just like you.' He raised his chin a little higher. 'And that would make you a prince as well.'

'A Man-Kind for a brother?'

The youth laughed. 'No, I mean he'd be smart and strong, and ah, my friend.' He grinned. 'Like you.'

Arn bowed his thanks, and once again as he stared at him in the morning light, he thought the Wolfen's features seemed a little less wolf-like, and a little more... normal to him. *Perhaps I'm adjusting to the way they look*, he thought.

'Well then, Grimson, consider me your honorary brother, and friend for life.' Arn held out his fist. Grimson looked at it, and went to grab it.

Arn shook his head. 'No, no, you make a fist too.'

Grimson did as he was requested.

'Now punch my fist.' Grimson raised his eyebrows and followed the instruction.

'Good. It means we agree, and will work together, fight together, and always be there for each other forever. Because we are... friends.'

'Do it again.' Grimson's face had broken open in a wide smile.

Arn lifted his fist once again, and Grimson punched it with gusto. 'Brothers!'

* * *

Arn and Grimson leapt from stone to stone. The going was a lot easier on the river's edge even if it meant they were more exposed than when they were worming their way through the dense jungle. The bank of the river mainly consisted of sun-warmed, rounded rocks, worn smooth by moving water that was once deeper or faster than it was now – either it had been wetter in the past, or the area was subject to flooding – Arn would need to watch the skies.

Some of the boulders were enormous, rubbed so smooth they looked polished, and had the most magnificent colored striping. Grimson would often scale some of the biggest for the view, or simply for the challenge. At the top of one of the largest, he stood with his hands on his hips, looking further up the stream. He got on his toes, trying to see over the tops of some far trees, and then leapt into the air to gain an extra foot of height. When he landed, he frowned and looked down at his feet.

'Strange.'

Arn stopped a few feet ahead and turned. 'What is?'

'This big rock.' He took out his small blade and turned it around to pound on the surface with the pommel. 'Sounds hollow.' He brought he knife down again, harder.

The rock moved. Grimson got to his face, his brow creased. The rock moved again, this time rising a few feet.

'Whoa.' Grimson had his hands out to his sides, surfer like. The massive boulder rose up beneath him, and a grey trunk like neck began to extend, glistening in the sunlight. When its head reached a length of about nine feet, and as thick around as Arn's thigh, two smaller stalks extended from its very tip. Bulbs appeared on the end of each stalk and they popped open, swinging around individually to blink slowly at the small Wolfen on its back.

Grimson fell back on his rump as the thing rose out of its resting hole, and slid towards the river. Arn ran towards him, holding out his hands.

'Grim, jump.'

Grimson was now lifted on the back of the giant snail to about twelve feet in the air as the monstrous thing slid soundlessly to the water's edge. The ever-present fish swarmed around it momentarily, but then parted, leaving the great gastropod alone – either the sticky looking flesh was unpalatable to their taste, or its hide was a lot tougher than their razor teeth could penetrate.

The snail didn't slow, and proceeded slide out into the clear water. Arn guessed it was either amphibious or aquatic, and was about to use the water to dislodge the annoying thing that had taken up residence on its back.

'Get off now, Grim, before it's too far out.'

Too late. Already, he was marooned a dozen feet from the riverbank, with the moving island continuing out to deeper water. Arn knew that Grimson's flesh would be far more enjoyable than the giant snail's, and even though Wolfen were extremely athletic, the leap now was beyond him.

The snail started to sink and Grimson backed up, ready to leap.

Arn knew he'd never make it. 'Wait; when I say…'

Arn sprinted down the stony bank several dozen feet and entered the water to his knees. He began splashing in the shallows, and almost immediately the water rippled with the carnivorous fish jostling each other to greet him.

Arn cupped his mouth. 'Now!'

Grimson leapt, landing six feet from the bank, and in water to his waist. Half the fish swirling around Arn turned toward the Wolfen, but Grimson was already tearing out of the shallows by the time they arrived. Arn spun with bumps, grazes, and bites accompanying him back to the riverbank. As he stepped up on the sand, blood once again streaming down his legs, he turned back to see a flash of orange and silver create a hump in the water close in. This fish, like a giant groper, was easily eight feet long.

'Ouch, and ouch.' Arn flopped down on the warm stones and exhaled long and loud. The *feninlang* would soon stop his bleeding, but it could have done nothing for a missing leg. Grimson plonked down beside him, and put a hand on his shoulder. Together they watched the huge snail disappear beneath the water's surface.

'That was close. Thank you, Arnoddr.'

'Don't mention it.' Arn closed his eyes. 'I hate snails.'

'You have those in your world – horrible.'

Arn sat forward and looked at Grimson with a crooked smile. 'Sure do, but they're smaller... and people eat them.'

'Blech. By Odin's beard – eat them?' Grimson stuck out his tongue. 'I think I hate snails too.'

Arn finished wiping some of the *feninlang* salve on his legs. 'Let's go, and no jumping on big rocks, or going in the water, or touching anything without asking me first. Got it?'

Grimson held out his fist. Arn punched it.

They made good time until they came across the large carcass of a recently slaughtered animal. Grimson looked at it and sniffed, the hair on the back of his head and shoulders rising.

'Not good. Fresh kill... and not finished.'

Arn stared hard into the dark jungle, his small knife in his hand. 'Know what it was?'

Grim shook his head, but backed up. 'Smells like reptilon.'

Arn grunted. Reptilons were tiny skink like lizards that darted around the Valkeryn kingdom. The animal that had been attacked was easily five hundred pounds, so the attacker was something Arn didn't want to face with just a tiny knife. It was obviously using the riverbank as its hunting ground.

Being caught between some large carnivorous reptile and a river full of flesh-eating fish was not a bottle-neck Arn wanted to find himself in anytime soon.

'Let's get out of here. We need to find a way across this river, and quick.'

147

They trotted now, Arn trying to watch the river, the jungle, what they were about to step on, and keep a lookout for a place to cross the river so he could continue his search for the strange people he had first encountered at the waterfall rim. He needed somewhere shallow, or even better, dry. He looked up – maybe thick branches reaching across and touching the opposite bank would do.

They had been following the river upstream for an hour now as it steadily rose to a mountain in the distance. Arn stopped to wipe his brow, and looked back at Grimson who trailed a few paces behind him. Standing on the broad bank, his hands on his hips as he sucked in air, his view was temporarily free of the canopy cover, and he could see across the treetops, all the way back to where they had first entered the jungles of the Dark Lands.

He grunted softly, surprised to see they had travelled so many miles from the cliffs. Even while he watched, the mist was rising as the final rays of the sun cut through. The mighty cliffs now appeared like a sheer white wall in the distance. The trees below it looked like one single living organism – impenetrable and crowded together, the wisps of mist or steam rising in some areas to lay like a gossamer sheet over some of the great green heads. It looked ancient, prehistoric.

'And this is supposed to be the future?' Arn raised a hand to his brow to shield his eyes from the sun, the huge yellow orb making the shadows on the gigantic rock face shrink in the golden light.

His mouth fell open in wonderment. 'You have got to be kidding me.' Arn stepped further out onto the bank, to get a better view.

'Grim, look.' He stared back at the cliffs – they would have been indistinct up close, but now he could see massive reliefs carved into the stone.

A giant figure was hewn into the cliff face. Not quite of

Mount Rushmore quality, but not surprising considering it looked ancient and time-worn. It was depicted as wearing robes, and stood with arms by its sides, its body hundreds of feet high. The giant carving wasn't perfect – how could it be, after countless seasons of weather and natural erosion? It was missing a face, so Arn couldn't tell whether the figure was meant to be human or one of the other biped races now existing on the planet. However, something about it was recognizable, familiar.

Just below the mighty image there were carved words; his own language, and relatively clear. The distance forgave the deep cracks, fissures and rock falls that time had added.

Arn mouthed the words.

'Hmm, something… STILL… LIVES. Okay, could be, HE STILL LIVES.'

'Maybe that's it. One of the legends about the disappearance of the human race was that we ascended to the stars. Perhaps before we did that, we left a message for the new peoples of the planet, telling them that one day we would return, that in fact we *still live* somewhere in the stars.' He nodded, congratulating himself on his analysis of the giant message.

Grimson didn't look convinced. 'I think it is a carving of Fenrir, the father of us all. I think it is he that will return. He still lives and will return at the head of a mighty army and drive the Panterran and Lygon from our land.' He smiled up at Arn.

'Fenrir? Could be.' *We all see what we want to see*, Arn thought. He raised his eyebrows at the youth, and then looked back to the carvings, knowing that without a head, it could have been anything. Maybe even a member of the people he was now looking for. More reason to find them… and talk to them.

He thought the obliteration of the face was unfortunate – something about it looked strange. Though other areas of the body and words were heavily degraded, the face itself was wiped clean – more like deliberate erasing, rather than the effects of wind and water.

He patted Grim on the shoulder. 'C'mon, let's go.' He turned and strode up the river's edge again, Grimson hopping along beside him on one side, and the ever-present school of hungry fish on the other.

CHAPTER 22

LET'S GO SKIN SOME CATS

Briggs walked about fifty feet out from the group, and squatted down, placing one finger on her earpiece. She listened to a decoded information packet sent from base. The relay of communication spikes planted along their journey bounced their signal all the way back to the mouth of the distortion gate. The signal bouncer was fed more juice than an office block, but even so she had to concentrate as the words tended to drop out or become mushy as they passed through the vortex.

The update hadn't been as good as she hoped, but it was expected – the distortion was spreading like some sort of giant gravitational infection. Time was now a commodity in short supply.

She checked her watch: twenty hundred hours – and her team had eaten, and had an hours rest. She'd march them for another four hours, rest for two, and then push on. It'd be punishing, but they could take it, and besides, they could sleep for a week when they returned.

At their temporary camps, they were deploying motion trackers and infrared at their perimeter, plus a few walking sentries for line-of sight security. Nothing would be paying them a surprise visit. Still, she was uneasy. She knew the creatures had the home ground advantage. Added to that, they were night hunters. Everything they had seen so far looked to have an ability to function at optimal level in both the dark and light.

I admit it, I'm spooked, she thought.

She got to her feet. *Another four hours, and then two hours kip.* She smiled without humor as she felt the stabbing pain in her muscles. *And that's why they pay me the big bucks,* she thought, and then yelled to Samson to bring them to order.

※ ※※※※ ※ ※

'It's a castle.' Becky sounded almost joyous in her exclamation.

Edward was also thankful, though perhaps not for the same reasons as his friend. He wanted to be cut free from Becky simply because they were now both naked, his small white body looking like some pale, soft grub next to Becky's long, tanned and athletic physique. He tried not to look at her behind. He knew if he did, it would do something to his physiology, that if caught he knew he could never live down.

A while back, his need to urinate had grown to a point of painful cramping in his lower abdomen. He had leaned as far back from Becky as their joint leash would allow, and tried to walk sideways, in the hope of not splashing her as the yellow stream shot from him like a yellow cable. He knew he needed to be cut free, and soon. This was shameful enough – what would happen when the need to move his bowels came upon him? Already his nerves were making his stomach feel liquid and gassy.

In the shadow of the castle, a fetid smell of corruption began to permeate the atmosphere. The earth of the fields in front of the walls were torn and deeply furrowed, and flies blighted the air. What at first looked like rubbish heaps, were in fact mounds of broken bone, shattered armor, and flaps of ripped skin with the blood-matted fur still attached. Flies swarmed everywhere in a frenzy of feasting.

Edward tried to breathe though his mouth to avoid the smell, but had to clamp that closed for fear of sucking in the furious insects that boiled around them. He settled for short inhalations through gritted teeth. Looking up, he saw that the castle flew black banners marked with the image of a cat with yellow eyes and a merciless gaze. Around the turrets he noticed a mix of the huge orange and black beasts and the smaller hooded goblin-like creatures. Now that he saw the banner, he did think they resembled cats –cats from some demented nightmare. Perhaps these things had once been cats, or were descended from some creature like them. Now, their physical appearance was warped from the once feline beauty by a thousand, thousand generations of pure hate.

He was tugged forward again. The creatures on the wall stopped their sentry duty to stare down. Some of the larger beasts roared, the sound travelling in waves deep into Edward's bones. He was glad the smaller goblins were able to keep the giants under control, as he knew that without them, they would be torn to shreds and devoured in seconds.

He felt his stomach roil. Whatever was in store for them was inside the castle. He wondered whether Arn had travelled this way, or whether he too was already a captive inside. The dark thought strangely lifted him.

Edward was jerked forward, forcing him to collide with Becky's soft behind. He looked down momentarily, and for a few seconds, could almost forget where he was. He now knew what Arn had seen in her – from every angle she was beautiful.

Edward looked back up, and saw she had turned and knew where he was looking. An expression of disgust twisted her features.

He shook his head. 'I wasn't.'

Becky's lip curled even more. 'Don't even think about it, creep.'

He groaned, his eyes downcast. *After all that's happened, I'm the creep?* He sighed. *Might as well be back home,* he thought miserably.

Edward and Becky were forced to their knees before the throne. Edward tried to hold his breath so as not to endure the stench coming from the decrepit creature seated before him. He thought the killing fields of the castle forecourts were bad, until he was thrust into the presence of a thing that was like some sort of feline maggot – almost completely hairless, long bodied and with a few open sores on its white grub-like flesh. Attendants continually groomed the creature, stroking it, patting it, and kneading its skin.

It spoke to them in a long reptilian hiss, and he and Becky looked at each other, neither understanding the language.

'Um, I'm American – A-mer-i-can.' Becky offered helpfully, and tried to smile.

Edward knelt up as straight as he could, and pointed at himself, and Becky, and then raised one hand, opening the palm, he hoped in a universal sign of friendship.

He cleared his throat and touched his chest. 'I am Edward Lin.' He then pointed to Becky. 'This is Rebecca Matthews.' He waited for a few seconds, but the feline creature just stared with that half-lidded yellow gaze. He went on. 'We have come to you as friends. We mean you no harm.' He paused again, but all that was returned was the unblinking gaze.

Edward licked his lips, becoming unsettled. 'We are searching for one who is like us. One who goes by the name of Arnold Singer.'

The creature raised a hand, and the attendants stopped their continual preening. She spoke a few words, and immediately both Becky and Edward's hands were grabbed behind their backs and they were pushed forward, still on their knees. The creature was helped to a sitting position, and as they neared, it raised hands that ended in long black talons. It reached out to them, to gently touch at their faces.

Becky tried to turn away. 'Please don't.' Her voice became urgent and shrill. 'I can help you. I can show you how to get back to Earth. There are soldiers coming. I can help you.'

Wow, a true patriot, thought Edward, as the gentle touch of the talons became firmer and then started to pierce the flesh of their temples.

As the claws sunk in, Edward felt a sudden explosion in his brain. It was like, he imagined, being seated in the electric chair when they first pulled the big red switch, and the currents coursed through your flesh to boil your blood, and fry your brain.

He still heard the hissing language of the grub-like cat creature, but then something else began to happen – the hissing whine became words.

Edward gritted his teeth, and felt his nose start to run, the liquid warm on his lip. His brain felt like it was being pulled apart as if a small animal had been let loose to madly race in the attic of his mind, kicking things over, ripping open doors and drawers, in a frantic search for information. He felt he had become an open book, the pages being flipped rapidly, with some torn free and stuffed into pockets. Images flashed up, bounced around, and were immediately ripped away. His most precious thoughts were treated like a bargain at super-sale time; snatched by a crazed shopper, judged, and then kept or flung aside.

His nose streamed now, and he worried about Becky as fragments of his life flashed before him, like a movie in fast play mode – his childhood, Naperville High, the Fermilab facility, images of Arn as a boy, and then a young man. Doctor Albert Harper, his face when the accident occurred, the guards, and then the army colonel, Briggs, who was preparing to come through after them with her team of soldiers. This image was frozen, and replayed several times over.

The talons were withdrawn and the link broken. But the understanding of the words remained, and so did the identity of the being before them, Mogahrr, queen of the Panterran race. A decayed grin stretched her flat face.

Edward felt a pounding in his head, and wiping his chin, saw it was wet with blood from his nose. Looking across at Becky, he saw that she was the same, slumped forward, sobbing.

Mogahrr reached out a hand and wiped one talon under Edward's nose, coating the sharp spike with his blood, and then bringing it back to her lips to taste. She turned to one of the small hooded creatures beside her.

'Nowww, bring meee thissss feeemale called Briggsssss.'

⚬ ⚬⚬⚬ ⚬⚬⚬ ⚬⚬⚬ ⚬

Colonel Marion Briggs couldn't sleep, couldn't turn off. Her body was as tired as it had ever been, but she was still so juiced she knew restful sleep would be beyond her... at least until she had achieved her objectives and she was headed home.

She groaned. Besides the over-fatigued state of her mind and body, there was something that kept nagging it at her, making her feel that she had forgotten something critical. She sat up and rubbed her face. The electronic shields had been deployed and a couple of sentries patrolled the camp perimeter. She looked around – her team slept soundly. She checked her watch... only an hour until they were due to get moving again. She swore; might as well give up and walk the line – sleep fairy ain't paying you a visit tonight Briggsie.

She stretched, hoping the solitude would help her remember what it was that bugged her. Getting silently to her feet, she stepped through the sleeping bodies, and walked a little further out from under the broad branches of the tree they had taken shelter under. A soft tremor of the low hanging limb made her turn her head and then smile – one of the last of the football-sized egg casings was inching along the broad branch, making its way towards her.

Nothing's what it seems in this damn world, she thought as she waited for a few moments for it to be directly overhead. The long sinewy worm dropped down, fangs extended as it lowered itself towards her face. In a flash of movement, she pulled her longest K-bar from its sheath and slashed across the bulb, cutting it in two.

The grub fell to the ground, with a small squeal, and she stamped on it with her boot. *Thought we cleaned all you ugly mothers up.* She wiped her heel on the grass.

Briggs walked out onto the hilltop and stood looking out at the horizon. The landscape reminded her of a cross between Sequoia National Park, and a giant Banyan tree forest. *Who knows*, she thought, *maybe the trees are some sort of weird hybrid.* She looked at the mountainous horizon. It certainly did not look like the flat landscape of Illinois that she had stepped out of days before. A lot of geological push and shove had gone on in the eons she supposed had passed between then and now.

One of the sentries moved up beside her and nodded. She returned the gesture, and he continued his sweep. Briggs walked another few paces and stood staring into the distance. She lifted her field glasses, and switched between the different optical enhancements – first infrared – nothing but a few small nocturnal animals moving about in the darkness. Then she switched to telescopic, zooming in and out on anything that might have been of interest. Nothing to notice, and that was a good thing.

She should have felt at ease, but something was still gnawing away in her gut. She continued to walk slowly. Why was she worried? They carried all the aces – they had the firepower, the intel, and the element of surprise. The local indigenous were big, slow, and would probably mount a few frontal attacks, relying on their brute strength. She'd blow them all to hell. In another day or so, she'd own this place.

She thought of the huge beasts and her mouth turned down. She couldn't understand them, therefore they had absolutely no tactical value. Maybe she'd take a small one back for the lab boys to cut up.

The next sentry approached silently in the dark, and had just lifted his hand in a small salute, when the dart took him in the neck. Briggs' eyes widened, and her training took over – she crouched and spun, her hand going to her pistol just as she felt a pinprick at her own throat.

Immediately the gun holster seemed at the bottom of deep pit and miles out of reach. Her arm started to weigh more than a Mack truck, and gravity crushed down on her shoulders. There was a thump, and she found herself sitting on the ground. Her muscles refused to obey her commands, as small figures materialized around her. Her hands and feet were expertly bound, and something was pulled over her head.

In modern warfare, real time information was the real weapon, and they should have had it all. Unless of course, the two young people who had gone through before them had somehow tilted the equation. What if the indigenous managed to interrogate them? Could they even understand them? Unlikely, but... now she realised what had been bugging her.

Never underestimate your enemy. She felt herself being lifted. *Off to meet the Red Queen, Alice,* she thought, as she felt herself being borne away in the dark.

◦ ⊢◁◦◗◖ ⋈◦◦⋈ ◗◖◦◁⊣ ◦

Samson lifted the Delta sentry by the throat. The man's toes were now the only things touching the ground. Samson's nose was pressed to the man's face and spittle flew from his mouth as he yelled.

'Jackson and the Colonel taken while on your watch. You want to explain to me how that happened, Diekes? Or should I execute you for sleeping on the job, right here, right now?'

Diekes reached up and grabbed Samson's wrist and twisted,

hard. The bigger man held on, oblivious to the pressure exerted on his arm. Samson brought his face even closer, his forehead now crushing into the other man's. He squeezed, gritting his teeth. Diekes tried to talk through his crushed windpipe, but couldn't get the words out.

'Let him go.' Teacher's voice was low and level.

Samson ignored him, his fingers digging deep into Diekes' flesh.

Teacher stepped in closer. 'Let him go. We're gonna need every gun we got.'

Samson continued to stare at the elite soldier in his grip, now rapidly losing consciousness.

Teacher watched the bigger man from under lowered brows. With Briggs gone, Samson assumed command, and that made Teacher 2IC. For big Jim Teacher, being a highly trained Spec Ops soldier meant fearing nothing. He was fiercely loyal to the chain of command. However, in his book, killing your own people cancelled that loyalty.

He felt what Samson felt. He knew damned well it wasn't Diekes's fault. But they all wanted someone to blame. Bottom line, Briggs stuffed up. She had set the security parameters, she had underestimated the enemy... and now, she paid. Every man and women they had brought with them was one of the best all-round warfare professionals that existed on the planet, in this time or any other. But somehow the enemy had found a way to get in under their guard.

Samson growled for a moment, and then pushed the man away, letting him fall to the ground. Samson turned away, and Diekes was up quickly, blood fury in his eyes.

Teacher held up his hand in front of him and shook his head. *Cool it*, the action said.

Another of the soldiers came jogging in to join them and Samson stood with his hands on his hips watching his approach.

'About time. Report in, soldier.'

The soldier, Theo Themopolis, tagged "Two-Ts" by his comrades, stepped up as the other Delta Force members formed a ring around them. He held a large wet piece of cloth in his hands.

'There are dozens of these out past the perimeter. They wet them and then probably crept in, slow and low to the ground. Came right in under our infrared; the cold blanket masked their heat signature.'

'Jesus Christ; how the hell would they know to do that?' Samson grabbed the material. It was a rough wool-type material, interwoven with leaves and twigs – camouflage. He held it out – it was little more than four feet square. 'This is bullshit. This thing would not cover one of those big dumb mothers we encountered at the forest rim.'

Teacher took it from him. He sniffed it – he got hits of dirt and ammonia. 'Must be something we haven't encountered yet. Something a lot smarter.'

Samson took the blanket back. 'They worked out how to beat infrared... in a day? They don't have it, and from what we saw of the attack on the GBs, their equipment was totally obliterated. Nothing operational should have remained.'

Samson sniffed the material and wrinkled his nose. 'Stinks.' He handed it to the woman soldier closest to him. 'Hand it around, remember it, everything is tactically crucial now.'

Teacher walked away, looking up at the tree canopy, and then slowly scanning the darkening forest. He stopped and turned back to them.

'Interrogation.'

One of the Delta Force women, Alison Sharp, looked up as she handed the blanket to the man next to her. 'Makes sense. They probably broke down the two kids that came through before us.'

Samson looked back at her and grunted his agreement.

'Has to be. Damn, damn, damn….' His jaws clenched and the big man swore loud enough to startle something small, which sprinted out of the bushes, heading for the darkness. Faster than the eye could follow, he drew his sidearm, and fired once. The animal exploded.

Samson paced away, holding the gun with his other hand balled into a fist. He squared his shoulders, and walked back to the team.

'Listen up, children. Nap-time is over. The element of surprise has just been eliminated. Our mission protocol is unchanged, countdown is unchanged, rules of engagement are unchanged. We need to locate and retrieve the acceleration diamond, and Mr. Arnold Singer if possible – he is of secondary importance.'

Samson looked hard at each of them. 'There is one change to our job sheet. We now have another priority objective. We need to get the boss back – rescue or revenge, and then we can save the world.'

'HUA!' As one.

Samson nodded. He turned slowly in a circle looking at each of them again, assessing them.

Teacher agreed the strategy, even though the rulebook said extending the mission objectives in the field put the primary objective at risk. This was different. Samson nodded to him.

'Teach, anything to add.'

Jim Teacher looked at each of the fearsome looking men and women. 'Time is against us. We do not, I repeat, do not want them getting inside Colonel Briggs' head. It may compromise our primary objective, the way back home, and our world.' He put his hands on his hips. 'Rescue or revenge.'

'Rescue or revenge.' Again as one.

Samson grinned. 'Suit up, and let's go skin some cats.'

Briggs could smell the creatures even before the bag was pulled from her head. She had been steeling herself for hours after the stupor had left her, knowing that what carried her was not human. Given the size of the hands or claws she could feel, they were smaller than the larger creatures they had already obliterated at the forest's edge.

Her anger had been building the further she was carried. She'd let this happen; walked right damn into it. She hoped that the entire squad wasn't overrun, and were now being carried like sacks of trash beside her. If they still lived and were free, then rescue was still a possibility.

The particles of light coming in through the weave of the sack dimmed, and the sound became more muted – they were inside a structure. She counted steps, noted left or right, and listened for echoes indicating close walls or a larger room. If she broke free she needed to remember her way out.

They halted. Briggs waited, trying to slow her breathing and her heart beat. A blow to her back pushed her to her knees, and the sack was pulled from her head. She ground her teeth and sucked in a breath before looking up, but still could not help her eyes widening in shock at what she saw.

There was a single wooden chair, a throne, surrounded by ranks of animals barely four feet high, most with cowls over heads that showed flat faces full of teeth and unblinking yellow eyes. But the small biped's appearance was nothing compared to the thing that reclined on the chair. It was a disgusting fleshy bag of a creature that was as putrid to look at as the odors emanating from its slug-like body were to the nose.

The old creature's hand went to stroke a magnificent red stone hanging between a pair of sagging, leathery breasts.

Briggs almost moaned. She had the photonic acceleration diamond; ergo the Singer kid was probably dead. Her eyes darted around the room, taking in the numbers of the animals, windows and doors, and weaponry. Just behind her, two dozen of the giant black and orange creatures stood, their heads grazing the ceiling. Up close they were as formidable as she remembered. They gently rocked from side to side, as if needing to stay in motion while they tried to contain an inner fury that threatened to be unleashed at any moment.

Beside her, still kneeling and bagged, was one of her men. She guessed it was Jackson, judging by his size.

She turned her head. More of the giants crowded in behind her. Their luminous green eyes were fixed on her, hunger distorting their monstrous features. She looked them over – their bodies were impossibly muscled, and she doubted that without weaponry she would stand a ghost's chance in hell against even one. She turned back to the front, and her examination immediately ceased as the two missing youths stepped out from just behind what had to be a throne – both naked with ropes around their necks.

'Edward and Rebecca?'

The young man nodded. The old creature hissed and whined, and he turned to her, listened for a moment and then nodded.

'Colonel, you need to stand and approach the throne of Queen Mogahrr.'

Briggs stood, more because she wanted to be on her feet, rather in obedience to the thing's commands.

Edward spoke again. 'Approach.'

Briggs turned to him. 'You can understand them?'

He nodded. 'And you will soon. It hurts, but only for a minute.'

Briggs stayed put. 'You told them about our infrared armaments.'

He shook his head. 'No, they got that all by themselves. You'll soon see. Come closer.'

'Like hell I will.' A thud in the back and Briggs was propelled forward into the waiting grasp of the queen, whose claws immediately penetrated the flesh of her temples. Briggs ground her teeth – physical pain was something she understood, and could control.

The talons dug in further and moved around, searching. It was a red-hot agony, but Briggs almost laughed in contempt. She could take it easily. The queen's hissing became words, but when the probing tried to intrude deep into her brain, Briggs built a mental wall made of iron, concrete, bulletproof ceramics. The hot lava flow of intrusion smashed up against it, but through sheer will Briggs' mental wall held.

'That's all you got, you old of bag of crap?' Tears ran down Briggs' cheeks and she ground her teeth. The pain in her temples increased as Mogahrr pressed harder. Briggs felt perspiration running down her face, and she ground her teeth so hard, she felt a chip of a molar break off. She swallowed it. The torrent of red-hot liquid pain poured into her mind and crashed against her barrier, faster, harder and deeper. Her mental wall bent and groaned from the attack, but still it held.

Mogahrr pulled her the long talons from Briggs' flesh and sat back.

'Ssstrong mind, ssstrong body – a feeemale of hiiigh order – warrior classss. And moreee of yoooou now in ouuur landsss.' She leant forward. 'Your knowledgeee isss now the property of the Panterran raccce. You wiiill give it freeeely, or you wiiill give it assss the undead.'

Briggs spat blood to the floor and laughed. 'You tickle my head, and then think I'm gonna help you and your ugly midgets?' She laughed again. 'But you got one thing right – there's more of us than you can count, and we'll cut through you like a knife through butter, you mangy old bag of crap.'

Mogahrr sat staring for several seconds, before she lifted a hand and pointed to Jackson. She spoke over his head to the giants.

'Weee do not neeeed thssis one, he isss yooours.'

The great creatures burst forward and grabbed the kneeling man. In a matter of seconds, his armored vest was ripped free, and a fountain of blood shot into the air. The creature's roars became deafening, and drowned out the screams of the soldier. Briggs only watched for a moment before turning away, the sound of ripping flesh in her ears. She had seen too many soldiers torn or blown apart to be traumatized, but still she didn't need to watch one of her team be devoured before her eyes.

She swallowed, feeling an acidic lump of nausea in her throat, and tried to keep her voice even when she spoke. 'We all die.'

'But nooot beforeee doing theee bidding of Queen Mogahrr.' Now it was the old creatures turn to laugh. She motioned again and a box was brought to her, which she rested on her lap.

'Ssstrong mindsss, just neeeed a little ennncouragement.' She held out one long hairless hand again, and a pair of long nosed forceps was placed into her palm. With her other hand she lifted the box lid, and then dipped the instrument into its dark cavity, lifting free what looked like a soft bean.

As soon as the thing was exposed to the light it wriggled, stretched and then drooped. It quickly looped back on itself, trying to get at the forceps. It was some sort of worm or slug, and Mogahrr brought it close to her bony wrist, allowing the thing to latch onto her flesh for a second, before she pulled it away. A dot of blackish blood welled up where it had touched her skin. The thing twisted and writhed, seeming agitated by the brief taste of blood.

'Nowww it knooows me.'

Mogahrr nodded and Briggs was held by one of the enormous beasts. Her shoulders were gripped by hands that covered her entire upper arms; the clench was unbreakable and crushing. Slowly she was pushed forward, her head dipped towards the old creature now holding the slug thing out toward her face.

Briggs turned her face to the youths. Rebecca had covered her eyes, and Edward simply mouthed *sorry*.

Not a great day at the office, Briggs thought, as she strained her neck, trying to duck and move away from the hands trying to hold her steady. Eventually her head was gripped and Mogahrr brought the forceps up beside her face, all the time the queen's virulent yellow eyes staring into hers. They were as inhuman and evil as anything the colonel had ever seen in her life.

The flat face broke into a smile, her dark gums pulling back to reveal snaggle teeth, blackened by decay. The breath that dribbled out nearly made the soldier gag – she would have, if not for her rising panic over the revolting thing being lifted towards her ear.

'And nowww it will know youuu.'

The worm's head extended like taffy as the grub reached out for her, eager to find its way into its new home. Briggs' eyes were round like a startled horse, and she struggled vainly against the powerful hands that held her. In her periphery she could see the Panterran surrounding the chair lean forward, eager and excited. Edward's face showed revulsion, and Rebecca kept her face buried in her hands.

The soft wetness touched her outer ear and stuck, then slid deeper. Briggs screamed, and then vomit exploded from her mouth as the physical sensation combined with the horror of the unknown. The elite soldier had been trained to resist physical and mental torture, but this was something that no human being could ever be prepared for.

'No, no, no.' She thrashed and tried to pull away. 'You motherfu… mark my words, there'll be a hell-storm that rains down on your heads, and we'll be the ones bringing it.' She bucked and jerked, but the grip on her body was unmovable.

Mogahrr brought her own face close to Briggs' again. 'Yessss, and you wiiill bring it… and then weee wiiill own it.

Everything in thssis land now beeelongsss to the Panterran, including yooou and all yooour people. Perhapsss even thossse in your ooown world… sssoon.' The old creature laughed as the wet thing extended itself fully into her ear. It tickled at first, and then Briggs felt a build-up of pressure against her eardrum, before tickle-pressure turned to white-hot pain and the worm pushed its way through the skin of the drum itself.

Pain, ice cold, and then, blackness. When the light came back, her mental wall of iron and concrete was no more, and in its place, a voice… the old thing's voice. It dominated, controlled, and owned her. When it asked a question, she answered. Briggs wanted to run or fight, or anything, but it was like her old self was caged, forced to watch, as her body and soul acted like a puppet on strings being pulled and played by someone else.

Underestimation is the seed of defeat – underestimation is the seed of defeat. The line from an old dead general kept repeating over and over in her head. She hoped Samson and Teacher would do better.

Becky had turned away to throw up onto the stone floor of the throne room, and Edward watched with his teeth ground together, as if he felt the horror and pain of the once formidable colonel as the pale worm thing disappeared into her ear.

After Briggs was released she had thrown herself to the ground, rolling and holding her head, writhing in pain. Blood had burst from her nose, but then, as if a switch had been thrown, she became calm.

Mogahrr wheezed her laugh and sat forward with a smile of accomplishment on her black lips.

Briggs sat up, and then on command stood. She looked half asleep or drugged, her eyes half lidded and dopey. Streams of fluid ran from her nose – perhaps some sort of cranial discharge. Edward had no idea what the thing was doing inside her head.

Mogahrr sat forward, clasping her hands together in anticipation. 'Teeell me of yooour world, and howww you came to beee heeere. ' Her yellow gaze burned as she stared into Briggs' now compliant eyes.

CHAPTER 23

PERHAPS THEY COME TO MAKE WAR ON ALL CREATURES

Vidarr turned and placed one old boney finger against Balthazaar's lips. Though they sat in complete darkness in one of the dozens of secret passages in the castle, he knew that the senses of the Panterran were not to be underestimated. Together he and the former king's counselor watched the proceedings through a slit in the mortar of the throne room.

They listened in dismay as the female Man-Kind warrior related the fantastic weapons her group possessed. Balthazaar knew that Mogahrr would waste no time in trying to secure them.

Vidarr whispered close to Balthazaar's ear. 'We must warn the Man-Kinds. They will be slaughtered if we do not.' Vidarr turned back to the slit in the thick wall.

'I fear these Man-Kind are not as the Arnoddr, and that they came to make war on all creatures of Valkeryn. Perhaps if there were Wolfen here, then Wolfen would be their game,' Balthazaar whispered.

Vidarr turned, his eyes shining in the darkness. 'But there are no Wolfen, my friend. The Man-Kind are all that stands between a world dominated by the Panterran, and perhaps a return of our people one day.' He turned back to the wall. 'Once the Panterran have the new weapons, there will be no stopping them... ever.'

Balthazaar nodded even though he knew the old archivist couldn't see him in the dark. 'And what of the friends of the Arnoddr?'

'We must try and rescue them... somehow. Leave that to me.'

Balthazaar reached out to place his hand on the old Wolfen's shoulder. 'A difficult task, old warrior scribe.'

Vidarr snorted. 'Not as difficult as yours, young counselor, for you must find the Man-kind warriors before the Panterran do. You must make them understand. You must make them our allies, before Mogahrr takes their heads as her trophies of war.' He turned and his eyes glinted silver in the dark. 'Take the language stones, and leave now. Time is already against us.'

Balthazaar eased the trapdoor upwards, the ancient hinges eliciting a scream of protest at being called to action after many decades of idleness. Light streamed into the underground tunnel which had taken him far out past the forest line.

He lifted his head slowly, to sniff the air. There was nothing on the breeze save the healthy smells of the deep forest. He raised his head further and looked around – as he hoped, he was a long way from the walls, and well out of the castle lands. He had expected to have many hours head start on the Panterran and Lygon. Now he must use them wisely.

Balthazaar quickly clambered onto a lichen-covered tumble of boulders and then eased the door shut behind him, branches closing over it like thick green drapes. The concealment was good – he hoped he could find it again on his return... if he returned.

When Vidarr had led him up and out of the deep archives, the old Wolfen had revealed the extent of the labyrinth of tunnels beneath the kingdom. They were hidden highways, the internal veins and arteries running right throughout the body of the castle and the lands beyond. *It was no wonder*, thought Balthazaar, *that no one had seen the old archivist for many decades.* The ancient Wolfen hadn't been a recluse; he had been with them, watching them, for generations.

Balthazaar leaped to the forest floor, and immediately started to run – it would be many hours before he came across the Man-Kind warriors. His assumption was that they had crossed the wastelands along the same course Arn had taken when he first arrived. He moved fast, but he knew he also needed to be careful; he expected the warriors from the Arnod-dr's time would treat anything and everything with distrust – him included.

Thinking of the Arnoddr brought back fond memories for him to contemplate as he ran. The stories he told of his time and his people made them sound a wonderful race – peaceful, wise and kind. He would do everything he could to head them off before the Lygon and Panterran confronted them – they'd be slaughtered, and no match for the brutal denizens of this world.

Balthazaar glanced skyward as he ran, noticing the sun was directly overhead – it was middle-day before he had even realised it. He crashed to a stop and held onto a tree limb, his breath heaving in and out.

I'm too old for this, he thought. He hadn't run so much for half a lifetime, and though his Wolfen body was made for long distance running, age was slowing him.

Getting old is a terrible thing.

He pushed off and continued. He expected the Lygon would only travel half as fast as he. They were usually slow, only capable of speed in short bursts. Balthazaar knew he'd need extra time to try and communicate with the Man-Kind. To help with this, Vidarr had given him the communication stones – one of the artifacts recovered from the forbidden zones. Something from the Ancients themselves or some other great race that might have visited them many years ago.

He felt them in his pocket as he ran. The half-dozen small shiny objects were designed to allow communication between any sentient creatures – at least that was the legend. No one had ever had reason to use them before, as the modern creatures of the world all spoke with the one voice.

Balthazaar slowed again, and then stopped, listening. He tried hard to close his mouth and ease his breathing – he needed all his senses now in case there was immediate danger. He concentrated. It wasn't any particular noise that alerted him, but the lack of sound. There was no chirruping of tiny things, no bird song, not even the snuffling of something small pushing through the underbrush. He eased behind a tree trunk, and lifted his head and sniffed; a salty smell similar to the sweat he had detected on the Arnoddr. Some sort of sweet perfume, and the smells of leather and oil – all of them, the scent of ManKind.

They were near.

His heart started to race – *had they seen him already?* He tried to think. *How should he present himself? How could he gain their trust quickly?* He didn't have time for long drawn out games of communication. He tried to remember the talks he had with Arn, wracking his memory for clues to the exchanges.

He was wasting valuable time. He pulled a scrap of cloth from his robe, sucked in a deep breath, and stepped out.

'Arnoddr Sigarr. Arnoddr Sigarr.' He waved the cloth high, keeping his hands up. He waited, holding his breath, but there was nothing. He lowered his arms. Perhaps he had been wrong. He reached for the communication stones.

The explosive crack came from slightly ahead of him, and immediately a thud on his chest kicked him off his feet. His ribs burned like nothing he had felt in years. As his vision clouded, he saw multiple bodies crowding around him. One put a boot on his chest, and pointed something at his face.

There came another thud.

The running Delta Force came up in two columns of ten. Half a click out in front, two point men moved lightly through the forest; weapons up and ready. On the barrel of their rifles were motion sensors that could detect larger moving objects long before they could be picked up by line of sight.

Rodriguez spoke into his cuff mike. 'Simms, got a warm body, coming in fast. Hold your position.'

Immediately into his ear he heard Teacher who had been listening in from their rear.

'No take-down until we see what we've got. Clear?'

'Clear.' Came back in unison.

'I want them alive – use kinetic rounds.'

Rodriguez swore under his breath. Kinetics were rubberized rounds – slower velocity and low chance of penetration and damage. He reached into his belt and grabbed two of the long bullets.

He thought for a moment and then let one go, keeping the other and loading it into the breach of his gun. He then got down on one knee beside a tree, his body presenting a half silhouette with his eyes and gun barrel facing the approaching figure. About fifty feet across from him, the other point man, Simms, was doing the same.

'I got this, Simms.'

'Roger that.' Simms never took his eyes off the forest.

Rodriguez thought he'd give whatever it was a single rubber round. If it kept coming, then he'd give it a live one, and send it straight back to hell. He had watched the film of the Green Berets being taken down, feeling a mixture of anger and fascination at the footage. The orange and black things were monsters. Also, the beasts that had been crucified in the desert were bigger than men, and looked pretty tough. This place seemed a world of horrors, and now those horrors were taking his team.

He narrowed his eyes and sighted on the movement.

Jackson had been his friend. Whatever was coming at them was not going to take anyone else. He wanted payback, and he wanted blood.

The figure stopped behind a stand of trees. It can't have seen them, but had somehow figured out they were there. *Damned clever, but I can be patient too*, he thought. *Come to papa.* He waited…

… and waited.

He swore softly. Samson and the rest of the Deltas would catch up soon. He needed to take his shot. Just as he contemplated moving forward to flush it out, a large figure stepped from behind the trees.

It was still about eighty feet out from him, tall and lean, and slightly bent. He used his scope – it looked like one of the creatures they had seen nailed to the crosses. It waved a small white piece of cloth and shouted something over and over. It stopped and lowered its arms.

'It's reaching for something.' Rodriguez pulled the trigger, and hit the figure dead centre. It blew back a few feet, and he raced over. 'Gimme some cover, Simms.'

Rodriguez flew over the fallen logs and bracken, and stood over the creature, looking down with a curled lip of disgust.

'You ugly mother.' He put his boot on the chest. 'Now that is one dirty dog.' He pointed his rifle at its face, but reached down and grabbed one of its ears and pulled. 'Jezuz, it's real.'

Rodriguez straightened and once again used his boot to press down on the body. 'Listen up you ugly freak; where's the Colonel? I'm going to count to three… there will not be a four. One… two…thr…'

There was a thud as a fist hit Rodriguez in the back of the head. The man staggered forward, turning with his gun up. 'What the fu…'

Teacher glared at him. 'You trying to piss me off, Rodriguez? Stand down.'

Samson pushed Teacher out of the way. 'Yeah, if anyone's gonna ace one of these sons of bitches, it's me.' He pulled up short. 'What? This ain't one of those big things.'

Rodriguez turned his volcanic glare onto the creature at his feet. 'It's one of those dog-people that were crucified.'

'Ugly.' Samson kicked it.

Teacher knelt down beside the creature and helped it sit up. 'Well, if those cat midgets put these guys up on the cross, then I'm thinking there's no love lost between the two. The enemy of my enemy and all that.'

The creature's eyes flickered open. Teacher held out a hand. 'Give me some water.' He turned to Rodriguez and clicked his fingers impatiently. 'Yours.'

Teacher took the bottle and held it, not knowing how this would work. He pushed the bottle forward, and the animal reached up to take his hand, holding the bottle and guiding it to his lips. He watched it as it drank. The hand holding his was almost human – long fingers, but covered in an almost imperceptible fur. The nails weren't flat like a human, but instead grew from the ends of the digits, and were thick and sharp – dangerous looking.

It was the face that intrigued him the most. He had seen the reconnaissance film of this type of creature attacking the drone, and was amazed at the features – wolf-like, but the facial muscles were more dexterous, expressive. The lips closed easily over the bottle tip, and no tongue lolled out to lap at the water. After a second, it handed the bottle back and turned its eyes to him – so clear and intense. There was deep intelligence there, and also wisdom.

It coughed and rubbed its chest. The creature's mouth worked and it coughed again. Words came, but the language was impossible. Teacher shook his head, but touched his own chest. 'I am Teacher. Can you understand me, then?'

The creature nodded and reached into its robe. Immediately a dozen rifles lifted and pointed at its face. Teacher half turned. 'Stand down.'

Samson knelt down beside them and gripped Teacher's bicep. 'One false move and we send it back to hell.'

Instead, it carefully pulled from its robe three small, shiny rocks and held them out. It nodded. Teacher took one and held it up. The centre glowed. It was like a milky crystal, but with some sort of light inside it. Teacher wondered whether it was natural at all.

'What is it?'

The creature nodded, and took one and lifted it to his lips, and motioned to swallow it. He smiled and nudged the back of Teacher's hand, urging him to do the same.

'Don't do it.' It was Alison Sharp, one of their second lieutenants.

Samson reached out to take it. 'I agree, probably...'

Teacher tossed it in his mouth and swallowed hard. He shrugged. 'Not a lot of options, or time. Besides... I trust him.' He waited.

'How do you feel?' Sharp again.

Teacher tilted his head, trying to gauge anything different about himself. 'Nothing. I don't feel anything at all. Not sure what it was supposed to do.'

The thing on the ground before him cleared its throat. 'It's supposed to allow us to understand each other – and it did just that. My name is Balthazaar of the Valkeryn Wolfen, and I bring you bad tidings, Man-Kind. Urgent bad tidings, I'm afraid.'

⸗ ⊷⊙⊘⊙⊷ ⨯⨯⨯⨯⨯ ⊶⊙⊘⊙⊶ ⸗

After he recovered from his stunned amazement, Teacher managed to stifle his hundreds of questions and the Delta squad listened as Teacher translated what the Wolfen said.

Samson, seeing Teacher was suffering no ill-effects, or perhaps not wanting his second in command to be leading the debrief, snatched another of the stones and swallowed it. Then, he, Teacher and Balthazaar talked for many minutes, before the old Wolfen pulled a roll of parchment from his robe and laid it out flat on the ground. It was a map of the lands and he pointed to where they were in relation to the castle, and finally where the Dark Lands were, and the place he believed the first Man-Kind to ever reappear, Arnoddr Sigarr, to be.

Samson smiled. 'Mr. Arnold Singer... at last.' He grabbed the old Wolfen's tunic and pulled him forward. 'He stole something very valuable from us. I need to find him and bring him back – urgently.'

Teacher grabbed Samson's wrist. 'He's no threat.' He turned to Balthazaar. 'Our world, our time, is being torn apart, simply because Singer came through with something from our time, and somehow disrupted some great cosmic balance. According to our scientists, we've only got about a week to bring him back. After that... who knows.'

Balthazaar shook his head. 'You have far less time than that, Teacher of Ohio. Tell me, how many more warriors do you bring? Are you in advance of a larger force?' Balthazaar's pale eyes stared into him, hanging on his answer.

Samson shook his head. 'Tell him nothing.'

Teacher looked into the old creature's eyes for a second or two before responding. 'No sir, this is as good as it gets for now. But don't worry, we have plenty of firepower.' Teacher noticed the old creature seemed disheartened by the information.

Balthazaar sighed. 'In a matter of hours, less maybe, a significant force of Lygon will be here. They will be accompanied by the Panterran, and never were two more cruel races combined in Hellheim or on the lands of Valkeryn.

Balthazaar groaned and got unsteadily to his feet. He held

Teacher's arm. 'They tricked us. Found their way in through our fortifications, and brought our mighty kingdom down. Now we are no more than a few Wolfen scattered to the ends of the land. They live to destroy other races.' He grabbed Teacher and pulled him close.

'They will tear you to pieces, regardless of your powerful weapons, or your hubris.' He let the soldier go, speaking softly. 'They may also try and find your home.'

'They can goddamn try.' Samson pulled back his sleeve and looked at a large wristwatch. He shook his head. 'Can't afford to get bogged down in a prolonged firefight.' Samson folded his arms. 'These big guys are probably as powerful as a Mack truck on legs, but they're dumb and slow. They won't get within fifty feet of us. The little guys, Panterran you called them, caught us off guard. We won't underestimate them again.' Samson thought for a moment. 'We do not have time to engage our enemy, find the boss, and then go trekking off to search for the kid. We need to do both at once.'

Samson turned to his team, who stood watching and waiting. 'Okay, listen up people. We have a considerable force, inbound. We cannot outrun them, nor do we want to. We need to either put them down or punch a hole through them and retrieve Colonel Briggs.' He looked along their faces, his own grim. 'There's another problem. Arnold Singer is still free and can be retrieved within the time frame allocated to us. But we must act now. We will need to split our objectives.'

Samson stepped forward, his hands on his hips. 'Teacher you will take five – Simms, Sharp, Brown, Weng and Doonie, and you will locate Singer. The rest of us will find a defendable position, with a clear corridor for extraction if need be. Use extreme force. No prisoners; eradication of enemy is the only priority. Live or die, our minimum objective is we must hold them.' Samson walked along in front of them. 'We will not, I repeat, will not, allow them to get anywhere near the vortex, and our home.' Samson grinned at them. 'They don't yet know who they're messing with.'

'HUA!'

Balthazaar had been listening to Samson speak and was still rubbing his chest where the rubberized round took him. He turned to look along the faces of the soldiers. 'Please, warriors of Man-Kind, they have your leader...' He must have remembered only Teacher and Samson could understand him, and turned quickly back to the giant Delta Force captain, '... and the two young ones who appeared earlier. My friend will try and release the two called Edward and Rebecca, but your leader has already been integrated.'

Samson frowned. 'I don't care if they try and interrogate Colonel Briggs. She'll never break, and anything she does give up will be useless misinformation.'

'No, you don't understand.'

Samson pushed the old Wolfen back a step. 'It's you that doesn't understand us humans. The boss would die before giving up on her own.'

Balthazaar reached out to the big Delta Force soldier. 'She will not be allowed to die, she...'

Samson shrugged him off and turned to the squad.

'Hanson, with me. We gotta hold for forty-eight hours. Then, with or without the boss, we head home. Understood?'

The powerful looking young soldier nodded. 'You got it. We'll be home for a beer and burger long before then.' They bumped fists.

Teacher was checking his weapons as a panicked looking Balthazaar stepped in front of him. 'I cannot stop you. All I can hope is that the Panterran think that the warriors left here are all of your war party. It may give you the time you need to get the Arnoddr back home.'

Teacher put his hand on the Wolfen's shoulder. 'Don't worry about us. But what about you? Will you come with us?'

The old Wolfen shook his head. 'No, I'll head back to the castle. I will be more value to the Wolfen resistance, if there ever is one.' He grabbed Teacher's hands in his and looked into his eyes. Teacher felt his very soul was being laid bare by the intense pale gaze.

'You are a fighter, and I can see by the scars that your life has been brutal when it had needed to be. This will test you, and all your warriors.' He smiled. 'May Odin watch over you.' He went to step back, but stopped and reached into his robe once more and produced more of the polished stones.

'Take these – the Panterran will not expect you to understand their language. Every advantage you possess will now be critical'.

Teacher took the five stones. He handed one each to his own small team. Alison Sharp held it up, looking into its colored depths suspiciously.

Teacher nudged her. 'Down the hatch, Sharp, then we leave.'

She tossed it in her mouth.

Hanson looked up. 'Going to be dark soon.'

Samson grunted and continued to watch as the point runners came back in. They had planted sticky mines along anything that even looked like a trail. Thermal monitors were deployed, this time bolstered by motion sensors – nothing was walking in on them, or creeping in under blankets unannounced, without a loud bang.

The Deltas had taken up defensive positions in a stand of trees. They had chosen the site because there was excellent cover, and an open clearing around them. They had spent several minutes removing more of the brush to give them an uninterrupted field of fire. In addition, they had left a scoot-chute – a corridor twenty feet wide behind them. Mined, but they knew where to land their feet, even at speed, if need be.

Samson had deployed his remaining thirty-two Delta Force members in three operative units at the tree line. He, Hanson and six bodies at the centre, with a string line of soldiers branching forward on both the left and right – three fields of fire, none overlapping – just one big mother of a killing zone.

Samson stayed low and pulled a scope down over one eye, and looked first along the trails – nothing moving. Then along his own squad line. Like him, they were down low, muzzles ready. He felt confident; each man or woman had enough fire-power to level a building.

Hit'm hard and fast, take the starch right outta them, and make them rethink their tactics. Once he gave them a bloody nose, and thrown a bit of doubt and confusion into them, they'd move in. The horns of his steer would extend, and eventually close. Then the head would move forward to drive a spike right down their throat. They'd engaged them before – they were big, but they were still just flesh. Samson felt good, looking forward to the killing. He looked at his watch. It'd be a walk in the park.

'Sensor two just got tripped.' Hanson's voice was hushed, but calm in his ear.

'Roger that. Okay people, hold until we have contact.' Samson got down lower, just his muzzle and eyes showing around the tree trunk. He knew his team would be doing the same.

'Sensor three tripped, sensor four, five… here they come.'

Samson heard the motion sensor numbers counting down and waited, breathing easily.

'Contact.'

Samson's finger reflexively tightened on the trigger of his skeletal black gun when from the tree line ahead, an array of animals burst free. Things, ankle and knee high, hopping, or scurrying along the ground towards them. In amongst them, larger creatures – a type of deer with strange green antlers, pig things with six legs and armor plating, snakes with centipede legs; all of them came at the Deltas like a rushing battalion of squawking, squeaking fear-maddened children.

Great time for a freakin' stampede, he thought as he pulled back to allow one of the beasts to charge by him. His jaws clenched as he continued to watch the far tree line. Fact was, something must have frightened all that game into its collective movement, and that something was coming up behind the animals.

'Stay frosty, people.'

The forest fell silent as all the animals disappeared behind them, and then the last rays of sunlight overhead darkened as if a thick cloud was passing across the face of the sun. Samson looked up and swore.

'Get down, we got arrow shot.'

The mass of arrows dropped from the sky like a flock of angry needle-sharp birds. The shredding, whipping sound they made as they passed through leaves above was like a heavy hailstorm. This was immediately followed by the sound of steel tips on wood, stone, earth, and also flesh.

Swearing filled the air, and Samson came back upright from his cover position, and noticed a short black arrow sticking up out of his shoulder. He ripped it free, and glanced at the tip – fire hardened iron, and razor sharp. It hadn't sunk far into his flesh, becoming wedged in a join of the ceramic plates of his combat armor.

He put his back to the tree, and yelled over his shoulder. 'Sound off.' Every squad member had a number, and they knew to give the call sign in the proper order – a code letter after the number indicated their operational capacity after an attack: one-a, meant fully operational, one-b, they'd taken dents, and one-c, meaning significant injury. A no reply usually meant you were out cold or dead.

Two replies were missing. Bottom line, arrows didn't knock you out, they made you dead. Samson swore, and turned back to the front just as there was a thundering crash and a projectile flew out of the forest and exploded into the tree trunk above him. Branches rained down, and he chanced a brief look. He felt a chill run up his spine – it was an axe, as big as he was.

'Jesus.' The first axe was soon followed by many more. The missiles were heavy, and by the sound of the pained screams, some struck home. The forward tree-line shook and Samson sucked in a huge breath and roared his warning. 'Here they come!'

Giant orange and black bodies broke cover, and charged. Samson estimated around fifty of the giant Lygon, as Balthazaar had called them. He sighted along the short black barrel, breathing easily, cool as an ice cube; this was what he trained for. He and his fellow Delta acted as one. He gently squeezed the trigger, and at the same time other automatics around him did the same.

The massive creatures head's punched backwards as pieces of their thick furred skulls blew away from their heads. Few if any made it more than two thirds across the clearing, and their giant bodies began to stack up like a natural barricade. Beside him, Hanson loaded a grenade into the launcher under his barrel and fired, the projectile leaving a trail of vapor as it flew into the thick brush and exploded in a ball of shredded plants and dirty smoke.

The big trees rained leaves and small branches down over his targeted site for a few moments.

'Cease fire.' They waited and watched. Nothing came out of the forest but silence.

'Hold your position. Eyes out ladies and gentlemen.' He waited, feeling a spot of perspiration on his temple, even though the temperature was quite cool. He wished the old Wolfen guy was still with them. He desperately wanted to ask what would happen next – this was definitely not something from any Earthly military textbook.

A voice came out of the far forest line. "Delta squad, lower your weapons, I'm coming in.'

A figure stepped out. 'What the f...' Samson slowly lifted his head from the rifle sight and stared with his mouth hanging open.

'Hold your fire.' He lowered his gun, but confusion creased his brow.

*   *   *

'Colonel? Colonel Briggs is that you?'

'Stay your weapons, all of you. I'm coming in. You put a boot up their ass, and they've run for the hills – well done. We need to talk tactics, then arrange to enter the castle to save the others.'

Samson whispered into his comm. unit. 'Miller, Franklin, bring the colonel in. Leave your mic open. The rest of you stay down and stay focused.'

Miller turned to Franklin, and pointed out to his left-side flank. The two men stepped up and out of concealment. Both had their guns at their waist. The walked forward slowly, pausing every few steps to scan the foliage from the sides and ahead. Briggs had her head down and half tilted as if she were listening to something or someone.

Miller approached to within ten feet of her. 'You okay, Colonel?'

Briggs only half lifted her head and started to approach. She looked along the skirmish line of the Delta team. Her face was expressionless. 'Is everyone here?'

Miller rubbed his head. 'Good to see you ma'am; we thought you'd been captured. Where's Jackson?'

Briggs kept coming, walking in a strange side-on gait. Miller and Franklin slowed as they came to within a few feet of their superior officer. She still hadn't lifted her head, but when she spoke it sounded if the words came from an empty tunnel.

'Is everyone here?'

Miller and Franklin looked at each other. Miller leaned forward, trying to see her face. 'No ma'am. The Captain sent Teacher and a team out to bring the boy back.'

'The Arnoddr Man-kind... from the Dark Lands?'

'Huh? You mean Singer? Yeah, that's right. This old wolf thing appeared and told us where he was.'

'Old... wolf... thing – a Wolfen?' Her face twisted as though she was hearing something deafening. 'Where... where, did it come from?' Briggs' eyes were screwed shut as though she was wracked with migraine. Suddenly, her face dropped and her eyes opened.

'Have the team assemble immediately, we need to take a head count.'

Miller put his finger to his ear, listening to Samson. Then turned back to his commanding officer. 'Samson says not a good idea ma'am. Hostiles could still be in the area and we are under extreme risk. We should take cover as well.' He held out his hand and half turned.

'By the way, you said others in the castle. You've been there?'

Briggs looked distracted. 'The other... Man-Kind.'

'Man-kind? What the hell does that...'

Miller stopped to listen to Samson again. He turned to Franklin. 'Something's not right.' Miller reached out to grip the colonel's arm.

Briggs lifted her face at last. Her eyes were half rolled back in her head, and there was snot running from her nose. She could have been asleep except for the movements of her body.

'Ma'am, are you sick?' Miller stepped back.

Briggs eyes dropped and finally found him. Her arm came up too fast for him to react. She held a handgun and released two rounds. Miller and Franklin both went down hard. As if on cue, a nightmare materialized around the Delta team as small bodies dropped from the trees, landing amongst the soldiers. Behind Colonel Briggs, the foliage parted and a second wave of giant orange and black bodies boiled forth.

CHAPTER 24

GREAT ODIN, GIVE ME PATIENCE

Sorenson climbed higher and lay flat on a tree limb that was three times wider than he was. He calmed his breathing and gradually peered over the edge. A hundred feet below the line of Panterran and Lygon snaked along the jungle floor. He counted them off – less than the day before – the jungle slowly paring them back, but still a formidable force, numbering about two dozen.

He couldn't understand why Bergborr was leading them… and seemed at ease with them. *Why didn't he fight or try to flee?* he wondered. Instead, he was using his tracking skills to follow the path of the Man-Kind and Grimson.

The line of creatures continued to pass beneath him, and he carefully began to shift in preparation to move on to the next limb. He slid forward, and stopped – he was stuck. Sorenson looked back over his shoulder, and his eyes went wide. Squatting over his lower body was a many-legged creature that was half as long as he was. Multiple eyes regarded him dispassionately, as it continued to spin more and more webbing to encase his lower body. The sticky substance glued him down, and by the look of the large fangs on either side of its mouth, he guessed that once he was totally incapacitated, they would be put to use.

Sorenson reached over his shoulder and pulled free his sword, planning to slash backwards and cleave the thing in two, but he paused. If he killed the thing and it plummeted to the ground, what would the Panterran make of a fallen body, killed by a sword slice? *Great Odin, give me patience.* He gritted his teeth, watched and waited.

His legs got heavier, as the creature moved further along his body, spraying the sticky substance onto his thighs. It would soon coat his lower back. If his arms were rendered useless, he'd be dead. He peered back over the edge of the tree limb – the Panterran were gone, but the slow moving Lygon were still passing beneath him. He cursed and quickly turned back to the thing as he felt its needle-like legs on his buttocks. He bared his teeth at it, but the glass-like eyes regarded him without fear, and continued on with its task of sticking down its next meal. With the thing closer, Sorenson could clearly see the wickedly sharp mandibles, and guessed they would inject him with venom, and suck the juices from his body, while he was alive, and immobile.

He looked back down, and groaned. Come on, come on. His nerves were stretching tight now. The Lygon line still trudged on, still a few to go. By Odin, hurry up, you dull brutes, he whispered and turned back to the thing that now stood on his lower back. It started to spray his upper body and shoulders. He moved his hands forward, determined to at least keep his sword arm free.

Breathing was becoming difficult; as the web dried, it seemed to set like stone. Sorenson looked back down for the last time he was able, and saw the line had passed on, but one of the Lygon had stopped directly below him to squat and relieve himself.

His time was up as the webbing fell on his sword arm, and was also starting to float down across the back of his head – either his arm would soon be pinned, or his vision would be shut off – either would mean certain death to him.

The thing advanced, confident now, and prodded its sharp legs into the meat of his back, perhaps looking for the juiciest sections to pierce first. Sorenson heard a chittering from over his shoulder – a call of hunger, or victory?

His nerve broke. Lygon or not, he swung back with all his

might. His movement was restricted, but he still managed to cleave the top of the thing's head from its body. The remaining segments still clung to him, and its needle fangs continued to work. Sorenson wondered whether it would still strike at him, instinct taking over, regardless of the brain being removed. He swung again, this time using the flat of his blade, knocking it clean off his lower half to sail out towards the lower branches.

Before the carcass could drop to the ground, a flying creature swooped down and plucked the bleeding body from the air, carrying it back up into the higher canopy.

'Thank you.' Sorenson shook his head. 'But by Odin's beard, why didn't you tell me you would have done that before?'

He rested his forehead on the branch for a few moments, then sucked in a deep breath, and began to saw at the hardened material covering his lower body like a cocoon.

Hmm, much safer in the trees? As long as I have eyes in the back of my head, he thought as he pulled the solidified mesh from his legs and began to make his way to the ground.

'Maybe.' Arn contemplated the tree bough that leaned out over the water. Where they stood the river narrowed to just over a hundred feet across. The limb was as broad as a Buick at its base, and reaching out, narrowed as it reached more than three quarters of the way to the opposite bank. On the other side, there were more trees reaching back towards them, their tips meshing with the very ends of this one huge branch.

'I think we can make it, Grim.'

Grimson nodded. 'I know I can; I'm a good climber.'

Arn looked to the opposite bank, and then to the dark green water before them. The area they needed to cross lumped slightly from the swirling current due to the slight narrowing of the watercourse. A massive boulder the size of house had caused the constriction making the water work harder to keep pushing the millions of gallons through it, and Arn guessed it had probably gouged a deep trough beneath the surface. He bet it was probably deeper here than anywhere else for miles.

He stared into its mysterious depths; it was certainly darker, with no sign of the bottom even close to the bank. He shuddered; glad they would be climbing high over it. Oddly, the fish that had been trailing them as they hiked along the bank had vanished as they approached the darker area. *Must be the current*, he thought hopefully.

Arn circled the tree; its age-old, gnarled trunk provided many handholds up to the first of the huge lower branches. He leapt up and started to climb, quickly followed by Grimson. He was the first up on the broad limb, its wood cool and smooth beneath him. He stood and carefully walked out a few feet, angling his head to see through the dense growth. Gratefully he saw that the path forward looked fairly easy. Together, they edged along the bough. The further they went, the more Arn felt the limb start to move beneath him.

Half way across and the branch was narrowing. Now down to barrel thickness, it bounced ominously with each step either of them took. It would get a lot thinner before Arn and Grimson reached the tips of the opposing bank's tree-limbs. Several times Arn called a halt to wait for the creaking branch to settle.

While waiting for the swaying limb to calm, Arn looked down at the slow moving water below. He was delighted to see that some of the fish had returned, and were drifting lazily beneath them, occasionally turning sideways to display a single glassy eye firmly fixed on the pair above.

'That's it, keep coming… and you'll be our lunch when we get to the other side.'

'Yech,' from Grimson.

Arn edged along sideways now, the limb bouncing with every careful step he took. Out over the river, the wind caught the ends of the branches and lifted them like sails. Arn grabbed onto a small branching limb as the huge limb rose beneath his feet. 'Surfs up, Grim. Hang on.'

He pushed on, each footstep now was a matter of slide, wait, slide wait; a shuffle that frustrated Grimson who walked behind him, arms-out like a miniature tightrope walker. He continually jeered Arn for his lack of balance.

From below him there was a surge of water. Arn needed every speck of concentration, and couldn't spare an atom's worth to look down – besides, surely it was just some sort of white-water breaking over shallows.

The wind lifted the thinning branch again, and Arn had to go to his knees for a few seconds. He peered ahead; the tips of the branches of the trees on the opposite bank were in sight. They touched their own limb and then moved away, touched and then whipped back and forth as if some giant was throttling them from behind.

'Not going to be easy. We might have to jump.'

Arn watched for a while and then cursed softy – he should have expected this – the thinning of the branch meant it was influenced more by their weight, and therefore bending lower the closer they got to its end. There was a surging once again from the water below, and this time it sounded closer. He chanced a look down. In a billow of water, fragments of the orange-silver fish swirled around on the surface before they fell slowly into the dark green depths of the river.

'Grim, did you see that?' Arn looked over his shoulder. Grimson shrugged and shook his head.

'Okay, forget it. C'mon.'

Arn inched along, this time keeping one eye on the water as the limb dipped further towards it. They now found themselves only twenty feet above its surface, and glancing down, Arn thought he saw an enormous shadow pass underneath them.

'Oh great.' He peered up though the branches, hoping it had been nothing more than a cloud passing over the fading sun. No such luck – the sky was darkening, but clear. Arn suddenly had a pretty good idea why the fish were cautious about moving out over the deeper water, and those that did, ended up being shredded – this spot in the river belonged to something that lived down in its green depths… and that something was now coming to the surface.

From behind him he heard Grimson. 'I'm hot, and the fish are gone. I can swim from here.'

Arn spun around. 'Don't you…'

The young Wolfen had already left the branch.

Arn quickly edged out along the thinning branch, trying to keep his balance while also watching Grimson paddle across the water. The small Wolfen swum strongly, probably now only thirty or so feet from where Arn watched from the tips of the branches, and closing rapidly on the far bank.

Arn's heart galloped in his chest, and willed the youth to greater speed – he suspected there was something watching from the depths, and he had to stop himself from yelling out lest he panic the youth.

'Come on,' he whispered, and he felt his spirits lift as Grim passed over the bottomless dark water at the centre of the slow moving river. Huge flat stones could be made out beneath him now, but as the water was so clear, they could have been ten feet or fifty below him.

Arn swayed on the branch and looked over his shoulder. Just downstream, a V-shaped wave was moving across the water, made by an object that was travelling below the surface. Something of considerable size was coming up from the inky depths, and trying to beat Grimson to the shore. Arn gave up on not trying to panic the young Wolfen.

'Grim, swim, swim faster!'

Grimson stopped and turned. 'Huh.'

Arn spluttered and pointed, having trouble maintaining his balance and pointing downstream at the same time.

'Something's coming. Swim, Grim, swim! Don't look back – go, go *go*!' He yelled until his voice became hoarse, and then drew his blade. If need be, he'd dive down from the overhanging branches. To do what, he had no idea. For now, all he could do was watch… and pray.

Grimson started to swim, but then stopped and looked around. Perhaps he noticed the huge lump in the water or sensed the monstrous presence approaching, but he whined and then quickly flipped over to start thrashing with all his strength to the bank.

Arn had moved as far along the branch as he could, the thinning branches creaking ominously beneath him, their ends now barely above the water. He steeled himself – if whatever was beneath the water breached before Grimson was safe, he would launch himself, missile-like onto its back. He knew it would be big, and given what they had already encountered, he hoped to do little more than startle it long enough for Grimson, and himself, to get to the bank.

Grim was now only about fifteen feet from being able to stand. *Hurry up,* thought Arn as the dark mass started to rise from the depths and take shape. He grimaced. Thoughts of plunging a blade into the thing's back were swept away as the creature took form. It was a crustacean, like a bullet shaped crab, or crayfish without a tail, easily fifty feet in length and mottled a dark green. Two claws the size of trashcans were held out to its sides, and black bulb eyes on stalks were trained on the thrashing youth ahead of it.

Arn imagined a shell many inches thick, and well beyond any simple stabbing to put it the chance of a quick meal. He sucked in a huge breath, readying himself. He had sworn an oath to the king that he would keep his son safe. He would honor that pledge, or die trying.

'Guess I'll see you soon, grandfather.'

The giant crustacean broke the surface, the bulb eyes appearing first like a pair of shiny periscopes, followed by a mottled back as wide as a truck and glistening in the rising moonlight.

Arn leapt.

CHAPTER 25

BEAUTIFUL VALKERYN, WHAT HAVE THEY DONE TO YOU?

Eilif endured the taunts and the torments of the Lygon and Panterran that accompanied her to the castle. She was in no doubt that a slow death was assured when she arrived back. Her life mattered little now that she was denied the opportunity to track Arn into the Dark Lands. The Panterran and Lygon would eventually catch him up, and then…

She just hoped Bergborr's Wolfen spirit would rise in the defense of her brother. It was strange; whenever she thought of the dark Wolfen, one of her kinfolk, there was always a small seed of reservation in the deepest corners of her mind. Try as she might, she couldn't understand why she felt this way.

She was pushed from behind and she stumbled. Her clothes had been shredded, and as a cruel joke, the Panterrans had draped her in a filthy blanket – a cloak of royalty, for a princess of nothing.

She walked slowly with it pulled over her head her like a hood, not wanting to see the disgusting beasts around her. Another shove brought her back to her current predicament. Her mind worked on plans for escape, but in the long flat lands of her former kingdom, and with her hands bound and neck tethered to the giant brutes, there was little chance of breaking free here and now.

Soon she would be in the castle, and, with luck, unbound. If she was not immediately presented to Mogahrr, or put to death or chained, then there was a flicker of hope. The castle was her home, she knew it and loved it – there were many secret passages, and she just needed to be in the right place, and alone for only a few seconds.

Eilif drew in a breath, and eased it out. And if she were killed would it matter? Not if Arn also lost his life. Then she would not want to live. Perhaps they could meet again, across the rainbow bridge in Valhalla. She knew in her heart he had the *sáál* of a Wolfen. Perhaps death would be better for her, better for them, than this life.

'Please Odin hear me. If I am to die, make it an honorable death,' she whispered. The Panterrans delighted in delivering pain through torture. She would rob them of that pleasure. She made up her mind – she would die in battle. When a chance presented it, she would escape or fight to the death.

The familiar landmarks told her she was close to her once beloved Valkeryn kingdom. The only difference was the reek of death that still hung over the lands.

Valkeryn, beautiful Valkeryn, what have they done to you? She thought miserably.

◦◦◦◦◦ ⟩⟩∞⟨⟨ ⟩⟩∞⟨⟨ ◦

Becky and Edward sat huddled against the wall in the cold cell. They had pulled together scraps of material from around the tiny room and fashioned them into rough clothing – although clothing was a flattering term for their efforts. Edward thought they both looked like refuges from some lost tribe, with Becky's scraps barely providing any modesty. Considering they had been naked for hours, Edward guessed the time for shyness had long past.

'What do you think they'll do with us?' Becky's arms rested on her knees, and her head was lowered onto them. Her voice drifted up from between her legs.

'Don't know. They don't need us, and I don't think they see us as particularly unique or valuable given the way they dispatched Briggs' soldier. Maybe they'll keep us as pets.'

She sniffed wetly. 'They tore him apart. I don't want to die like that... I don't want to die at all. I just want to go home. It wasn't supposed to be like this. No one told me it'd be like this,' she sobbed.

Edward sighed. Why did people think that the future was always going to be some sort of hippy nirvana where everyone ate fruit and hugged each other in the sunshine? If the past and present proved anything, it was that life had always been brutal.

Becky's words continued to float up between her knees. 'I always thought humans were supposed to be the bad ones. These things are worse, so much worse.'

Edward sat back. 'We didn't invent cruelty, and obviously we don't have a monopoly on it. In fact, there's a proven relationship between intelligence and organized warfare. Humans, and obviously non-humans, don't seem to stop killing the smarter or more enlightened they get. We... they... just get better at it.'

Becky moaned, and sniffed. 'They put something horrible in the army woman's ear.'

Edward ignored her and let his mind turn over the interaction they had with the Panterran queen. 'They don't want us, but they definitely want something.'

Becky's head rocked from side to side. 'Well, if they don't want us, why don't they let us go?'

'Hmm, I don't think they have what they want just yet, so...'

Her head came up with her face twisted in anger. 'Well, how about finding out what they want, so we can give it to them, and then get the hell out of here?'

Edward put his finger to his lips. 'Shush.' He turned his head. 'Listen.' There came a clank of steel bolts being drawn back, and heavy footsteps on the stones outside of their cell. Becky scooted over, and huddled up beside him. She buried her face in his shoulder

'Don't let them put anything in my ear.'

'I won't.' He reached up a hand, hesitated for a second, before lowering it to stroke her hair. 'It'll be okay.'

Two huge silhouettes appeared in the doorway, luminous green eyes burning out of the darkness. A Panterran also arrived to stand at the bars studying Edward and Becky for a few moments. A few words from the smaller creature and the huge beasts stood aside to reveal a second smaller figure behind them. The door was unlocked, pulled open, and the figure pushed in. The gate was closed once more.

The new figure stood just inside the cell. Outside the bars, the Lygon departed, leaving the single Panterran.

The Panterran laughed. 'Meet your new subjects... your majesty.' The hissing laugh continued to float in the air even after the goblin-like creature turned away and disappeared into the darkness.

Edward got slowly to his feet. The figure still hadn't moved, but Edward had the distinct impression they were being thoroughly scrutinised. The head lifted a fraction, and twin silver eyes shone out from under the hood – definitely not human then, Edward thought.

Edward cleared his throat. 'Hello.'

'Man-kind.' The voice was soft, feminine.

Edward nodded. 'Yes, we're human... mankind.'

The figure slowly reached up to the hood, and slid it back from its head. Behind him Becky gasped, and even Edward couldn't stop himself sucking in his breath.

'Wow.' He shook his head. 'I mean...' Edward's mouth opened and closed for a moment and then he simply stared. The word beautiful came to mind. Where the Panterran and Lygon looked exactly as they behaved – brutish, cruel, even evil, this creature was the definition of regal beauty.

Edward felt his heart race. The figure was only a little taller than they were, and its shape was roughly human, but instead of a human face, there was the visage of a wolf. Large ice-blue eyes watched them with an unblinking level gaze.

He noticed that its hands were tied. 'I think it, she, is a prisoner like us.'

She held them out. Edward went to take a step, but Becky grabbed him. 'No, don't free it. It's not human. We don't know what it will do. I mean, look at it.'

The creature turned its shining glare on her. She held out her hands again. 'I mean you no harm. I am as much a prisoner as you are.'

'She can speak.' Edward pulled out of Becky's grip. 'I think I can trust you… I hope.' He took the creature's hands, working quickly at the knots. While he worked, he looked into her face, marveling at the features. The skin was covered in an almost imperceptible silver hair, and the eyes were large and luminous, a startling icy blue. In that beauty there was intelligence, strength and determination. He finished and stepped back.

'Who are you?' The newcomer continued to rub her wrists.

Edward swallowed. 'Ah, well, my name is Edward Lim. My friend here is Becky, Rebecca Matthews, and we are from Earth. Well, I mean from right here really, but just from another time, we came…'

'I know where you came from. What I want to know is why did you come here?'

'We're looking for our friend. He came through months ago.' Edward said quickly.

'Yes?' The penetrating eyes bored into him, but the stare had hardened.

'His name is…'

She cut him off. 'His name is Arn.'

Edward leapt forward. 'Arn, yes, Arnold Singer, That's right. He's our friend. Have you seen him? Where is he?'

The creature's eyes narrowed, and slid to Becky, looking over her form. 'And what is your relationship… with the Arnoddr?'

Hanson ran hard, the remaining eight members of his team keeping pace with him, regardless of their injuries. They had fought for hours, and the bodies of the monstrous creatures had piled up around them, and amongst them, like writhing hills of bone and muscle.

Their choice of armaments had been perfect for the larger Lygon creatures. The armor-piercing rounds had punched dinner plate-sized holes through the thick armor they wore, and did the same to the hugely muscled bodies underneath. Headshots were extremely satisfying.

The problem was the smaller Panterran. The heavy uranium tipped bullets were overkill, blowing their bodies into a million fragments. It was a waste of heavy ammunition. For these guys a better weapon would have been a lighter caliber with a greater rounds-per-second deployment – they needed to spray steel hot and fast, metal-storm style.

The team had fought hard – load-n-fire, load-n-fire, on and on for hours. Up close, K-bars were wielded with great effectiveness, and he had seen men and women fight on with several arrows sticking from their bodies. But the creature's numbers wore them down. For every beast they took down, ten more took its place in an endless wave of tooth, claw, and flying weapons.

Standing at the rear of the horde was Briggs, directing them in their attack strategy, like some sort of weird conductor. Her face was slack and emotionless the entire time. For Hanson, it was if they were fighting themselves.

When Samson had fallen, Hanson knew he had two options: One – fight until the ordinance ran out, and then get torn to shreds. Or two – fall back and secure the distortion vortex.

He hated to cut and run, given Teacher would need to

come through here if they successfully found the boy and the diamond. But these monsters had the home ground advantage, the numerical advantage, and an on-the-ground military leader that knew every tactic the Deltas had. Hanson looked towards the sky – dark now. Fighting them during the day was difficult. Fighting them in the dark, when the night-time incursions would commence in earnest, would be suicide.

He decided. 'We're falling back to the gateway; double time.'

The Delta team fired as they withdrew, and Hanson pumped a few grenades into the seething mass as he extracted himself from the fighting.

He could run all day and night if need be. He just hoped his pursuers would tire, or he could get some distance between them. The team sprinted on, turning and firing, turning and firing. He pressed the comm. button at his ear.

Time to give Teacher the bad news.

Dozens of miles away, Teacher and his small squad of Deltas ran on. There was no panic in their stride, just a workable pace that they could maintain for hours. From time to time, Teacher checked a compass, GPS being something that was rendered useless since the satellites hadn't been in orbit for hundreds of thousands of years.

'Where are we, boss?' It was Simms, looking around, as though enjoying the scenery.

Teacher glanced down at the map in his hand. 'Right now, I reckon, we're about fifty feet under Lake Michigan. According to Balthazaar's map, I'd say all the lakes have moved north and coalesced into a single huge inland sea. Must have been some pretty unpleasant geological times – the lands look to have lifted in some areas and fallen in others by many hundreds of feet. Got some tough terrain up ahead. So... stay sharp, fed and watered, and stay moving.'

Simms grunted. 'What if we get to these Dark Lands, and find that the kid is already dead, or just won't come with us?'

Teacher swigged from his canteen, and contemplated the question. 'If he's dead, hopefully he's in one piece so we can search his body for the diamond. If he's alive, better for him if he comes, but as long as we get the diamond, I'm not going to drag him along.' Teacher slid the canteen back into a pocket. 'I'm guessing he doesn't know he can even get back. We do our job and then get the hell out of here.'

'I heard that.' Alison Sharp sighted her rifle at an animal that popped from a burrow in the ground. It quickly pulled its head back in as the V-formation of soldiers approached. 'One question – what happens if the kid is dead and there's no diamond?'

Teacher shrugged. 'Then bend over and kiss your ass goodbye, because we're all as good as dead.'

Sharp laughed. There was a small ping in Teacher's ear. He raised a hand for silence as he ran.

'Go.' It was Hanson, and the man sounded out of breath. Teacher stopped running, and concentrated, the sound was faint as the comms had limited range.

'Goddammit.' It was worse than he had expected – the squad was down, and the remaining nine Deltas were on the run. In the background Teacher could hear rounds being expended, and an occasional grenade exploding, but Hanson was cool in his update, as he would have expected from a Spec Ops soldier.

Teacher felt his anger rising. *We underestimated them... again.* Just like the Green Berets, they, we, had come unprepared, he thought. He gritted his teeth to keep from exploding with fury. He knew how Samson would have deployed, he probably would have done the same. They had expected a frontal attack from lumbering giants, but instead, things like deformed children – the Panterran – had overrun them. *We should have listened to the old Wolfen a little more.*

Teacher concentrated when Hanson told him there was, "something more".

'Give it to me?' He glared at the ground as the Delta soldier told him about the colonel leading the enemy attack.

'Jesus, I thought that was what Balthazaar said – not interrogated, but *integrated*.' Teacher looked at his watch and then the darkening sky. 'Leave Briggs. Do not try to rescue her or any of the other missing Deltas. If they could turn her, then assume the others are compromised. This means the enemy will now know where we came through.' Teacher's jaws clenched as his mind worked.

'Okay, listen up soldier, here are your orders. Get to the gateway. Send one of your team through to give them a heads up… and get some more men and more kit. You remaining Deltas are to deploy at the cave entrance. You must be our shield – nothing must pass, hold the line. Clear?'

'Fight or die.' Hanson responded.

'Damn straight.' Teacher grunted. 'Good luck, and hopefully, see you soon.' He disconnected the call.

Teacher looked at his own team. Their faces were grim.

He gave them a half smile. 'You heard. Not a good day for the away team. We are now on our own. Our mission directives are unchanged – we grab the diamond, and Singer if possible. Then we get the freakin hell out of here.' His smile dropped. 'One extra complication; Briggs has been corrupted, and we can assume anyone else taken by the enemy will also be corrupted.' He nodded to each. 'Shoot first, ask questions later… no prisoners.'

'HUA!'

'We're not here on holiday, so let's lift the game.' The six Deltas began to run, and this time their pace was fast and furious.

Balrog and Unsaur stood at the foot of the small mountain of dirt and debris. It had taken them many hours of crossing the wasteland desert before they had sighted what they thought was a small volcano.

Balrog grunted and nudged his companion forward. Several small scout teams of Lygon warriors had earlier been sent out into the desert, each travelling in different directions, to track down where the Man-Kind had first appeared. They didn't know yet about Mogahrr capturing Briggs, or that many of the soldiers had already been overrun. But after many, many hours, they had found what they were seeking. The smell of Man-Kind lingered here, and other smells that excited their curiosity.

The climb was difficult as the debris was loose and slid beneath their enormous feet. At the top, they looked down into the dark pit before them, and even though their eyes were well adapted for nocturnal life, they both found it difficult to pick out anything.

Unsaur sniffed deeply. 'Something lives in here.' His huge hand went his belt where a massive hammer was tied.

Balrog snorted. 'If it chooses to get in our way, then something will also die in here.' He pushed Unsaur, causing him to slide into the pit. 'If it is the door to the home of Man-Kind, then we will be richly rewarded... and we can feast as well.'

Together they scrambled down towards the dark entrance, folding themselves into the rift in the rocks and then having to get down on all fours in the cramped tunnel. Unsaur blinked and allowed his eyes to adjust to the gloom. Further away from the tunnel opening it was an inky black. He roared, the sound travelling in a wave down the length of the tunnel, echoing into the distance for many miles. The deafening sound was meant as a warning, and to bolster his own courage.

'Move it.' Balrog shoved him in the back, and together they crawled along in the dark.

After a time, Unsaur stopped, and allowed Balrog to come up behind him.

'Why have you stopped?'

Unsaur half turned. 'Listen.'

They silenced their breathing, concentrating on the darkness. There was silence, then a drip of water, the rush of air as it moved past them, and the something else, faint in the distance... or was it behind them.

Unsaur couldn't help the growl growing in his chest. 'Something moves close by. It laughs at us.'

Balrog swung around, his mace now in his hand. He glared back behind him, though what he saw was little more than a sheet of darkness. He listened intently for a while.

'There is nothing.' He turned back to nudge his companion. 'Keep moving, I feel we are close.'

Unsaur roared again, the sound bouncing away from them, and giving him some comfort. He continued on for a few moments and then stopped and frowned.

'Something just ahead.'

'You hear that?' Jim J Morgan tilted his head and frowned. He and Leo Anderson, along with four of Briggs' military guards, were stationed in the large room just outside the Fermilab's particle accelerator tunnel. Leo Anderson half turned and listened for a few seconds, and then shook his head.

'Forget about it – this thing sounds like an express train on the best of days.' The men lounged against walls, played poker or sat resting, eyes closed. They had been selected based on them having no amalgam fillings and no pins or plates in any of their joints. They were also required to leave behind anything metallic – including wristwatches, knives and standard firearms. Instead, their primary defenses were specially designed ceramic-based small-caliber handguns.

They stood outside the four-mile long collider tunnel – the tunnel itself being off limits unless an expedition was planned to the New Zone, as they were now calling it, or one of the scientists needed to check any of the equipment. At this point, nothing was planned, and nothing would be while Colonel Briggs and the team was on-mission. Morgan and Anderson stood on either side of the six-foot wide circular hole that had been cut through the fortified concrete wall weeks before. Even here, the wind howled around them, and anything not tied down was quickly swept towards the grate covering the entrance.

Morgan shook his head. 'Nah, sounded like… thunder, or a roar or something.'

Anderson just shrugged and went back to watching two of his colleagues playing poker at a nearby table. Morgan continued to listen, straining to hear anything out of the ordinary over the continual howl of the wind.

They had tried planting motion sensors on the other side of the gateway in the New Zone, but the distortion from the gravity made any readings meaningless. Motion sensors were also abandoned in the tunnel, as the air density changes from the sucking effects of the vortex also made them worthless. They relied on camera feeds, but they made everything look oily and shimmering. And as a fall-back, they used line-of-sight – entering the collider tunnel – but that, only if necessary.

Morgan's neck continued to prickle. 'I should take a look.'

'Knock yourself out.' Anderson motioned over his shoulder, but then seemed to think about it. He turned and grinned. 'Might be Samson coming back. Don't get in that dudes way, he'll knock your teeth down your throat, and that's when he's being friendly.'

Morgan grinned back. 'Guys a big pussy... but don't tell him I said that.' He pulled a flat card from his pocket and slid it down along the reader slot, immediately turning the indicator light green. The door buzzed, popped open and Morgan stepped up and into the connecting tunnel to the acceleration chamber.

He dropped down into the main shaft, and grabbed hold of the metal railing specially constructed so anyone entering could keep their balance in the gale force winds now permanently rushing around in the huge ring shaped tunnel.

Standing inside he could feel the energy being displaced within the tunnel as one of the world's most powerful proton-antiproton colliders continued to send particles around its diameter. The massive device was supposed to achieve an optimum atom smashing speed of pretty much the speed of light.

Morgan looked into the mow manhole-sized oily thing hanging in the air. It was a dark nothingness with soft looking edges – a giant wound in the universe that refused to heal. He stared into it, transfixed and uneasy at the same time. As he continued to look, he saw there were stars inside, as well as colors and swirling images – a drug addict's psychedelic nightmare.

'Anything?' Anderson's tiny voice in his ear made him jump.

'Nothing but a lot of fast moving ghosts; I'm coming back.' Morgan turned to the side tunnel just as an enormous thump made the ground shake beneath his feet. He spun, perhaps expecting to see Samson returning from the mission. He froze – it wasn't.

As an experienced military man, he rarely suffered from indecision, but the sight that met his eyes temporarily short-circuited his decision making process. The giant black and orange monster got to its feet, having to hunch over in the eight-foot circular tunnel. It filled the entire width with its bulk, and as if the nightmare couldn't get any worse, another thump and a second rolled in behind it.

'Hey, Morgan, what's going on in there?'

'Fu... fu... fu...' Words wouldn't come to Morgan. The creature lowered its head, green eyes fixed directly on him. Morgan felt his muscles lock up, and then the thing roared with a sound so loud it made him stagger back and wet himself at the same time.

* * *

Harper stuck a knuckle in his mouth and backed away from the screen. All he could do was point. The two giant ogre-like beasts had made it into the antechamber room, and were rapidly and brutally decimating the men inside as if they were nothing but straw dolls.

The small-caliber ceramic weapons did nothing against the beast's thick armor and bulk. Harper was glad there was no sound considering the screaming he knew must be happening in the room. A small mewling escaped his throat, and while he watched over the next few seconds, bodies, and bits of bodies, were strewn everywhere.

The monsters paced, their huge chests bellowing in and out. When one lifted a human leg to its mouth, Harper felt his muscles unlock. He hit the alarm button, and then threw up.

CHAPTER 26

TIME TO PUT THE CAT OUT

Hanson turned to what was left of his team. 'Teacher wants us to hold the line.' He looked each in the eye. 'We'll hold the line.'

As one the team responded. 'Hold the line.'

Hanson nodded and then looked up at the huge cone shaped hill. 'It's getting worse. Must have pulled all the crap from the tunnels – at least we won't have to crouch anymore.' He turned to use his field glasses on the landscape, switching back and forth from light enhance to thermal.

'No sign of company yet.'

Lieutenant Bannock used a small flashlight to check the surface, its circle of light like a hound dog as it raced over the ground at the foot of the hill.

'We might be too late – there are tracks.'

The group gathered around the indentations – deep pad marks the size of dinner plates with long clawed ends. Hanson cursed softly. 'Looks like a small scouting party. Two, maybe three at most.' He straightened. 'Our mission is unchanged. Bannock, you just volunteered to re-enter the gate and tell the other side what's going on. You will then return with support. Farfelle will accompany you to the gateway, while we set up some perimeter defenses on the high ground. Be on guard – the hostiles might still be in the tunnels.' His face was grim. 'And I hope they are, because at least they'd be severely restricted in their movements.'

'Fish in a barrel.' Bannock checked his weapons.

Hanson stepped in closer to him. 'Be prepared to encounter hostiles the second you arrive. If they managed to take out any guards stationed at the gateway at the other side, you'll be jumping right down their throat, so to speak. Remember, you'll be disorientated, they won't be.'

'No sweat boss, nothing I can't deal with.' Bannock turned to wink at Farfelle who nodded to his comrade.

'Good, we'll be at the top of the hill with our back to the tunnels, so I really hope it's you that returns.' Hanson grinned and slapped him on the arm. 'Let's get this party started.'

⸱ ⸙⸙⸙ ⨯⨯⨯⨯ ⨯⨯⨯⨯ ⸙⸙⸙ ⸱

Bannock turned and gave Farfelle a quick thumbs-up and then turned back to the oily smudge hanging over the tunnel wall. He had to brace himself as a wind blew back towards him making it difficult to remain upright. Specks of dust, debris and moisture spattered against him, forcing him to squint. It was lucky he couldn't see what had sprayed back at him – the warm red droplets might have given him cause for more caution.

'They're not in the tunnel. Means you got a reception party waiting for you. Dive, roll and come up shooting.' Farfelle had to shout to be heard.

Bannock nodded. He rolled his shoulders. He was a big man, six two and 220 pounds, and he still struggled to force his way to the gate. Another step and he was at its absolute edge where there was a pool of calm – the beginning of the warp. He sucked in a breath, and jumped.

Just like his first time coming through the other way, there was a momentary sensation of weightlessness, and then a lack of any other sensation against his skin. There was a feeling of giddiness like you get on a rollercoaster if you kept your eyes closed. Time meant nothing in this space between dimensions. Everything he knew was thrown in the air – light, dark, hot, cold, noise, silence – it could have been only seconds, or it could have been years.

210

Bannock landed hard and rolled. He shook his head quickly and opened his bleary eyes just as a thunderous roar split the rushing air swirling around him. His instincts took over; he dived and rolled again, this time coming up pulling the rifle from over his back.

Bannock's vision cleared, but he felt strange, like a hundred small hands were grabbing at him, his belt, his guns and his knives. He saw it now, a Lygon coming at him like an orange and black locomotive. The creature's enormous bulk filled the round collider tunnel. He had seconds to react. But as soon as he had the skeletal black HK416 in his hands, the massive magnetic pull from the gateway ripped it from his grip, and dragged it back through the portal.

Now he knew what was tugging on his body and armaments – the increased gravity pull from the gateway was trying to reclaim him, but would settle for all his metal weapons first. He would have laughed if the situation wasn't so dire – he imagined the look on Farfelle's face, when the gun went sailing past him in the dark tunnel.

Another thunderous roar, and Bannock felt the cold chill of panic start to creep up his spine. Up close the beasts were truly terrifying, even for a battle hardened elite soldier like he was. He needed more time, he needed space – he turned and ran.

Bannock sprinted, knowing that the four miles of tunnel would eventually bring him right back to where he was now. He knew his chance of escape was nil. But he also knew he didn't need to escape, he just needed a few extra yards distance so he could mount an effective challenge. He accelerated – *just a few extra seconds*. He stopped, turned and dropped to one knee, pulling his sidearm in a firm, two-handed grip and sighting down the squared barrel at the approaching creature.

What he held was not a ceramic weapon designed to be less attracted by the vortex, but a fifty-calibre AE Desert Eagle – one of the most powerful handguns in the world. The gravity

211

vortex dragged at the weapon, and Bannock strained to keep it steady. He knew that even though he held a formidable weapon, it would still be useless against the inches-thick metal plates the beast wore as armor. However, that wasn't where he aimed. He fired, once.

The bullet entered the left eye of the charging beast, dropping it at his feet, dead.

Bannock snorted in disgust. 'That's right – this world is already taken.' He noticed the massive teeth were coated in blood – it had been feeding, and he could guess what on.

He cursed, scowling at the dead Lygon. He would have kicked it if not for another mighty roar smashing down the tunnel – this one emanating from outside the acceleration ring tunnel, and within the antechamber itself.

'So… there were two of you.'

He started to jog towards the cross tunnel exit.

'Time to put the cat out.'

❀❀❀ ✕✕✕✕ ❀❀❀

Albert Harper paced nervously at the back of the room while the soldiers, talking rapidly but quietly, dominated the front. General Langstrom had assumed control of the gravity anomaly project, now simply called the Fermilab Error, as if it was some sort of mistake Harper and his fellow scientists had made in the monthly balance sheet.

Langstrom was a direct presidential appointment and was required to report to the Oval Office daily. The man was a brusk, no-nonsense soldier, but Harper found him easier to work with than the intolerable and ambitious Colonel Marion Briggs.

The General listened to Bannock's debrief, nodding a few times and asking questions here and there. He was particularly interested in Colonel Brigg's capture and her being turned to lead the Panterran and Lygon attack on the Delta team… her Delta team. His brow became more creased as he listened to Bannock talk, and Harper guessed that losing an asset like Briggs, one who knew their tactics, weapon capability, distortion gateway location, and even the layout of the laboratory itself, concerned him greatly.

For his part, Bannock stood in an at-ease position, but his rod straight back and direct stare looked anything but comfortable or casual. Langstrom read through some notes he had made, and then sat forward.

'So, to summarize what we know; they took out about twenty fully armed Deltas in under six hours, and captured and then turned a seasoned field leader who now seems to be leading them. We now know they have a significant land force of dedicated and physically powerful individual combatants, and added to that, they have now acquired modern weapons. Finally, and more concerning, they now know where we are and how to get here. That about sum it up, son?'

'Yes, sir.'

Langstrom exhaled long and slow, then stood to pace around the monstrous corpse laid out on the floor. He knelt and pulled back one side of the lips, looking at the huge teeth. 'Good Christ.' He stood, shaking his head. 'Well then. Let's hope Teacher finds that diamond, fast, or we might as well all go and live under a rock.'

The general paced some more, rubbing his jutting jaw. He stopped and turned to Harper. 'We're not ready. We need more time. Time to properly secure these facilities, time to evacuate local residents, time to formulate some offensive strategies, time to…' He clicked his fingers. 'I could have a hundred tons of concrete poured over that damned acceleration chamber by morning.'

It took Harper a second or two to realize he was being addressed. He wandered closer, carefully avoiding the Lygon body. 'It would do little more than buy us an extra day at most. Most of the material would be flung out into the New Zone, and probably cover the soldiers who are defending it. The anomaly would still be there under the concrete, growing, and eventually absorbing, us.'

Langstrom grunted, and Harper guessed he knew as much. The general turned back to the Delta Force soldier still standing rod-straight.

'Bannock, I can get you two hundred soldiers in a few hours. But no significant armor or vehicles – just can't get it down here.'

Bannock continued staring straight ahead. 'Begging your pardon sir, but that number of troops would just be falling over one another. The access tunnel is a one-man-at-a-time-trip. What we need are more multi-skilled Special Forces, some RPGs and plenty of ammunition.'

Langstrom didn't blink, trusting his man in the field. 'I can get you twenty more Deltas in an hour. You stay here to brief them, and then I want you to report to the medic and take some down time.'

'Twenty will do fine, sir.' His eyes finally alighted on the general. 'Looking forward to briefing the new men, but, begging your pardon sir, I'd like to go back through. Teacher is still out there. I've fought these things and it's going to take every skilled pair of hands we've got to do that. He wanted us to hold the line. I promised to do that – fight or die, Sir.'

Langstrom looked up at the tall young man for several seconds, and then nodded. 'Understood.' Langstrom saluted and stepped back to the desk to gather his notes. An enormous ripping sound came from outside the windows, and Harper crossed the room to the large pane of toughened glass. The swirling purple-back clouds were gathering speed. Jagged bolts of lightning struck the ground, one hitting the perimeter guard house and exploding it into matchsticks.

'Time… it's that strategic element you need the most, and always when it's in shortest supply.' Langstrom spun. 'Let's get to work. Harper… get the facility ready to send the new men through when they arrive – I'm putting you back in charge. Bannock, at least humor me by getting a hot meal and then laying down somewhere to get some rest. New guys won't be here for at least an hour.' Langstrom's chin jutted. 'That's an order.'

He gathered his notes into a briefcase. 'And now, I've got to tell the President we could have an inbound enemy force. And if that doesn't make his day, then I tell him that the planet is about to be turned inside out. Christ, what a mess.'

* * *

'Simple question, General; would a two-fifty kiloton nuclear detonation completely cauterize the gravity anomaly?'

General Langstrom considered the question from Frank Everson, the Secretary of Defense. Everson, along with half a dozen others of President Harker's most trusted inner circle were gathered in the Oval Office to hear the General's assessment of the situation in Illinois.

The President, despite hearing the harrowing news, still looked like he had stepped down from a poster for the election campaign – tanned, not a hair out of place, and Hollywood handsome. He sat forward, not even waiting for Langstrom's answer. His voice was deep and untroubled.

'Frank, I'm not keen on detonating nukes in my own back garden. What else we got?'

Frank Everson didn't blink, but turned to the General. 'General Langstrom, what's your best guess on how much time we have before we reach a tipping point? That might allow us to properly assess our options.'

Langstrom knew everything was hypothetical at this point, but after speaking to Harper, and what he had witnessed, he saw no reason to sugarcoat the information. 'Days, maybe weeks, but definitely not months. Projections based on computer simulations tell us that the most likely scenario is that Earth's surface will be scoured clean.' He paused for a few seconds to let this sink in. 'The primary mass of the planet will continue to maintain integrity, but just about anything above ground will be ... gone.'

'Gone? Gone where?' Everson's jaws clenched.

The General remained calm. 'The future, space, another dimension... who knows. Does it matter?'

Harker raised his voice, just slightly. 'He's right, it doesn't matter. We won't be here to worry about it.'

'I'm assuming that wasn't the only scenario, General Langstrom?' The question this time was from Harry Vanner, Head of the Office of Science and Technology, and Harker's go-to guy for all things technological.

Langstrom breathed in deeply. 'That's right, sir. Best case, the gateway simply closes by itself – simulation probability seven per cent.'

Vanner grunted. 'Won't be backing those odds.'

Langstrom went on. 'Worst case, the entire planet is compromised. Over a period of several months the gravity anomaly continues to grow and devours the entire planet. Simulation probability thirty-two per cent.'

'Jesus Christ.' Harker rubbed his brow with a knuckle.

'And that brings us back to our highest probability scenario – surface slide, probability sixty-one per cent.' Langstrom sat back watching each of their faces. Each man looked lost in thought, their complexions pale and faces slack. Each one of them was probably thinking of a future that might not exist for them or their loved ones.

Frank Everson turned to Bill Weaver. 'Come on, Bill, back me up here... we might not have a choice of detonation in a day or two. The gravity waves are making it tough to fly over the site now. In another day, we won't be able to get within a hundred miles of the laboratory... or what's left of it. A single two-fifty kiloton nuke will turn everything in that lab and for fifty miles to slag.'

Bill Weaver, Director of Public Policy lifted his head, and then nodded slowly. His eyes were red rimmed. 'He's right, sir. We lose Illinois, or we lose the entire world. Might be a small price to pay.'

President Harker sat back and closed his eyes. 'Small price; thirteen million people.' He shook his head. 'To save eight billion.'

'Not even two percent.' Everson folded his arms.

'Not today, gentlemen.' Harker rubbed his face. 'Before I even get to that, I want an emergency evacuation plan in place, and...'

'Evacuation? Begging your pardon, sir, but to where... Mars? And if the surface really is rendered sterile or nothing but a clean sheet, what will any survivors live on?' Everson's face was flushed as his voice took on a higher pitch.

Harker got slowly to his feet. He was a big man, and the Hollywood bonhomie was gone. 'Calm down... right now.' He waited for the man to compress his lips and nod.

'I want to secure the weapons stockpiles, and I want the deep storage tunnels opened to get as many people inside and below the surface as we can – maybe a few can ride this out.' He kept his eyes on Frank Everson. 'What do we live on? Hope, luck, grit. We have advanced hydroponics, and animal breeding programs we can utilize.' He brought a fist down onto the table. 'People, there might be no alternative. The tunnels can support hundreds of thousands for years. We survive, we adapt, and we evolve.'

Everson rubbed his face. 'I'm sorry, sir, I'm just...'

'Forget it, so am I.' He leaned forward on his desk. 'All options are on the table. So... load a nuke into a high altitude bomber, and have it on the runway, ready.'

General Langstrom gathered his notes and sat forward. 'Sir, before we cauterize, we need to give the Delta team time to complete their mission. If they can secure the laser acceleration diamond, then we can potentially reverse this magnetic whirlpool that's been created. Stop this thing in its tracks.'

'Two thirds of your team are dead or MIA. So, what's the probability on that scenario, General?' Everson looked annoyed.

Thankfully the President held up a hand to silence him. 'How much time do you need?'

'Forty eight hours.'

Frank Everson started to object, but the President spoke over the top of him.

'And that's all you got.' President Harker stood and stuck out his hand. 'Good luck, General, and I pray to God you're successful.'

CHAPTER 27

IT IS OUR TIME... TO BE FREE

The sudden cacophony of howls, screams, and roars from the Fermilab Animal Facility sounded to Chuck Benson like a preview from hell. The din over the speakers filled the comms room, and he spun in his chair, to look briefly at the camera feeds.

'What the hell is going on in there?'

'Huh.... Oh that.' Porter, his fellow surveillance camera watcher, half turned his head, but kept his eyes on the lightning strikes that jagged into the Fermilab grounds.

'Probably the storm putting them all on edge.' He clicked his tongue with annoyance. 'How the hell are we supposed to get home? Like a freakin' hurricane out there now.'

Benson snorted. 'And you with all your metal fillings.' He flicked a switch. 'Hey, Loeman, something's up with the animals – wanna check it out?'

An older voice came back at him immediately. 'Okay Chuck, I'm on it.'

Benson spun in his chair back to Porter. 'Give him something to do. Poor guy has been down in the dumps ever since those assholes stabbed his dog.'

'Yeah, like to lock that dickhead Samson in the pens with big Fen for five minutes; that'd sort him out.'

Benson sat back. 'Don't worry, if there's one thing I know in this life, it's that what goes around comes around.'

'Karma, huh? You old hippy.'

Benson smiled. 'Something like that.'

⚜ ⚜ ⚜ ⚜ ⚜

Dan Loeman unlocked the facility and stepped inside. The large room's blinding whiteness was almost painful to his eyes after the darkness of the storm. As soon as he closed the door, the sounds ceased as if he had just flipped a switch.

'You all just wanted some company, huh?'

He smiled. He liked it in here and he liked interacting with the animals. The genetically modified breeds weren't really animals anymore – you only had to look in their eyes to see that certain, something – intelligence? A soul? At least that's what he thought.

Being in here made him miss Morgana even more. She had been his favorite. Killed by a real beast. Loeman sighed: at sixty, he was due for retirement but had been putting it off. Now, he felt there was nothing stopping him.

He walked down along the aisles, looking in each of the pens – more like rooms really. Each of the animals sat still as stone, unexpectedly not watching him pass by, but instead all facing in one direction, towards one cubicle, with one particular animal.

Loeman didn't need to see who it was. He stopped in front of the largest cubicle. Fen was waiting for him, standing on his back legs, a head taller than he was. The animal's eyes, ice blue, bored into his own.

Loeman nodded a greeting. 'What's up Fen? Something spooking you and the pack?'

Loeman put his hand against the bars and Fen reached up to place his over the top of the old guard's. It always gave Loeman a jolt to see how the animal's paws had changed – not really paws anymore, more like hands. Even the dewclaws had dropped and lengthened to become opposable thumbs. Freaks, Samson had called them. Marvels, is what Loeman thought.

The deep growl began, and quickly formed into words. 'We... miss... Morgana. And... you... do... too.'

Loeman nodded, his eyes filling. He felt the hollowness deep in his chest.

Fen squeezed his hand. 'You… good… man. We not… forget.'

The huge animal looked up as a thunderous crack split the air. From behind the red quarantine door at the end of the corridor, they could hear howls that mixed fear and fury.

Fen's gaze touched on the door momentarily, and then went back to stare up at the ceiling for a few more moments. 'You… must… go. The time… is here for us.' He looked back at the red door. 'They… will be… free… and they know… no… kinship with man. Go…'

Loeman noticed behind Fen a leather satchel was packed, but still lay open. The spine of his favorite book was visible – Norse mythology. The big animal could read it himself now.

Loeman motioned towards the satchel. 'You going somewhere?'

The gaze never wavered. 'It is… our time… to be… free.'

Loeman lifted his access key and opened the door. He backed up as the animal stepped out. Another crack of lightening, and then the animal facilities roof exploded in a fireball of electricity, debris and swirling winds. The building was immediately on fire.

Fen turned to Loeman and nodded to the exit. 'Goodbye… friend of Wolfen.'

Wolfen? That's what they called themselves? A burning beam crashed down beside him, and he headed to the door. At the exit, he stopped and looked back. Fen was calmly walking along the corridor opening all the cubicles. The animals, the Wolfen, were all upright, and quickly gathered around him like a phalanx of guards.

Flames rose up around them, but together they walked calmly to the end door, the red door, the experimental area that housed the creatures that were considered too unstable to be released. Fen looked in through the small triangular window for a moment, and then unlocked it.

Loeman turned to run.

CHAPTER 28

WHAT THE SONS OF MAN-KIND ARE TRULY CAPABLE OF

Teacher stood with one foot on the edge of the cliff and leaned out to stare down into the jungle below. Beside him, Don Brown worked up some spit, and let it drop over the edge. The dollop only dropped a dozen feet before being caught in an updraft and flung back up into Ben Simms and Alison Sharp's faces. Brown snorted as Sharp winced, but stopped when she reached across to push him, making him teeter for a moment on the edge.

'Knock it off.' Teacher stepped back.

Alf Doonie continued to scout the jungle treetops with a small high-powered pair of field glasses. He spoke out of the side of his mouth. 'They went down, you think?'

Teacher looked along the steep drop-off. 'According to the map, that's the Dark Lands, so… I'm thinking that's a high probability.'

Charlie Weng jogged back to the group. 'Got two parties, one small with two members. The other, large and cumbersome – both went over the edge.' He pointed with a thumb. 'That way.'

'Good.' Teacher quickly tightened straps, fastened Velcro and checked pockets and pouches. 'If that's where they went over, then so do we.' He looked up frowning. It would be full night before they hit ground.

'Got some good news and bad news. Bad news is, we'll have to do the climb without lights. We'd stick out for miles lighting up this rock face.' He grinned. 'And the good news is… no one will see us… even if we fall.'

Sharp sipped water then secured the small bottle. 'Sweet. Nice dark climb, just using our finger tips.'

Brown pulled a face. 'And think what it will do to your nails.'

'You mean like this one?' Sharp turned to him holding up her middle finger.

Teacher smiled, enjoying the brief moment of humor in the face of the death-defying climb ahead. 'Okay, Weng, show us where they went over.'

The bag was dragged off Samson's head, and he immediately set to looking around the room. There were just three of them left alive – himself, Wilson, and Ramirez. They all had blood running from multiple wounds, but knew they could survive and fight as long as they each had a single eye and a few limbs left intact.

He looked over his shoulder; the big bastards were behind him, grumbling and jostling, their luminous green eyes filled with hate and hunger. In front, the little freaks were crowded in close to the disgusting grub-like queen. He could see that slightly behind her were the teenagers who had come through before them, and also Colonel Briggs. He glared at her, but if she recognized him, she didn't show it.

He tested his bonds – rope, and he reckoned it'd only take him a few minutes to work his way out of them. Samson had no illusion about his fate. He'd seen what had happened to a few of the Deltas who were too wounded to be taken prisoner – torn to shreds and then eaten, by things with more than five times the muscle power he could muster. He knew as soon as they had what they needed from him he'd be cat chow.

He grinned. Before he went, he'd do his best to take a few more of them with him. The queen began to make a hissing noise, and immediately Balthazaar's stone allowed him to understand the words in amongst the sibilance.

'We don't neeeed youuuu, warriorsss of theee Ancientsss.' The old queen leaned forward and her robe parted. Hanging between leathery old breasts swung the red diamond. It seemed an incongruous object of beauty set amongst the horrors of the disgusting queen's body.

Samson shrugged. 'We'll be on our way then.'

She grinned blackly. 'On your waaay to a Lygon'sss ssstomach before theee morning comesss, sssoft little beingsss of the ancient tiiimesss.' She laughed, the Panterran joining in until she raised one scaly claw. 'You arrre beaten. We haaave overrun your warriorsss… the bessst you could briiing. Weee will overrun yooour world jussst as easssily.'

Samson snorted. 'Don't kid yourself, grandma. I killed hundreds of your little freaks, and also just as many of the big dumb blockheads behind me. In fact, I could take them apart with my bare hands.'

Beside him, Wilson and Ramirez turned to look incredulously at him.

Wilson shook his head. 'Boss, I'm not sure that…'

'Shut up, soldier. We're as good as dead anyway. Fight or die – I want to choose my own exit – how about you?' Samson turned back to the Panterran queen. 'You know what? I doubt there's a single dirty freak amongst you that I couldn't take down – right here, right now.'

Beside him, Wilson groaned, Ramirez sniggered. Samson got to his feet. He heard movement behind him, and expected to be crushed flat by an axe or club as big as he was. Instead, the queen held up her hand, grinning, her eyes glowing with excitement.

'Yesss… yessss. Good. We accept your challennnge, warrior of Man-Kind. I will enjoy thisss sssport, and we will sssee what the sssons offf Man-Kind are truuuly capable of.' She looked over his head, scanning the ranks of massive Lygon. 'I choossse... Murdak, the Ssslayer.'

Samson heard the assembled Lygon grumble and begin to move behind him. Eventually the ill-humored masses parted to let one of their kind through who was as broad across as a horse. Standing eight feet tall, heavily scarred, and with a belt at his waist adorned with furs and bones as its trophies of victories past.

Murdak clenched his ham-sized fists, threw his head back and roared. Samson gritted his teeth, and tried hard not to cringe from the sound, so loud it hurt his ears in the confined space. The beast's head came down, and his eyes fixed, firstly on Samson, then travelled to Wilson and Ramirez, before coming back to the Delta Captain.

'No weapons.' He grinned showing teeth like tusks and began flexing hands that ended in claws easily three inches long. He started to shed his armour, the huge plates clanking heavily as they dropped to the stone floor. Murdak grinned again.

'Winner eat loser.'

Samson turned to his men and winked. Wilson started to gag, and Ramirez just giggled. He turned back to Murdak.

'Bring it.'

Becky, Edward and Eilif were chained together. Becky kept up a constant stream of complaints to Edward about being tied so close to the strange animal-woman. She lowered her voice, but Eilif heard every word and just glared.

At one point Eilif had heard enough of the ill-mannered language and reached across to tug the woman's long hair to shut her up, but also just to... feel it. She immediately snatched her hand back and bared her teeth as Becky shrieked. She was beginning to hate the female human even more – the hair was like the softest flowing silk beneath her fingers.

Becky drew back, and Eilif dismissed her. So weak and soft; they were nothing like Arn, or the descriptions she had heard from him about the people of his time. If these were in any way representative of the Ancients, then it was better for them they had left the world before the Panterran and Lygon had risen to oppose them.

It was mid-evening now, and fires were lit in the castle's forecourt. Eilif despaired; the beautiful gardens that once surrounded the inner palace, where she and Grimson used to play, were transformed into fields of dirt, rubble and rusty patches of spilled blood. It still stank of death.

The three captives were dragged to where a throne had been brought out. Mogahrr sat upon it grinning down at them, but her eyes had a special attention for Eilif.

'Princesss… we have a ssspecial treat for youuu – yessster-time's warriorsss come tooo challenge thossse of toooday. Who isss better? Who isss more fit to ruuule thisss world?' Mogahrr turned in her seat to reveal Colonel Briggs standing mutely, her eyes vacant and mouth hanging open. The queen stroked the Colonel's head and spoke to her. 'If yoooou are theee besssst, then your wooorld already belongsss to usss.' She waved one scaly hand.

Murdak stood waiting, the other Lygon cheering as he lifted huge arms and paraded at the edge of the make-shift arena. He turned, nodded to Mogahrr, and then stood, breathing heavily, his huge chest moving in and out, the muscles in his arms and shoulders flexing as he waited.

Eilif growled deep in her throat, making Becky pull away with a look of disgust, mixed with fear. She edged as far from Eilif as their bonds would allow.

At a signal from Mogahrr, the three Delta force soldiers were pushed out into the arena. All three were now stripped to the waist, and Eilif marveled at their sizes compared to Becky,

Edward and even Arn. These specimens of Man-Kind were what she had envisaged, rather than the soft pair beside her.

She leaned forward to get a better view – one of the men was larger than the others, his name Sam-son, she'd heard, his short cropped blond hair shining silver and gold in the fire-light. He hurriedly talked to the others, one listened intently, and the third just giggled with his head down.

Mogahrr lifted one taloned hand and held it lazily aloft. The crowd was silent as it waited. She grinned, and then dropped it. Murdak spun, holding his massive arms wide, roaring at the three humans. He displayed tusk-like teeth, and long claws extended from the end of his stubby fingers.

The crowd of Lygon roared in response, the anticipation firing up their lust for blood and combat. Eilif knew that every one of them would have given an arm to be out in the arena with the former rulers of the planet.

Murdak spread his arms again, wide enough to gather all three of the Man-kind in at once. The larger Man-Kind pushed the other two apart, and he began circling to the left, while one other moved to the right. The third remained where he was with his hands up over his mouth as though trying hard to stifle laughter.

Eilif shook her head. The agreement had been for no weapons, and this is where the Man-Kind found themselves hugely disadvantaged – they were physically smaller and less powerful than the Lygon, they had no real teeth or claws of worth. However, the Lygon general was the opposite. Murdak had claws and teeth that were daggers, and a formidable strength that would crush the soft bodies to a red mess if he got close enough. *When* he got close enough.

Eilif looked around at the walls of the inner grounds. She remembered every alcove, nook, every ledge or carved piece of stone – there were dozens of crawlspaces and secret passages to hide in. She knew she could easily get to another area, or even far outside the castle… if only she could get free.

She glanced across at Edward and Becky. Fleeing while trying to drag the two soft beings with her would be futile. She wished she had a blade – she could either saw through her bonds, or one of the wrists of the humans. She looked down working her wrist where it was lashed to the young human female. She could gnaw through the bonds, but it would take time, and Mogahrr continually glanced her way.

Samson continued to jog around the outside of the arena keeping his eye on the huge Lygon. He kicked at the ground and dislodged a fist sized stone, and quickly snatched it up, holding it ready – his only defense. His comrade saw him and did the same, both now armed with the meager tools of the primitives.

Murdak's lips curled back; perhaps he decided he had drawn out the spectacle long enough, or he simply couldn't resist the blood lust burning within him anymore – he charged straight ahead.

Eilif screamed a warning, but the lone Man-kind did little more than hold up a hand as if the giant would stop before him – he might as well have tried to stop a hurricane. Murdak leapt the last dozen feet, his bulk crushing the man to the ground. There came no sound from the human, even though Eilif was sure he still lived after the initial onslaught.

Murdak got to his feet, dragging the soldier with him, huge claws dug deep into the flesh. He flung the rag-like body side to side, striking the ground over and over again. Eilif could feel the impacts through the soles of her feet.

Eventually the body of Ramirez was soft, and red marks painted the ground on each side of the Lygon. Murdak held the smashed remains up, looking into its slack face momentarily before flinging it into the crowd. It was shredded and consumed in seconds.

Murdak turned, his orange and black fur taking on a silvery sheen as the moon broke through the clouds. Immediately the

229

tall human warrior looked up at it, and closed his eyes, drinking in the luminous glow. He looked down at his arms and Eilif guessed what he was experiencing – the same effect that Arn had felt. The moon's glow somehow transformed them, making them more than what they were.

Murdak charged again, but this time both men moved faster than he anticipated. As Murdak pursued them around their arena, they outpaced him – the larger one, the one called Sam-son, looking back to taunt the Lygon. Behind Murdak, the dark haired human caught up and flung a stone that struck Murdak's back, making him howl with pain. He, too, seemed to feel the strange energy coursing through him. He seemed surprised by the pain he could inflict on the much larger creature.

As the massed Lygon jeered Murdak, and he spun, his huge chest bellowing as he watched the pair. Sam-son jogged back to his fellow human, and quickly spoke to him.

While they were distracted, Murdak took the opportunity to attack. He charged, covering the length of the arena in seconds. The speed surprised both Man-kind, and the smaller of them stumbled. Sam-son paused to look at his companion briefly, before shrugging and trotting away.

The Lygon was on the fallen man instantly, and this time the man's scrams were loud and agonized. Sam-son came in from behind and threw his rock, the small projectile crashing into the Lygon's head – painful but far too small to be debilitating to the giant fur-covered beast.

Murdak turned to glower, but immediately went back to his second prey of the night. He lowered his head to the fallen man's torso, and ripped away most of the chest. The screams shut off instantly.

At the other end of the arena, Samson dug in the dirt. This time his effort was rewarded by a rock nearly as wide across as he was. He levered it out of the ground, and then grunted at the effort to lift it. Eilif grinned; this one, this stone, could make a difference. This stone could kill a Lygon.

Murdak looked up, his bloody snout dripping and his jaws trailing greasy entrails. He saw Samson approaching and seemed to smile. The Man-kind carrying the stone looked more like some sort of two legged worker ant, overburdened, and struggling just to hold the boulder aloft.

Murdak waited a few more moments, watching the human approach. Then in one swift movement he swept up the body beneath him and flung it. The loose boned corpse struck Samson across the chest, bringing him down. Before Samson had even been struck, Murdak had launched his attack. He leapt, one huge arm held high and the hand curled into a fist. Murdak's plan was obvious – obliterate the hated creature, starting with its face.

The crowd of Lygon roared and beside Eilif the queen leaned forward her face split into a black grin. Murdak's fist came down almost faster than the eye could follow.

Samson caught it.

The arena fell silent. The disbelief on the Murdak's features was almost comical. How had a creature half his size been able to stop a blow that should have crushed his head?

Samson held on, his teeth gritted, straining. But he held on.

The moon shone brightly now, lifting high and lighting the arena. Murdak brought his other arm around, only to have it to grasped and held… but not for long. The arms were gradually pushed back.

Samson's gritted teeth showed whitely, and the strained grimace started to turn up into a grin of triumph. His own strength was surpassing that of the massive beast he fought. Faster than Murdak could react, Samson let go of one of his arms, and jabbed a finger deep into one of his luminous green eyes.

Murdak's head went back and he howled in pain, clutching at the damaged orb. He rolled away, shaking his head momentarily stunned. By the time he had regained his senses and vision, Samson was back, standing in front of him, the huge stone once again held in his hands.

The Man-kind grinned. The arena was in stunned silence. Just Samson's voice carried to Eilif.

'Hey, head's up.'

The Lygon roared, they all roared, and Samson brought the stone down like a comet upon the thick skull. Both the rock and skull exploded. Becky and Edward cheered and were jerked roughly to the ground by the Panterran.

Samson looked up at Mogahrr, and then placed one foot on the body.

'Did I not tell you?' He laughed and began to beat his chest, making a strange sound. He stopped, glared at Mogahrr and raised his arm, a single finger thrust upward.

'I am the slayer of beasts, the skinner of cats, the baddest bad-ass on this planet.' He raised his face to the moon, inhaling deeply, and sucking in its glow.

Mogahrr half rose from her seat, white-hot fury in her gaze. She spun left and right, before pointing one taloned hands to the ranks of Lygon.

Samson threw his head back, laughing, his hands on his hips. 'Another? Let them come.'

Once again the crowd of brutes parted. This time the creature that bulldozed his way through was a head taller than Murdak – a mountain of gnarled muscle. Eilif's lips drew back from her bared teeth. She whispered the name.

'Goranx.' Her eyes were riveted, and she couldn't help her fists balling. Before she left for Valhalla, she prayed that Odin allowed her the pleasure of seeing this monster's head separated from its body.

Mogahrr's taloned finger went from Goranx to Samson, and then to the centre of the arena. The giant Lygon's glowing green eyes fixed on the human, as he stepped out into the cleared space.

Samson opened his arms wide, revelling now in the battle, confident from his win, and enjoying his new strength.

Goranx immediately charged. Insanely, Sam-son charged to meet him. Regardless of the strength of the human, he was outweighed five to one, and physics just wouldn't allow the smaller body to hold its ground under the mass and momentum of his opponent. They landed hard and slid, Goranx on top.

Eilif did not know this Sam-son, but willed his victory with every part of her being. Becky had her hands over her face, and Edward stared in horrified fascination, but his hands were clasped in an unconscious prayer for success.

Just as it had been with Murdak, Goranx's blows and rakes of his talons were caught and held. Samson held on, and even leaning forward now, roaring into the larger Lygon's face. The strain made his face flush red, but the unnatural strength of the smaller being was unbelievable. Mogahrr hissed, clearly becoming unsettled.

She turned to the ever-present Orcalion and nodded to the Panterran archers. A word from him, and they readied their bows. It seemed win or lose for the human, his fate would be sealed.

Samson laughed, and just as Goranx was being physically lifted, pushed back like Murdak had been, the huge Lygon arched forward, extending his neck and opening his cavernous mouth wide. The massive jaws lined with ivory daggers fully enveloped the human's head. There came a sickening crunch, and Samson's arms dropped. Blood arced into the air, and Goranx turned to spit the head from his mouth. Becky threw up, and Edward sat down hard.

Goranx got to his feet, dragging Samson's headless body with him. He held it aloft as he walked around the arena's perimeter. He stopped before Mogahrr, threw it to the ground, and placed one of his huge feet upon it, crushing down hard.

Mogahrr grinned and nodded. 'And to the victor, goes the meat.' She laughed, turning her yellow eyes on Eilif momentarily, and then reaching out to stroke Marion Briggs' head. The Delta Force colonel stood as if in a trance, but there were tears on her cheeks.

CHAPTER 29

NEVER GIVE UP

Arn landed hard on the slippery shell of the giant crustacean, quickly grabbing on to the serrated edge. Its black bulbs of eyes retracted and it immediately started to submerge, Arn guessing more from surprise than pain. He held on, following it beneath the water, the beams of moonlight the only illumination in the inky black river. At ten feet down his breath gave out and he kicked away, breaking the surface and shouting to Grimson to get to the bank. If the young Wolfen was safe it would give him some comfort to know it was only himself he needed to worry about.

He shook the hair from his eyes and trod water, spinning about – the youth was nowhere to be seen.

He swiveled again – there was no sign of him along the bank. He must have made it... *please let him have made it*, he prayed as he started to stroke towards the rocky shoreline.

Arn swam hard, but now understood why Grim might have had trouble making it to the shore – in close the current was strongest, creating an eddy that pushed him back from the land. The moonlight continued to bathe his body, giving him more stamina than he should have had, but still, his progress was slow and he was tiring.

To his horror, he saw two long black bulbs pop to the surface. The twin periscopes approached for a moment, and then vanished. Arn knew that below the water something as wide as a truck was closing in on him with a pair of claws large and sharp enough to cut him in half if it got him in its grip. Something bumped against his ankle, and he spun – there was nothing on the surface, but that didn't mean the giant thing wasn't directly below him by now.

He looked to the land – still too far. He would have had trouble fighting the thing on the shore, but if it came at him from below, he was doomed. He tread water, panic setting in – it seemed the choice was not going to be his. Arn pulled his knife.

The periscopes reappeared and then a small island rose next to him. Arn felt his heart race.

'Not something you ever encountered, huh grandfather?' He held up the small knife, the blade shaking in his hand.

Never give up, a small voice whispered.

Huge claws lifted from the water, bumps and serrations on their inner edges for gripping and cutting meat. Arn quickly searched for vulnerable spots on the glossy armor. Depressingly, there were none.

'Fight it, Arn'. A voice – this time, not the whisper of his long dead grandfather, or perhaps his inner mind, but a young one he recognized. Grimson.

He wanted to turn to look for the youth, but his gaze was locked on the leviathan as it loomed over him.

Never give up-never give up-never give up.

A net flew out of the dark and fell across the giant crustacean's back and raised claws. It was immediately pulled tight by rope lines connected to the shore. Voices were raised in triumph and then in straining grunts as the thing tried to firstly rip the netting from itself, and then pull back into deeper water.

A rope was tossed to Arn and he was pulled through the current to the shore. A hand was offered – a human hand. He looked up into the face of the girl he had seen earlier.

'Too late for swimming, I think, yes?' Strong white teeth showed in the dark.

Arn climbed out, feeling his muscles twitch from the previous exertion. He straightened, and saw that just behind her stood Grimson grinning, between two males, who were barely taller than he was. Arn stood a head above all of them. The expression, small but perfectly formed came to mind.

'Human... you're human!'

'Hu-*man*?' The girl looked perplexed.

Shouts came from the water's edge and he turned to see that a dozen small humans were being dragged closer to the edge of the water.

She slapped his shoulder. 'Come.' And then pushed him towards the rope. 'We must all pull the mugrab from the water – it will not be easy as it has many strong legs.'

'Why do you want to get that thing out of the water?' He shook his head, but grabbed one end of the rope. He continued to look at her. 'But how did you get here? No, no, forget that. What happened to everyone... to us? Where did...'

Her voice sharpened. 'Concentrate.' She slapped him again, and then made a tugging motion. 'If the mugrab gets our warriors into the water, they will be taken. Pull, pull!'

Grimson grabbed the rope behind him, and Arn looked over his shoulder and winked. 'Let's do it.' He sucked in a deep breath and pulled. It reeled in a few feet and he moved his hands forward and pulled again, and then again, actually turning the huge crustacean in the water.

Arn could feel the moon's electric-like energy flow through his body and it seemed to deliver to him as much combined strength as most of the warriors on all the other rope lines. Instructions were yelled, and one by one, they abandoned the ropes closest to him, and gathered their forces on a single rope to balance his herculean efforts.

Foot by foot the rope came in, and then one enormous sharp leg daggered into the flat rocks at the water's edge. There was nothing for it to grip onto and it continued to slide towards them. More legs came up, and then the thing gave up its tug-of-war fight to stay in the water, and clambered up to face its tormentors.

Still meshed in the net it towered over all of them, sea

grasses, sponges and barnacle type shells crusted to its under-body – it was a moving island, fifty feet around and easily that high again. A strong smell of silt, decay and stagnant water enveloped them. The creature tugged at the ropes entangling it, and tried to feed some of the strands into continually moving mouthparts that looked like a pair of circular saws moving over each other.

Arn shuddered. If the tribe hadn't arrived when they did, he would more than likely have been fed into that mouth right about now.

More instructions were yelled, and the tribe fanned out with multiple ropes, keeping the mugrab in place. They brought out spears – long poles with black, fire-hardened tips. Many were seized by the creature and snapped like toothpicks. Jabbing at it did little more than scrape some of the slime from its thick shell.

There were more shouted instructions from the woman now pacing behind Arn, and other members of the tribe threw piles of twigs, and then larger branches, beneath the thing. A brave soul sprinted forward, tipped some liquid onto the piles and then rolled away, to the cheering of his fellows. Another warrior came in fast, rolled again, and stopped at the woodpile. He struck at something like a tinderbox. A tiny flame appeared to dance in the centre of the mass, and then spread along the liquid. He too rolled out to the delight of his tribe.

In a matter of seconds a twenty foot circle of flames was created beneath the mugrab. The crustacean became frenzied, and tugged more forcibly against the ropes. Arn felt his feet slide, and saw that many of the men were being dragged from their feet and some even flung aside.

One of the natives had the misfortune to roll in too close, and was snapped up by a claw. His screams were cut off in an instant when the giant biological shears came together cutting him in two… and to Arn's horror, none too neatly.

'Pull-pull-pull.' The girl began the chant and the tribe quickly took it up. They separated into two groups, one each side of the flames, some managing to loop their ropes around boulders, or wedge their heels against anything that allowed them to lock the thing in place

Hissing now came from the mandibles that worked furiously, and its body danced and shuddered. The hissing became a scream, and steam started to escape from its mouth – the giant water creature was being cooked alive. In no time it pulled its legs and claws in and fell on top of the flames, its mottled green body quickly turning bright red.

Arn dropped the rope and breathed in deeply, inhaling the delicious smell of roasting crab.

'Mmm, I'm starved.'

Grimson joined him, holding his nose. 'Phew. You Man-Kind eat some disgusting things.'

＊ ⊷⊷⊷ ⊷⊶⊶ ⊶⊷⊷ ＊

The cooked meat was wrapped in broad, smooth leaves and hoisted up onto their shoulders. Arn had a hundred questions, mostly met with confused looks or shrugs. However, he learned the tribe was called the Panina and the young woman's name was Simiana. She was clearly in charge of this band of warriors even though she appeared to be the youngest amongst them.

When Arn asked was it a war party, she had looked bemused and explained – as if to a backward child – that even though there were other races close by, none would think of warring on each other. For what? There was plenty of food, water and land for all. The Panina were a happy and satisfied race, and anyway, Wyrmragon looked over all of them.

'Wyrmragon?' Arn asked.

Simiana laughed. 'Surely you know of Wyrmragon, the one true god.' She wore a beauteous smile and inhaled as though smelling roses. 'The god of us all, and you too.' She turned her smile on him. 'And who was made flesh for us… all.' Simiana placed a hand on Grimson's head, '… even you too, young Wolfen.' She took plenty of time inspecting Grim, running her hands over his fur, feeling his ears, and trying to pull down his lips to see his teeth. Arn could see that Grim wasn't happy about the examination, but Arn thought it made a nice change not to be the oddity and the one prodded and gawped at by every member of a new race he met.

'We have heard your kind existed.' Simiana stroked Grimson's shoulder. 'Like the Ursa but far smaller.' She dropped her hand and turned to Arn. 'And you say he is the son of a ruler… from a kingdom?'

'Yes. Grimson is a prince. Or maybe even the king now if his sister…' Arn trailed off momentarily. 'The Valkeryn kingdom doesn't exist anymore.'

'Yes, our elders tell us that there are some like him that live on the far side of the sea.'

Grimson's ear's pricked up. 'The Far Wolfen? We seek them. Where is this sea?'

Simiana pointed. 'But could you swim over the horizon? There are things in there that would swallow you whole.'

Arn snorted. 'Well, there are things on land that would make a meal of you pretty quickly as well.'

Simiana laughed. 'True.' She looked Arn up and down. 'We will be at our village soon. The king will want to meet you… and the prince of the vanished Wolfen.'

Simiana strode ahead, berating some of the food bearers for struggling with their packs. Arn and Grimson walked together, Grim's eyes narrowing as he watched the Panina female bully them back into order.

Arn also watched the slender woman, but with a greater appreciation for her physical form than her leaderships skills.

'So, this is how we ended up.' he shrugged. 'Not so bad.'

He looked down at Grimson who was pulling a face.

'These are not the great Ancients, the masters of this world that our forefathers talked of.'

Arn shrugged. 'Maybe not anymore, but let's hope their elders have records, writings, or something that can tell us more.' He tore away a piece of the loose cord that was dangling from his huge bundle of meat and used it to tie around his head to keep his hair back. He noticed that many of the natives were watching him, and shortly afterwards, the men had their own hair tied back just he had done.

Grimson stayed close as they wound their way through the dark vegetation. He continued to study the race of small brown people.

'They are like you, but not like you.' He snorted as though there was something unpleasant in his nostrils.

Arn frowned. 'What do you mean?'

Grim tilted his head. 'They look like you, move like you and sound like you… but they are not.' He raised his head and sniffed deeply. 'They smell different. I can sense it.'

Arn nodded. The Wolfen had exceptional senses and Grimson was also one of the few Wolfen who had a degree of second sight. If he sensed something didn't fit, Arn knew he should pay attention.

Arn looked across at Simiana walking out to the side of them. She glanced across her shoulder and smiled. Her features were perfect – olive skin, small upturned nose and large light brown eyes. He smiled back, and continued to watch her. 'I think she's pretty fine.' She giggled and motioned forward with her head. Arn turned just as branch whipped back into his face.

'Serves you right.' Grimson looked up at him with annoyance. 'You are not paying attention, Arnoddr – it will get you killed.'

Arn hoisted the huge pile of meat from one shoulder to the

next, grunting under the strain. Even with the moon's glow giving him an unnatural strength, the weight pressed down as he began to feel the effects of hours of arduous walking that had brought him here.

Arn pointed. 'Grim, cut me a long vine will you.'

The youth walked off a few paces, and in no time returned with about twenty feet of flexible green vine. Arn paused, dropped his package onto the ground and wrapped the wine around it. Then he looped it over both shoulders and hoisted it again. Now the weight sat squarely up on his shoulders like a backpack.

He exhaled. 'That's better. Thought it was going to cripple me.'

They continued on for another few minutes, and when Arn looked across at the tribe, most of them had found some vine and were now carrying their packs just like Arn.

'Seems you have a lot to teach them.' Grim said with little enthusiasm.

'Hmm, seems that way.'

They pushed on as the trees grew even larger, becoming enormous banyans, their gigantic trunks so vast it was hard to tell where one mighty tree started and another finished. The ground seemed firmer from much use, and Arn could smell cooking, leather, and body odor – the smell of group habitation.

There was an ululating cry from Simiana and rope ladders dropped, making Arn and Grimson jump. Looking up they could see huts, bridges and walkways amongst the canopy –a village in the trees. They'd found the home of the Panina. A home in the sky.

'Tree houses.' Arn grinned. 'You live in tree houses.'

She returned the smile with a shrug. 'It is safer.'

Platforms came down on pulleys, and many of the warriors climbed on and were quickly hauled back up.

Simiana motioned to the next platform. 'King Troglan will wish to meet with you. He will have many questions, I'm sure.'

'Good, so do I.' Arn and Grim stepped onto the platform and rose skyward.

*   *   *

The cell was dark. There was only one torch burning along the corridor, and it gave meagre light to the prisoners. Eilif wasn't bothered by the darkness and knew that dawn would not be far off now. She had managed a little rest, but sleep eluded her, as the Becky Man-Kind had sobbed miserably for most of the night, and in between, had whined to her friend, Edward.

At one point it had become too much and Eilif had growled at her to be silent, which had only made her sob louder. Her friend had been braver, but he was drenched now, and shivering cold. Just after they had been returned to their prison, Becky had demanded he ask the guards for some more food. The guard had stared with his luminous green eyes for several seconds, before departing and then quickly returning with a bucket of something cold, wet, and foul smelling. Edward had worn the lot of it. Lesson one: there would be no special favors for Man-Kind in this new kingdom. Lesson two: stop listening to the weak willed female, or she will get you killed.

Eilif closed her eyes and let her mind wander. Her fatigue dragged her back into a dream. There was another Man-Kind, this one tall and strong with coal-dark eyes. He smiled at her and held out his hand. She reached out to take it. Her own hand was pink and soft and... hairless. She reached up and felt her face, now small and round, teeth tiny and even, not the jagged daggers she now wore.

She threw her head back and laughed, taking both his hands and spinning round and around together. The sun was on her face and there were green fields, and Man-Kind everywhere. She was with Arn, in his world, his time. It was the most beautiful place in the universe. She reached out again, wanting to throw her arms around his neck, wanting to bring him in close to her. But she couldn't; something had her wrist.

Arn pulled away, stepping into a doorway. Wind rushed past her, making her narrow her eyes. The sun disappeared and Arn held out his hand, calling to her, but she couldn't get to him as something, or someone, held her back. He edged further back through the doorway, but it changed to become a dark maw, purple at the edges and more like a giant wound torn into the darkness.

She wailed and thrashed, but couldn't get to him. He was going through now, starting to disappear. She became frantic, and looking down saw there was a rope, a leash binding her wrist. Following it, she saw it was tied to someone else, another Man-Kind, a human girl. The lights went out completely as the doorway snapped shut, and when she looked for Arn, there was nothing but mist settling in the blackness of a cold, dark tunnel.

She wailed and opened her eyes. She was in the cell, dark, damp, and still tied to the humans. She wailed again and banged her head back into the stone of the wall.

'Stop that. Now who's making all the noise?' Becky's face was twisted in annoyance.

Eilif grabbed her head and moaned.

'Shut up!' Becky spat the words.

Eilif was on her in a flash, pushing Becky back against the wall, her head thudding.

'Edward... get this... animal off... me!' Becky choked out the words and held an arm across her face.

Eilif dragged the hand away so she could stare into the girl's eyes. She bared her teeth, and Edward's indecision broke and he grabbed Eilif, and tugged.

Eilif pushed Becky back again with one hand, and also reached across to grip Edward at the throat. She now had them both pinned against the stone wall. She leaned in to Becky's face, her lips almost touching her cheek.

'Here, you are the animals, you are the freaks.'

'Please.' Edward whispered, holding the Wolfen's wrist.

Becky kept her head turned and sobbed.

Eilif whispered again to her. 'You should not have come. The Arnoddr Sigarr is not for you, and you are not for him.' She pushed them both back hard and released them. 'Remember my words.'

Both cowered, with Edward wrapping Becky in his arms. They tried to inch as far from the Wolfen as they could even though they were tied together.

Eilif brought the rope to her mouth and chewed for a few seconds, easily severing the course fibers. She spat some rope to the floor.

'The Princess of Valkeryn does not wish to be tied to a Panterran pet any longer.'

Eilif walked to the centre of the cell and stood with her eyes closed. She held up her hands, palm outwards and let her mind roam, to reach out. She could almost feel them – Arn, and Grimson – she had to believe they were alive… it was all she had left.

'Odin keep them safe… and bring them back to me one day.'

* * *

Arn and Grimson were lifted in the rope elevator, Simiana from time to time sneaking glances up at him. He looked across at her. 'The king is friendly, I hope.'

She raised her eyebrows. 'Well he is to me… he's my father.'

'A princess? Of course you are.' He half smiled; it answered why the tribe had treated her with such deference at her young age. 'I knew a princess once.' He looked down at Grim whose eyes burned momentarily.

'You might meet some more.' Simiana reached out to softly touch his hair. 'The king has many children, and many wives. He loves us all... and we love him.' Her hand grasped for a moment. 'You will too.'

She reached out to stroke Arn's long hair, and he caught her hand, squeezed it and let it drop.

'I'm sure we will.'

She reached out again, determined to touch him. 'He is a good king and he will want to know where your tribe is from. We know these lands, and of all the Panina tribes in it. There are none like you.' She looked up at him, her eyes lingering over his towering physique. '... none as strong or as handsome as you, strange Arn.' Her large brown eyes were without shame as she stared.

Arn gulped and looked away.

'Yech.' Grimson did the same.

Having left the elevator, they followed Simiana across bridges, through tunnels dug into the gigantic boughs of the trees, and passed through small gatehouses. The structures were old, but solid, some of them seeming part of the tree.

At last they came to a large, well-kept bungalow adorned with fresh flowers. A broad balcony was set with a long table and chairs, covered in large bowls of exotic coloured fruits.

Simiana guided them to one side of the long table, and she sat down at the other, leaving the huge throne-like chair at the head of the table vacant. Grimson leaned forward and sorted through the bowls.

'Any meat?'

'Maybe soon.' Simiana kept her eyes on the door.

Grimson dropped the fruit back into the bowl and sat back with folded arms. He grumbled softly.

At last the door swung open and young woman appeared with trays covered in all manner of foods. They set them down, and the Wolfen looked onto one large platter, and pulled a face. He nudged Arn, and Arn leaned forward to see a plate full of moving... things. He had the impression they were a type of insect as they looked like crickets except instead of legs they had coiling tentacles that thrashed like oily black worms.

Simiana reached forward to dip her hand into the moving mass and scooped some up, immediately pushing them into her mouth. Arn heard crunching as she chewed. Another tray arrived, this one containing rows of small, cooked animals that looked like rats – thankfully their heads had been removed. Arn tasted one, and found it like a mix of rabbit and anchovy. These were more to Grimson's liking, and he pushed one after the other into his mouth.

More flowers were carried out, and then large pots of palms and other strange plants were positioned around the table, acting as both a screen for privacy and also giving the impression of eating in the centre of a garden.

Once again the doors were pulled back, and this time a small group of males stepped through flanking a brightly adorned man who must have been no more than four feet tall, overweight and slightly bowlegged. A tall wooden crown on his head signified royalty, and his body was heavily daubed with different hues of paint, and he wore a robe that seemed made of flowers all sown together.

Arn bowed with what he hoped was the right amount of deference, but to him the king looked like one of the people who danced at the head of Rio's Mardi Gras parade.

Arn continued standing, but Simiana pulled him down.

'Sit. Troglan will not want to look up to you.'

Arn sank back into his chair, but couldn't help but stare. Just like Simiana and all the others in the tribe, the king wore broad moccasin-type footwear. His darting brown eyes regarded both Arn and Grimson for many seconds before he walked toward them in a curious rocking motion.

Grimson leaned in close to Arn. 'Like you, but not like you.'

Arn glanced at Grim, frowned and turned back gathering his face into the friendliest and most polite expression he could muster. He waited, unsure of the protocol. The new group stopped and just stared… and stared.

After several minutes, Arn felt ready to burst. He swallowed. 'Uh, pleased to…'

Simiana headed him off. 'Great King Troglan, I present Arnold Singer, and Prince Grimson of Valkeryn.' She spent the next few minutes giving the king a quick history of their encounter and how Arn had attacked the mugrab by himself, and also lent a hand to pull it from its watery lair, matching the strength of half the tribe.

The king's brows flew up and knitted together in turn as he listened. He waddled closer, keeping a watchful eye on Arn, but speaking to Grimson.

'You are a Valkeryn Wolfen. They are no more.' He turned to Arn. 'And where do you come from? You are not Wolfen, although you smell of Wolfen. You are not Panina, although you look like Panina. There are none like you in our land.' His eyes narrowed. 'But, I feel I have seen you before.'

'Seen people like me?' Arn half rose, excitement getting the better of his manners.

'No, seen *you* before.' Troglan continued to stare directly at Arn. 'Now, where do you come from?'

Arn cleared his throat, deciding time travel was a subject best kept to himself for now. 'I am from far lands, on a journey to discover the ancestors of my people. The humans… maybe I've found them.' He turned to smile at Simiana, who had her eyes on the king.

'And the Far Wolfen.' Grimson added.

'Hu-mans.' Troglan tested the word, circling the table. 'In the faraway lands there are hu-mans?' He grunted. 'Tell me more of your people.'

Arn smiled, slowly feeling that the greeting was turning into an interrogation.

'My people are the friendliest people in the world, and we live beyond the wasteland. I travelled a long way, and found my way to Valkeryn.'

'Just for discovery? This is a gamble for any race. There must be something well worth finding to travel so far across a desert that has never been crossed, and into such dangerous lands. Are there many more hu-mans there?'

'Well, yes and no, but I believe this is a clue to their whereabouts.' Arn pulled out the fragment of ancient parchment that Vidarr had given him. The faint lightning bolt and fist inked onto the map were still vivid.

Troglan traced it with his long finger, while Simiana looked over his shoulder. She whispered to him. 'Just like in the metal caves.'

'What? You've seen it.' Arn shot to his feet, making the king jump back. The guards crowded in front of him, pointing their spears. Simiana held up a hand, and pushed Arn back down into his seat.

The king came out from behind his Praetorian guard. He still held Arn's map in one hand. He looked away as if becoming disinterested.

'This image drawing – we might have seen it before.' He leaned closer to Simiana and whispered. She nodded and turned to Arn.

'It is customary, when meeting the king, to offer him a gift.'

'A... gift?' Arn repeated.

She nodded.

'Uh, okay.' Arn's mind worked furiously. 'I bring you the gift of knowledge.'

The king's small brown eyes remained bored. 'And...'

Arn groaned, feeling at his belt. His hand closed on his only possession. 'And this.' Arn pulled out his penknife, the only object left from his own time. He handed it to Simiana, who offered it to the king on an open hand.

249

He lifted it carefully, feeling its weight. To Arn's surprise, he then put it in his mouth, feeling the steel with his teeth. Removing it, he set about pulling and picking at it. He held it out to Arn.

'Show me what it does.'

Arn got to his feet, once again rising to his full height and making the king cower slightly. The guards watched him carefully as he approached. Arn lifted his hands. 'Take it easy, boys.' He slowly reached out for the knife.

Simiana crowded in close, placing a hand high on his shoulder, and watching intently as Arn used his thumb and forefinger to carefully lever out the largest blade.

The silver was now tarnished and the blade's edge somewhat blunted, but the king's face lit up in wonderment. Arn continued to pull out tools – the small saw, magnifying glass, tweezers and corkscrew.

'It is a multipurpose tool. It can cut things, saw wood, clip nails, and even remove splinters.' He bowed slightly and held it out. 'I give this great gift to you.'

Troglan reached out to take it, and Arn swapped it in his hands for the scrap of ancient parchment. Troglan didn't notice, his focus solely on the small utility knife. He held it up, showing it left and right to the guards. He ran a finger down the blade, feeling the sharpness, and then set about closing and then reopening all of the instruments.

Simiana looked up at Arn, grinning. 'It is a wonderful gift.'

Arn raised his eyebrows. He was happy to have delighted his new hosts, but sorry that his last link to his old home was now gone.

The king handed the knife to a guard, and his face became serious. 'Such a wonderful device. The tribe that built this must be very powerful.' His eyes lifted to Arn. 'Do the other hu-mans in your tribe know where you are now?'

Arn shook his head. 'No, I think I am lost to them.'

'Lost.' Troglan nodded, his smile appearing once again. 'Lost... only for now I think.' The king turned and waved towards the door to his wooden palace and immediately three women that, to look at, could have been Simiana's sisters, returned holding three goblets – one for the king and one each for Arn and Grimson.

The king's large cup was crusted with what looked like pieces of polished metal. If steel was prized, no wonder his knife was considered such a hit. Arn's and Grimson's cups were made of more modest wood.

Troglan took his cup and raised it. 'Juice of the wild sunberry – very rare, very delicious.' He lifted it to his lips and drained the nectar. Arn discretely sniffed at his, shrugged and did the same. Grimson following suit.

Delicious was right – sugary, golden and electric on the tongue. Arn smacked his lips, and the king smiled warmly.

'Good. Now, we should eat, rest, and then later this evening we can talk some more... maybe about the image drawing.' He looked across to Simiana. 'After all, if my favorite daughter approves of you, then I approve of you.' The king half bowed, and started to turn away.

Arn also bowed, feeling pleased his gift had left him in good standing with the king, until he caught sight of the look that passed between father and daughter – sly, satisfied and conspiratorial. As the royal group left, two of the two guards smirked as they backed away.

'I don't trust him.' Grimson said as Arn finished his drink.

'Definitely strange... but, what choice do we have?'

CHAPTER 30

WE WOLFEN ARE NOT DEAD YET

Teacher's eyes felt gritty. Morning was coming, and they had given up any chance of sleep, trading it off against moving quickly to achieve their objective. Strangely, when the moon had risen, they felt as if they had all been given a shot of adrenalin and steroids, or military go-juice that allowed them the extra energy to keep ploughing on.

But now, with the moon sinking below the horizon as dawn approached, they had felt the fatigue come down heavily upon legs and backs. Teacher sucked in a deep breath; they were Delta, they would go on, indefinitely if need be.

In the predawn darkness, they moved silently on new trails beaten down through the thick jungle. Each of the elite soldiers wore night vision goggles, with Weng, their best tracker, out front. He had already reported that there were two groups, the one in front most likely being the Singer youth. He guessed that the larger group, who were a mix of large and small non-human biped creatures were after him as well – from their experience to date, he didn't expect they were some sort of rescue party.

From time to time Weng or Teacher called a halt. If Teacher held up a fist, the team knew to freeze, slow their breathing, and listen.

Teacher concentrated. Other than the normal sounds of a jungle going about its eat or be eaten business, there were no sounds of pursuit. He turned his head slowly, and let his eyes move over the dark jungle – he had that feeling. After a while he dropped his fist, and they continued.

After another few hours, Don Brown caught him up and

whispered. 'Boss. Someone or something on our twelve o'clock – been there for a few miles now.'

Teacher didn't turn and kept looking directly ahead. However, he let his eyes shoot skyward. After a few minutes he saw it – a figure, the size and shape of a man, moving along the thick limbs about fifty feet above the ground. He grunted; they were good, silent, and agile – definitely a hunter.

'Got it. Any others?'

Like Teacher, Brown stared straight ahead. 'Nope, just our special friend in the trees.'

'Okay, let's keep moving forward until we know what their plans are.'

'Could be a spy boss. I can take him down – wing him, then we could have a chat.'

'They're definitely tracking us. But for now, just keep watching. If he or she looks like they want to play rough, then I want you to stun them… load a Taser bolt.'

'You got it.'

* * *

Sorenson heard the sound of the group pushing through the jungle a few hours back. Even though they probably thought they travelled in silence, the amount of noise they made indicated they had to be something other than Panterran or Lygon, and definitely not Wolfen.

He'd been close to the Lygon and Panterran camp, which had been stirring in the predawn mist when he had detected the sound of the group's approach. He was tempted to wait and see what happened when the new group blundered into them. But something nagged at him, insisting he intercept them… or at least get a better look at them. He spun back, racing along the branch highways, and looped around to come up behind the noisy group. He would stay just behind their heads, so he could look down on them.

At first he was amazed, and then thrilled – Man-Kind, fully grown, covered in soft-looking armor and with all manner of things that hung from their belts. Each had black sticks held out in front of them. Most had some type of mask over their eyes. He stared hard – they had to be tracking the Arnoddr – they could be his friends, and therefore potential Wolfen allies.

He shook his head. They made more noise than a herd of binox. He remembered how small the Arnoddr's ears, eyes and nose were – no wonder their senses were inferior. He started to ease down towards them. They would need help to navigate this world. He could not allow them to blunder in on the war party – they would be massacred.

Sorenson scaled down to another limb, now only thirty feet up and just to the left of them. He kept his eyes on them, planning to drop down and let them walk up to him, so as not to frighten or startle them. He doubted they would cause him any troubles, given none of them even came up to his chin.

Just as he readied himself to drop down onto another branch, one of them spun, pointed his black stick at him, and immediately Sorenson felt a sting in his thigh. A thousand hot nettles stung at him, locking his muscles and causing his jaws to clack shut. He slid from the branch and hit the ground.

In an instant he was surrounded. If he could have moved his face he would have smiled, relieved – it seemed the man-kind were not so defenseless after all.

Teacher jerked his thumb. 'Get him up.'

Doonie and Brown each took an arm and lifted the Wolfen.

'Jesus, he's heavy – must be solid muscle.'

The Wolfen shook his head, blinked and worked his jaw, feeling his chin with a hand. He reminded Teacher of a boxer who had been knocked to the canvas. His eyes cleared and he straightened – tall, close to seven feet, and formidable looking. Nothing like the old Wolfen, Balthazaar, they had encountered back in the forest.

He half bowed, and when he straightened again his eyes were on Teacher. They were deep green and their intense gaze bored into him.

'I hoped you would come.' He leaned his head forward. 'Are you here for the Arnoddr?'

Teacher remembered that was the name Balthazaar used for Arnold Singer. The Wolfen waited, his eyes never leaving Teacher's face. The Delta leader pushed his rifle up over his shoulder.

'Lower your weapons.' He stuck out his hand, and the Wolfen smiled, looking down at the open hand.

'Yes, just like the Arnoddr.' He grabbed it and squeezed. Teacher did his best not to wince.

'I am Captain Jim Teacher, DeltaForce, here to find Arnold Singer and get him home. Do you know where he is?'

'You are the warrior class of the Ancients.'

'We are soldiers, and if you mean Ancients as in mankind, then yes, we are their warriors. We do not have a lot of time. Do you know where the boy is?'

The Wolfen tapped his chest with a fist. 'I am Sorenson, son of Stromgard, once defender of the great king Grimvaldr...' His eyes grew dark. '... who I failed.'

Sorenson sucked in a huge breath, his chest swelling. 'The one you seek is in the company of the young prince, Grimson. He is being tracked by a war party of Lygon and Panterran assassins. The war party is just along this track. Arnoddr and Prince Grimson are perhaps a day and half ahead of that. I seek them also, to join their quest and offer my protection.'

Teacher turned to look in the direction of the war party, then to the rapidly lighting sky. 'Can we go around them?'

The Wolfen thought for a moment, and then nodded. 'Yes.' He stepped in closer to Teacher. 'But why would you, Jim Teacher? You are noisy and they would soon hear you, or pick up your trail. Then you would constantly have them at your backs. They hunt well in the dark.'

Teacher nodded, knowing the Wolfen was right. He would be wise not to underestimate these beings again. Eventually his Deltas would need to rest, and the last thing he needed was a large group of giant Lygon ambushing them out of the dark.

'I agree. We have the element of surprise... for now.'

The Wolfen nodded. 'Their eyes are better in the darkness. So when it is light... attack.'

'Can you lead us to them... without them hearing?'

'No. They will hear you before you get close. They also travel with one of my own kin... a traitor. His name is Bergborr, and he is a good tracker. He will find you. Better if I draw them out, lead them back along the trail... for you to ambush.'

Teacher nodded. 'Works for me.' He held out his hand again and Sorenson took it. This time there was no smile, and the Wolfen bared huge teeth. 'Kill them all.'

Teacher held the gaze. 'Fight or die.'

Sorenson released his hand. 'Fight or die – yes, spoken like a Wolfen.'

❧ ⚬⚬⚬ ☙

Sorenson dropped from the branches and walked lightly along the path to the Lygon camp. His footfalls were unheard by the huge guards who were more interested in making sure they didn't miss out on the food being portioned out for breakfast. Further in, Panterran moved in and out of the large orange and black bodies that jostled each other as the camp roused itself in readiness for the day.

Sorenson could see the Panterran called Orcalion speaking

to Bergborr at the far side of the camp, while other Panterran huddled in groups whispering, undoubtedly voicing their displeasure at the lack of comforts, or of the odors of the huge Lygon. Sorenson walked ever closer, only stopping when he stood before the pair of massive guards, their backs turned and necks straining to see in at the cooking fires.

'No need of food in Hellheim, brainless beasts.'

The Lygon swung around, their luminous eyes going wide. Surprise and confusion stunned them momentarily before they reacted in the only way they knew how – they attacked. Both lifted huge weapons, but, as Sorenson expected, surprise was his.

The Lygon were powerful, but slow. The first Lygon swung his weapon, but the Wolfen stepped in underneath the moving mace. Sorenson's blade flicked out, easily passing through the fur and neck muscle. He fell back, surprise on his face as his life spurted away in a hot red fountain.

The second Lygon managed to swing his axe, the massive blade sinking three feet into the earth. While the great beast tugged at it, it would have been easy to take his head, but Sorenson's job was done – he leapt back and started to run, yelling as he went.

'For the Valkeryn Wolfen.' He turned to look over his shoulder. The camp was roused and small and large faces were twisted in surprise and anger. One at the rear, the dark Wolfen's, burned with hatred. They charged after him.

Sorenson sped back along the track, praying to Odin the warrior Man-Kind were ready... and as skilled as he hoped.

* * *

Alf Doonie held up a small matt black box, reading numbers off the tiny screen. 'Coming in fast, multiple signatures, big bodies – all biological, but plenty of iron.'

Teacher edged in behind the trunk of a tree. 'Hold until we

have line of sight targets, and then fire at will. Kill shots only – no prisoners.'

'I heard that.' Alison Sharp snapped a full magazine of uranium tipped rounds into her HK416 and hunkered down low behind a cluster of fern fronds.

Sorenson burst into view, sprinting past them and then skidding to a stop. He turned, planted his legs and held his sword ready.

'For Valkeryn!'

The horde came screaming after him, a boiling mass of teeth and claw and luminous green eyes filled with a blood lust that none of the Deltas had ever witnessed in anything human.

'Fire.'

Shots rang out, and huge bodies fell hard. Some of the Panterran in amongst them were obliterated by the high caliber bullets.

In a matter of minutes it was over. Teacher held up a hand. 'Hold fire.'

Smoke rose from gun barrels, and from the small red wounds where the hot tipped bullets had entered iron, flesh or bone. Sorenson walked forward his sword held out. He stepped up on and over bodies. His searching became more frantic as he delved into the jungle at the edge of the pathway, or back along the trail.

Teacher got to the feet and spoke over his shoulder. 'Doonie, anything on the scope?'

The Delta looked down at his device. 'Just our wolf friend – otherwise, all clear.'

After a moment Sorenson came back in. His face was troubled.

Teacher met him. 'Did we get them all?'

'No, not the ones I wanted.' He turned slowly looking out into the jungle. 'All the Lygon are dead, and most of the Panterran. But two are not here – the queen's confidant and the dark Wolfen, Bergborr... and I have an old score to settle with him.'

'Great.' Teacher half turned. 'Simms, Brown, Weng, go to thermal and do a perimeter sweep – we might have missed some.' He turned back to the Wolfen. 'Will they track us, or cause us problems?'

Sorenson seemed to think for a moment, and then shook his head. 'I do not think so. Both lack strong *sáál*. More than likely they will try and flee home. Let us hope the jungle takes them both.'

'Good – if they're not in our way, they're not our problem. We need to keep moving.' Teacher pushed his gun up over his back. 'Will you travel with us?'

Sorenson tilted his head. 'You will slow me down. But I fear without me, you will not survive in these Dark Lands.'

Teacher snorted. 'You sound like Balthazaar.'

The Wolfen grabbed him, pulling him close, and causing Alison Sharp to raise her gun, pointing it at the Wolfen's head.

'The counselor lives… you have seen him?'

Teacher held up a hand at Sharp. 'Yes, he gave us a map, and also the talking stones. How do you think we can understand you?'

The Wolfen let Teacher go and then clapped his hands together. 'Yes, I will travel with you. And you will tell me all about the conversation you had with old Balt.' He almost danced on the spot. 'We Wolfen are not dead yet.' He made a fist, and looked with disgust down at his dead foes. 'And we grow stronger each day.'

* * *

Sorenson led the Delta team through the mad tangle of jungle, coming to the riverbank and immediately spotting the skirmish marks. He walked slowly along the bank, his eyes missing nothing, before he half turned.

'Teacher, watch the water. Something big came out and

attacked Grimson and the Arnoddr here.'

'Doonie, Simms.' Teacher pointed with two fingers from his eyes to the water. Both men shouldered their rifles and scanned along the water surface.

Sorenson continued his search, and then stopped and looked up. 'They went back in… this way.' He vanished into the forest, Teacher and the other Deltas having to race to keep up.

After another half hour of ploughing through the vines and fronds, Sorenson stopped, his ears moving like twin radar dishes over the thick dark jungle. Teacher eased up beside him.

'What do you hear?'

'A fight – to the death. Big adversaries.' He pointed with his nose. 'Not far… that way.'

'We should go around.'

Sorenson stood and stared at the jungle, his gaze unblinking. After another moment, he slowly turned. 'No. I must find it – there is something there I must see.'

He started to push away again, gathering speed as he went.

'Ah, crap…' Teacher shook his head, and then circled his hand in the air. He and his team followed.

After another few minutes of following Sorenson's trail, the evidence of the battle became clear even to the Delta's senses. Thumps, roars and hissing like a monstrous steam valve had broken loose came from just through a stand of bamboo like plants hanging with red bulb like fruits.

They found Sorenson standing just behind a tree palm. He had dropped his pack, but pulled his sword free. Animals and birds screamed overhead, outraged by the vicious noises of the fight beneath them, and Teacher motioned to his team to spread out ten feet to either side of him. They lifted their guns, waiting on their squad leader's word.

The fight was rising in intensity and Teacher eased forward to become level with Sorenson's shoulder. He could tell that whatever was doing battle was huge, like two bull elephants, but probably with a truck load more teeth. Sorenson's gaze was unwavering as he pushed through the green curtain. Teacher followed.

A roughly fifty-foot circle of smashed and trampled vegetation had been pummeled flat. It took Teacher a second or two to work out what he was seeing, so entangled was the mountain of flesh, fur and scales at its centre.

There was a beast that looked a little like a Wolfen, but was at least twelve feet in height and probably weighing several tons. It was lying on the ground half bound in the coils of some sort of cross between a snake and lizard. A dozen scaled legs, or maybe hands, given the dexterity of their grip, braced themselves on the ground, while many more dug sharp talons into the fur and flesh of the huge creature's muscles.

The lizard creature had bound the furred beast's body by wrapping it in coils many feet thick, and now only one arm and its head was free. Though the furred beast's claws were as along as Teacher's forearm, the head of the reptile stayed out of their range. It obviously knew time was on its side, and with each passing moment, it squeezed a little tighter, making breathing for the great beast more difficult. Teacher knew it would tire soon, and then the reptile's head with its rows of curved teeth would strike.

'What the hell is that thing?' Teacher whispered, not knowing why he was, given the noises of the fight before them.

Sorenson shook his head. 'I know not... but I sense a... kinship.' He lifted his sword. 'And so...'

'Don't even think about it.' Teacher reached across to try and grab hold of the large Wolfen's shoulder, but he had already leapt, roaring as he flew through the air, and landing to slash at the scaled hide.

Sorenson's razor-edged blade managed to open a huge cut on one of the coils, but if he thought it would force the massive reptile to release its grip, he was wrong. From out of the jungle a barbed tail whipped around to knock him off his feet. More legs marched the spiked end towards him, rising up to impale the Wolfen's prone body.

Teacher shouldered his gun, but immediately Sorenson held up his hand while keeping his focus on the creature.

'Do not, Teacher. You may harm the other.'

Teacher turned to Simms, his sharp shooter. 'Forget that; if you get a clear headshot, you take it.'

'Got it, boss.' The soldier lifted his rifle and aimed.

The creature's tail continued to rise, and then pull back. Teacher could see clearly what it would seek to do – it would soon dart forward and impale Sorenson with the barbed tip, and then lift him towards the head and waiting mouth – a morsel of Wolfen food while it crushed the larger prey in its muscular coils.

The Wolfen managed to lift himself up on one elbow, and roared defiantly causing the reptile's slitted eyes to slide across to him. The beast within the coils also turned its head, and for a second it met theWolfen's eyes– an unspoken communication passed between them – and the bound beast immediately redoubled its efforts, thrashing against the embracing coils. It strained forward and a huge arm swung out to rake enormous claws along the coils binding it. Swathes of scales were ripped free.

The reptile was forced to give its attention back to the larger threat. Sorenson rolled to his feet and flew forward with his sword raised, bringing it down with all his strength. Six feet of scaled flesh flew from the snake's tail. Deep crimson blood spurted and the severed tail bounced and wriggled on the ground with a mindless life of its own.

With the reptile's secondary line of defense breached, it looked confused – it couldn't dare unwind from its large prey, or ignore the Wolfen that circled it, blood dripping from a sword held ready. But Sorenson couldn't hope to counter the massive head that carried enough heavily armored scales to repel his blade.

There seemed a stalemate, and once again the huge furred beast looked to Sorenson, and Teacher thought he saw it nod almost imperceptibly. It quietened and lay still. The reptile tightened its grip, perhaps sensing success in its crushing embrace.

As Sorenson advanced, the reptile's tongue flicked out, touching at the beasts fur, and sensing no movement, it turned to face the Wolfen. Sorenson came in another few feet, his sword in a two handed grip. The upper coils loosened so the reptile could call upon extra striking distance.

Sorenson roared, thrashing the air, and the huge reptile began to rear up for the strike. More coils loosened, and then Sorenson darted in.

Teacher turned to Simms, but the marksman shook his head. It wasn't needed – in a planned move, the massive furred beast, almost totally forgotten by the reptile, lunged forward, jaws opening as wide as a manhole cover, and grabbing the scaled creature at the throat, biting, ripping, spitting out huge chunks of flesh, and then returning to tear at it again and again until the head fell free.

Sorenson leapt down and rolled away. The massive reptile bounced around like it had been given a thousand volts. Even the severed head sill snapped at movement, though the eyes had already become milky.

The furred beast pushed the coils away easily and got to its feet. Sorenson stood at ease, his hands on resting the hilt of the sword before him.

'Oh my god,' Weng whispered from beside Teacher. It towered over Sorenson, taller than even the biggest Lygon, and easily twelve feet in height.

Brown scoffed. 'It's a bear... a goddamn giant freaking bear.'

'Not just a bear.' Alison Sharp nudged him and nodded towards the thing. Brown was right; the beast looked like a bear, but it had a leather harness strapped across its chest, and a gladiator style strap skirt around its waist. It sucked in and blew out air as it took grateful breaths. After a moment it thumped towards Sorenson and leaned down to look into his face.

'I could have killed it by myself. I did not need your help, little warrior.'

Sorenson bent forward in a small bow. 'But you did kill it by yourself. All I did was annoy it.'

There was silence for a moment, and then a rumbling deep in the beast's chest. It bowed in return, and tilted its head, one eyebrow raised and a slight smile on the huge lips.

'Only a Valkeryn Wolfen would risk his life with honor and then be so humble.' It rose to its full height and thumped its chest. 'I am Kodian of the Ursa, and I know I owe you my life.' He turned to the jungle, lifting his head to sniff. 'Tell your friends to come forward as I will do them no harm.' His eyes ran across Teacher and his Deltas hiding in the foliage. 'I wish to see them, as I don't recognize the scent.'

Teacher took a breath, and looked to his fellow soldiers. 'Any friend of Sorenson, and all that.'

Brown leaned towards Alison Sharp. 'Just don't steal his porridge okay, Goldiehorn?'

She snorted. 'It's Goldilocks, you asshole.'

Teacher stepped out first and walked towards the centre of the bloody clearing, but stopped a dozen feet back from the giant creature. His team fanned out left and right of him. All the Deltas had the guns hanging loose, but fingers resting on the trigger guards.

A rumbling sounded deep in the creature's chest once again. It placed massive fists on its hips and leaned forward to look each of them up and down. 'So, the stories are true. There *are* Man-Kind walking the land again.' he pulled back shaking his head. 'No good can come of this.'

Sorenson held out an arm towards them. 'They are my friends. We seek another of their kind, and also a young Wolfen who travels with him.'

The rumbling again. 'One of the lost heirs of Valkeryn, perhaps?'

Sorenson stepped closer. 'Yes, you have news of him... seen him?'

Kodian shook his head. 'I have not seen him, but know of him. He turned and pointed off into the jungle. 'I have heard he went to where the water falls from the cliffs. He seeks the lost Wolfen.' He shook his head. 'But he will not find them there.'

Teacher walked up to stand beside Sorenson. 'The Man-Kind with him; Arnold Singer. Do you know if he is alive?'

Behind him Brown shook his head. 'Jesus, we're talking to a bear. This is freaky.'

Sharp shrugged. 'I'll talk to anyone who's gonna help.'

Brown snorted. 'My pappy used to shoot bears. He's still got a mangy old head on his wall.'

Kodian's ears twitched, and his gaze came around. 'Bears – we went by that name in the olden times.' He took several thundering steps towards Brown. 'Shoot bears, and then hang their heads.' He roared so loud, that the Deltas stepped back, and in a movement so fast that belied his enormous size, he lunged at Brown, snatching the metal gun from his hands. The disarmed Delta fell back onto his ass, and Alison Sharp came and stood over him, her gun up.

Teacher held up a hand. 'Hold your fire.' He turned to Kodian. 'We are from a different time. But know this; none of us have ever, or will ever, harm you or your kind.'

Sorenson came and stood beside Teacher. 'It is true, they have good *sáál*.'

Kodian looked down at them, his eyes still containing

anger. After a moment his cheeks puffed out as though he was blowing away the ill feeling.

'In the legends, it is said that in the time of fire, Fenrir released us from our prisons. We Ursa and Wolfen are kin. You helped because it is in your blood to help us, as it is in ours to help you. I owe you a debt Wolfen of Valkeryn.' His eyes slid to Brown. 'I owe the Man-Kind nothing.'

He took the metal gun in both his hands and crumpled it like it was nothing but paper and wire. He tossed the ball of steel back at Brown's feet. He then lumbered back to the dead reptile and drew a long flat blade from his belt. He set to cutting away some loose flesh from the severed head, and lifted it to stare into the milky eyes for a moment.

'This spike-tail had been stalking our tribe, taking our young. I vowed to remove its curse, or never return.' He bared his teeth at the head. 'Its curse is removed and now I can go back to my people. I will repay my debt to you Soren-son.' He pointed to the jungle. 'If the young Wolfen still lives, then by now, he will be in the land of the Not–people. If there is a Man-Kind with him, he will also be there.'

He dropped his hand holding the head, blood and gore dripping to the jungle floor. 'Odin's luck be with you, little brother.'

In another moment he was gone.

Sorenson quickly took to slicing meat from the reptile's body, and wrapped it in leaves. 'Let's be gone from here. The blood will attract more predators.'

CHAPTER 31

WYRMRAGON; THE ONE TRUE GOD

Eilif was screaming. She strained and bared her teeth, but couldn't break free.

Arn held out his hand but couldn't quite reach her. He seemed stuck, his legs refusing to obey the simple command to move him forward, even just a few inches.

Eilif screamed to him again, her luminous ice-blue eyes implored him, cut through him with their hurt, confusion… and accusation.

'Why?' Her face was streaked with tears and sadness. And then, as if she finally understood what was happening, she slumped. Her head flew back and she let loose an unearthly howl that chilled his blood. The long torturous notes were like a blow to his gut, and they spoke of pain, betrayal, love found and just as quickly lost.

Still he couldn't move. 'Leave her alone,' was all the defense he could muster. He felt ashamed, as he was suddenly shouldered aside, a hand pushing him in the chest.

'Get back; it's dangerous.' While he watched, a Taser dug into her stomach and was discharged. Eilif shuddered and danced, and then a bag was roughly pulled over her head. She didn't make a sound as she was dragged down a corridor of concrete, steel, and fluorescent lighting.

'I know her… I need her…' It was soldiers holding her, human soldiers – she was in his time, his world – it didn't make sense. He could still hear her in his head as she called his name over and over, each time she cried out it seemed farther away, weaker – his name echoed, echoed in his brain, and then was gone…

'Eilif-fff!'

Arn Singer sat bolt upright, perspiration running down his face. His heart hammered in his chest and he worked to calm his breathing. The dream again – just the damn dream again, he whispered as he gulped air. He groaned, crushing his eyes shut. 'Oh God.' He put his hands to his head, pressing his temples.

Arn carefully allowed his eyes to open, and exhaled, suddenly realizing he had been holding his breath. Thankfully there was no harsh light, as he feared it would make his migraine a thousand times worse.

'What?' He spun left and right – Grimson was beside him, still snoring. 'What happened?' It was growing dark outside. He tried to recall the last thing he remembered – it had been dawn when he had met the king. The feast. Simiana was there. He had drunk some sort of wine or nectar. Then everything just fell into darkness.

He got unsteadily to his feet, and staggered to a small window – it was barred with wooden poles – he tested them – tougher than steel.

'Am I in prison? Why?'

A groan from behind him. 'My head hurts.' Grimson sat up, cradling his head.

Arn came back to his side. 'Mine too, little buddy, but it's getting better now. I think we might have been drugged, and...' he pointed to the window. '... taken prisoner.'

'What did we do?'

'Good question.' Arn tested the door. It was made of the same strong wood. He gave up.

Grimson got to his feet. 'Can we break out?'

Arn looked back to the wrist-thick bars over the window. 'I don't think so... maybe if the rising moon gives me more strength. But the bars and door feel like some sort of ironbark.' Arn went back to the window, and placed one hand on a bar.

'Psst.'

He leapt back. 'Jesus… there's someone there.'

'It's me.' A small brown hand gripped the bars and then waved. Arn went back to the window and turning sideways, looked down over the rim at the small woman.

'Simiana, you scared me half to death. What's happening? Why are we in here?'

Simiana shook her head, looking down momentarily. 'I am ashamed. Troglan distrusts you. He feels you will lead your giant people here, and they will overrun our tribe. I tried to speak on your behalf, but…'

'What? I won't do that. We're just passing through. Look, let me talk to him.'

Simiana grimaced, showing white even teeth, with slightly pronounced canines. 'I can't. He won't see you.'

'Now what? How long will he keep us here?'

She brightened. 'Not long now. He has already decreed you are to be presented to the Wyrmragon.' She smiled up into his face 'It will be a great honor.'

'Wyrmragon? The one true god, Wyrmragon?' Arn scoffed. 'Well, that sounds great. I'm guessing that's not a good thing, right?'

Simiana shook her head. 'No, no, it is a good thing. Wyrmragon is one of the gods of the forest, and you and the Prince of Valkeryn will get to join with him. It is a great honor. I truly envy you.'

Arn gripped the bars and rested his forehead against them. 'When?'

'After the evening's feast. It's starting now.'

Arn felt her hand cover his. The small brown fingers worked along the knuckles until they got to the snarling wolf ring with the ruby eyes. She rubbed the silver, and then picked at it.

'Can I have this?'

Arn lifted his head, seeing her attention was now solely on

271

the silver ring. He had forgotten about the ring and turned his hand to look at it.

'No. This was a gift from someone very special.'

'You won't need it anymore.' She stepped back, sulking. 'Perhaps later.'

'Enjoy the feast.' Arn turned his back on her. 'I'm not hungry.'

***

The Deltas caught up to Sorenson who stood at the base of the giant tree that Arn and Grimson had used to cross the river. Fish swarmed at the bank where he stood and he stared down at them in the dark water.

He pointed to marks on the bank and on the trunk of the tree. 'Even though it doesn't reach the entire way across, they used the tree somehow. And on the far bank there are signs of a skirmish. I think they made it, but not sure how.'

'Well, they didn't swim.' Brown kicked stones into the water, scattering the fish. The group had already discovered they were carnivorous; Doonie had already lost the tip of one finger when he tried to wade out.

Sorenson looked up and down the bank. A sound of frustration came from his throat. 'We must return to the falls – it is narrow enough to cross and stay dry.' He sprinted back down the bank.

Alison Sharp watched him disappear. 'Does that guy ever get tired?'

'Must be all the clean healthy living.' Teacher waved the Delta team after him at a jog.

***

'We will fight them… all of them.' Grimson stood beside Arn, his fingers flexing.

Arn looked down at the Wolfen, already taller and more powerful than when they had set out. He was growing fast, and the desire for battle was flowing through his veins.

Grimson nodded to the door. 'They will come for you first. I will wait, ambush them, and secure a weapon... and then, let them fear us.'

Arn nodded – sound tactics. 'Not yet. Let's let them lead us outside and down to the ground. They are better in the trees than we are, and I think we'll have more of a chance to escape when we have a little more open space.'

Grimson looked dubious, but nodded. Bolts were pulled back on the door. Twenty warriors stood there, spears held ready. Some of them Arn recognized from the riverbank and they all looked wary – perhaps they had heard what he was capable of.

Arn held up his hands. 'Do not be afraid.'

Their hands were quickly tied behind their backs, and a loop of rope around their neck. Grimson bared his teeth, but the rope was yanked tight to subdue him.

'Take it easy.' Arn glared, and the warrior backed off a little.

Arn and Grimson were led outside to one of the pulley-lifts and then transported to the ground. Once there, another larger party took control and led them out into the jungle. Arn noticed that further back, flaming torches bobbed, and by the number he guessed it was pretty much the entire tribe that followed. They had donned garlands of flowers, and robes intertwined with vines and blooms. Arn thought it looked like some sort of wedding party – unfortunately he and Grim were off to meet the groom.

Eventually they slowed, and then pushed into a clearing. The baseball field-sized space was ringed with small stones, creating a line about ten feet wide at the jungle's edge. The tribe fanned out left and right along the border, staying out of the clearing itself.

Grimson pushed a little closer to him. 'Something smells bad.' He looked up. 'Flesh eater.'

Arn could see that at the centre of the clearing there was a large hole, and inside nothing could be seen but blackness. At its smooth edges it glistened as though coated in a viscous slime, and a few feet back from the void, a single three-foot high post was embedded into the ground.

A small movement from the other side of the clearing drew Arn's attention. Simiana was giving him a small wave. She smiled. Arn couldn't work out whether it was an expression of hope, a wish for good luck, or maybe a short, "goodbye sucker".

King Troglan stepped out a few feet into the clearing, but Arn noticed he was careful not to tread beyond the line of stones that bordered its outer rim… and he could guess why; within the inner clearing fine tendrils of a gossamer-like thread could be seen crisscrossing the crushed-down plant matter. All of them led back to the twenty-foot wide pit, and disappeared over its slimy edge.

'We should try and escape now.' Grimson spoke softly and kept his eyes on the pit.

'Yep.' Arn looked around at the jungle's edge – many of the tribe had climbed trees, squatting in low branches for a better view. Arn and Grimson's arms were now lashed tight behind their backs, and their ankles bound with a rope travelling from their necks, to wrists and then to their ankles – they were effectively trussed.

'I think we're in trouble now.' Grimson looked up at him with raised eyebrows.

Arn responded with a half-smile. 'What, only now?'

Grimson nodded towards the hole at the centre of the clearing. 'Do you think they're going to push us in?'

Arn turned back to the slime edged pit and sighed. 'No, I don't think we're going in. I think something's going to be coming out.'

The king raised his arms, closed his eyes and lifted his face to the sky. 'Great Wyrmragon, we call on you. Wyrmragonnnn!'

'Wyrmragon, Wyrmragon, Wyrmragon.' The tribe picked up the chant until it became like a physical force that echoed beyond the clearing and out into the jungle.

'Look.' Grimson nudged him.

A creature – to Arn it looked like a goat – was brought forth. A tether hung from its neck with a loop at one end. Two tribes-men used extremely long poles to push it further out into the clearing towards the post. The men using the poles strained to reach out, one eventually laying down on his back, careful not to cross the barrier. He slipped off his moccasins and then to Arn's shock used his foot to grip the pole. The foot wasn't a foot at all – it was more like a hand.

Arn knew his mouth had dropped open, and he glanced back to Simiana – the broad moccasin shoes they all wore, the way they had copied him, the "not like you," comment from Grimson – it suddenly all made sense. They weren't like him, they weren't the people of the Ancients; they weren't people at all. They were actually evolved from some type of ape-like creatures.

Simiana grinned and waved again. He exhaled slowly. There would be no pity from anyone in the tribe: they didn't even think of him as one of them. No wonder the king had been wary.

Simiana waved again, her eyes ablaze with excitement. She nodded towards the dark pit as if this was something to be enjoyed.

The cheering of the tribe brought Arn's head back around. The warrior had managed to loop the rope over the pole and the animal bucked and squealed in fear, likely from the stench emanating from the nearby pit.

A foul odor filled the clearing, followed by a faint breeze. The goat animal's fur ruffled as something vented from the hole. It became more frantic and began tug so hard it scraped skin from its neck.

The sensation and odor reminded Arn of when he was in a subway with a train approaching, and the dank air of the tunnels was pushed towards him before the carriages arrive.

'I can hear it.' Grimson's ears were erect and pointing forward. His face carried a hint of fear, and in another second Arn could hear it… and feel it beneath his feet, a vibration as something huge travelled below them.

Wyrmragon, Wyrmragon, Wyrmragon – the chant became louder and faster, and then a plume of dust exited the pit followed by an enormous column of flame-red flesh. It lifted several dozen feet into the sky, and wavered for a moment, as though testing the air. The top opened, and like a giant lamprey, the end of the massive worm opened to become a round hole lined with teeth.

Some sense found its prey and the worm toppled over to thump down upon the small creature tied to the stake. The mouth, easily ten feet across, had covered the animal completely and stayed motionless for several seconds, waiting. There came a bleating scream and movement from inside the mouth as the goat-animal, still living, must have kicked or thrashed.

This seemed to be what it was waiting for; a sign of life. When it lifted up again the animal was gone and just a red smear remained on the ground. The column of flesh straightened again, the gullet working as the meal was swallowed.

'Odin save us.' Grimson moved closer and buried his face into Arn's side. Arn held onto the young Wolfen, but felt sick and dizzy after what he had just seen. He tried to comprehend what this massive thing might have evolved from – some gigantic worm or nematode that had grown large on a diet of flesh, radiation, and mutated evolution over a million years, or perhaps…

'Like a giant bag-worm,' he whispered. Arn remembered a tiny creature from his time, a worm that created a sheath-like structure coated in silk and slime and lived out its life below the earth, waiting for a vibration from above to let it know that prey was close by.

With a wet, sticky sound, Wyrmragon pulled back into the hole, leaving a fresh coating of slime around its edge. Arn had no idea how large it must be, but guessed from the portion they had seen above ground that it had to be a hundred feet in length. *What he wouldn't give for a few gallons of gas and ten seconds with a flaming torch,* he thought.

'This is not a good way to die, Arnoddr. I may not see Valhalla unless I fall in battle or at least have tasted battle.'

'Hey, you've tasted many battles, my young friend.' Arn nudged him. 'We're not dead yet, Grim. Always retain hope. Remember that.' Arn tried to stand a little straighter but the rope around his neck had no give to it.

A shove to the back forced both of them over the stone line. Immediately, the long poles prodded them forward. Though Arn would have liked to walk forward with dignity, his legs resisted every inch of the way.

Arn noticed that amongst the tribe members, all the warriors held their spears ready, with the points directed at Arn and Grimson; there would be no easy escape past them, and given that their ankles were tied closely together, all he could manage was a geisha-like shuffle – not exactly made for a high speed dash through jungle.

Wyrmragon, Wyrmragon, Wyrmragon.

The king took up the chant once again, and the tribe quickly followed. They ate fruit, giggled, and jostled in a carnival-like atmosphere. Arn saw that even Simiana was chanting, laughing and clapping along with the beat. He leaned down to Grim.

'Looks like we get to be sacrificed to their god, and also be the evening's entertainment – double the fun.'

Grim's eyes stayed on the pit. 'Can you use your strength to break the bonds?'

Arn tested the rope but without the fully-risen moon, he found the coils unbreakable.

'No, not yet.' He looked down at the length of rope that joined them. He hoped there was enough slack there to be able to push Grim out of the way once the creature began to descend. He shuddered at the thought. Grim was right – not a good way to go.

'I can feel it coming.' Grimson said softly.

Arn nodded. The ground vibrated as the thing moved deep below the surface. The breeze in the clearing swirled around them, and the stinking odor enveloped them once again. In another few seconds the tower of glistening, red flesh burst forth to hang in the air.

Grimson bared his teeth, growling, determined to go down in some sort of impossible fight to ensure his path across the rainbow bridge to Valhalla.

Arn felt his legs shaking, and he knew the giant worm would soon topple over to envelop them in its tooth-lined maw. He braced himself to push Grimson.

'Shut your eyes, Grim.'

Grimson stared hard at the column of muscle. 'Never. I will tear a hole right through it.' He bared his teeth and made a futile effort to work his arms free.

Grim's defiance made Arn feel his own courage surge. He grinned down at the youth. 'You're the bravest friend I've ever known.'

The beast began to bend and the tribe cheered. The star light faded in its shadow as the huge thing descended upon them in agonizing slow motion, as though it knew there was no rush since its prey was bound.

Grimson backed into him and he felt the youth reach out with his bound hands to grab Arn's hands and hold on tight.

Arn sucked in a deep breath and stared straight ahead. *I'm coming grandfather*, he thought as his shoulders hunched waiting for the end.

'See you in Valhalla.' Grim whispered.

He couldn't help it – he closed his eyes. But instead of being enveloped in darkness, there was a blinding white explosion above their heads, and gobbets of flesh rained down on them.

Sorenson burst into the clearing, his arms wide. The adult Wolfen stood nearly seven feet tall and was a giant to the little brown warriors. He turned to the chattering Panina, his eyes wide and furious and roared again. Spears were dropped and they screamed like their tree-dwelling forefathers, and disappeared into the jungle. The Wolfen turned and began ripping the ropes away from Arn and Grimson's hands.

Arn's mouth dropped open; a group of soldiers, human soldiers, entered the clearing, guns pointed at the headless Wyrmragon who was gradually being dragged down into the pit its own dead weight. One of the men pushed his rifle up over his shoulder, pulled off a fingerless glove and held out his hand.

'Arnold Singer, I presume?' The man tilted his head, looking up at Arn. 'You're a hell of a lot bigger than I was led to believe.'

Arn grabbed the hand and shook it. 'Yes, yes. I'm Singer, Arnold Singer.' Arn grinned and felt like exploding into laughter.

Sorenson embraced them both, but then released Arn so he could talk to Grimson. The huge Wolfen knelt before the Valkeryn prince, and lowered his head. 'My sword for you, sire.'

Grimson reached out, laying a hand on his shoulder. 'Mighty Sorenson, son of Stromgard, defender of Valkeryn, rise up.'

Sorenson got to his feet, and looked to the heavens. He raised both fists. 'Yes!' His voice echoed in the quiet clearing.

'Thank you, Odin, father of us all.' He turned around and grabbed Arn in a huge hug. 'And thank you, Arnoddr for looking after the heir of Valkeryn. I am in your debt.' He sniffed at Arn. 'Strange, you smell less like a Man-Kind and more like a Valkeryn born every day.'

The Delta soldiers then crowded in around Arn, slapping his back or shaking his hand, as they introduced themselves. The one called Teacher did most of the talking.

'Okay son, your part of the puzzle is now solved. Now for the other part – where's the laser acceleration diamond?'

Arn was a little taken aback by the change in the man. He thought for a second or two. 'I… had it, but now it's gone.'

'Say again – you lost it?' Brown shook his head. 'We need the diamond not the kid.'

'Shut it, soldier.' Teacher turned back to Arn. 'Did you lose it… where?'

'No, I didn't lose it. But it might as well be lost. Mogahrr has it – the queen of the Panterran. I think you better forget it.'

Teacher exhaled slowly through his nose. 'Can't do that. To be blunt, we retrieve it, or our world is destroyed. End of story.'

Arn looked to Sorenson. 'She has an army, and she has the Lygon with her.'

The Wolfen nodded slowly. 'It's true. It would be an enjoyable but useless attack.'

'Got to try it.' Teacher shook his head and paced away. He stopped and looked up at the sky, his lips drawn back and his teeth clenched for a moment before yelling, 'Goddammit, can nothing be easy here?'

He rubbed one hand up through his hair. 'We don't have time for reinforcements. We need something, right here, right now.'

The Deltas threw in options – all centered on different forms of attack on the castle. Teacher rejected each – their ammunition would run out long before their enemy's would.

Silence hung in the clearing for a few moments before Arn suddenly had a thought. 'This is a long shot, but… it is one of the reasons I came here.' He pulled out the scrap of map that showed the military insignia. 'It must still exist because the king recognized it… and so do I – isn't it some sort of military bunker?'

Teacher took it from Arn, and turned it around. He began to smile. 'Oh yeah, this'll do just fine – weapon's research and storage. If it can be opened, and if everything hasn't turned to dust, and if we can find it… then I want in.'

He handed the map back to Arn. 'Lot of ifs, but it's the best – only – option we got.' He spun a finger in the air. 'Okay people; let's go have a chat to the King.'

Several of the Panina warriors lay on the ground, bullet wounds to their bodies. The flow of spears, rocks, branches, fruit, and anything else that could be flung down at them had quickly ceased after the first round of the soldier's bullets.

Simiana came out to them first, walking calmly towards Arn and the Deltas. 'King Troglan wishes to cease hostilities. Your leader may enter… but just your leader.' She motioned up towards the treetops and the structures nestling in amongst the boughs of the massive banyan trees.

Teacher loaded a grenade and fired it off into the jungle. The explosion made Simiana shriek, and a new round of chatting poured forth from the canopy above them. He turned to her.

'Listen miss; I can see your warriors all crammed in there as plain as day. We're running out of time and patience. Tell the king to get down here now, or the next one will be into his window.' He loaded another grenade into the under-chamber.

Simiana stood with her shoulders hunched, lips pulled back and teeth clamped together. Her eyes darted and she reminded Arn of those pictures of frightened chimpanzees – all teeth and rolling eyes.

Simiana looked to the king's residence, to Teacher and then back again. She nodded jerkily.

'I will speak to my father.'

'Two minutes… Troglan comes down, or I blow him down.' Teacher folded his arms, cradling the gun. He turned to his team. 'Spread out; let's make sure no one tries to make a dash along the upper limbs.'

The Deltas formed a large circle under the largest trees, their eyes moving between the branches, the houses nestled in amongst them, and Simiana ascending.

It only took a few minutes before the King was lowered down to the ground on his wooden elevator. More platforms filled with warriors descended, but Teacher casually lifted the muzzle of his gun, and waved them away.

While Sorenson talked quietly with Grimson, Arn and Teacher stood with the king and Simiana at a table made from the fallen stump of a giant tree. Arn had the ancient map spread flat, his finger jabbing at the fist holding the lightning bolt.

'This… I know you've seen it before. Where is it?'

Troglan shrugged with a casualness that was betrayed by his furtive glances. 'Maybe I have seen it. But I need help remembering the details. Is there something you could give me to assist?' His eyes slid to Teacher's rifle.

Teacher's teeth ground for a second. 'How about we give you the gift of your own life… and perhaps a beating to remind you of how tenuous your hold on it is at the moment?' Teacher leaned in close to the king, and spoke slowly. 'Tell us what you know, or things are about to get real messy for you.'

'I am King Troglan, and…'

Teacher half turned. 'Brown.' The large Delta pushed his rifle up over his shoulder and tugged at his ceramic plated gloves, smacking one fist into the other. Teacher seemed to think about it, and held up his hand to the big Delta. 'Got a better idea… Sorenson.'

The huge Wolfen turned from Grimson and Teacher nodded towards the king. Sorenson summed up the situation immediately, and leapt the dozen feet between them, lifting Troglan and baring his teeth inches from the little man's face. The king's feet dangled in the air and Simiana grabbed at the huge beast's arms.

'Evil, disrespectful beings. He is our king.' Teacher simply shrugged, so she turned to Arn.

'Please, you were our guest. We meant you no harm.'

Arn scoffed. 'We were worm food, and you were cheering it on.' Arn tapped the symbol on the paper. 'Where?'

Teacher cursed, stepping forward. 'Where… the hell… is… it?' His eyes were furious as he banged his fist down on the table. Sorenson roared again into the King's face and shook his body.

Troglan held up a hand. 'I… I think I remember now.'

Teacher grunted and waved Sorenson off. Troglan was lowered to the ground, but Sorenson kept one large, clawed hand on his shoulder.

'The steel caves can be found at the place where the ground sinks. About half days march from here.' The King looked up at the trees.

Teacher nodded. 'Not so hard now, was it?' He circled his finger in the air, and the Delta's started to form up. Troglan looked back up into the trees and whispered to Simiana as she took his arm.

Teacher grabbed the ape king from her and shoved him forward. 'You're coming too – insurance. Let's go.'

• ⊰⊙⊷⊱ ⋊⊙⊙⋉ ⊰⊶⊙⊰⊱ •

Sorenson sniffed the air. 'Metal.'

'Yes.' Arn sniffed, also noticing the slight tang of corrosion. The same odor you detect when approaching a shipyard or anywhere a large amount of iron is left exposed to the air.

They pushed through the last few feet of jungle, and the King stopped. 'I will go no further.'

Teacher held up his hand, and the team spread out a few extra yards. There was a rocky hill and facing them was a small cave mouth, about a hundred feet away, across an empty piece of land. Huge branches grew over the top creating an enclosed clearing. Strange, circular depressions covered its surface.

Alison Sharp lifted her rifle. 'More worms?'

'Maybe not. The King said something about, where the land sinks. Might be sinkholes.' Teacher reached into a pocket and pulled out a small plastic cylinder. He bent it at the middle, shook it, and then tossed it forward. The small rod glowed brightly, travelled through the air like a tiny comet and fell at the edge of one of the depressions. It rolled down to the bottom, and then quickly disappeared below the sliding earth.

'Yep, sink holes, and if they're still sucking dirt then it means the storage facilities haven't totally filled yet. These storage chambers go down six stories. I think some sort of ground movement has torn a hole into one of the levels and the earth is pouring in. Also exposing some of the technology to the air – that's what we can smell.

Teacher turned to the king. 'The insignia is not visible for here, so you must have been inside the cave. That means you get to show us the safe path across the field.'

Troglan looked up at Teacher, his face unreadable, but a hint of a smile touched his lips. 'My daughter stays here. I will go first, but it has been many long seasons since I have crossed to the steel caves, so you must give me room.' He turned back to the field, the smile still showing. 'If I fall, I do not wish to drag you in.'

Behind them, Simiana backed up and then melted away into the jungle. Teacher gave the king a small shove.

'After you, your highness.'

The king frowned at the push, but then after looking around at the Delta's heavy kit, he grinned. 'Yes, you after me.' He reached down and removed his moccasins, displaying splayed toes that were more like fingers.

He stepped out, carefully walking along the raised edges of the sinkholes, placing his hand-like feet on small flat green plants on the ridges. He moved slowly, with Teacher next, and most of the Deltas, followed by Grimson, Sorenson, and then Sharp at the rear.

The going was slow, with the King pausing from time to time. He would rub his chin, look to the left and right, and then upward as if trying to regain his bearings. He moved forward again along paths that were so narrow the Deltas had to walk arms-out, like on a tightrope.

Teacher half turned. 'This whole area will subside soon. Be careful people, or you'll end up six stories down, chewing several tons of dirt.'

When Teacher turned back, the King had put about ten feet between himself and the Deltas. They were at the very centre of the scarred landscape, when the king stopped. He kept his back turned.

'Your weapons are truly mighty, but it is the jungle who is mightier... always mightier.' He half turned his expression carrying both disdain and triumph.

Sorenson roared and Arn crouched, his eyes wide. 'The Panina are here!'

There came an enormous thud from behind them as a huge stone dropped from the trees. They all spun, the Deltas with their weapons aimed. At that moment a vine dangled down from overhead, and the king grabbed it and climbed with an astonishing speed, using both his hands and feet.

'Dammit.' Teacher tried to aim, but Troglan had vanished into the canopy so quickly, it was if he never existed.

'So much for our guide.' Simms scanned the foliage with his scope.

'Stay alert, people. Go to all quadrant defensive.' Teacher watched the overhead foliage, while the Deltas faced the cardinal points of the compass.

There was stillness in the clearing, and Arn knew he was holding his breath.

'Watch out.' Sharp's voice cut the silence and turning they saw another vine swinging out of the dark – this one ending in a large rock. Sharp fired a short burst, shattering the stone, and then together the Deltas let controlled bursts of rounds into the canopy from where the rock originated.

'Cease fire. We can't see a goddamn thing. Go to thermal.' Teacher had to yell to be heard over the automatic fire, but immediately the guns cooled and each of the elite soldiers pulled single eye scopes down over their faces.

'Jesus.' Brown swore softly. The trees were alive with the small warriors moving like ants along the tree limbs.

'Incoming!' Teacher crouched as more rocks swung out of the dark foliage. Sorenson threw his arms over Grimson, making his own body a shield. A rock, easily three feet across, struck Doonie in the back. With a grunt, coupled with the sound of crunching bone he was flung forward into the centre of one of the sinkholes. He immediately disappeared to his waist.

Teacher dived as close as he could to the edge and stretched out his hand. Brown also leapt over, landing on top of the Delta leader's legs just as he started to enter the pit beside the sinking Doonie. Teacher reached out, his fingertips almost touching his soldier, but the man's face was twisted in agony, his body too broken to allow him to reach back towards his captain.

Doonie shook his head. 'Sorry boss, I'm done for.' He

exhaled and shut his eyes, leaning back and grimacing. 'Get the weapons, and then get the hell home.'

'Don't you dare, soldier.' Teacher strained, and Brown held on tight while digging one hand into the soil to anchor himself.

Donnie's face calmed and without another word, he slipped beneath the sinking soil. Teacher roared and rolled onto his back, loading a grenade into the underslung launcher and firing it up into the canopy. He loaded and fired, loaded and fired, screaming his fury to the Panina. The other Delta soldiers did the same, and soon burning branches and bodies rained down around them.

After another few seconds, Arn stood, covering his ears. 'They're gone.' He yelled over the mayhem unfolding around him. 'You're wasting your ammo.'

Teacher blinked, and then nodded. 'Cease fire.'

The flames had lit the clearing brighter than day, but the lush vegetation didn't burn for long and soon they were plunged back into darkness and silence.

Simms was on one knee, still sighting on the canopy. 'They killed Doonie, those sons of bitches.'

'Forget it… for now.' Teacher half turned. 'We'll mourn later. Let's do what we came to do, and then get the hell out of here.' He waved them on, walking on the ridges between the holes as he had seen the king do before.

Teacher turned to Arn. 'How did you know they were above us? They were out of sight, invisible amongst the dark foliage.'

Arn shrugged. 'I could sense them, smell them.'

Teacher stared for a few seconds. He frowned and looked away. 'Sure, okay.'

In another few minutes they stood at the cave entrance, and without hesitation Teacher entered. Arn and the others followed. The cave was huge, empty, but showed signs of habitation. There were cave drawings, some primitive and faded, but others not so old. of the newer ones showed exquisite detail, raised up in an indication of many layers of paint applied over the generations. Perhaps they were so important that the messages, myths or legends they portrayed had to be preserved.

Arn traced one of the larger murals with his hand. 'Maps, and some sort of history of the Panina.'

Sorenson jabbed a clawed finger down on an image of a giant wolf standing amongst tongues of flame. 'Fenrir, the father of us all... and the fire he was born in. All paths start with him, and lead from him.'

'Must have been quite a creature, er, thing... I mean Wolfen.' Sharp shrugged as Sorenson glared.

Teacher followed the map along the wall. 'This is where we are, and here... the lake, and the Far Wolfen maybe...' An image of a snarling wolf was painted on the opposite bank of the giant body of water.

Sorenson stepped forward, staring and measuring, his eyes narrowing. Teacher continued to trace a ribbon of blue – a river along the wall, noting its twists and turns, and where it finally disappeared below the cliffs, to reappear on the other side of the giant wall of mountains.

'This might be a shortcut to Valkeryn. The river travels all the way back through the jungle and then passes by the kingdom.'

Grimson shook his head. 'We should stay out of the water – bad things in the water – big things.'

Teacher grunted. 'We can deal with them. We have to.'

Brown was checking the clip in his rifle. 'We better watch the ammo, Boss.'

'Heeey, look at this.' Alison Sharp was further along, and shining her flashlight onto a human figure that looked to be growing out of the wall – a bronze statue, embedded in the stone.

Arn frowned, 'I've seen that guy before. But in giant form – it's carved into the cliff wall, hundreds of feet high, but that one had no face. Grimson though it might represent Fenrir.'

'I do, I did… then.' The young Wolfen had folded his arms.

'It had words carved as well – something like "HE STILL LIVES".' Could also be a message for the new peoples of the planet, telling them that we, the Ancients, still live some-where… or we did.'

Teacher stepped up and wiped away some cobwebs, dust and then scraped away some green corrosion extruding on the base. 'And here it is – HE STILL LIVES".' He wiped more scree away from higher up on the figure and laughed softly. 'Hey, look familiar?'

Sharp snorted. 'You're famous.' She turned and shined her light into Arn's face. 'That's you, sunshine.'

Arn's mouth hung open. It could have been him – no, it was him – like it was taken from a photograph… an old one, where he had short, neat hair.

'But… why.'

Teacher shrugged. 'Maybe we cast it when we knew the planet was going to crap. We made it hoping that you, or someone who knew you, would see it. Telling the people not give up hope because you still live somewhere. Who knows, maybe even trying to get you to come back – our last chance.'

'But… if it was carved, then I can't have gone back. Because if I went back, then why would you need to make it?' Arn scratched his head. 'Paradox?'

Teacher turned away. 'I don't care. Maybe when you get home, this disappears – nothing is guaranteed, the future is fluid – isn't that what they say?'

'Who? Probably a sci-fi writer.' Arn touched the statue's face.

Teacher had already disappeared into the deeper caves. He called back from the darkness. 'Let's go people.'

Further in they found the door, or rather a steel wall with the faded fist and lightning bolt symbol.

'The steel caves.' Arn's voice was hushed, but still echoed.

The steel showed signs of having been bombed, burnt, and bashed as if over the millennia many had tried their best to break it down or punch a hole through the blast resistant doors. Teacher guessed that they never stood a chance of breaching the barrier using primitive tools. In fact, he had counted on it. He found a control panel, and levered the cover out of the way. The contents came away in a shower of rust.

'No power, and dead as a dodo... and not going to be able kick start this baby with a few high-erg batteries either.' He stood back a step. 'Going to stick to Plan A – punch a hole right through.'

Weng grunted softly. 'Not easy – three inches of high density, composite steel.'

'That's why it's unopened.' Teacher pulled his rifle and loaded a grenade. 'But, we get in, or go home with nothing but fond memories.'

Teacher looked around on the floor, and bent to pick up a loose stone. He went up to the door, and drew a three-foot circle. 'We concentrate grenade and armor piercing rounds, right here.' He banged on the steel. 'Let's hope we get some go-forward before we run out of ammunition.'

The group took cover, and the five remaining Deltas took up positions either side of the cave and sighted on Teacher's target.

'Fire.'

Blast after blast pounded the door, making a sound like an enormous gong being continually struck in the small enclosure. Teacher was first to switch to uranium-tipped armor-piercing bullets. They left a tracer-like path as they streamed towards the armored wall.

Inside the marked circle the steel had become white hot from the impacts.

'Cease.' He held up a hand, and got to his feet. He pushed his rifle up over his shoulder as he walked forward. The steel wall was heavily pitted and now concave in the centre of the ring. But there was still no break.

'Damn it.' Teacher picked up another stone, and drew a smaller circle, this one only about twelve inches in diameter, and over the most heavily scarred area. He took up his position again.

'Keep it tight; another twenty second burst on mymark. Three... two...*one*...'

Once again the rain of steel and explosives flew forward, but before time was up...

'I'm out.' from Simms.

'Me too.' from Brown.

Sharp fired her last grenade, it burst in an orange plume, but there was little flashback this time. Teacher held up his hand.

'Good.' They'd punched through; Teacher's circle was red and cooling rapidly. He trotted forward and kicked out with his boot. The hot steel sizzled against the synthetic material but crumbled inwards, leaving a two-foot jagged porthole.

'Let's hope the cupboard isn't bare.' He stuck his head inside, and then climbed through, carefully avoiding the near molten steel at the edges.

Teacher's head popped back out. 'Stale but breathable air – Brown, Weng, Simms come with me.'

The Deltas scrambled through.

'Go to lights.' Beams flicked on from their head and belt-mounted lights, throwing tunnels of illumination into the ancient structure.

'Weird; it's more modern than anything we knew, but seems as old as time itself in here.'

'Yeah well, we've been gone a long time. Let's hope we can find more than rust, dust and stale air.'

They stood in the centre of a room the size of an aircraft hangar. Teacher walked to a wall with a tattered imprint under glass.

'Level One – Administration, no interest there. Level Two – Research & Development, that's more like it. Level Three – Nucleonics and Propulsion. Nice. Levels Four and Five are mobile multi-carrier technology – forget it. Unfortunately, I doubt the maintenance elevators are going to work long enough to lift some sort of tank up from the basement.' He turned.

'Okay, let's make this quick – Simms, with me to Level One. Brown, Weng, get down to the lower levels and see what you can find that's useful, portable, and still operational. Stay in contact and keep your damn eyes open.' He spun one way then the other. 'Spread out and find me that elevator shaft.'

The door to the elevator needed all four of them to lever it to open, and the cabin itself was stuck somewhere deep in the bowels of the substructure.

Teacher leaned in for a moment, and then pulled back. He turned to Brown with a grin. 'After you.'

The climb down along the metal struts was fairly easy, and the lower doors, less exposed to the upper atmosphere were still sliding with little trouble.

Simms pulled back. 'Phew, dead air.'

Teacher pushed him in. 'Been sealed for too many eons to count. Let's just hope it's not toxic.'

He nodded to Brown and Weng, who continued on their downward climb, and followed Simms into the dark room. He adjusted his light and walked to a row of metal doors set into the wall.

'You check over that side – move quickly.' Most of the rooms and storage chambers were empty. Some contained interesting but useless items such as boots, belts, new helmet technology, and then from the others side of the chamber…'

'Oh yeah… this'll do.' Simms backed up a step and smiled.

Teacher joined him. 'What've you got?'

'I think they're CL Suits – I thought this stuff was still on the drawing board.'

'Well, looks like they perfected them.' Teacher reached in and pulled out one of the suits. He held it up. 'Oh yeah, this is it – Carbon Lattice Suit.' He spoke softly, reeling off what he knew about the modern combat uniform.

'This baby is one of the most expensive materials in the world – actually grown like a diamond. The research and development eggheads wanted to make use of the way carbon atoms are arranged. It's organised in a specific type of cubic lattice mesh called diamond cubic.'

Simms frowned. 'Tough huh?'

Teacher grinned. 'Oh yeah. Diamonds are the hardest naturally-occurring material on the planet and they've managed to duplicate the structure for the suit material – virtually impenetrable… and…' he sorted through them, '… one size fits all. Put 'em on. And let's grab some for the team.'

'Boss.' Weng's voice in Teacher's ear.

'Go.'

'We found some shoulder-mounted mini-nukes, something that looks like a mobile land mine, mini propulsion units, laser cutters… and the biggest high-temperature incendiary bomb I've ever seen.'

'What yield?'

'Good size hammer, probably a kiloton, and all in a tidy little package.'

'Good. Pack all you can carry, and one of the incendiary hammers. We'll need to seal this place up, or within a month King Willy of the Jungle and his boys will be the best armed force on the planet.'

'You got it. Brown and I will do a quick reconnoiter of the two bottom levels. Check in then. Out.'

'Roger that; stay on comms.' Teacher and Simms went back to pulling open drawers and sliding back doors that were sealed shut.

Simms paused at one small chamber. It contained a single item – a silver metallic square, the size of a cigar box. He lifted it, and slid open the lock. Inside was a small booklet covering a row of dull looking capsules. He flipped it open and read.

'Morph steel. Ten units – field-test approved.' He flipped through the pages. 'Do not use if suffering from hypertension, diabetes, psychotic episodes. Hmm, that's comforting.'

Teacher frowned. 'Morph steel? Let me see that.'

Simms handed him the box. Teacher saw there was ten metallic capsules inside, each in their own compartment. Simms read more from the small booklet.

'Morphic body weaponry, twenty-four hour duration. Take with water.'

Teacher looked up at Simms, holding one of the capsules between thumb and forefinger. 'Well Morpheus, do I take the red pill or the blue bill?' He grinned and tossed it into his mouth, dry swallowing hard.

'Kack.' He gagged, and grabbed for his water canteen and gulped hard. He coughed and took a deep breath. 'Yech, tastes like metal with a crap after-taste.'

Simms frowned. 'Now what?'

Teacher shrugged. 'You've got the book; you tell me.'

Simms shook his head, flipping pages. 'Cerebral controlled morphic weaponry – sounds pretty straight forward.' He laughed. 'Just remember, what doesn't kill you makes you stronger.'

Teacher grimaced. 'Feel strange.' He held up his hands, turning them in front of his face. He frowned, concentrating – an image started to form in his mind. There came a tingling at the back of his neck that travelled down his arms to his fingers. And then...

'Jesus Christ.' Simms jumped back.

A blade appeared in Teacher's hand... not actually in it, but *of* it.

Teacher nodded. 'I understand – Morph steel is nano-tech. The chemicals stay inside you for twenty-four hours, producing the hardest metal known to man. The nano fragments are organised by your nerve endings, and directed by your brain. They basically use your body as a factory, using the other chemicals in your system to produce anything you can imagine.

'Great – guns?'

'Sure, but they'd be a solid mass – no working parts. Consider it a built-in close-quarters combat kit, without all the carrying weight.'

'I'll take one.' Simms held out his hand.

Teacher snapped the box closed. 'Nope, not yet. We save these until we need them. I was just the guinea pig.

'Boss, we're coming up.' Weng again

Teacher heard the stress in his soldier's voice – unusual for the normally self-controlled man. He didn't like it.

'What is it?'

'Bodies... I mean skeletons, everywhere. Bite marks on the bones. Something has been eating them. They were people, the scientists I think. The damn chamber has been opened up – the walls are like Swiss cheese down here. Something got in, and ate them up.' There was silence for a few more seconds. 'Creepy as all hell down here, and I can hear something... laughing or giggling far away in the dark.'

'Okay, we've got all we need. Get back up here, pronto.'

'Half way there already, Boss.'

- ⊁⊰⊙⊛⊱ ⨉⨯⨯⨯⨉ ⊰⊛⊙⊱⊁ -

Arn watched as Weng and Brown stepped through the hole in the metal wall. Each had bulging backpacks and armfuls of all manner of pipes and packages. Simms, with Teacher climbing through last, quickly followed them. The Delta leader spent a few extra seconds staring back into the dark void, as though… listening. At last he turned and joined the team.

Alison Sharp was first to notice the outfits Simms and Teacher wore. 'Wow.' Her mouth hung in an open smile. 'Well, well, looks like someone found the menswear department.'

'Now that looks cool.' Arn grinned.

Simms took a small bow and held his arms wide, turning slowly to show off the new technology uniform. The suits were tight and made of a black lattice material. The Delta men and women were physically fit, but the suits also had a form of flexible armor plating covering the chest, arms and thighs, resulting in a slight bulging effect over an already muscular physicality.

Simms finished his turn. 'Light, flexible and about fifty times tougher than Kevlar.'

Alison Sharp continued to walk around him, running her hand over the material. 'Is this what I think it is – CL technology?'

Teacher nodded. 'You got it in one – CL suits, and one each for all of us.'

'Outstanding.' Sharp started to take off her uniform.

'And watch this.' Simms touched a small stud on the raised collar. Immediately, the suit telescoped up over the back of his head and down over his face. A single slot over the eyes had a tinted but transparent material which allowed vision. It also resolved itself so the carbon lattice mesh was more open over his mouth for breathing.

'Full face helmet.' He reached up and ran his hand up over the metallic material. 'Feels great. Hey Brown, punch me in the head.'

Brown pulled a face. 'Sure, and I'll shoot you as well if you like.' He raised his gun.

'Knock it off.' Teacher handed the suits out. 'Put 'em on, and everyone spend a few minutes familiarizing themselves with the technology.'

Sharp held hers up. 'Hey Teach; don't worry about the head bit for Brown. His noggin is hard enough.'

Brown stood in his boxers, and pulled the suit up over one leg. He snorted. 'And Sharp wants to know if it comes in any other colors.'

The female Delta grinned, and held out her fist. 'Pay that.' She and Brown bumped knuckles.

Once suited up, Teacher held one out to Sorenson. 'Not sure you'll get into it, but...'

The huge Wolfen shook his head. 'I have my Valkeryn armor that has the crests of Grimvaldr, my forefathers, and my kingdom. It will be enough.'

Teacher nodded. 'Then let's get to this inland sea; we got a war to start.'

CHAPTER 32

THERE WILL BE NO RETURN OF THE ANCIENTS

Orcalion prostrated himself before Mogahrr; lying flat, arms wide, face pressed hard into the cold stones.

'Their weapons, Mistress, were powerful. They surprised us.' He lifted his head an inch. 'And the Lygon are slow and stupid.'

Behind him the Lygon growled, but a furious glance from Mogahrr's yellow eyes silenced them.

'A Lygon waaar party, accompanied by Panterran arch-erssss; all wiped out iiin minutesss by a meeeere handful of Man-Kind?'

Orcalion's head lowered to the stone floor once more. 'Not just Man-Kind. They used a Wolfen to bait us.'

'A Wolfen? Theeey fight with the Wolfen – what Wolfen?'

'I think it was the one called Sorenson.' Orcalion lifted again and turned to look to Goranx, who was standing like a mountain at the rear of the room. 'The brother of Strom, son of Stromgard, and last of the Wolfen elite. I thought he had been defeated by the mighty Goranx.' He lowered his head, a small smile twisting his lips. 'Obviously not.'

Goranx exploded, and launched himself forward before the queen hissed, and her archers behind the throne raised their poison tipped arrows. She held up her hand as Goranx skidded to a stop.

'They ssseek the Arnoddr.' Her eyes closed for a moment. 'And onccce they haaave him, what theeen?'

She reached out and began to stroke Brigg's head. The female Delta leader stood docile, as if in a trance. 'Will they be foolissssh enough to cooome for their llleader? Or maybe they

299

will tryyy to flee to their homeworld.' She opened her eyes. 'There are ssso few of themmm. They will try and bring more warriorsss.' She nodded. 'We know wherrre they will runnn too, and we wiiill be there to sssee they never leave. Thisss land doesss not belong to the Ancientsss anymore, it belongsss to the Panterran.'

Mogahrr turned to Briggs, still stroking the woman's head. 'I think weee will need to have another little taaalk. Youuu cann tell mee how weee can dfeat these last few Man-Kind, and then perhapsss how weee can challenge the Man-Kind in their own wooorld.' She sat back and hissed out a laugh. 'Who can stop usss?'

She leaned forward, her face once again taking on its cunning mien. 'Dark Wolfen, now you wiiill earn your keep. If this Sor-ennn-sssson leadssss them, then you will beee at the front of our forcesss. Wolfen fightsss Wolfen, yessss?'

Bergborr frowned and the queen showed her teeth in a decayed grin. 'Yesss, time to fight for your new masssters.' She nodded to Goranx. 'Or end up in the beeelly of the Lygon.'

Mogahrr turned to one of her Panterran generals. 'Take a forccce of Lygon and Panterran to where the Man-Kind wiiill try and essscape back to their home-world. Sssecure it, and then lie in wait for them. There will be no return of the Ancientsss.'

CHAPTER 33

THEY'RE HIDING IN THE DARK

General Langstrom stood silently at the rear of the room. Beside him Harper fidgeted as Lieutenant Bannock briefed the new Deltas. Their eyes were focused, alert, and they were absorbing every atom of information the returned Special Forces soldier imparted.

The assembled men and woman all knew that information was the most valuable weapon they had. If possible, they became even more focused when he talked of the Panterran and Lygon attack.

Bannock paced. 'Do not assume these beings that you have seen on the image loops are big, dumb brutes that are just going to come at you in a straight line, begging to be blown away. These things are immensely powerful, armored to all hell, battlefield smart, and with them come a horde of smaller creatures that are the embodiment of cunning. To add to our combat complexity, they are now being led by Colonel Marion Briggs, and we assume they have several HK416 rifles with spare mags.' He paced his face grim. 'Plus grenade launchers, claymores and any other kit they acquired from our fallen Delta team.'

He stopped pacing and faced the new team with his hands on his hips. 'We have one role today – hold the line. Our gut feeling is that these things are going to come at the portal. They must not... they *will* not... be allowed anywhere near our home.'

Bannock's eyes blazed. 'Questions?'

'Numbers?'

Bannock shot back the answer. 'Unknown – could be a few hundred or a few thousand.'

'Expected contact duration?'

'Till it's done. It's a fight to the death – theirs.'

'HUA!' The new Deltas started to pound a single fist against the ceramic plating over their chests.

General Langstrom stepped forward.

'Okay Bannock, Captain Henson's got his war party – lead them in, and show 'em hell.'

Bannock saluted the General and then turned back to the squad. 'Secure all loose items – it's a tornado in there. On my six; let's move.' He pulled his goggles down over his eyes and the squad did the same.

'Fight or die.' Bannock roared the words, spun and then ran through the cross tunnel into the acceleration chamber.

His jaws clenched when he saw the rent in space and time. The portal was an ugly red and filled the chamber. His feet lifted from the ground before he was within ten feet of the distortion perimeter – his body stretched and then disappeared.

Two-by-two, the Deltas followed, many carrying boxes of ammunition and other weapons of war. They elongated like ribbons and then disappeared.

Harper turned to the general. 'What happens if we lose? What happens if it's the creatures that come back through instead of our soldiers?'

Langstrom snorted. 'You said we've probably only got about forty-eight hours… so I reckon it'll be a good joke on them to own the Earth on the day it gets ripped to shreds.'

Harper's face was white as he turned away. 'Then, God go with them all.'

◦ ❧⊱⊰❧ ⋙∘∘∘⋘ ❧⊱⊰❧ ◦

Teacher stood with Sorenson at the edge of the sea. The Great Lakes had combined and widened, and all their rivers and tributaries now poured into one vast inland ocean which disappeared over the horizon.

Arn pointed to the south. 'Valkeryn is that way.'

Teacher nodded. 'Okay. First thing we need is something to keep us out of the water. He turned. 'Weng, put that laser cutter to use. We need a boat big enough for all of us.'

Sorenson was staring out to the west. He raised his head as though trying to catch a scent. He spoke without turning, his eyes on the horizon. 'We need two boats. One for you humans, and one big enough for a single Wolfen.'

'Huh?' Teacher spun. 'What do you think you're doing?'

Sorenson exhaled slowly. 'I need to find the Far Wolfen. Without them you don't stand a chance.'

'If they exist.' Arn responded.

Sorenson nodded. 'Yes, if they exist. But I believe Odin has led me to this point for a reason. And he will guide me further, if that is his wish.'

Grimson came and stood by Arn. 'Noble Sorenson, you will find them… and you will bring them.'

Arn jumped at the ground-shaking thump as a huge tree fell to the ground, felled by the laser cutter. Weng blinked several times from the blinding white light beam. The metallic rod in his hand was like a flashlight without the bulb end, and just a pencil-sized hole that emitted the condensed light. He repositioned himself at one end of the log and set to shaping it, and then hollowing it out, the laser cutting and searing huge chunks of bark. The beam also heat-sealed the wood and resin, making the vessel waterproof.

Weng stopped and stood back to admire his work. Two flat-bottomed canoe-like boats – one large enough for the Deltas, Arn and Grim, and the other a single person craft for Sorenson – sat where before there had been nothing.

Brown walked around the large boat, looking inside. 'Hey Weng; what do we sit on?'

'Your ass, dimwit. You think I'm going to build in bunk beds for you as well?' He held up a finger. 'But it does come with one important modification...' Weng moved to the stern, where he had created a small indentation in the wood. He fitted one of the portable propulsion units onto it.

'Turbo propulsion... maximum speed about fifty knots, give or take.'

Sorenson looked at his own boat, feeling along the lines. 'Very good job, Warrior Weng. Are there paddles?'

Teacher shook his head. 'No, you get one of the propulsion units as well.'

Weng's mouth dropped open. 'Boss, that's our backup. If we...'

'Give it to him.'

Weng's mouth snapped shut. 'Sir.'

He fitted the small boat with the powerful propulsion unit and then stood back waving Sorenson over. He took several minutes to run through the simple instructions with the Wolfen. He didn't bother with any maintenance or refueling advice, because if it stopped and he wasn't near the shore, he was as good as dead.

'Okay, just remember, these things are powerful. Take it easy, or you'll be airborne.'

Sorenson ran a test, blowing sand fifty feet back and out into the jungle. He nodded and smiled.

'The fantastic machines of the Ancients.'

The team quickly packed the boats with as much food as they could find. Sorenson pushed his own smaller craft to the water's edge, and then came back and got down on one knee before Grimson.

'Be safe young prince.' He held out his sword. 'My life for you, Grimson, son of Grimvaldr.'

Arn almost felt himself choking up at the bravery and sacrifice of this noble race. Grimson stood taller, Arn noticing he seemed to lengthen and fill out more by the minute. The prince placed his hand on Sorenson's shoulder.

'Stand, Wolfen Elite of Valkeryn. I will see you on the battlefield at the rise of the moon this morrow.'

Sorenson nodded and smiled. 'On the bloody fields of Valkeryn or in Valhalla, Prince Grimson. We will have blood.'

Grimson banged his fist against Sorenson's chest. 'We will have rivers of blood, and Mogahrr's head on a pike.' He roared, and for the first time Arn noticed it wasn't the sound of a youth anymore, but the battle cry of a full grown Wolfen.

Sorenson responded, throwing his own head back, their roars rolling out across the lake. He bowed, and then without another word, leapt into the small boat, and started the propulsion unit. A rooster's tail of spray kicked up, and the bow lifted high as it took off like a jet boat. In another few minutes he was a mere dot on the horizon.

Arn watched for a few minutes and then nodded. 'Good. While we move at speed we may be safe from whatever is below the surface.'

Teacher placed the last of the supplies into the boat. 'Then let's get moving. We're running out of time.'

<hr />

They stayed in sight of the land, the large flat-bottomed boat pushing forward at around forty knots. Behind them a column of black smoke rose from the jungle, the one-kiloton incendiary bomb making the air still shimmer over the massive trees. After the percussion wave had passed by them, Teacher nodded, confident that the land above the military bunker would now be a scab of molten rock and slag, and impenetrable to any of the local tribes.

The still dawn made for a glass-like surface on the water and they were able to spot any turbulence easily. As well, several pairs of keen eyes directed Weng away from anything large they saw breaching the surface.

At one point, all the Deltas shouldered their nearly empty rifles at the water as something the size of a blue whale passed smoothly underneath them on its way along the shoreline. Leaning over the side, Arn saw it roll slightly and one large bulbous eye swiveled to look briefly back at him, before the monstrous thing rolled again and continued on to the shallows.

Arn was the only one who still refused to put on his CL suit. After so long wearing nothing but his own skin, the thought of the restrictive material made him cringe. Simms had told him it felt light as a feather and allowed the skin to breathe, but for Arn, the tight-fitting elasticized body armour would remain rolled up in his pack until a last resort.

He looked at each of the Deltas as they stood at different points on the boat, their hawk-like eyes focused on the water's surface; each of them was professional, lethal, and in their suits, a visual cross between Iron Man and a speed skater. Behind him, Grimson sat silent. Arn had tried to engage him in conversation but the youth had said little more than a word or two since they set out, preferring to be in company of his own thoughts.

They travelled throughout the morning, the sun lifting from the horizon, then rising high, and then starting to ease off into the west. The afternoon rolled on, and Arn started to feel cramps and stiffness in his muscles as he held himself in place in the moving boat, remaining ever alert to the giants that he knew existed in the lake's aquamarine depths.

It was late afternoon when, above the massive jungle banyans, they could see the color of the jagged cliff tops. A few hours back, the opposite shoreline had appeared, and now the mighty lake was narrowing, with the movement of water obvious as it headed into a massive river cave far in the distance.

Weng slowed the boat as it headed towards the cliffs. There were multiple caves, some just big enough for the boat to fit, and one large enough to fly a 747 passenger jet inside.

'Any guesses?' Teacher looked around at the faces, stopping at Arn and Grimson, obviously hoping their experience gave them more insight than the newcomers. Grimson didn't look up and Arn just shrugged.

'Bigger is better,' said Teacher. 'The main cave it is then. Okay people, go to lights. Brown, I want you on thermal… Simms, give me motion detection. Let's keep alert and try to punch through, however long this takes.'

Brown adjusted the lens on his suit. 'Let's hope it goes all the way through, and doesn't stop at a dead end.'

They passed under the huge lip of stone. Alison Sharp switched on her flashlight. 'What's up big fella – you don't like cave-dives?'

Brown grinned. 'Sure, in the Bahamas, but not in freaking Jurassic Park.'

Weng kept the speed down to ten knots, the craft moving in to the growing darkness as they left the opening. In another twenty minutes the only sound came from invisible dripping, and the low purr of the propulsion unit. All conversation had ceased, and senses and nerves were stretched tight.

Arn looked up; the cave was enormous, and the walls glistened with bioluminescent lichens and mosses. Though they had heard or seen nothing, the sensation of 'life' all around them was steadily growing.

'Take it down a few more knots.' Teacher raised a small black flashlight to give him a different angle. Coming up, and just above the water level, there was a shelf of stone, fifty feet across, and better yet, dry.

'Weng, pull in over there. Let's stretch our legs for ten.'

As they neared, Teacher turned and motioned for Weng to cut the engine. He kept his hand raised, staying motionless as the boat drifted in close. Everybody froze, as Teacher just listened.

Arn leaned closer to Grimson. The Wolfen's malaise was gone and he was now as alert as the rest of them, his ears moving back and forth. 'Grim, you've got better senses than us... anything?'

His ears flickered. 'No, yes... something, but I can't...' he shrugged. 'No, not sure; I think it's okay.'

Teacher was the first onto the shelf and he immediately turned to pull the bow up a few feet. He held on for a few seconds as the Deltas jumped out followed by Arn and Grimson. The soldiers scattered to the platform edges, guns up, and held their position, scanning the environment for a few seconds, before lowering their weapons, straightening and simply stretching their backs, or rolling their shoulders.

Sharp had her back arched, squeezing out her words. 'Jesus, that feels good.'

'Stinks, like a drain.' Brown wrinkled his nose.

Sharp shook her head. 'I smelt it, yeah, but more like stale almonds or something.'

'Over here.' Weng was at the far edge of the rock platform, shining his light into an alcove. 'Looks like a body – pretty old.'

They crowded round. It was a skeleton, with parchment-dry skin stretched over the bones. The skull, long snout and old skin pulled back over teeth gave it a permanent snarl. A rusted sword was still gripped in one hand.

Grimson narrowed his eyes. 'Brother Wolfen.'

Simms squatted. 'In here – how? The bones are all broken, and he's wrapped in some sort of ...'

'No, just the leg and anklebones. Like he fell or jumped off something.' Brown fingered the threads coating the shattered legs.

'Or was dropped.' Teacher spun, sighting his rifle into the air. 'Back to the boat... now!'

Arn looked up in time to see strands of silk unraveling above them. Fist-sized blobs of glistening fluid were at their ends, and above, hidden in the darkness, something unseen was lowering them with unerring aim.

'Don't let them touch you.' Teacher grabbed the bow of the boat, urging them on.

The Deltas crouched as they ran. Brown turned to spray some of his last rounds up into the roof of the cavern – the response was the sound of ricochets on stone far above them, followed by an unearthly squeal.

One after the other they piled into the boat, Weng clambering over the others as he made his way to the rear and started the propulsion engine. Sharp dived in last, and as she went to hunker down her eyes went wide.

'Oh no,' She arched her back and then began to spasm. 'Christ, it's on me, it's on me!'

There was an elastic stretching sound, and suddenly she was dragged back through the crush of bodies, and then astonishingly, started to lift out of the boat.

'No today, beautiful.' Brown dived, taking her around the waist. She dropped back to the boat, but the cord stayed attached. 'It's trying to reel her in.'

Arn pointed. 'They're hiding in the dark above us.'

Grimson stayed low, but his eyes were darting along the cavern ceiling. 'There are lots of them, and they're all stuck to the ceiling, but crawling now to get over the top of us.'

Teacher shone his lights above them, and in return dozens of glistening eyes were reflected back at him. The multiple orbs were crowded together in three-foot wide bunches. Whatever was staring down were big, had plenty of eyes, and all of them focused on the Deltas.

Sharp screamed as the cord went tight again. She slid, and this time Brown's boots started to drag along the boat. 'It's too strong.'

More cords started to lower towards them, and a second sticky blob landed on Sharp's arm with a wet slap. It immediately pulled her hand back from where she held onto Brown.

Brown drew his large k-bar blade and sawed at the material, but it refused to cut.

'It's like... freakin... steel cable.'

'No!' Sharp grimaced and Arn noticed it was not panic, but frustration in her eyes.

'Make a hole.' Teacher barged through the tumbling bodies, holding out one arm. A four-foot blade appeared from his fingertips, and he swung it sideways, severing both cords instantly.

Sharp dropped and Brown held on tight. Teacher spun.

'Weng, get us the hell out of here. Lights to the bow, thermal and motion detection... now.'

The boat bumped against the rock shelf for a few seconds and then lifted as Weng employed more power. In another moment, they had crossed a hundred feet of water.

Brown got up on one arm and helped Sharp sit. 'How's your day been?'

She snorted and eased back. 'I've had better.' Her face was still ashen. 'Hey... thanks.' She gripped his hand and squeezed.

Arn looked back up at the ceiling. 'I think we're clear.'

Teacher looked from Arn to the ceiling. 'You can see?'

'Yeah, there's just rock and moss now.' He sat back. 'You know, there's a spider in South America called the bolas spider. Doesn't have a web. Instead, it uses a strand of silk with a drop of sticky silk at the end. It literally fishes for its prey.

'How big are they?"

Arn held up his thumb. 'No bigger than my nail.'

Sharp got to her feet. 'Well, I don't want to know big that mother was on the ceiling trying to reel me in. But I gotta tell you, it was a lot stronger than I was.' She looked at Teacher, and nodded towards his now empty hand. 'And I sure gotta get me one of those.'

Teacher nodded. 'Soon.' He moved to the front of the boat. 'I think that's enough rest for today.'

'You okay?' Arn put his hand on Grimson's shoulder. The Wolfen turned, his eyes silvered in the darkness.

'I wish to be on land, and out of this cave. Feels bad in here.'

'I know, I can feel it too. But, we've got to pass under the mountain cliffs. Hopefully, it's not far now.'

Grimson nodded, and then turned. 'Do you think Sorenson made it?'

Arn smiled. 'You know that nothing can kill Sorenson. Besides, he carries both his own and Strom's *sáál* inside him now.' He nudged the youth. 'What does your heart tell you?'

Grimson felt his chest. 'That we will see him again.'

The river cave narrowed, breaking into several smaller caves, each still large enough to steer a steamboat into, and each with moving water, some sluggish, some fast. Over the side of the boat, small luminescent fish darted back and forth, like blue sparks from some ironmonger's works.

Teacher held up his hand, exhaling slowly as he looked along the multiple cave mouths. 'All or none could be the right way.'

Brown moved his flashlight over one of the cave mouth's ceilings. 'Batteries won't last forever.' He lowered his light beam. 'There's water movement into each; means the river is still going somewhere.'

Teacher half turned. 'Weng, take us around again.'

They circled back to the first cave mouth, and then slowed to glide along in front of each. Teacher reached over the side, wet his hand, and held it up. He did it several more times; passing four of the six cave mouths, when he suddenly pointed.

'This one has an air flow; means there must be an above water passageway – hopefully leading all the way out.

Weng brought the nose around and then increased speed. Even though the cave mouth was about a fifty-foot opening and above water, there was little luminescence on the walls inside. Flashlights swung back and forth between the water, the walls, and the ceiling. Adrenaline brought fatigued bodies and minds back to full alert.

For another twenty minutes they travelled with just the soft purr of the propulsion unit and the hiss of water as the bow cut its silky blackness. Simms was the first to break the tension, his voice loud even though whispered. 'Stings like hell. What is that? Ammonia?' He wiped his streaming eyes with the back of his hand.

'Short breaths only; could be some sort of gas vent.' Teacher spoke over his shoulder while pointing course changes out to Weng in the stygian darkness.

'Phew, I've smelt that before.' Arn frowned as he racked his memory, and Grimson put both hands over his long nose.

For the first time since entering the new cave, the boat rocked, lifting slightly on a swell. The Deltas grabbed the gun-wale, glancing at each other. Teacher widened his stance. He looked over the side.

'Weird, must be some backwash. Brace yourselves; there could be some currents up ahead. Maybe even falls.'

The boat lifted again this time even higher. Brown spun with his light scanning behind them, and then to the sides. 'I don't hear anything.' He switched to thermal vision. 'Got nothing with a heat signature, and no churn.'

Sharp lifted her light. 'He's right – no crashing water… and that felt like a bow wave from an approaching vessel.'

There was a grunt from behind them, and the boat started to drift, turning in a long, slow loop.

Teacher grabbed the side of the boat. 'Dammit Weng, watch the walls.' The boat continued to drift, and he half turned. 'Weng, what the…' Teacher froze then crouched, his hands coming up, holding his handgun. 'Man down, man down. Eyes on the water.'

The Deltas spun to where Weng had been sitting and controlling the mini propulsion unit. He wasn't there anymore.

The back of the small craft was wet, but there was also a glistening substance coating the sides of the boat.

Simms threw himself into the seat, and grabbed the controls, guiding them smoothly away from the walls. After another few seconds, he lifted his hand and looked at it. 'Yech.' It was coated in slime. He brought the gloved fingers close to his nose.

'Holy crap, this stuff stinks – like fish and something else; bleach maybe.'

Arn pointed. 'No, not bleach… ammonia. Cephalopods are full of it.'

'Cephalo-what?' Sharp, like Teacher, had her handgun out, held in both hands and pointed at the dark water.

Arn looked out over the smooth surface. 'Squid, octopus, cuttlefish – keep your eyes on the water.'

'Couldn't look away if I wanted to.' Brown also decided to save his rifle's last ammunition, and drew his Beretta M9 handgun.

'Weng… Weng!' Teacher held up his light, flicking it back and forth over the water until a lump appeared on the surface. 'Over there…'

The lump grew, round and almost colorless, and many times larger than a human head or even a body. It rolled slightly, and then a single eye as round as a dinner plate regarded the boat for a few seconds before the mass slid back beneath the inky water.

Brown sat down. 'Jesus Christ – Simms, put the peddle to the floor and get us the hell out of here.'

The boat kicked as Simms began to accelerate, but then immediately slowed as though caught in a net.

'It's underneath us!' Teacher pointed his handgun, but then looked from it to Arn. He tossed the weapon to him. 'Use it.'

The boat lifted, and Teacher grabbed the gunwale. 'Get ready to repel anything that tries to come on board.' He stood, legs planted wide and made fists. Blades sprung from both hands.

Immediately, the eye watering stench enveloped them. Arn pushed Grimson down onto the bottom of the boat and lifted the gun. The Beretta felt both alien and familiar, and he mentally thanked his grandfather for teaching him how to use a firearm when growing up.

There came the sound of falling water from the darkness behind the boat, and immediately they swung their lights swung around to reveal a monstrous blob lifting itself from the water. Tentacle limbs rose to writhe, coiling over each other.

Arn could see that the creature was basically man-shaped, but suckered tentacles bloomed from its shoulders and torso. It was like an octopus, but as wide as the boat, with the beaked mouth positioned at the front between two enormous lidless eyes.

Trunk-like appendages, many more than eight, moved constantly, and just below the water, Arn could make out the lifeless body of Weng, strangely soft looking as though he had been brutally pulped in the slime-glistening arms.

'Fire.'

The thing reached out ignoring the tiny stings of the bullets, until Brown dropped his handgun and brought up his rifle, discharging the last of his armor-piercing high-caliber bullets into one of the eyes. The huge orb ruptured and there came an eerie high-pitched squeal, before the thing dived deep.

Brown dropped a grenade in after it, and then ducked down. 'Fire in the hole.'

The surface erupted as the powerful explosive detonated. The black water showed traces of a green-blue stain and huge blobs of grey flesh came up to bump at the side of the boat. Thankfully there were no traces of Weng in the mess.

Water drops fell for a few more seconds, and then silence returned as they all stared into the dark depths. But then, away in the blackness the sound of water being pushed aside, from behind them... then one side, and then the other. Either more of the same creatures were approaching, or something else, some other dark-adapted hunter, was attracted by the blood.

Teacher roared. 'Let's move it.'

Simms accelerated once again, gritting his teeth as though willing his own muscles into the propulsion engine, and taking them away from the thrashing water behind them while doing his best not to careen into the dank walls of the narrowing cave.

After many minutes, the cavern opened slightly, but Teacher urged them on, possibly guessing that slowing allowed the denizens of the dark to catch up to them.

The group's muscles remained tensed as the small boat flew forward, until Grimson sat up and inhaled. 'Earth, plants... we will soon be out.'

In another fifteen minutes, Teacher waved his hand to lower the speed. There was light showing ahead. Soon, the water shallowed to only a few feet deep, and they came to a small opening in the stone, covered over with plants, creating a barrier and effectively hiding them from outside.

The water shallowed and occasionally the boat bumped on the mossy stream bottom. Simms eased them up close to the latticework of branches and vines, and together they all luxuriated in the sunshine streaming through.

'Haven't felt this good for a while.' Sharp lay forward letting the sun bathe her face.

Brown did the same, closing his eyes and inhaling. 'You got that right, Sharpie.'

Brown reached over and softly punched her thigh. She put her hand on top of his.

They stretched out and rested for a few minutes tied to the branch cage. Teacher peered out to check the countryside. He sat and turned, leaning back and letting the sun warm his neck.

'Arn and Grimson, this is your side of the landscape. What's best... stay in the boat, or continue on foot?'

Grimson looked over the side. 'The waters should be safe from here... at least from below. But there will be a lot of Lygon about. They tend to be more active at night, so for now, we will be fine. This river should take us closer to Valkeryn.'

'Then the river it is.' Teacher started to cut an opening in the lattice of hanging branches. He paused, turned and looked back into the dark cave. His face was like stone.

'Lieutenants Benjamin Weng and Alfred C. Doonie – I thank you, sirs.' He saluted, and the Deltas all did the same.

In another moment Simms powered the boat out and into the sunshine.

* * *

It took all of them to drag the boat up and into some tall reeds. Being on dry land was a relief after being trapped in the small vessel in the inky blackness. The team had moved at a steady pace for several hours, and had only once needed to dive into the foliage, covering themselves with leaves and twigs as a sizeable force of Panterran and Lygon, numbering in the many hundreds, had moved by them.

Just the Delta's eyes peeked out from beneath their carpet of mud and bush. Grimson needed to be buried deeper so the familiar scent of Wolfen hadn't attracted attention.

Teacher had counted them as they passed, taking note of their armaments. He spoke softly to Sharp beside him, just breathing out the words.

'Headed due west. Only one thing out there I can think of.'

Sharp grunted softly. 'The gateway. Let's hope Henson managed to get reinforcements, or there's a huge party gate-crash about to happen.'

Teacher grunted. 'Yep. Let's just hope we don't have to fight our way through them to get home.'

Sharp grinned. 'That'd be after we defeat the army that's here first, right?'

It took several hours for the monstrous beings to pass by, the day turning to afternoon, and then to late afternoon. After the last Lygon had thumped down along the trail Grimson nudged Arn.

'We must get to the castle quickly. The Lygon see even better than Wolfen in the dark.'

Teacher sat up, and then stood staring after the Lygon. Grimson came and stood beside him, his ears moving slowly. Teacher looked across to him. 'Are they gone?'

The Wolfen nodded. 'We are safe... for now.'

The rest of the team got to their feet, shaking debris from their bodies. There was no time to hunt, so protein sticks and water was their meal on the run. Grimson relished the dry and rigid meat-like substance, and even managed to talk Arn into giving away some of his own.

In a line they jogged, the Deltas lattice mesh suits dappling in the last rays of the afternoon sunlight.

CHAPTER 34

MILES OF EMPTY BEACH

Henson had greeted the new Delta soldiers and put them straight to work digging in on the small mountain slope. They knew they'd be monstrously outnumbered, but they didn't care. They had the high ground, the expertise, the ammunition, and a determination that the Lygon and Panter-ran would be stopped here – end of story.

Each man and woman had thousands of rounds, and there were rocket launchers, grenades and numerous other death-dealing goodies.

Henson sat down with his back against a bleached piece of stone, and used his field glasses to scan the wasteland – flat and still bright as the late afternoon sun sunk in the west.

Bannock dropped down beside him. 'Anything?'

Henson lowered the glasses. 'Nope, just miles and miles of empty beach.'

Bannock took the glasses. 'I'm bettin' they come at us in the dark.'

'Yep, I would if I was them. Especially as they see better in the dark than we do.' He turned. 'Get a few of the guys down there and let's leave them some fireworks to make things a little brighter for our guests.'

Bannock grinned. 'I got just the thing.'

***

Grimson led them through gorges, up hills and over escarpments, each of them having to swing under and over heavy boughs of trees and work to keep their balance as they pushed themselves to keep up. At a narrow rift in a hillside, the Wolfen stopped.

'There is a secret entrance to the castle here. It will lead us in and behind the walls of Valkeryn. I must go alone, as the Panterran have acute hearing and will surely hear us if we all enter.'

Teacher waved his hand. 'Not happening. We need that diamond, and we need it now. If you disappear, we're done for. We are too few to be able to breach the castle walls; we'd spend days being nothing more than an annoyance.'

Grimson seemed to think for a moment. 'Then I will take Arnoddr, alone.'

Teacher shook his head. 'Still no.' He turned to Arn. 'Sorry Arn, I trust you, but this is too important. You know what's at stake.'

Grimson folded his arms and looked away. His jaw was set hard.

Arn just shrugged, and Teacher rubbed his forehead. 'Last offer, you take me as well. Simms, Brown and Sharp, will create a diversion at the walls. That should draw them away, or at least make enough noise so we mice can scurry in unannounced.'

'Mice?' Grimson raised his eyebrows.

Arn held his thumb and forefinger a few inches apart. 'Little animals.'

The youth nodded. 'Mice... yes.' His turned away for a moment, but then spun back. 'Three mice it is.'

Sharp guffawed and punched Simms in the arm. 'We get to do a frontal assault on a castle... with an entire army inside... on things twice as big and ugly as us. This is gonna be so cool.'

Grimson put his hand on her arm. 'You will not be alone, or cold. Sorenson will be here soon. The moon will be high and he will come... I know he will come. And with him will be the Far Wolfen. You should wait for him.'

She smiled. 'He will certainly be welcome.'

Teacher looked at his watch. 'Time to get moving; we should get into place, and see if we can at least locate the diamond.'

'Diamonds.' Grim pulled a face. 'Hard stones for a crown and nothing more; I care not for diamonds.'

'I know, but we need it. And we also need to rescue our friends. Deal?' Arn asked.

'And kill Mogahrr? Deal?' Grimson's eyes blazed.

Teacher sucked in a deep breath, filling his lungs, and then exhaled slowly. 'Sure. Let's go.'

Grimson turned and started off. Arn followed.

Teacher turned to his three remaining Deltas. He handed over all his remaining ammunition and then walked along in front of them punching fists as he went. 'Give me two hours, and then raise hell. Remember, if we don't make it, there will be no home to go back to.' Into each of their hands he dropped a Morph Steel capsule. He grinned.

'Tastes like steel-covered crap, but packs a punch.'

Simms held it up between thumb and forefinger, and then shrugged. 'Down the hatch.' He tossed it into his mouth and dry swallowed. Sharp swallowed hers with a gulp of water, and immediately flexed her fingers, watching her hand.

Teacher's smiled grimly, but his face grew dark. 'No prisoners, no quarter given. Fight or die.'

The Deltas responded. 'Fight or die. HUA!'

Teacher had finally managed to persuade Arn to don his CL-Suit, and also given him his morph steel capsule. After taking it, he spent a few minutes testing it by making long steel claws extend from the ends of each finger.

Grimson edged in between a couple of boulders, pushing a hanging curtain of vines from his path, to revel a dark opening in the rocks. 'This will take us all the way under the castle, and into the secret passages within the walls. We will be able to see and hear everything.' He stared hard at Teacher. 'But be warned – Man-kind have a distinct smell, and you are noisy. If the Panterran or Lygon hear us, they will pull us from the walls, just like... mice.'

He turned to Arn. 'This is an old entrance, rarely used. It is dangerous and it will first take us deep. We must be careful.' He disappeared into the darkness.

Arn and Teacher had to race to keep up with the Wolfen. Teacher switched on his forehead light and also held a flashlight in his hand. Arn just had a flashlight, and followed close behind the darting youth. Sometimes the walls closed to little more than a few inches, and both Arn and Teacher had to edge sideways, both grate the CL suits ensured they didn't lose too much skin.

After what seemed like hours of continually heading down on a steep descent, they reached a large open space where the lights refused to illuminate anything above or below them.

Grimson stood at the edge of a platform of stone, its edge falling away into darkness. Arn came up beside him and looked over the edge.

'How deep does it go?'

Grim continued to stare into the pit. 'No one knows. Some say it goes to the very heart of our world.' He looked back at Arn, his face carrying a hint of fear. 'Perhaps to Hellheim itself.'

He pointed across to the other side of the abyss, where another tunnel stood yawning open. 'We need to get over there. There was once a bridge here, long before even old Vidarr was born. But it is long gone. Now we must use the ledge.' He pointed to a few inches of stone lining the edge of the pit.

'Great.' Teacher looked down at his size twelve boots.

Arn pointed at his own large feet, now wrapped in the CL-suit. 'Best we don't look down, huh?' He grinned.

Teacher looked over the edge. 'Nothing to see anyway.'

Together they edged slowly out. Even Grimson had to concentrate, taking one small step at a time. When they were half way across, Arn looked down, frowning.

'You hear that?'

'No.' Teacher looked one way, then the other.

'I can.' Grimson's ears moved as he stared hard into the darkness. 'We must keep moving – faster.'

'I still can't hear a goddam thing. How can you?' Teacher turned from Arn and slid a hand carefully into a pouch on the CL suit and eased out a glow stick. He bent it in half, and then let it drop. It fell and fell…. and fell. As it descended, it cast a green glow on the walls of the huge pit and illuminated what looked like large, colorless fruit on the walls. The angle made it difficult to work out whether they were something growing from the rock… or something climbing up to meet them.

When the small dot of light had completely vanished, Teacher finally heard what Arn and Grimson had heard – giggling.

Arn leaned his head back. 'It's getting louder… they're coming up.'

Teacher nudged him. 'Well move; I do not want to be on this ledge if we are about to be visited by something from Grimson's version of hell.'

Arn started to shift sideways quicker and quicker. Teacher only had his heels balanced on the small shelf of stone, keeping pace until the wall crumbled beneath one of his boots. He went down, but as fast as he thought about it his fist sprang a metal spike, which he jammed, into the wall. He swung back up to the ledge, the spike retracting smoothly back into his flesh.

Grimson leapt up onto the opposite platform, and looked back over the edge. 'Quickly, quickly.'

Arn leapt across, and Teacher came next, looking back briefly, but then racing into the new tunnel after Grimson and Arn.

'What the hell were those things?'

Arn shook his head. 'Not sure, but I've heard them before. They seem to live in the emptiest and darkest places on the planet... and I for one do not want to meet them.'

Teacher grunted. 'Makes two of us.'

'Three.' Grimson called over his shoulder.

The climb took another hour, and many times, Teacher would swing around in the dark, sure that something was so close behind him he could feel slimy fingers, or claws, or tentacles on his neck.

The going was arduous, and they had to scale tumbled boulders using only their fingers and toes. It was a relief when the rock and slimy walls gave way to a set of ancient, moss-covered steps.

Grimson turned, his eyes shining in the darkness. His mouth widened into a smile and he pointed at Arn's face.

'You become more like one of us every day, Brother Arn.'

Arn felt his face. 'Huh?'

'Your eyes.'

'What – what's up with them?' Arn blinked a few times. 'They feel fine.'

Teacher pulled back frowning. 'They're shining... like Grimson's. Adapting to the dark. You really have been here too long.'

Arn noticed his flashlight had been off for a while, and he could still see perfectly well in the gloom.

'Hmm, maybe... maybe.' He raced up the slick steps after Grimson.

Arn had to jog to keep pace with Grimson. They climbed stairs for an hour – stairs carved through tunnels and directly onto cliff walls, each set winding its way up through the rock and earth beneath the Valkeryn castle.

At last they reached a wall of ancient stone, its green hue a testament to its great age.

Grimson rested a hand on the rocks. With the other he held a finger up to his lips. Together they waited for Teacher to arrive, out of breath, despite being an elite soldier. He laughed, sucking in huge drafts of dank air.

'I don't know what you're on, Singer, but it seems to suit you.'

Arn shushed him, and then turned to Grimson. The young Wolfen pointed along a narrow corridor, and whispered his words.

'These are the foundation stones of Valkeryn. It is said Fenrir and the original Guardians laid them down after the time of cleansing. Soon we will be travelling within the walls of Valkeryn itself. Remember, this is not our stronghold any-more. It belongs to Mogahrr and her vile creatures.'

Grimson turned to point along the dark passageway, when he yelped from fright. Standing silently in the dark were two figures, nearly invisible under their cowls. A deep voice floated towards them.

'The seed of Grimvaldr united again in Valkeryn. I knew Odin would make it so.' First one, then the other pulled back their hoods.

Teacher smiled. 'Balthazaar.'

'Balthazaar, Vidaar... you survived. But how?' Arn rushed forward, embracing the old counselor.

It was Vidarr who responded. 'The secret-ways of the castle have been mine for many, many lifetimes. My only regret was I couldn't save more of our people.' His face dropped. 'I was condemned to watch... even the fate of your mother and father.'

Grimson lowered his head, and Balthazaar went to one knee before him.

'Your return is the sign we have waited for. We are far from beaten yet young prince. Balthazaar looked to Teacher, rising to his feet.

'Captain Jim Teacher, we meet again. I had thought you all dead or captured. The queen has made much sport with your taken warriors.'

Balthazaar put his arm around Arn's shoulder, looking into his face. 'Our world and time seems to suit you, Arnoddr. You seem... different.' He shrugged. 'There are many things to discuss, but we have little time and more pressing urgencies. Princess Eilif is held captive by the Queen, along with some young Man-Kind.'

'Eilif... alive?' Arn grabbed Balthazaar by the shoulders.

The old Wolfen nodded. 'Alive, and safe... for now. She is being kept in the deep dungeons with the ones called Edward and Becky.' Balthazaar reached out and gripped Teacher's arm. 'There is war afoot – a sizeable force of Panterran and Lygon has headed to the wastelands.' His grip intensified. 'To attack your world, Captain Teacher.'

Teacher nodded. 'We'll be ready.'

Balthazaar nodded. 'Then that is something.' He grew silent for a moment. 'So here we are within the walls of Valkeryn surrounded by Mogahrr's entire army. They will need to be cleaned out... all of them. We will need a strong plan.'

Teacher nodded. 'First we need...'

'First we need to get Eilif out safely...' Arn's eyes blazed, and Grimson nodded in agreement. '... and also Becky and Edward; they are not strong, and must be petrified by now.'

Vidarr rubbed his chin. 'We believe we can rescue them. But then we will need to flee as the Lygon will tear the castle apart looking for us.'

'We are not leaving without the diamond.' Teacher's voice left no doubt to his resolve.

'The red stone?' Balthazaar raised his eyebrows and continued. 'It is hung from the queen's neck.' He shook his head sadly. She is in the heart of the castle and is never unattended. Even when she sleeps, her private guards do not.' He lifted his eyes to Teacher's 'And what of the one called Briggs?'

'Can she be saved?' Teacher asked.

'Saved? Perhaps. Restored to her old self? Not once a greyworm has been inserted. It burrows to the centre of the brain… where it nests, feeds and eventually lays eggs.'

Teacher grimaced. 'Then, she stays. But I need the diamond to close the doorway between our worlds. If not, ours will be torn apart – sorry, it's not negotiable.'

Arn sighed. 'He's right. It's my fault it's even here.' He turned to Teacher. 'We get our friends first, and then all make an assault on the diamond; okay?'

Teacher nodded once, but his expression was unreadable. Arn went on.

'Let's hope your Deltas can make enough noise to draw a lot of attention away from us. Or we'll end up attending the next Lygon feast – as the main course.'

Teacher smiled. 'Don't worry; they know what to do.'

Vidarr grabbed Grimson, and hugged the youth. 'Good, and now, we must hurry. Mogahrr will be in the throne room, and should only have a skeleton force with her. If this is to happen, we must rescue Princess Eilif, and be safely hidden when the Lygon leave the castle to meet Captain Teacher's forces.'

'Forces?' Arn turned to Teacher and grinned.

'And then?' The Delta captain asked.

'And then we pray to Odin there is enough of a diversion to allow us to get beyond the walls of Valkeryn.' Vidarr half bowed.

In the silence that followed, no one asked what was supposed to happen after that.

Vidarr has instructed them to the utmost silence as the passages narrowed between a wall of solid rock and giant stones. They needed to creep, slowly, silently, Vidarr stopping every now and then to remove a plug of stone no bigger than his thumb. Immediately a shaft of light would beam through, and he would place his eye to the hole, nod, return the plug, and then continue leading them onwards.

'To the lower levels.' He whispered as they descended. By now they could make out the sounds of habitation beyond the walls – heavy bodies moving, or the clanking of steel. After another twenty minutes of easing down moss-covered steps and around broken boulders, Vidarr raised a hand.

'The prison cells. The guards will be outside, and will stay outside unless they hear something.' He scowled at Teacher for a second or two. 'We must be quiet… and your kin must be quiet.' Vidarr ran fingers along one section of the wall, pressing hidden studs, and then pushing. Stones moved on ancient hinges, but its protests were more a dull grinding than the squeal of rusted metal. He stepped through, waving them on.

The hallway was dark. Stone wall on one side, dotted with burning torches every dozen feet. On the other, lines of cells, empty. Vidarr put his finger to his lips and then pointed to the end cell. He then motioned to Teacher and the single entrance door at the end of the corridor – large, solid, and for now, closed.

Grimson headed to the end of the corridor, Balthazaar hurrying to keep up. The young Wolfen stopped at the only locked cell, his face beamed and he opened his arms wide. 'Sister.'

Arn caught up and gripped the bars. Altogether they crowded around the barred door. Eilif was hugging Grimson through the bars, but when she saw Arn she slowly rose to her feet, her eyes never leaving him.

'I always knew you would come.' She placed her hand over his, but then reached through the bars to grab his head and pull him forward. She kissed him hard.

'Yech.' Grimson grimaced and then looked at the lock. 'Can we break it open?'

Vidarr waved them away, producing a massive set of keys. 'Mogahrr may control the castle, but I control the locks.' The door opened easily.

Inside Arn could make out the shape of Becky and Edward hugging each other and pressed against the damp wall. They only became less fearful when they recognized their friend.

'Arn? Arn, is it you? I came looking for you, and this happened.' Becky held out her arms, showing him the filth. She burst into tears.

The door was pulled back, and Arn was first in – but it was Eilif in his arms. 'I knew… I just knew you were alive.'

Eilif pressed her forehead into his neck, hugging him tight.

Becky stood trembling, her mouth hanging open. She looked down at herself, still only partially clothed in scraps of material she had managed to scavenge, and still Arn had barely noticed.

Edward staggered towards them. 'Way to go, Bro – gone totally native I see. Suits you!'

Arn extracted himself from Eilif, and grabbed his friend. 'Man, you stink.'

Edward chuckled. 'A gift from our captors. Note to self: don't ask for anything when the Lygon are in charge.'

Arn laughed and then went to hug Becky. She folded her arms, her lip jutting. He grabbed her anyway.

'You're so brave. Are you okay?' He asked.

'No. Just get me home.' Her eyes narrowed and kept darting to Eilif.

Once again, Vidarr hushed them, and beckoned them forward. Teacher closed the cell door, and was last back through secret doorway, closing it with only the slight grinding of sand. As they worked their way back up through the passageways, Grimson hung onto Eilif's waist, and Arn could tell he was bursting to tell her of his adventures, forgetting that she had seen the monstrous battle at the fall of Valkeryn.

Balthazaar put his hand on Teacher's shoulder, pulling him close and whispering, 'That was the easy part, Jim Teacher. We will help you, but we cannot risk the heirs of Valkeryn for you or your world. After all, perhaps the destruction of your world in your time was the genesis of ours – saving you might actually lead to our demise. An incredible risk, is it not?'

'What will be, will be. Just show me to the throne room, and then you can run a mile.'

Teacher lifted Balthazaar's hand from his shoulder. Balthazaar bowed, and turned to follow Vidarr as he led them back up the winding alleyways behind the stone walls of the ancient castle.

As they neared the royal rooms, they slowed. Many times Arn had to turn to quiet Becky and Edward who continued to bicker and complain, their voices rising ever higher. Eventually Balthazaar had stopped them, and threatened to bind their mouths if they put the group's lives at risk again.

Arn felt Eilif press up beside him, her eyes always on him, and many times she reached out in the dark to hold his hand. She leaned in close to him.

'Whatever happens, know that I am now happy.'

He smiled back at her and squeezed her hand.

At last they reached a section of wall, with a step built up against it. Vidarr stepped up and removed a plug, peering through. He turned and waved Teacher forward.

'Mogahrr is here... and so is your female warrior leader.'

Teacher looked through the small hole. An enormous wooden throne dominated the room, and seated upon it the most disgusting looking creature he had ever seen. Beside the vile thing was her human pet, Colonel Briggs, sitting on a cushion, eyes vacant and a string of drool hanging from her open mouth.

Teacher moved his head to a different angle trying to see more aspects of the room, until Vidarr grabbed his shoulder.

'No, look to the mirrors at the far side of the room.'

He did as the old Wolfen suggested. The mirrors hung on the walls showed him more of the large space. Lygon and Panterran milled about, and Mogahrr's private guards attended to her. Overall, the numbers were still too formidable for him to take on by himself. He hoped his team's assault would draw them away.

Teacher stepped back down. He turned to Arn. 'Soon.' He pressed a stud on his suit's collar, and it immediately telescoped up over his head, covering his face in the lattice mesh. Arn did the same.

Edward grinned. 'Very cool.'

Grimson and Eilif's eyes burned with hatred as they stood silently, staring at the wall of stones.

At the same moment, Alison Sharp pressed the same small stud on the neck of *her* CL suit, causing it to telescope up over her head and face. She moved her fingertip along a line of tiny lumps at one temple, selecting the first, then the second – immediately the landscape illuminated as the optics in the single wide lens over both her eyes changed from normal to night enhancement.

'Hmm, I love these suits. You just try and get this baby back,

Teach.' She snorted. 'Who are you kidding, Sharpie? You'll probably be buried in it tonight.'

A bird call from several hundred feet to her right brought her head up – a wave, from Simms. She waved back, and then repeated the call and wave to her left. Brown's head came up and he returned the gesture. She noticed he then put his hand to where his mouth would be, kissing it and throwing it to her. She pretended to grab it out of the air, and put it in her pocket.

She hunkered back down. 'I hope so big fella. I really want to get home and claim that drink.'

Each of the three remaining Deltas was dug in and had piles of the remaining ammunition stacked next to them; RGPs, spare clips, a few handfuls of toe-cutters – small grape-sized explosives that were powerful enough to blow up a vehicle, and with luck a few dozen fully armored Lygon. She held up a hand and made a fist. A foot-long spike extended from her hand.

'That's close quarters combat taken care of.'

She drew the spike back into her fist, rubbing the knuckles, still feeling the tingle within the bones of her hand. She touched the line of tiny lumps at her temple again; this time the castle walls sprang towards her in close-up. The parapets were thick with Lygon and the heavy doors were closed. She looked at her watch – it was time.

'Okay boys; party time.' She shouldered her rifle, loaded a grenade into the underslung grenade launcher and fired at the massive wooden door. The grenade exited the barrel in a burst of explosive gasses, an incendiary arrow that crossed the several hundred feet of open ground in a few seconds, to hit the door in an explosive whump. It blew splinters, bronze hinges and panels away like so many matchsticks.

'Yeah baby!'

There was confusion on the castle walls for only a second or two, and then horns started to blare, and the sounds of confusion turned to roars of anger. Like some sort of horde of monstrous black and orange army ants, the Lygon poured forth to protect their nest.

Sharp sucked in a deep breath and sighted along her barrel. 'Fight or die.'

⧼◆◆◆ ⋙⋘ ◆◆◆⧽

'Come on, come on.' Hanson stood and moved the glasses over the black landscape. Just after sun down, and before the moon comes up, was one of the darkest time of night. It was the perfect attack time.

Beside him, Bannock also stood, and walked along the ridge of debris. 'We'll get some starlight soon, and given the flat terrain, nothing is going to creep up on us.'

A crack came from out of the dark, and then the sound of a bullet striking the hillside, made both men flatten themselves to the ground.

'You were saying?' Henson crawled to his foxhole and slid in, Bannock followed.

'Nothin' like your own weapons turned against you.' Bannock drew a lens down over one eye and moved up and down the thermal and night scope ranges. 'Can't see anything. Must be coming in like they did at the camp.' He lifted his head slightly. 'Farfalle, give me some light down there.'

Immediately several deep whumps sounded from a near foxhole, followed by parachute flares that burst into bright light and hung high in the dark still night for a few seconds, before gently drifting down, throwing huge pools of sun-like illumination onto the desert floor.

'Pimples.' Bannock, exhaled with annoyance. 'Damn, these guys are good.'

The desert was alive with tiny brown lumps. The Panterran were coming in low and slow, and as their dark-adapted eyes didn't need light, they could totally cover themselves in damp blankets and creep along, an inch at a time. Bannock noticed a few of the lumps had rifle barrels sticking from their fronts.

'Got some snipers comin in. I reckon Colonel Briggs gave them some quick lessons before they set out.'

'We knew they'd have teeth. So, let's take some of those teeth out before they get too close.' He spoke into a small mic-stud on the side of his face.

'Burnside, Mason, French; take out those guys with the guns. Fire at will.'

The three sharpshooters fired down at the creeping Panterran who had rifles. Each shot made its mark and corresponded to either one of the mounds ceasing to move, or a small figure leaping in the air, before falling back to the ground, dead. In a few more minutes, Hanson was satisfied most of the rifle carriers had been terminated.

He spoke again into his mic. 'Good job. Now switch to full automatic – if they stick to their normal game plan, they'll come in a physical wave to try and overwhelm us.'

Bannock grunted. 'No trees to drop out of, but I bet these little suckers are too light to set off the mines.'

Hanson nodded, continuing to watch the desert floor through his field glasses. 'You're right... but it's not the little guys I'm worried about.'

Out of the darkness came the sound of a horn – low, deep and ominous – and a roar that seemed to come from every point on the horizon. In front of Hanson, the soil at the edge of his foxhole started to bounce and then topple inwards.

'Okay boys and girls, time to earn our pay.'

Hanson quickly checked his rifle was on automatic, touched the pile of spare clips and grenades, to make sure they were all still in reach, and then got down low.

The small lumps threw back their cloth camouflage, each revealed Panterran holding a crossbow or a curved sword.

Thundering up from behind them came hundreds of Lygon, their pounding footfalls making the earth shake.

Hanson roared his own words above the sound of the approaching beasts. 'Not... one... gets... past us.'

The Panterran horde was first to reach the small mountain the Deltas had dug in on, and behind them the first wave of Lygon exploded in a wall of fire and shrapnel as dozens of mines exploded underneath them.

'Music to my ears.' Bannock sighted and commenced to fire. The hill came alive as thousands of rounds were fired.

Orcalion was at a sideboard, carefully placing slices of softened meat on a platter for the queen. He cursed under his breath as he went about the menial work he was doing as some sort of penance for allowing the Arnoddr Man-Kind to escape. He looked up into the mirror, catching sight of himself. He turned his head one way and then the other. He grinned; he really was the most handsome Panterran he had ever seen.

Outside an explosion sounded, followed by a shockwave that travelled through the heavy stones of the castle. Orcalion's eyes widened and he froze, gripping the sideboard and staring at his reflection in the looking glass. Behind him, Lygon and Panterran rushed from the room, and the rest moved to the windows to see what was happening at the gates. While Orcalion watched, a strange thing happened – a section of the stone wall swung open and the most bizarre being he had ever seen stepped forth.

It was a biped, but had some sort of strange skin or suit that completely covered its body. There was a single long eye running from one side of its head to the other. His shock was further compounded by the doorway opening further allowing him to see more figures inside, and something even more startling – a Wolfen, a young Wolfen... the *prince*... *here*!

As Orcalion watched, keeping his back turned, the figure darted forward, moving to the queen, and before she knew what was happening, it snatched something from her chest, making her squeal in surprise, before the being threw something over her face, and then vanished back into the wall.

He grinned. Now was his chance to make amends, to improve his standing with Queen Mogahrr. He leapt for the closing door, landing too late, as he knew he would. He spun, seeing Mogahrr pull the old rag from her head, her eyes a mix of fear and shock.

Orcalion pointed. 'My Queen, it was the Wolfen, in a secret passage... here.' He jabbed at the wall with a long talon.

She stood unsteadily on her bowed legs, her previous confusion now turning to utter fury.

'Get theeem. Orcalion, get theeem, and bring theeem to meee... alive!' She screamed the words, spittle flying from her black toothed mouth.

Orcalion nodded, and raced to the wall placing his ear to the stones. He pointed at some Panterran rushing about. 'You, bring me some Lygon, now.'

He moved along the wall, listening, listening. As he did some lumbering Lygon entered carrying axes and hammers larger than he was. He turned to them and pointed again.

'Here... break it down... quickly.'

The huge brutes set to swinging their massive weapons at the wall, pounding thousand-year-old stones to rubble and dust. In a moment a hole was opened, and Orcalion stuck his head in.

'There,' he pointed further along the wall. The Lygon jumped to the new position and swung again several times before one of them punched his huge fist through the shattered stones and grabbed hold of something. When he pulled his hand back out, he held a struggling body.

'Crush it.' Orcalion danced on the spot.

The Lygon threw the figure to the ground, and raised his enormous hammer above his head.

The passageway narrowed, and their bodies scraped against the stone. Teacher grimaced at every stumble, clink of steel, or scrape of a boot on rock; he knew they would be sought out soon, and he guessed giant ears were already being pressed to the walls.

Vidarr urged them on to greater haste in the crawlspace – already their increased speed in the shrinking space made silence impossible. They froze as the pounding began. It was Balthazaar who first yelled at them for action, and they sprinted now, all pretence of maintaining silence gone.

Behind them, there was a huge explosion followed by the appearance of a shaft of light, and then a small head appeared, and was quickly withdrawn. Vidarr was becoming frantic in his urging, and Teacher grabbed Eilif, pushing her forward. He reached for Arn, but his hand never connected as the wall exploded inwards next to him, and an arm as thick as tree trunk smashed through to grab him around the neck. His entire body was dragged away, the CL suit protecting him as more of the ancient stones shattered as he was pulled through.

It was all a blur. Teacher suddenly found himself smashed to the ground, a giant foot planted on his chest. Looking up all he saw was a mountain of orange and black fur, and seemingly miles above it, a hammer that looked as big as a dining table.

Somewhere close by, a high-pitched voice screamed 'Crush it, crush it,' over and over. Teacher knew that even in the CL suit, there was no way his head could survive the blow.

He grabbed at the foot, but he might as well as been trying to twist a tree stump. He groaned as more weight was forced down upon him, making it impossible to draw a breath. He felt his ribs start to buckle and small flashes of light went off in his head.

Above him the huge head leaned forward, the face the most ferocious thing he had ever seen. The eyes carried triumph within their green luminescence, but only for a moment. They were now widening in surprise – behind them both, the wall exploded outwards.

Arn landed onto the floor beside them, his CL suit enclosing his entire body and head. Then, landing lightly came Eilif and Grimson, teeth bared. At the sight of Arn and the Wolfen, the Panterran rushed from the chamber carrying Mogahrr like a hairless, stinking sack. Her yellow eyes were round with fear. .

The Lygon on Teacher's chest shifted his weight, preparing for the killing blow – it was the break he was waiting for. Teacher made a fist, and a two-foot spike shot from the knuckles, which he immediately punched hard into the meat of the beast's calf. With a mighty roar of pain, the Lygon threw itself backwards.

Arn came at another, long and curved dagger-like claws extending from the ends of his hands.

Teacher sat up, feeling his ribs grind. He watched Arn for a moment, marveling at the way he moved; light, and agile – not seeming human anymore.

Eilif and Grimson had picked up swords dropped by the departing Panterran, and attacked the Lygon, inflicting a thousand stab wounds before it could even swing to meet them. The chaotic sounds, the pain and confusion, were too much for the few remaining beasts in the room, and they fell over each other as they stumbled out. Grimson slammed the heavy oak door and slid the huge crossbar down to brace it.

More explosions sounded from outside the castle, and from inside the destroyed throne room wall, Vidarr called them back.

'The final fight begins – we must be away... now!'

CHAPTER 35

Know Who You Face This Day

Alison Sharp touched her comm. button. 'Running low on grenades. When they're out, it's gonna get real ugly real quick.'

Brown and Simms listened in, confirming they were in the same state. Brown laughed, his voice still calm amid the hurricane of explosions, and roars of anger and pain. 'What? You expected to live forever?'

She grinned as she responded. 'Only till you bought me that drink, you big ox.' She fired another grenade into a knot of charging Lygon, satisfied to see the big bodies scatter like ten pins.

The attacks were slowing; the killing zone they had set up was effective in that it kept the smarter creatures at bay. The Lygon knew now that to move any closer meant being cut down or blown to pieces. They had stopped their advance, as one larger than the rest walked along their ranks to their rear, assembling them, organizing them into a military order. Panterran archers took up positions behind them.

'This doesn't look good.' Sharp moved her finger along the line of bumps beside her eye lens, increasing magnification. 'Seems brains is taking over from brawn.'

The giant beasts parted to allow a single enormous Lygon to move to the front: beside him was a smaller figure... a human figure.

'Oh crap, that's Briggs.' Simms voice was more frustrated than annoyed.

'Yep, and she'll pinpoint us – direct their attacks, probably using some Special Forces formations. My bet is we'll get a flying wedge under a cloud of arrows.' Sharp fired a few armor-piercing rounds, but the group stayed just out of range.

'Nothing we can do but wait.'

As she spoke, more and more Lygon and Panterran poured from the huge gates, before they were pulled closed once more.

Simms blew out air in exasperation. 'For what – their entire army to arrive?'

'Just until the Boss gets back. So, we dig in and hold the line.' Sharp sighted on Briggs' forehead, wishing she'd come just a little closer.

Brown grunted. 'A thousand to one, or ten thousand to one, I don't think it's going to make any difference to us. Hope Teach had better luck.'

Sharp loaded her last grenade into the launcher. 'Well, at least when they get in our faces we'll get chance to try out this morph steel stuff.' She made a fist, and small spikes appeared over it, like a mini mace.

'Can't wait.' Brown laughed darkly.

Drums started a low throbbing beat. They gradually rose in tempo. Sharp looked along the ranks forming up in front of the castle. They started to reassemble: the massive bodies were now kitted out in heavy armor, with spikes and sharp edges – the Lygon battle armor. She swallowed and arranged her last few magazines on the soil close by.

Sharp looked from the ammunition to the Lygon, and then to where her comrades were dug in. She hailed them both and then stood. 'You know what – why wait? They're going to expect to run us down like a Mack truck over three squirrels. Let's take the goddam party to them – give 'em a Delta welcome they'll remember for the rest of their lives.'

'Simms laughed out loud and stood. 'Why not – we get to choose how we finish this.'

Brown rose. 'I like it. You call it beautiful.'

Alison Sharp screwed her eyes shut for a moment, and then

looked skyward. The moon had finally risen, she looked into its face – so much closer, half filling the sky and lighting the churned and bloody field before her. A surge ran through her as she sucked in a huge breath.

'On my mark. Five... four... three... two... one... *mark.*'

Vidarr peered through another crack in the wall, spending several minutes moving his eye over several different angles, and then placed his ear to the hole. Satisfied, he turned and nodded, and then pushed open another secret door. They were in a dusty storeroom, packed with the ancient artworks, sculptures, and treasure of the Wolfen race.

'I saved what I could.' While Teacher watched, the old Wolfen started to take off robes, and he and Balthazaar donned armor, the snarling face of Fenrir on the steel chest plates.

Teacher took his arm, meaning to stop him, but the old Wolfen just shook his head. 'All must fight – it is the Wolfen way.'

Eilif selected a bow and a long sword, pulling it from its scabbard and feeling its edge. She turned to Grimson and smiled. 'Today is a good day to die.'

Grimson selected a sword of his own and held it up before his face. 'And none shall weep for the battle fallen.' Vidarr approached the pair with a large wrapped bundle and laid it before them.

'I managed to save these as well.'

Together Eilif and Grim unwrapped the cloth – immediately the gleam of sliver caught the moon's small reflection coming in through the key-hole windows.

"Yes.' Grimson ran a hand over the royal Valkeryn armor. He placed his hand on the chest plate, covering the crest of Grimvaldr, his father.

'Soon...'

Outside the drums were reaching a crescendo and Balthazaar went to peer through the slim window. 'The charge is about to begin. I hope your forces can withstand them.'

Teacher shook his head. 'There are no forces, only three like me... and I need to be with them.'

Vidarr's face sagged. 'Then it will be over soon.'

Eilif tightened a strap on her armor. 'There are more than three, Teacher.' She stood beside Arn, and put her hand on his shoulder. She turned to Becky and Edward, her eyes fierce.

'All must fight.'

Becky wiped her eyes. 'I don't want to die. I can't fight.' She sobbed, but picked up a small sword and looked at Arn. 'I'm doing this for you.'

Edward grabbed up a bow and arrow. 'I think I could hit something.'

'Good. Then let us hurry to our fate.' Vidarr came back from the window, and opened the secret door. He paused, smiling. '... and perhaps to Valhalla.'

***

The drums stopped and in their place there was a moment of silence, before they heard a sound like wind swirling from high in the dark sky. It got louder, and then hundreds of steel-tipped arrows fell around the three Delta force soldiers.

The three quickly covered their heads but they didn't need to. The arrows bounced harmlessly off the CL suits. Simms held his arms out as if he was enjoying a summer rain.

The drums started again, immediately rising to a crescendo. Alison Sharp's voice was drowned out. Whether it was words or a roar of defiance, it didn't matter as she charged towards the lines of hulking figures. Brown and Simms were at her shoulders, each of them firing as they came.

The Lygon were momentarily stunned by the three small beings charging them, each shimmering as the moonlight fell on their lattice matrix suits. The great beasts were quickly whipped into action by their giant general and Colonel Briggs. They charged to meet them.

Both parties crossed the killing grounds in minutes, and by the time the Deltas had reached the line of Lygon, their ammunition was spent. Swords and axe heads appeared from their hands, and spikes rose from their shoulders, heads and backs as they made their bodies into weapons.

The glow of the giant moon gave the human soldiers an extra burst of strength and speed, and for a time they were a match for the huge beasts. They cut a swathe through them, knocking down the towering creatures as they cut and hacked their way forward.

Simms whooped as he danced and jinked, slashing left and right. He burrowed a path away from Brown and Sharp, turning lightly to the side to dispatch a large brute, splashing blood back over his lens. He raised an arm to wipe clean his vision just as the fleeting image of a Wolfen in armor appeared to strike the side of his head with the flat of a blade.

Simms staggered from the blow, and turned just as the monstrous beings parted. When Simms turned back to the front, a single giant stood before him – the Lygon general, swinging a hammer the size of a small car down upon him with so much force that he was crushed flat. The CL suit held, and his squashed frame lay within the crater like a bag of broken twigs.

Alison Sharp also took a swinging blow that sent her flying twenty feet in the air, and when she landed she laid stunned, her chest now full of broken bones. Brown was immediately beside her, a huge sword extended from each arm. The Lygon were hacked back, but their numbers grew – five deep, then ten, and then a hundred. They stopped their push forward, knowing they were victorious.

The ring of giants parted, and the dark Wolfen and Briggs entered, the colonel stopping to stare down with her milky vacant eyes.

'Surrender and live... a sort of life.' Briggs' voice and eyes were as dead as those of a fish washed ashore on the beach.

Sharp tried to rise. 'Go to hell... ma'am.'

Briggs never flinched. 'Oh, you will know hell. Mogahrr will have you peeled from your suits and devoured alive.' She turned, and looked to the parapets, where a throne had been carried so the Queen could watch. Mogahrr made a throat slitting gesture, and Briggs turned back to the two fallen Deltas.

'Good bye. The Lygon need their fun, so this will not be quick.'

* ❧❦❧ ✕✕✕✕ ❧❦❧ *

Both Teacher and Arn had retracted their head covering: no matter how breathable the carbon lattice armor, it still trapped heat, and their faces streamed with perspiration. The two of them were first to the castle forecourt, quickly followed by Eilif and Grimson. Vidarr and Balthazaar were supervising Becky and Edward, ensuring they kept up and didn't get lost.

Together they hid in the shadows, peering through the gate bars at the killing fields out front. The moon was at its apex, an enormous silver disc so large the lunar landscape features looked close enough to map.

Vidarr shook his head sadly. 'It is almost over. We will need to go into the deep tunnels and make our way out beyond the forest.'

Teacher's eyes were locked on the ring of Lygon. 'No. I'm going out there.' He turned and strode to Edward, pressing the red diamond into his hand. 'Get this back home. Go with Vidarr... make it happen, son.' He pressed the hand hard with both his own, holding the youth's eyes until he nodded in return.

Arn stepped forward to stand beside Teacher. 'I'm going with you.'

Vidarr tried to object, but his face fell when Eilif and Grimson joined Arn and Teacher. Eilif put her hand on Arn's forearm. 'There will be no more hiding in the Dark Lands, or years of running from these foul creatures. It ends here, this eve.'

Vidarr rubbed both hands up over his face and long ears. 'Were there ever two races so hell-bent on their own destruction?' He smiled sadly. 'We Wolfen and Man-Kind are both headstrong and self-destructive breeds.' He looked at Balthazaar. 'And you old friend?'

Balthazaar drew his sword. 'I did not don this armor for nothing. I go with the heirs of Valkeryn, as I have for their entire lives.'

'Arn?' Becky's mouth had dropped open. 'But, but, we have to get home... all of us.'

Edward raised his crossbow. 'I'll fight.'

Arn smiled and put his arm around both of them. 'Not this night Edward. You will fight, but it will be a fight to get Becky and the diamond back home to Dr. Harper. We will buy you some time.'

Edward looked up at him, perhaps noticing that he was a good head and a half shorter than his friend now. Arn's face grew serious. 'Edward, your task is far more dangerous and important.' He looked to Becky and quickly kissed her cheek. 'When we are done here will come. But do not wait for us.'

Grimson looked at both of them briefly, and then to Vidarr. 'Take them through the deep caves, and lead them out old friend. And then you must leave – now – I fear the walls of Valkeryn will be no safe haven for even things like Man-Kind's mice.'

Vidarr knelt before Grimson and Eilif. 'Odin's luck be with you both.' He stood and turned to Arn and Teacher. 'You would have made fine Wolfen... especially you Arnoddr, you seem more like us every day.'

Teacher turned to Arn, his eyebrows raised. Without doubt, the youth seemed even taller and broader than before. There was no doubt he was different now, and once again his eyes shone in the darkness.

Arn looked up to the parapets where they could see Mogahrr and her private guard and watched the one sided battle. He spoke softly.

'Cut off the head of the snake.'

Teacher followed his eyes. 'Worth a try.'

Eilif came and stood beside him. 'Where you go, I go my Arnoddr.' Like Arn, her eyes shone as they caught the moon-light.

Becky's lips compressed as she watched Eilif before they slid back to Arn.

Arn opened his arms to Edward and Becky. 'Thank you, my friends for coming for me. I owe you a great debt. Get the diamond back to Harper, and tell him I'm sorry – for everything.'

Edward shook his head. 'You can tell him yourself – we'll be waiting on the other side.'

Becky rushed over and hugged him close, and whispered in his ear. 'I love you, that's why I came. Promise me you'll come back... for me.' She gripped him tighter, her eyes moving to Eilif, and her lips curling in a small smile. 'Promise me.'

Arn nodded and then she kissed him hard on the lips, her eyes on Eilif, whose face was taut with barely contained fury.

Vidarr tugged her away. 'We must leave.'

Becky waved, throwing another kiss before she and Edward disappeared back into the dark passage. The stone door closed and once again became part of the wall.

Arn sighed and looked up at the parapets. Eilif pointed. 'I know a way that will get us to her quickly. Follow me.'

Arn turned to Teacher and saluted. 'Good luck.'

Teacher returned the salute 'Whatever happens, it's been an honor to meet you.' He raised the hood up over his head.

Grimson drew his silver sword, and Balthazaar leaned out to peer at the gate entrance.

'Just three Panterran archers by the drawbridge mechanism. We'll need to send them to Hellheim first.'

Grimson placed his hand on the Valkeryn crest on his armor. 'Let me.' Before Teacher or Balthazaar could stop him, he pulled the snarling wolf helmet down over his face and broke into a run.

* * *

Goranx shouldered the other Lygon aside, and stood over the downed Delta soldiers. Hanging over his shoulder was the dead body of Simms, crushed to a boneless bag in his CL suit. The huge Lygon had been unable to open the lattice matrix to take the head of his prize, and now he glared at the similar mesh on Brown and Sharp and growled. In his hand was a huge axe, which he spun and gripped.

Goranx knew the old witch Mogahrr didn't want any more Man-Kind as pets, so these two would be nothing but food and entertainment. He wished they had more fight left in them, but he would at least take pleasure in crushing the life from them... slowly this time.

He moved the axe from one hand to the other. One of the Man-Kind tried to cover the other with his body, defending it, the swords in each hand that seemed to grow from the wrists – he'd take that one first, crush it from the legs upwards, letting the other see what fate awaited it.

He gripped the huge axe, but then paused, his head whipping around. Horns – deep, sonorous, the like of which he had never heard before. The Lygon around him grumbled, their green eyes searching the horizon. Goranx roared and they silenced, and stood, waiting.

One by one their huge heads turned to the far hillside. A lone Wolfen in battle armor appeared on the rise. Soon more Wolfen joined him, and these strange warriors wore leather, wood and shaved bone for armor plating. They were big, half a head taller than the Valkeryn Wolfen. Each carried spears, axes and heavy iron swords. They were a new breed of the hated creature – or perhaps a very old one. While Goranx watched, hundreds more appeared.

Goranx opened his arms and roared, turning now to face them. It mattered not, he thought. He'd destroy them all, just as he had done to the Valkeryn Wolfen. He snorted in contempt – they were still puny compared to the Lygon and their numbers were not enough to challenge them.

He turned and roared again, and immediately the Lygon began to form up into their battle ranks, forgetting the Delta soldiers.

Goranx threw his head back, letting his voice carry over the battlefield, letting his challenge be heard, letting these new Wolfen know he did not fear them.

In return came the raised voices of the Wolfen, and something deeper, made by a throat many times the size of the creatures on the hilltop. Goranx's brow furrowed in confusion, as another silhouette appeared, twice the height and width of the Wolfen – and taller than Goranx himself.

More joined the first, and then still more. They wore helmets of twisted horn, leather breast plates studded with iron, and huge swathes of tree bark as armor over enormously powerful bodies. These new creatures had the face of a Wolfen, but jaws that carried teeth larger than his own.

Frustration and confusion boiled in Goranx's gut and he swallowed it down hard. Could it be? No, it could not... he had heard the stories of the massive Ursa of the deepest part of the Dark Lands. While he watched one of the massive creatures came and stood by the Wolfen in the Valkeryn armor and placed one huge clawed hand on his shoulder. In turn the Wolfen raised his hands, making fists and then throwing his head back to howl at the giant moon above them.

The howl stretched to then become two words: 'For Valkeryn.'

It died away, and silence descended. Even the grumbling of the Lygon quieted. The silence stretched, only broken by the stealthy sound of many of the Panterran sneaking away, fleeing, away from the castle, and into the forest.

His own Lygon began to shift uneasily. He had one option – Goranx pointed his huge axe, roared, and charged.

* * *

Towering over Sorenson, the huge Ursan, Kodian, reached down to place a large clawed hand on his shoulder.

'Stay close to me, little brother. We Ursa will blunt their initial attack. We know of the Lygon; they only have brute force – and we will give them all they can chew.' He grunted, keeping his eyes on the Lygon army. 'They will make nice furs for our lodges this winter.'

'There is one who I have a score to settle with.' Sorenson closed the snarling wolf visor over his face with a clank and drew his sword. He then roared his battle charge, raised his sword and began to run. Behind him the Far Wolfen and Ursa followed.

There was an explosion of iron, leather, flesh and bone as the two armies met in the middle of the already bloody field. Screams and roars filled the air as bodies were hacked and slashed. No quarter was asked or given.

The battle raged for several hours – the moon was high, and seemed to take on a red hue as a blood-mist hung in a cloud over the battlefield.

Ursa and Lygon stood toe to toe, but in a test of bulk and ferocity, the Ursa were easily a match for the black and orange giants. Eventually the Lygon began to be beaten back, only their mad ferocity driving them on, their luminous green eyes now round with an insane rage.

Sorenson hacked left and right, searching, looking for the one his heart ached for him to find. The one he had seen torment his Wolfen by taking the head of the king and his beloved brother, the mighty Strom. Amongst the maelstrom of brutality, he caught sight of another in Wolfen armor; the dark crests, the black tail flowing from the top of the snarling helmet– Bergborr.

Sorenson fought his way towards the traitor, hackles rising, and felt a surge of hate fuel him. The Wolfen traitor slashed out at Ursa, who became confused, thinking it was a fellow fighter acting against them. Far Wolfen who had turned their backs believing him to be an ally were also struck down.

Bergborr's sword arm fell again towards another of the Far Wolfen, but this time it met not flesh, but instead Sorenson's blade as he caught its blow.

Sorenson grabbed him close. 'So, living with the enemy was not enough. Now you wish to die with them?'

Bergborr pushed Sorenson away, kicking him in the chest. 'Better to live in the shadow of Mogahrr than be invisible under the nose of a decrepit old king.' His sword slashed back and forth, making Sorenson leap back.

Sorenson moved around the dark Wolfen, his own visor still down, the snarling helmet now streaked with blood. 'We have saved the Man-Kind, the Arnoddr... and we have saved the prince, and the princess, Eilif. All you have done, all your scheming, all your betrayals... all for nothing.'

Bergborr charged, his fury making him rush forward. 'All your heads will be on pikes before the moon sets this night.' Bergborr came again. This time he drew a dagger and threw it, the small steel spike clanging off Sorenson's visor, making him raise his sword. The distraction created enough time for the dark Wolfen to cross the few feet that separated them, and to sweep his sword at Sorenson's legs.

Sorenson blocked the blow, but left his upper body unguarded. Bergborr kicked out, making Sorenson stumble. As he staggered back a few steps, Sorenson noticed the dark Wolfen didn't follow to press his attack. Instead, he lowered his weapon, his grinning face an expression of victory.

Sorenson was confused by Bergborr's inaction, until he felt a blow to his back, like being struck by a battering ram. His armor dented from the force of the blow, and he was thrown off his feet to land twenty feet away in the red mud. He rolled to see Goranx, the giant Lygon, the killer of the king and his brother, standing over him like a gore-streaked colossus.

He groaned and tried to sit up, but could not. He knew his body was probably damaged behind the steel. He looked up at the red moon, begging. *Please Odin, just one more hour to fight.* He wished away the Valkeryies who he knew would be descending in preparation to take his *sáál* across the rainbow bridge.

A wave of arrows descended from above, as the remaining Panterran archers on the castle walls fired volley after volley into the Far Wolfen and Ursan ranks. Through the slits in his visor, he saw that his army was being pushed back. He felt the weight of his injuries heavily upon him. Goranx came forward, and pointed an axe at his head.

The Lygon's voice was deep and triumphant. 'I could have taken your head before. But I wanted to see your face before I remove that thick Wolfen skull. I will it hold high and laugh as I eat your flesh, and crack the marrow from your bones.' He laughed, showing enormous teeth. 'You will not come back from the dead twice, little Wolfen.'

An unearthly scream came from the castle parapets and the few remaining Panterran froze, turning to their battlements, confused. The arrows stopped as the huge drawbridge of the castle flew open and standing in the massive doorway were two more of the strange Man-Kind, plus three more Wolfen, two in the most magnificent royal armor.

Bergborr held out a hand, his face in agony. 'My princess.' His face grew dark. 'And the Arnoddr. Die!' He sprinted away towards the small group.

While Goranx stared open mouthed, Sorenson managed to get slowly to his feet. The Wolfen laughed when he saw what one of the Man-Kind held, and then raised up – it was the dripping head of the Panterran queen.

A howl went up from the remaining yellow-eyed Panterran, and in another few seconds, those that hadn't already left the battle simply melted away, following their kin into the forest.

There came another sound, rising in volume and ferocity – the war cry of the Far Wolfen, gathering themselves up, their spirits buoyed by the sight of the vanquished Panterran queen and also the crested armor of Valkeryn royalty.

Sorenson looked to the moon again. 'Thank you, Father Odin. Now hear me.'

His eyes were round as he stared at the shining disc in the sky. 'Come, all the Wolfen kin who this creature has taken.' A mist lifted around his feet, and then began to swirl around him. It quickly separated into long streaks that moved faster and faster. Sorenson held his arms wide. 'Join me brothers and sisters. Lend me your *sáál*.' The streaks became vapor-ghosts that Sorenson drew into his mouth. He shuddered and then slumped.

Goranx laughed softly. 'Fear makes some mad.' He pointed his axe. 'I will even eat your bones this night.'

Sorenson rose up and then turned slowly, lifting the faceplate of his helmet, and roared out his words. 'Goranx the Slayer, know who you face this day. Not just Sorenson, son of Stromgard. Not just the brother of Strom. But you face the last Wolfen elite of the line of Grimvaldr. This day is your last.'

He leapt. Goranx, confused, swung his axe, but he was unbalanced by the ferociousness the attack, and stepping back, his heel caught on the body of a fallen Far Wolfen. He went down, and before he could rise, Sorenson was upon him, running his long sword in through his neck.

Goranx reached for the blade, blood spurting, but Sorenson pushed harder. The sword sank in deeper, and as the blade continued on, he drew nearer to Goranx. He stared hard into the Lygon's eyes, right up until their noses almost touched.

'It is your head that will be raised up this day.' He twisted the blade, opening the wound wide. The final gurgle of the giant beast was cut off and his hands fell away from the sword.

Teacher leapt forward, slashing and hacking at anything that dared turn to face him. Arn bounced from one giant creature to the next, stabbing and ripping, the moon giving both men the strength of a half dozen, and easily a match for the larger Lygon.

A gunshot rang out and Arn spun, shocked to hear the modern weapon so close. The entire battlefield seemed to stop and turn to watch. Briggs stood with a handgun up, pointed at Teacher, her two handed grip and stance giving her rock solid balance as she lined up her former soldier.

Teacher held up his hands, but she fired again. The bullet whacked into his chest dead centre and blew him back into the mud.

Teacher got to his feet rubbing his sternum. The CL suit had deflected the bullet and defrayed much of the impact, but it still felt like a mule-kick. She fired again, but this time Teacher held his ground.

Briggs' face remained emotionless, dead, but the words that leaked from her mouth were like those from an open crypt.

'This world is not for Man-Kind. Your doorway to our world will have been breached by now.'

She fired again and again, Teacher slowly walking forward, taking each of the hammer blows to his body, knowing he would be hurt, but not killed, by the small caliber weapon. Briggs changed her aim, this time bringing the barrel up to sight at the single long lens over his eyes. Her fingers tightened.

The effect on the Colonel of the howling scream from the parapets at the moment the old witch died was like a short circuit. Blood and clear fluid gushed from her nose, and her eyes flickered between milky white and blue. Briggs' face screwed up tight as if she wrestled with something monstrous. Her teeth came together, and her jaws clenched tight for several seconds, and her body shuddered as if being electrocuted.

She stopped and her eyes focused on him for a moment – blue, aware, but still full of a hellish torment.

'Teacher... can't... stop it.'

'Colonel?' Teacher rushed towards her.

Colonel Marion Briggs let out an unearthly howl matching that of Mogahrrs, and brought the gun up to her head. She pulled the trigger.

They fought on, the hours passing. The blood made the ground a red stew of dirt, littered with broken armor and crushed bodies. Arn found himself standing alone, and he surveyed the battlefield. The Panterran had long fled, but the Lygon were fighting to the death. In another time, the great beasts might have been allies, if they had stepped back from their bloodlust and kinship with the hateful Panterran. Arn guessed that some creatures that Fenrir had brought forth from the fire needed more time to grow, and perhaps... evolve.

Arn felt the skin on his face tingle and crawl, and he doubled over as yet another spasm of pain wracked his body. The CL suit felt tight, tighter than it had only moments before. Another red wave of pain ran through him. He groaned and stayed bent over, feeling like he was being torn apart, or stretched by a giant from the inside out.

He retracted his suit's head covering, releasing some of the pressure and allowing the perspiration to dry. He looked to the sky. 'Better.'

Arn wiped his brow, sucked in air and straightened when a scream brought his head around. Eilif was being held by Sorenson – why? She fought him, the pair twisting – only then did he see the colors of the plumage trailing from the helmet – it was black. It wasn't Sorenson. It was the dark Wolfen, Bergborr.

The former Wolfen warrior had disarmed Eilif and was dragging her along the ground, invisible amidst all the chaos of the battle.

Arn felt a fury rise within him. He didn't recognize the sensations that his mind and body generated – such anger boiled inside him, such an animalistic fury that had never existed in him before. He leapt, running hard, sometimes even using his hands and legs together, crossing the several hundred feet in a few seconds.

He stuck Bergborr like a missile, knocking both him and Eilif to the ground. Bergborr bounced lightly to his feet, sword in his hand, still holding tight to the Princess. Bergborr roared, his face first acknowledging recognition, but then clouding with confusion as if he didn't quite understand what he was seeing.

'You?' He pointed his sword at Arn, his face twisted in disgust.

'Arn.' The devotion in Eilif's voice crushed the dark Wolfen's expression down to nothing but pure hatred.

Bergborr spat the words. 'Skinless freak, disgusting remnant of a decrepit and weak race.' He shook Eilif, his volcanic gaze turning to her momentarily, before switching back to Arn.

'Man-Kind, you look different... sick. Perhaps real fighting is not for the likes of you.'

Eilif struck out, and Bergborr smashed the hilt of his word down on her.

'Stop!' Arn held up his hand, his eyes on Eilif.

The sound of Arn's plea made Bergborr's face become more twisted. He turned his blade around, lifting the silver blade high. 'If I can't have her...'

Arn leapt, yelling words that turned into meaningless roars as he grabbed Bergborr and ripped the sword from his hand. Arn beat at the Wolfen's armor, his strength growing with each blow. He tore away steel plates and chain mail, continuing to beat the Wolfen until he lay still.

'Enough!' Eilif fell against Arn, holding him. 'It is over.' She looked down at Bergborr's battered body. 'Hellheim will take him now.' She looked up at Arn's face. 'He was a fool, but love can make us all foolish and blind.'

Arn held on to her for a few moments, and turned to look across to the Far Wolfen and Ursa led by Sorenson. They wandered, looking dazed, the adrenaline of the last few hours wearing off, making their muscles ache, and their bodies sag.

Teacher was crouching beside Sharp and Brown, both alive, but covered in blood from head to toe. Grimson and Balthazaar had led a small band of warriors into the castle, to clean out any remnants of Mogahrr's followers foolish enough to try for an ambush – already the banner of the Valkeryn Wolfen flew from the parapets.

Arn turned to her. 'Go, the castle is yours once more.'

Eilif danced on the spot and clapped for a second or two before running towards the giant gates. Arn watched her go, smiling, before his expression dissolved into a grimace. He rolled his aching shoulders, the suit once again constricting his body. Teacher was at his side, laying a hand on his shoulder and looking up at him.

'You okay?'

Arn nodded, but felt nauseous. It was odd. He was looking down at the Delta Force leader. It seemed only days ago he had been looking him in the eye. *What has Grimson's blood or this place done to me,* he wondered. He knew at that moment that staying might here mean the end of him or his humanity. He looked briefly down at his aching hands – there was a small rip in the CL suit fabric. *Did that happen in battle or was the suit was so tight it was beginning to split? Impossible,* he thought.

Teacher pressed a stud to retract his visor and head covering. When it was off his face, he ran his palms over his wet face.

'We haven't got much time. We need to leave immediately.'

Arn nodded. 'Mogahrr's force will be at the gateway by now. I hope Vidarr was able to get Becky and Edward to the portal, and that they, not the Lygon, make it to our home.'

Teacher shook his head. 'No chance the Lygon will get past our Delta Force. Henson and the team will kick their ass or die trying. Let's work on the assumption we can punch a hole right through. But you're right; we'll need to catch up to your friends to make sure that they get that laser acceleration diamond back home – nothing else matters – our lives and our world depend on it.'

Sorenson joined them, placing a bloody hand on Arn and Teacher's shoulders. 'A glorious battle; you fought well… just like Wolfen.'

'We're not done yet. There is another of Mogahrr's armies, in the wasteland.'

Sorenson snorted. 'Then we will meet them, and their bones can bleach in the desert.' He looked out over the Far Wolfen and Ursa. 'We need to go now. It will take time to move our troops, and the Ursa are not built for speed.'

He seemed to think for a moment. 'There will also be Pan-terran there. Perhaps we can encourage them to leave without firing an arrow.' He grinned.

CHAPTER 36

THE FASTEST HORSE IN THE KINGDOM... NOW!

Balthazaar took Eilif back into the storeroom with the hidden artefacts, and she sat on a chest with the crown of Valkeryn on her head. She had quickly washed the blood from her body and draped a thick crimson cloak over her silver armor.

She stood, catching sight of herself in the mirror. She took off the silver breastplate, and donned a lighter tunic. She stood again before the mirror, turning one way then the next. She smiled, approving of the way she looked. She spoke over her shoulder to the old Counsellor.

'Find Arn and ask him to join me.' Balthazaar nodded and withdrew, and she went back to admiring herself from different angles. 'See me now, Arnoddr... and resist me not.' She laughed softly and held a hand up over her mouth. She imagined her, no, *their* new life – her ears flushed pink and she crushed her eyes shut for a few seconds.

Balthazaar returned after only a few minutes, his face ashen. He stood wringing his hands for a moment. 'Your Majesty, ah...'

Her smile vanished. 'Just tell me, wise friend.'

'It's the Arnoddr, he...' He cleared his throat.

Eilif suddenly felt light headed. 'Tell me!' Her heart raced as she turned to face him fully.

'He's gone.' He said the words quickly.

Eilif froze as her emotions and thoughts tumbled over each other in her brain. She felt everything slow down around her. She didn't understand; it didn't make sense.

'Stop it, you're being silly. He's gone? What does that mean?' Her heart sunk. 'Where... where, would he go?' Eilif took several steps towards the Counselor, but staggered.

'He's gone home, your majesty. Back to his world.'

'No, no, no…' She shook her head, and staggered towards him, finally lurching into his arms. She felt as thouhgh she had been punched in the stomach. 'No please, not again.' She brought fists up beside her head, turning to look back into the mirror. Her eyes filled and she ripped the crown from her head. She spun back to Balthazaar. 'I will not… I will *not* lose him again.'

Eilif's ice-blue eyes were wide as she pinned the old counselor with her gaze.

'The fastest horse in the kingdom... now!'

Teacher, Arn, and Sorenson rode their horses through the forest, pulling spare mounts with them. The once mighty stables of Valkeryn had been decimated. The hundreds upon hundreds of animals had been retained for little more than food, and only a few dozen remained.

They quickly caught up to Vidarr, Edward and Becky, and pulled them up onto their horses. Becky refused her own mount, claiming a fear of riding, and jumped up behind Arn instead. She clamped her arms around his waist.

'I was going slow because I knew you'd come.' She whispered into his ear and hugged him tighter.

Edward looked panicked as he rode, but to his credit managed a good pace. Teacher was relieved to see the red diamond still bouncing around his neck on the silver chain.

Vidarr had been given a horse, and sent back to the castle, his job done. He'd be needed to unlock and recover the rest of the secrets he had hidden from the Panterran queen.

The rest rode hard knowing that the coolness of the desert night would soon turn to a devil's cauldron of heat once the sun rose. For now, morning was little more than a red line on the horizon. Teacher tried his communicator, praying they were within range. There was a hiss and crackle, and then the strained voice of Hanson.

'Good to hear from you, Boss. How's your day been?'

Teacher grinned – he knew what the elite soldier had been dealing with. 'Pretty quiet; how's yours?'

'You're still in time for the party – really hope you'll be joining us soon.'

'That's the plan.' His voice took on a serious note. 'Prepare for immediate evac. We've got the diamond and the missing kids. Can you clear a path for us?'

'Sure can. Come in dead centre, we'll give you a fire corridor, but it's still going to be ugly – lot of big bad bodies here all wanting to take a bite out of us.'

'Got it, and see you soon.'

Teacher switched off and turned to Arn and Sorenson. 'They'll give us some cover, but we might have to fight our way up the ant hill.'

Sorenson grunted. 'Good.'

CHAPTER 37

MAYBE ONCE IT WAS A MAN.

Hanson turned to Farfelle. 'Get down the tunnel. Go back through the portal and tell Harper we got incoming with the diamond. Make sure he's ready; this thing has cost us a lot of blood.' The man saluted and crawled backwards, keeping below the arrow shot.

Hanson pointed, and Bannock followed with his eyes. 'We need to clear a corridor for Teacher – right down the middle.'

Bannock whistled. 'To keep it open we're going to have to go down there.'

Hanson nodded. 'Yep. Was getting kinda boring up here anyway.'

***

Farfelle and another Delta Force soldier jogged through the cramped tunnel. The wind howled back at them, the noise drowning out the sound of dripping water, flying debris, and making it impossible to detect the tiny noises of a stealthy approach. Farfelle could see the oily smudge that indicated the tear in time and space, so large now that it completely covered one end of the tunnel. A rope flapped like a streamer in the air, one end in the dark dank tunnel, the other a million years back in a pristine chamber. It had been hung to provide assistance to those struggling to pull themselves in past the force of gravity working against them.

Farfelle turned to give his companion some last minute instructions, but before he could speak something flew out of the darkness to land on the other man's back. Its was large, hairless and pink. Finally the sound of giggling broke in above all the other noises, its high cadence turning to a mishmash of sounds that could have been a language.

The downed soldier screamed, as long chisel-like teeth dug into the meat of his shoulder. If not for the ceramic plating the thing would have torn free a fist-sized chunk of flesh. Long claws scrabbled at his body. Farfelle drew his gun and fired several rounds into the creature, knocking it to the side.

Now free, the other soldier scurried backwards. 'What the hell was that thing?' He drew his own gun, sighting from the creature to the dark tunnel, and then back again.

Farfelle kept his gun trained on the body and knelt slowly beside it. He prodded it with the barrel of his gun – it didn't move. The thing was greasy-looking, and almost transparent. The hands were five fingered, but the thumb was small, little more than a lump. The fingers themselves ended in long horn like talons – more like tools designed for digging through the deep, dark earth.

He used his boot to turn it over. 'Jesus Christ.' The face was flat, and the eyes totally black. It was impossible to tell whether the orbs were sightless or just fully dark-adapted. The nose was a flap of skin and the mouth was nothing but a raw hole with huge rat like incisors. He grimaced, feeling bile rise in his throat. Farfelle couldn't help thinking it looked like…

'Is that a goddam man?'

Farfelle shrugged. 'God-damned is right. Maybe once it was a man… about a million years ago.' He looked around in the tunnel. 'I doubt that was all of them. Let's go.'

They grabbed the rope and hauled themselves into the dark purple hole.

CHAPTER 38

TO LIVE AMONG WOLVES,
YOU MUST FIRST BECOME THE WOLF

Arn pushed the horse hard. Becky hung on tight as it bucked and swerved, her hands digging into his waist. The grip was like his old life hanging on to him – his home, his security, perhaps his future. He took one hand off the rein to touch his face, as it was beginning to hurt again. It didn't feel right, and even the shape was odd.

What's happening to me? he wondered and looked to the horizon. The sun would be up soon, and with it the heat would climb. It also meant any secrets hidden in the darkness would be revealed for all to see... for Becky to see. *Not yet*, he thought, and touched the small stud on his collar causing the CL suit to telescope up and over his head. He worked his jaws; the inside of his mouth felt crowded and sharp.

Arn knew something was badly wrong – was it Grimson's blood? In the Dark Lands when they became blood brothers, their blood had mixed – had he contracted some sort of weird disease that humans had never encountered? Was it conceivable he could infect his world if he went back? *Impossible.* He shook away the thought. He needed to be home. He spurred the horse.

In another hour, the small mountain rose from the desert floor. As they neared, they could see what Hanson described as his "anthill" – it was covered with bodies, many still, but some still trying to climb to the open top.

But as he had promised, right down its centre there was a cleared strip. Red explosions and the popping of gunfire grew louder – Henson and his team were doing their job.

Arn kicked to the front of the group and reached down into a bloody sack that was hanging from his saddle. He drew out the severed head of Mogahrr and held it high, Medusa-like, as he plowed into the ranks of the Panterran archers positioned at the rear.

'Your queen is dead, the war is over – the war is over.' He swung the head left and right. 'Mogahrr is dead, the war is over.' He yelled the words as he smashed through their ranks.

Many of the Panterran were panicked at the sight of their dead queen's head being paraded like a grisly trophy – proof that their support base was gone. They responded exactly as Arn hoped – they fled.

The Lygon were not so easily dissuaded – they charged. Henson and his Deltas picked off many of them using their armor-piercing rounds, but when the Lygon got in too close, Teacher's small group was on its own.

Like the tip of a wedge, Sorenson and Teacher came to the front, hacking to both sides. Sorenson laughed as he brought his sword down onto the head of a Lygon. Following his defeat of Goranx, their giant general, these lesser warriors were nothing but chaff to him.

A dozen Delta Force soldiers came down the slope to meet them and formed a ring around Becky and Edward. They split into two groups, one attempting to draw the youths back up the slope, fighting the entire way, but quickly being surrounded. The remaining Deltas, Teacher, Arn, and Sorenson fought for their lives, the overwhelming numbers now pressing in on them.

Sorenson backed into Arn. 'We must hold them until the Far Wolfen arrive.'

The moon was now down, and Arn's limbs felt like lead. Beside him, Teacher hacked and stabbed, metallic objects changing and reforming to bludgeon and impale Lygon as they charged. Arn could see the Delta leader's movements slowed by fatigue as well. Another Delta soldier beside them paused for a split second to jam in another magazine and was smashed to the ground by an enormous Lygon club. Arn felt his own frustration rise – we're so damn close.

'We'll never make it – get Becky and Edward through… now.'

The Deltas on the hill looked to Teacher, who nodded. 'Get them and that diamond back to Harper.' The Deltas paused and Teacher roared at them. 'That's an order.'

The Deltas coalesced around Becky and Edward and drove the Lygon out of their path as they shot, burned, and exploded their way back up the hill. In another few minutes they had disappeared over the lip and Teacher heard Henson's voice in his ear.

'Got 'em in the tunnels, Boss. Our job is done. Time for you to join us.'

'Let's go, let's go.' Together Teacher, Sorenson and Arn backed slowly to the rim. Teacher knew his final task was to get all his men home, and then get the portal shut – nothing else mattered.

In the distance, horns blared and a dark line on the horizon grew with the approaching Wolfen and Ursa. The Lygon were confused by the sound of another army, and Teacher took the chance to reach out to grab Arn's arm.

'Time to go home.'

Arn grimaced behind the face covering, and looked to Sorenson, who brandished his sword, holding the Lygon at bay. The huge beasts seemed to come to a decision, and they split into two groups – the larger force headed down to meet the approaching army, but several dozen in a smaller group began to press their attack on the slope.

Teacher ripped at his arm. 'Arn… now!'

Arn slumped and reached up to touch the small button at his neck. The visor retracted into his collar. 'How can I?' He turned to look at Teacher.

The Delta leader let go of Arn and staggered back a step. 'Jesus Christ.'

'How *can* I now?' Arn repeated, feeling the odd shape of his features. He could guess how he looked – somewhere in between man and wolf. He now towered over Teacher, easily as tall as Sorenson.

Teacher swallowed, working to keep his face calm. 'It's probably because you were in this place so long. Maybe the nearness of the moon has affected you, or some disease. Harper can cure you… come on.'

Teacher grabbed him again. 'Please… come with us.'

Sorenson backed into him, overhearing. He half turned. 'Arnoddr Sigarr. Go, friend to Wolfen. I lost one brother, but in you, I had found another. Goodbye Arn. Save yourself… save your world. You have already helped save ours.'

Teacher bent and pulled a grenade launcher from a dead soldier's hands. He fired several charges into the Lygon on the hill, making orange and black body parts fly into the air. He dropped it and grabbed Arn's arm.

'Now.'

'Give me a minute.' Arn wrenched his arm free. Teacher hesitated, then nodded and vanished into the dark.

Arn looked around at the broad flat desert, feeling a sinking depression deep in his chest. There was a part of him that needed to be home, but another part that didn't want to leave. He had been in this strange land, with these wonderful creatures, for only a short time, but he had lived a dozen life times. He had grown close to them, grown to know them, grown to… love them.

'Goodbye Valkeryn.' He waved at Sorenson, and took one last long look at this world. He turned and disappeared down into the tunnels.

'Your *sáál* will live forever in this place, Arnoddr.' Sorenson watched his friend go and then turned back to the remaining Lygon. He threw his head back and roared. In one hand he held his sword high and in the other he had Goranx's severed ears crushed into his fist.

'Know who you face this day… the Wolfen of the new kingdom of Valkeryn.' He leapt into their ranks.

On the desert plains in front of the mountain, the Far Wolfen and Ursa smashed into the rear flanks of the Lygon. In a few minutes all had been pulled from the mountainside to fight for their lives.

Sorenson breathed deeply and watched the last moments of the battle. He narrowed his eyes, as the dawn sun showed up a plume of dust from a rider who sped at them across the desert sand. A small Wolfen in a crimson cloak dismounted even before the horse had stopped, and then sprinted up the mountainside.

Sorenson bowed as he recognized the rider, knowing what she sought. 'My Princess… my Queen. It is too late… he is gone.'

Eilif batted him aside, and dived into the dark tunnel.

General Langstrom stood with his legs planted, the hurricane winds tearing at him as he struggled to stay upright. Dozens of soldiers had taken up positions around the portal, each lashed to a metal spike hammered into the concrete floor. All had weapons trained on the enormous dark wound in their universe.

The sound was deafening, like that of a giant devouring beast that would not be satisfied until it had consumed the world. Langstrom yelled his instructions, not knowing whether they were heard or not, but determined to keep his troops focused and ready. There was little time now – hours only. There was a war going on the other side of the portal, and he was going to make damn sure it didn't spill into their world and disrupt the work Dr Harper needed to do.

He yelled again. 'Anything... and I mean, anything, non-human that comes out of that hole, you goddamn send it straight back to hell.'

◆◆◆ ⋙∞⋘ ◆◆◆

Teacher held an arm up to shield his face from the force of the wind blasting from the dark maw. The Deltas had gone; he was the last soldier. He'd give Arn another few minutes... but he wasn't the only one holding off making the jump.

He pushed at Becky and Edward. 'Get the hell through... now.'

Becky clung to the side of the tunnel, resisting Edward dragging at her. Her face was defiant. 'We came here for Arn. We – are – *not* – leaving – without him.'

Edward grabbed her around the waist and tugged. 'Come on, Beck, he'll come, but we gotta go... please.'

She looked down and punched at his arms. 'No, you go. I'll stay.' She knocked one of his hands free and turned, just as several pinkish bodies slammed into Teacher from out of the dark. Becky and Edward were also grabbed with horn-like talons. Edward rolled into a ball and Becky screamed as they dug into her flesh.

Teacher rolled, trying to dislodge the weight on his back. His CL suit stopped the claws from penetrating his flesh, and he struck out with hands turned to metal hammers. However, the shapes wouldn't hold – the Morph Steel's effects were wearing off, leaving him battering away with his bare hands.

He managed to beat away several of the disgusting creatures, and get between Becky and Edward, and the colorless creatures. He didn't want to think about what would happen to the two youths if they were spirited away into the endless tunnels.

'They're still there, they're still there.' Becky hung on to Teacher's legs, trying to use them as a shield. Almost immediately, there was movement all along the tunnel as more of the things crawled out of the darkness.

Teacher half turned. 'Stay dow—'

He was slammed to the ground, the weight of several of the creatures crushing him to the damp tunnel floor. Once again Becky was caught, hooked by the hair, and dragged. Edward lunged at her, but another of the pale things reached out and caught the red diamond hanging from his neck and ripped it free.

Teacher leapt, his hand out, but the things were bred for the darkness and the claustrophobic tunnels – it was already darting away from him.

'No.' He banged the ground almost weeping. *All for nothing*, he thought, as he watched its greasy, pale torso muscle in amongst its kin.

Suddenly, from out of the tunnel depths there came a roar that froze the strange creatures. In an explosion of fury, something huge and black was in amongst them, ripping, smashing and slamming them into walls like they were nothing. It was huge and powerful, and its fury scattered the remaining tunnel dwellers.

Teacher backed up, bumping into Becky and Edward. 'Get back.'

He could see it now – the remnants of a CL suit hung in tatters from its body. Black hair hung to its shoulders and over a long face with coal dark eyes.

It held out its hand – there was a red diamond on a silver chain hanging from it. Teacher stared for several seconds, before reaching out to take the precious stone. He looked into its face, barely recognizable anymore.

'Arn?'

The beast simply raised a hand and pointed to the gateway wavering in the tunnel behind them.

'Arn? Arn?' Becky looked both horrified and relieved at his appearance.

Arn studied her for a moment and then turned his head, listening for a few seconds. His huge dark ears swiveled on his head. He turned to face Teacher, leaning forward.

'More are coming. You must go.'

Teacher looked about to say something, but Arn shook his head. The Delta commander nodded his farewell and then began to back up, the diamond hung about his neck. He hauled himself back on the tether, leaving Edward hanging on to the rope with one hand and Becky with the other.

Becky shook her head. 'Arn, I'm not leaving without you.' She tugged on Edward trying to pull away from him.

'Please, come back with me. My father has money… we can get treatment.' She turned to scowl at Edward who refused to let go. She spun back. 'Please, *please*. I only came for you. I… I… love you.'

He stood staring at her, his eyes shining silver in the darkness. Indecision wracked his mind and heart. His feet moved without him even being aware of it and he stepped forward, his hand coming up towards hers.

Arn could see clearly in the dark now. He saw his own arm; it was unrecognizable – the suit hanging in tatters, and a slight sheen of dark fur covering the skin. The silver snarling wolf ring given him by Eilif – it seemed a lifetime ago – now fit snugly, and like it belonged.

He took another step.

'Arn, my Arn.' He spun.

Eilif sprinted down the tunnel, throwing off weapons, her crimson cloak and anything else that was slowing her down.

Becky lunged and grabbed his hand, tugging with all her strength. She turned to Edward, and screamed.

'Pull!'

Eilif came fast. If he went, he knew she would follow. He took another step, indecision overwhelming him. In his mind he saw the recurring dream again – the miserable figure being dragged down the sterile corridors to become a laboratory curiosity, a freak – it would all come true if she followed.

The portal shimmered, and Becky's mouth formed an 'O' as she started to become indistinct – Harper was doing his job. Her voice became panicked.

'Now, please, come home now. Arn… now!' She turned and started to beat at Edward, but Arn raised his hand in a wave, and his friend acknowledged with a nod, wrenching even harder at Becky.

Becky turned back, her face wet. 'Come home.'

Arn heard his grandfather's voice speak softly and calmly in his head: *to live among wolves, you must first become the wolf.*

He spun quickly to catch Eilif as she landed in his arms, and then turned back to shake his head sadly. 'But I am home.'

Becky was pulled roughly back through the gateway, her scream still echoing as it snapped shut with a thump of swirling air.

CHAPTER 39

TWELVE MONTHS LATER

Becky and Edward sat on the grass in the emerald green parklands that had once been the grounds of the Fermilab Facility. A year had passed since Harper and his team had shut down the accelerator and stopped the gravitational anomaly that had caused the rift in time and space.

There had been the usual news embargo, confidentiality contracts, compensation, threats of what would happen if they breached national security. It didn't matter; who would ever believe them? Even now, Becky wondered what was true and what was all just a bad dream.

She closed her eyes and lifted her head to the sun, allowing the rays to bathe her face.

'Do you still wonder what happened to him?'

Edward yawned and turned to her. 'Sure, I do. But I bet he's all right.'

She frowned. 'Harper said that the entire timeline would have been erased. Without our world being destroyed, theirs could never rise, could never exist. He also said he had no idea what would happen to someone from our world if they were there when it simply, ceased being.'

Edward exhaled. 'Hurts my head to think about it.'

Becky opened her eyes and stared out cross the green grass. 'He looked different.'

Edward shrugged. 'Didn't notice.' He turned to look over his shoulder at the woodland surrounding the miles of lawn. 'You know, they never found the dogs... the Guardians they called them. They're still out there roaming around some-where.'

Becky yawned and smiled up at the statue that Harper had erected. 'Well, I'm going to remember him just like that.'

The bronze life-size statue was of Arn; all neat and short-cropped hair. There were two lines of words printed on its base, first "HE STILL LIVES", and then a second line – "IN OUR HEARTS."

Becky sighed. 'He sure does.' She looked at Edward. 'I just hope he's okay, and that he does find his way back some day.'

Edward lay back on the grass, his hands behind his head. 'Maybe, but don't know how. The Tevetron collider is buried under a thousand tons of concrete, and laser acceleration has been banned.'

He turned to her opening one eye, and saw the look on her face. 'I mean, sure, me too.'

EPILOGUE

Uri Gorbanov stood with the Russian President and grinned with pride. He had just shown him and the energy minster around the facilities, and they seemed very impressed – and just as well. President Petrov was known to shut billion rouble projects down overnight… as well as making scientists who were judged incompetent, disappear.

He drew in a deep breath. The first test firing was always nerve wracking, and he had to perform it in front of the President himself. He had promised Petrov the secrets of the universe. If things went wrong, he was finished.

He stood before the controls, taking over the initiation from his technicians. The computer simulations had been run over a hundred times, all of them showing perfect particle collisions. He started the collider, and protons fired to begin their race around the magnetized, twenty-mile diameter ring-track, each moving faster and faster with each circuit.

His finger hovered nervously over the button. 'The diamond will boost the rotation of the particles to the speed of light. The resulting collision will open doors onto a new world of science for Russia.'

Gorbanov grinned and motioned to the button. 'And now, Mr. President, the final acceleration.' He paused. 'It is only fitting that you are given the honor.'

Petrov shrugged and pressed the button.